Global
Raider

By James McKenna

GLOBAL RAIDER

Lone Cloud Publishing

Unit 1 Betjeman Close, Cowper Road,

Harpenden, Herts AL5 4XH

2014

ISBN 978-0-9928400-1-3

lonecloudpublishing@live.co.uk

Book cover design by BespokeBookCovers.com

The Unseen
The Uncounted
The Unwanted

James McKenna also writes for young readers

The Mind Traveller is the first in a trilogy of
action/adventure stories for 10-15 year olds

CHAPTER 1

Sweat trickled on Seb's face. In the still night a fly buzzed, stopped, buzzed again then settled on the barrel of his AK74 rifle. Lying in a hollow scooped from the desert floor, he squinted through his night optic sight, drawing a line of vision over the ambush square, waiting on the enemy, waiting on advanced warning from the UAV twelve miles in the sky.

Since hitting the dropping zone at 2300 hours and burying his parachutes, Seb had felt his adrenalin slowly gain in pressure to feed tension over fear. Fear would come later, when it was done and over. For now he blocked all negatives from his mental preparation. The Combined Agency Taskforce, CAT taught all or nothing and the eight-man ambush team from the Anti-terrorist Warfare wing would expect nothing less of him. He just prayed the outcome would not demand a cold blooded execution. This he knew was his trial for acceptance amongst the elite. These guys were ex-SAS, 9 Para, SBS, Airborne and Commandos, the very finest of British Special Forces; except ambush via US ground control in America and an unmanned aerial vehicle somewhere amidst the stars was untried. Tucked in his hole, Seb knew he was central to the operation's success, his orders deciding whether he and others of the CAT team lived or died. Tension in his body sparked every muscle and nerve which in turn pumped his sweat into the desert heat.

He brushed at another fly and heard Jock Anderson flick away the same irritation in the adjacent scoop, heard him puff when one settled on his lips. Seb considered him the babyminder but it did not detract from responsibility. Young he might be, but Seb was still the commanding officer. If he messed up, no one would forgive him. The outcome was a steel flask of anthrax en route to London, courtesy of one very dangerous al-Qaeda agent.

From the slit of the sand covered hole he looked up to

a star scattered heaven, the crystal air allowing vision thirty metres into the hot, velvet night. To his right lay undulating desert, to his left sand rock hills rose in stark silhouette, the tops shimmered by moonlight. On the lower slopes he had set the team's RV point and a two-man comms post manning the radio link to base. The team link was through UHF sets. More important was Seb's own link by satellite-com direct to Global Hawk ground control. Somewhere high above, an unmanned aerial vehicle watched over them like a guardian angel.

Again Jock shuffled his solid bulk, farted and set the flies buzzing.

"What the fuck you been eating?" Seb put a forearm to his nose, glad of the disturbance and the ease of tension.

"Beans." Jock turned his big square face and grinned. "I always eat beans before an op. Gives more velocity when I run."

Seb lifted his head and noticed all the flies had deserted. "You're more lethal than the bloody anthrax."

"In Al Razi's face, evil bastard." Jock laid the crook of his arm over the butt of a Barrett M82A1 sniper rifle, its .50 round capable of piercing an engine block.

"You think the Yanks are up there?" Jock asked.

"Somewhere." Seb rested chin to forearm and stared at a million stars. "They've been watching these guys by satellite for months. The stupid prats are still using mobiles. They're watching them now. Technology, that's what wins wars. When it works," he added in after thought.

"Still takes squaddies on the ground, some poor bastards to sort out the mess."

"For now. But it will change."

"We'll be dead by then."

"Hope not." Seb looked back to where a sand track wound its way around the hill at a hundred metres distance. He knew that four miles on the other side an al-Qaeda training camp held three hundred men. Somewhere over the track four of his own team lay waiting, each huddled in a scoop from the desert floor, each listening for his command to open fire. During the protracted silence the earpiece of Seb's sat-link whispered warning.

"Global Hawk to Desert Snatch. Convoy preparing to leave compound. Three vehicles, estimated enemy strength, eighteen. ETA, ten minutes."

Seb listened to the American voice of the UAV ground control, someone in a far distant place who watched this patch of desert through darkness and space.

"Roger that." Seb switched mikes and spoke to his team over UHF. "Eighteen players, three vehicles, ETA ten minutes. Pete, Mike, you take lead vehicle. Dave, Rich, end vehicle. Jock and I will do middle. Everyone to mop up runners. Barretts to stop vehicles," Seb paused. "Priority is the flask, probably in the central vehicle. Try not to cause fire. We don't want it red hot or broken. Some poor sod has to carry it."

"Guess who?" Jock grinned.

Ruperts do have their uses, Seb thought as he listened to the team's radio acknowledgement. In his mind he knew each person was aware that if a convoy took just ten minutes to arrive, so could three hundred al-Qaeda. A Puma helicopter with a second on standby would have been alerted for their run to the RV, waiting on his order to pick up when safe. For a clean withdrawal the time factors became crucial. He remembered words from his boss, Colonel Fox, that to lead men you had to be at one with them, mentally and physically. To give them confidence and get them the hell out of any position when they were being shot to pieces. "Stand to," he said and looked back to the night. The tension left his body under a surge of adrenalin. This was his life, what he had trained for. He felt totally focussed. The target was Dr Al Razi, a British mullah and long known supporter of al-Qaeda. Left to preach his hatred in London and travel at will, Al Razi had just collected some of Syria's stolen anthrax. His intended place of distribution, the British populous.

Seb shifted the butt of his rifle and took grip of the stock. As Rupert it was his duty to ensure Al Razi stayed in the desert. Long, silent minutes passed which left him time to think. Execution would need anger, hatred.

"Hawk to Desert Snatch, convoy now traversing hillside to your position. ETA three minutes."

"Roger that," Seb answered. He felt calm now, an inner control filled with solid determination. Every sense became alert to the stillness, the slow encroaching sound of engines. He wanted these bastards, this little shit Al Razi who would kill thousands in satisfaction of self-righteous bigotry.

"All positions fire on my action." Seb gave his last order and squinted through the night optic sight, watching the lead vehicle come round the hillside, a Toyota FWD with twin mounted machine guns over the cab. Full blaze headlights cut across their position and the desert floor, sweeping down the track as the second vehicle came into view, an enclosed landcruiser. Target vehicle, Seb was certain. He felt Jock shift the Barrett to aim at its engine cover. Last vehicle was an open truck carrying a dozen armed men.

"See you in paradise," Jock whispered.

"No way, we'll piss this." Seb took first pressure on his trigger and listened to the sat-com earpiece come to life.

"Hawk to Desert Snatch. A tracked vehicle has also left the compound, possibly an APC, repeat, armoured vehicle ETA your location eight minutes."

"Shit." Now or never. Seb squeezed the trigger and put a series of three round bursts into the landcruiser's side windows. Beside him the heavy calibre discharge of the Barrett imploded on his eardrums.

A crescendo of ear stunning noise came instantly amidst flickering darts of light. Flame spat across the black velvet sky from the single rounds of the massive Barrett sniper weapons while the snatched, chattering fire of HKG3s and AK74 assault rifles gave constant barrage. Seb shouted the last message from Global Hawk over his UHF.

Return fire from the convoy terminated within sixty seconds. Sergeant Pete Shaffer on the opposite side of the track called ceasefire. The sudden cessation of noise returned the desert to stillness, the silence only disturbed by the crackle of flames from the rear truck and intermittent cries of the wounded.

Seb pushed up from the dugout, Jock beside him, the heavy Barrett cradled in his arms. Half a dozen bodies shadowed the desert floor, fanned out from the vehicles like scattered clothes bags.

"Move it." Seb heard the order from Pete Shaffer as he came out of his hole. Figures emerged from the desert floor, all running at a crouch, all knowing they had minutes before an enemy armoured vehicle arrived.

Seb was within twenty feet when the fuel tank on the rear truck exploded. In the shock of fire, three of the supposed dead stood up and ran, four more figures leaped from the back, two of them ablaze. The team's response came immediately, their weapons raking the night with fire, twitching bodies as they scattered and fell. Seb kept running for the landcruiser, his sole objective to secure the canister of anthrax, the rest was now Pete Shaffer's; except for Al Razi, whom he hoped was dead.

The landcruiser sat fat and dark on deflated tyres, the windscreen and front side window shattered. Smoke and steam drifted from under the bonnet. Seb threw open the rear door and stood ready to fire. The driver was dead, so was the man beside him. In the back a thin bearded guy sat in petrified silence, eyes and mouth wide open, hands raised.

"Where is it?" Seb jabbed with his rifle barrel. Sitting in the back of the only air-conditioned vehicle this had to be Al Razi.

"I don't know what you mean." The cleric spread his

hands.

"Then fucking die." Seb took aim.

"Here." The guy grabbed a briefcase from behind the seat and held it in offering.

Seb snatched it onto the ground, flipped the catches and pushed up the lid. Inside lay a steel flask wedged by polystyrene. Jock had the tail open, throwing aside items while searching through other baggage.

"Is this it?" Seb took out the canister and pushed it into his shirt. "Tell me or I kill you now!"

"All of it, no more. They kept the rest."

"Nothing here," Jock said.

"Out, out." Seb grabbed the cleric's shirt, hauling him over the seat, trying to think of him as a mass murdered. He had never killed in cold blood.

Global Hawk sounded in his earpiece. "Sit-rep."

"Anthrax secure," Seb answered.

"Execute courier. Then immediate evacuation, additional firepower imminent," Hawk replied.

"Roger that." He turned the AK74 back to Al Razi. Seb wished to hell he had no conscience. He had to do this, had to. He took first pressure on the trigger, swallowed hard and paused, paused long enough to know he couldn't finish it.

"I have human rights. I am from London, British citizen, you cannot shoot me."

The air rocked and Al Razi's body jerked as his head disintegrated under impact from the single round out of Anderson's rifle. "Citizenship revoked." He looked to Seb and grinned. "Perks of being Rupert's nanny."

Seb looked to the splatter of brain and blood covering his hands and weapon but his relief was huge and thankful. "Withdraw to RV. Let's get the fuck out of here," he shouted, pushing the flask so it wedged against his skin under the strap of his belt kit, the same time counting heads as his team made a tactical withdrawal from the shattered convoy. No one down, he thought and called on his UHF link. "Pumas to pick up. Two minutes."

The clatter of a tracked vehicle became audible and a searchlight beam cut through the night. Seb answered with a snatched burst from the AK. The resulting darkness lasted moments before a parachute flare burst overhead. An APC stood ten metres back from the smouldering truck, its turret swinging before a heavy machine gun clattered round towards their retreating line.

Seb dropped simultaneously with the team. Again the night became a crash of noise, the ground pocked and chopped by the strike of rounds as the APC searched for range. Seb rolled, pulled a weapon propelled grenade from his kit, fitted it to the barrel of his rifle and fired. He was shouting, shouting as his men were shouting, their voices momentarily lost under the exploding grenade. This wasn't meant to happen. The al-Qaeda camp would be swarming by now.

Amidst the torrent of gunfire between APC and Seb's team, two silver bolts cut the black sky and turned the APC to molten metal. The eruption shuddered the ground, the sound vibrating through the air, impacting on Seb's eardrums so even his own voice sounded as if called from a distant place. Blood red flames billowed out across the desert floor, a rolling fireball veined with black acrid smoke. Within seconds the eruption had evaporated back into the stillness of night leaving small isolated patches of burning oil. The APC no longer existed.

Anderson stood. "Fucking hell, God's on our side. Where did that come from?"

Seb also stood. "I can guess. Additional firepower received," he said into his mike, transmitted by CP and sat-com to Global Hawk control.

"Hope it did the trick. Service courtesy of USAF."

"It did the trick." Sean looked to the star encrusted sky.

"Well yer ain't seen nothing yet. Just wait for Global Raider."

CHAPTER 2

General Jake Hammerton cast no shadow on the busy New York pavements. In the grey evening light he moved amidst the noise and glare of its human beings while keeping his concentration on events across the street, his mind on the kill.

Both he and the traffic stayed the same pace as Perry, his target, who strolled the opposite side of West 49th. Traffic clustered then stretched, rolling in a slow shuffle towards the intersection. The truck trailing Perry matched his progress, the driver carefully maintaining position to the rear, his wheels eighteen inches from the kerb. Training, Jake knew, brought perfection.

Amidst the congestion Perry occasionally drifted from sight, then Jake whispered into the mouthpiece of his body set, ensuring the two-man team that followed kept the target in view. Perry walked with positive steps, the black briefcase clutched in his right hand. Jake checked time and position. The target was five hundred metres from enemy contact and five metres from termination point. Lights on the intersection turned green and Jake took the opportunity.

"Execute immediately," he again spoke softly into the microphone on his lapel, stopping at the corner to watch the truck move forward, knowing four men from Walsh Security would be clustering in Perry's path. Somewhere ahead a siren wailed, a long, angry shriek cutting over the city noise.

Jake saw the annoyance on Perry's face and watched him side step in the apparent confusion of pedestrian confrontation. Next moment he was sprawling in the road, his head between the front wheels and those which followed, his body stretched facedown before the next set of wheels humped slightly. Jake heard the distinct pop of calvarium bone above the fading siren and watched the truck clear the corner to drive down 5th Avenue. He saw no sign of the four-man team. A woman screamed and people started to gather.

"Target down, briefcase swapped." Jake heard the whisper of one of his men over the earpiece and responded with a grunt of pride. Good men all of them, he thought, and strolled away in the opposite direction.

Henry Taylor had the Buick idling at the kerbside, his unlit pipe clenched between teeth, his expression bland. He released the locking mechanism and Jake slid his solid bulk into the back seat.

"Twenty seconds from time of command to execution. That team is superb," Jake said.

"Crowded sidewalk, just ain't safe no more." Henry sucked on his pipe.

"So perish all traitors." Jake lowered the rear window and took the black briefcase passed by one of his men from the pavement. "Fireback is rolling, Henry. One year down the line and Khalid is coming into target."

"You are now twenty minutes to rendezvous." Henry checked his watch and drove out into the traffic.

Jake opened the briefcase and looked through the contents, unfinished sandwiches, New Scientist magazine, business cards, correspondence. "Boring life he lived, Henry." Jake parted the magazine and found sheets of figures inside. "Flight details, we got evidence."

"You going to tell Mr Walsh?" Henry asked. "He'll find out."

"Only what I want him to know. Best he's kept out the frame. He's got problems enough." Jake looked to the pavement as they passed over the intersection. He saw police there, someone taking pictures of the uncovered body, a second policeman lifting a black briefcase. "Did you hear his head pop?" Jake asked. "Like a firecracker on the 4th of July. Real patriotic." Jake smiled and sat back in the comfort of his leather seat.

Twenty minutes later he slid shut the side door of a grey panel van. A fixed table and four swivel chairs filled the centre floor.   He nodded greetings to the three occupants but received scant acknowledgement in return. Forward of the enclosed cargo deck an FBI agent clicked the van into drive and pulled away from the kerb. Jake steadied himself, opposing the momentum as he sat in the empty seat.   A tall, hooked nosed block of a man with cropped hair and lined face, he gave the image of being stone cut.   His smile held no mirth and was not returned by the senior security agents opposite. Jake considered them Government hackers, pension men, eager for glory, scared of retribution.   He saw the three as scavengers, hooded crows, hunched and ready to pluck the eyes from any opponent.

"I must inform you, gentlemen, Operation Fireback is now active," he said, watching them flicker in apprehension as they realised the binding commitment.

"You could have told us." The speaker was Dalvarral of the Defense Department.

"We agreed the operation would be run only on a need to know basis. You didn't need to know, till now."

"You certain Khalid bin Qasem will bite?" Ratner, an assistant director with the Science and Technology Directorate of the CIA said, observed Jake with convex eyes.

"You told me your department was getting a lot of electronic chatter, that's al-Qaeda worried over the money they put in," Jake said.   "Well, thirty minutes ago I terminated Khalid's source of information.   To obtain lock-on, he must act before any navigational codes are changed.   That's effectively after GR4's penultimate test flight. If he obtains lock-on during the test, he'll siphon enough information to strike again on the inaugural flight."

"Are we sure?" Ratner asked.

"Defeat or humiliation of American's ultimate weapon will give him world acclaim. Every country supporting Islamic militants will fund him. To win he has to bite, because if he doesn't, al-Qaeda will bite him."

"Then why arrest Perry, for God's sake?" Dave Shalk of the FBI pointed his finger, the nail manicured, his hand white and soft. "I threw you the guy because the FBI knew him as an Internet paedophile, ideal for blackmail. If you've arrested Perry, he'll talk, Khalid will find out. He may back off or sell the information we passed. That's long term damage."

Jake resisted the temptation to snap the man's finger off. "I said, his information source was terminated. I saw no point in creating paperwork over this." Jake watched the FBI man shrink back, saw him realise. The finger wavered.

"We have no jurisdiction over the police," Shalk warned. "If you commit a crime, don't get caught."

"We are at war." Jake looked between them. "That's total commitment. You've all given input. FBI finding Perry as the patsy, CIA's infiltration tipping him to al-Qaeda for blackmail. But it was me who had to set the sting while limiting damage. I placed two guys in his department, guys of his sexual inclination, which made it easier for him to recruit them, security men who could smuggle stuff out. That way Qasem only got what we wanted. Both Perry and his boss, Crawley, had access to lift classified data from the loop. The fact they're both shirt lifters makes it look like a faggot conspiracy. And you're right, Perry would have talked. So exit Perry, job done. I had to protect my men and our own interest. And you did hint at Heaven's approval."

"I said Heaven had been informed of a covert operation to wipe Khalid bin Qasem out, to destroy a group central to the terrorist circuit," Dalvarral said. "They made no comment. You might note, this meeting is not held in a Government office. Don't that tell you something?"

"Deniable operation, glory or bust. Perry got run over by a truck." Jake watched the three crows draw down their hoods. Knowledge compromised them. He felt nothing but contempt. "If you join battle, gentlemen, ain't no point pussy-footing behind the stockade. Since 9/11 we've been at war. If a traitor hands secrets to the enemy, he pays the consequences. You don't like it, you're in the wrong game."

"Don't doubt us, Jake," Ratner said. "But on home ground we got limitations."

"Al-Qaeda brought the battlefield here and set the ground rules. Let's not forget, we play a double game using a double-edged sword. With Government approval the security of Walsh Industries is my responsibility and as Walsh developed Global Raider or GR4, so security on the aircraft is also mine. On your suggestion and with your co-operation I've allowed a controlled leakage of information to ensnare an enemy. That puts us into a conspiracy, gentlemen. And those in a conspiracy stay close, or fall by their own hand."

"Double-edged swords cut two ways, Jake. We have to ensure it doesn't bounce back. We are all involved," Dalvarral said.

"In that case, I suggest we all take a firm grip. Perry is dead. Fortunately I lifted the documents he carried and replaced them with others to which he had sole access. The upside is Dr Max Crawley, Perry's boss, is going to shit himself when he learns his chief assistant is the source of a major leak. That leaves him vulnerable as planned. The downside is, Wat Walsh will also hear. That causes problems."

"So we cut Walsh in." Ratner tapped the table and sat back. "He's a patriot and it will make our lives easier."

Jake shook his head, listening to the grind of traffic as it passed outside. "Last time Khalid crossed with Walsh, you guys let Khalid execute the man's wife. That's a lot of rage to suffer, even for a patriot. Wat Walsh don't forgive or forget. Your agency's got no credit with him, that's why he's paranoid over the safety of his daughter. He don't trust the security services. The first hint of Khalid and he might well lock down, ground GR4 and kill our operation. He has that power."

Shalk made to speak but Dalvarral interrupted him.

"Walsh and his daughter are important, but small fry. Expedience surpasses them both. What do you advise?"

"Perry's death will out the supposed impossible, enemy infiltration. If Khalid is suggested I'll need to satisfy Daddy Walsh over the absolute safety of Juliet Walsh. I've been planning to shift her to a secret place under maximum security, but now I've only got nine days to persuade her, otherwise this could fold."

"You saying the whole operation is dependent on some spoilt brat?" Shalk's finger was outstretched again. "For God's sakes, lock her up."

"Juliet Walsh don't lock up or shut up easy. Of course, I could remove her father's paranoia by throwing her under a truck. Alternatively, you guys could use influence in your departments and get me some co-operation from Heaven. And I mean immediately."

In the Back Bay district of Boston, USA, Lisa drove the Mercedes away from the elegant, brownstone house Lucas Kean had rented solely for Juliet's visits. Settling for the long drive Juliet curled both legs beneath her, tugged ineffectually at the hem of her mini skirt and half turned towards her bodyguard. She knew Lisa wanted comment, something to report if questioned by Papa. Papa always wanted to know, Papa had expectations.

"He has nice eyes and a cute butt," Juliet said finally, rewarding her friend's patience. "And he kissed me, twice."

"Eyes for you only, Sweetpea, you have him at your beck and call."

Juliet shrugged and let the darkness of night hide her grimace. "I'm not sure I want to call. My father sees himself as emperor, Lucas the power. Truth is, I'm just the trinket in between." She fondled the gold cylinder hanging on a chain around her neck, the metal encasing an emergency pull switch and transmitter.

"Come on now baby, lighten up." Lisa glanced momentarily from the road, the city lights reflecting over her blue eyes and short blonde hair. "You have yourself a maestro. He's clean, sharp and flying so fast others burn in his tail fire. He's in your palm. Number one bachelor of America. Every female socialite wants his name in her diary."

"But would you marry him?" Juliet asked, twisting the tracking bracelet on her wrist. "A white President with a black wife. I'll be the symbol of a united America. After the first black President that's what Lucas is after; and all very noble. But I don't want to be a symbol, I want to be a woman, a wife and a mother."

"And First Lady! I tell you, Sweetpea, if I were in your place I'd swallow the guy. But I'm from the wrong side of the track and I ain't pretty like you."

"Yes you are. Even Lucas eyes you up. You're striking, you have presence." Juliet smiled and touched Lisa's shoulder, leaving her hand there for reassurance. Lisa was tall with razor cut blonde hair and boyish features. Years of training had developed a solid but statuesque figure, one hundred and twenty pounds of silken muscle capable of flooring three assailants in as many seconds. Sometimes Juliet allowed herself the mental and physical capitulation of being encapsulated by that strength, not the brute power but the essence of domination which lay beneath. It came with tenderness, a touch, a caress, a kiss that lingered seconds too long. Over the years while Lisa had guarded her during time at the university, Juliet had exercised the boundaries of intimacy and friendship in tandem with caprice. To hide her own uncertainties and to maintain the bond of intimacy, she made frequent play of platonic, sisterly union. She knew this was cruel to Lisa but she did not know how to cope with her own tangle of emotions. She had few people to love and Lisa was her rock in isolation.

"You're kind, Sweetpea," Lisa said. "But what I generate is simple lust. You're different. You have that essential feminine sway, that prettiness which draws men. They want to protect you, yet same time find themselves captivated by your little girl smile. Men see me as fantasy sex. You're the girl they want to marry. I watch men, the way they watch you. And Lucas watches you with an open need. I see it in his eyes. For him, you're the perfect partner for his perfect marriage."

"His perfect marriage, Papa's perfect marriage. But you ain't got anything unless you've got love. And I don't love Lucas."

"Love! You're kidding me, Juliet. What's love got to do with it? In the perfect marriage, love is what the P.R. men pull out of the package when you go before media. Love is messy. You have to show clean, be snappy."

Juliet shrugged. "Maybe I'm old-fashioned ... husband and kids, a family." She suddenly wanted to busy herself and found superficial distraction by unpinning her long black hair before shaking it to fullness.

"Come on, Sweetpea, let's stay real. Love is for dough-heads. Super couples don't love. They have sex and try not to bite each other."

"Momma always talked of marriage and love." Juliet fished a white, elasticated ribbon from the glove compartment and slipped it over her wrist, pulling her hair to form a black, gleaming ponytail which she twisted through the band. She listened to Lisa's lapse of silence before feeling friendly fingers squeeze her arm.

"'S'OK, baby, I understand."

Clear of central Boston, Lisa turned the Mercedes up onto the freeway, heading south towards Plymouth and Cape Cod. Juliet did not want silence, she wanted Lisa's counsel.

"The truth is, I don't have a choice. I'm Juliet Walsh,

daughter of Wat Walsh, richest nigger in America, probably the world. I'm as much a part of his empire as any other commodity. There for use or disposal in securing or expanding the greater whole. But if forced, I want Lucas on my terms, not Papa's. That's why I need to stay here this summer I want to know the man I'm expected to marry."

Lisa's hand came up over the back of her neck, gently massaged between thumb and forefinger.

"You want my advice," Lisa said. "You're right. But you been going with him four months now. Time to take a break and reflect. Listen, Jake Hammerton's been on the line, he asked if you've considered the proposed trip to England. It'll mean two weeks out of the cage. Also time to look up universities for your PhD."

"Tempting, but I'm determined to sort Lucas. I have to do this, Lisa. Lucas wants Papa's money for his campaign. Papa wants a son-in-law who will be President of the United States. Little Sweetpea is the connection. When Lucas asks me to marry, I'm going to face a lot of pressure. I can only handle that if I know we have a chance."

"And who says romance is dead?" Lisa moved her hand back to the steering wheel, a soft smile on her lips. A sad smile, Juliet thought. She stared to the roadside emergency lane, vision and thoughts lost in the blur of passing darkness and light. Now she felt bitter, her own words having explained her position as the bartered bride. Lucas was charming, kind and courteous, but also fifteen years her senior. He treated her like a child bride in waiting, the pretty princess being groomed for the media. During that evening in their one brief moment of privacy, he had embraced and kissed her, then set her aside as if duty done and courtship satisfied. She would have been happier taking him to her bed, warming him, discovering him woman to man as she had done with other boyfriends during moments of freedom. She wondered if Lucas had ever been a boy, or always a hard-boiled contender for the presidency of the United States.

"You'd think he'd want me in his bed," she said out of her thoughts. "Any man would want to try the goods." She shrugged and grinned. "But maybe he ain't got the balls for it. Next time I'm close, I'll grab the senator's jumbo; see if I get a reaction."

"That's my baby. You're beginning to see the light."

Juliet began to giggle. "As my best friend and confidante, you can have the honour of judging. I'll move in close and give a come on squeeze. You watch his face, see if his tongue pops out, then we'll know he's for real."

"Sweetpea, for that show I'll carry a surveillance camera."

"And I'll let you know if the future President has balls enough for the job."

Juliet laughed, then put her head on Lisa's shoulder, clasping hold of her arm as she closed her eyes.

Jake brooded as the Sikorsky helicopter juddered its way towards Cape Cod, its turbulent frame stimulating memories of Iraq and Afghanistan. A time he remembered when a soldier knew his duty, knew the meaning of patriotism and endeavour, a time he considered the most important in any man's life, a time of war. Ten minutes after his call from the mortuary, he dialled Wat Wash on their personal link. Jake dispensed with pleasantries.

"We have ourselves a situation. Max Crawley's chief admin officer, Luke Perry, got himself run over by a truck; dead and gone." Jake listened to the silence of shock, then Wat's gravelled voice came over the transmitter, no hint of African origins, just moneyed New England.

"Does his family know, does Max know?"

"Nothing out yet. But when the police found Perry's security pass they called the FBI who called Walsh

Securities on account of his briefcase. Inside were copies of classified documents."

"You check their grade?"

"They originated from somewhere high. Looks like we got enemy in the compound."

"Shit. Has Max Crawley been informed?"

"I'm about to relay the news."

"If the FBI are onto this, we need to contain damage. I suggest we put the towers on maximum security."

Jake imagined the dapper little man pacing his Philadelphian mansion, his fists clenched, his eyes closed as he calculated the cost to his bank balance.

"Negative, Wat. Let's keep this wrapped. Maximum security would have the media on our ass. I'm putting the doctor and his department under twenty-four-hour close watch surveillance. If we can identify an accomplice, we can interrogate."

"God damn, this had to happen right near completion. Where's Juliet?"

"The tracker bracelet puts her heading for Humarock after a visit with Lucas. She's safe, but I think we need her in deep cover, at least until Raider is handed over."

"Agreed, but I can't force her. She's determined to stay and her liaison with Lucas is important."

"Kids sometimes need direct persuasion," Jake said, and looked out into the darkness.

"Get a meeting set up with Max, my office 0800 hours," Wat said.

Jake listened to the contact go dead and knew he'd torn the great Mr Walsh apart, divided between the safety of his two loves, GR4, unmanned stealth bomber extraordinary and Juliet his daughter, an exasperating female. Jake pressed buttons for Dr Max Crawley, wondering if the little faggot was lying on pink satin.

"Bad news, Doctor. Your chief exec just got himself run over, dead." Jake smiled down to the scattering of lights two thousand feet below and heard Crawley gasp in disbelief.

"How in God's name?"

"Tripped on a kerb. Now he's slabbed out in the city morgue with a head like a pancake."

"This is awful."

"Worse, he was carrying classified documents from your department. We got a meeting in Wat's office at 0800 hours tomorrow. I know you and Perry were close," he paused. "That will mean awkward questions. I'll be in my office from 0700 hours if you want to look in, it may save you grief."

Jake switched off and returned the mobile to his pocket whilst smiling. Across the cockpit, Navro jockeyed the craft through the glow of silver moonlight. "You know," Jake said. "I think I upset the guy."

"Are we rolling, sir?" Navro asked.

Jake felt real pleasure in his smile as he looked to his subordinate. Navro was a sculptured mass of muscle who kept the light in his eyes hidden behind dark glasses. Ex-marine captain and expert in martial arts, he was the kind of man Jake trusted. A good soldier, from a good army. Jake took pride in hand picking his men. No one would push Walsh Securities, not even Delta Force. "We will be, Navro," he said. "I'm just about to apply a little direct persuasion."

"Stop!" Juliet's scream came the same instant she saw the flash of feline eyes, then the Mercedes was over it. In reaction, Lisa swerved into the emergency lane, stopping amidst a squeal of brakes and rubber.

"Did I hit something?" she asked. They were stationary beneath a high, concrete rampart. Juliet was out of the car even before it stopped, running from Lisa's frantic warning.

"For Christ's sakes, get back into the car. We're on the fucking freeway."

Juliet ran twenty metres before she found the cat crouched under a cable duct. It appeared in a state of bewilderment, its belly down flat, its teeth bared in retaliation to fear. She was unable to judge if it was hurt. The animal hissed warning.

"Come on little thing," she coaxed, keeping her voice gentle, her hand in offering, not touching. "You're going to get squashed out here. Come to Juliet." Taking a chance, she tentatively stroked the animal's head.

"What the hell are you doing, girl? Will you get back in the car!" Lisa came beside her waving a Glock automatic.

"Don't yell, you'll scare the cat," Juliet said, trying to maintain gentleness in her voice.

"Fuck the cat. You're in a high-risk zone. You want me fired?"

"I don't think it's hurt." Juliet slowly reached and carefully scooped the frightened creature into her hands. Lisa was on one knee, automatic at arm's length, threatening any passing traffic which slowed.

"Return to the car, Miss Walsh, or God help me, I'll strap your ass so hard you won't sit for days."

"Take no notice of her, she's only bluffing." Juliet gently turned the cat to cradle its back. "Maybe it's sick. Do you think it's sick, Lisa?"

"Are you listening to me, girl? For Christ's sakes, move it." Juliet was grabbed by her arm and dragged upwards. The cat seemed content to remain cradled as both were marched back to the Mercedes. Fifty metres ahead, a second car had stopped, its driver leaning on the roof, looking towards the approaching traffic. In the darkness, the myriad of passing lights flickered his silhouette. Lisa only took her eyes from him during the seconds she checked the abandoned Mercedes and thrust Juliet inside.

"Don't you like cats?" Juliet adopted her best little girl smile, watching Lisa climb in opposite before slamming her door.

"Don't you butter me up. You had me shit scared."

Lisa returned the automatic to its holster then swung back into traffic, checking the parked car as they passed. The driver was out of sight. "You might have got run over, snatched, shot. Did you see that guy watching? Jesus, I'm going to give you such a spanking."

"I think I'll call him Lucas," Juliet said.

"It's probably got fleas. Anyway, how do you know it's a boy?"

"Because he's smiling at me."

Lisa answered with silence, increasing speed, continually swapping lanes and checking her rear mirror for a tail.

"Sorry," Juliet said finally and touched her arm. "Didn't mean to upset you."

"You forget young lady, you're the most precious thing in your daddy's life. If he ever hears I let you out on the freeway, my butt will be down the road and you confined in your gilded cage."

Juliet stroked the cat, not looking at Lisa as she held up the tracker bracelet locked around her wrist.

"I've never been out of my gilded cage; not since Momma died." She heard Lisa's protracted sigh of resignation and knew she'd won. She stroked the cat and took comfort from its acceptance of her while lights from other people's lives and houses passed in the night. She let silence calm Lisa's mood.

A month previously her father had rented a summerhouse overlooking the ocean near Humarock, Massachusetts. It was, he said, a place of her own to entertain friends. But her friends were all hand picked from the empire, approved by security and never allowed to break the rules of conduct. If they did, they were out, whether Juliet liked it or not. Neither did she believe the house was hired for her personal benefit but to allow an exchange of visits between herself and Senator Lucas Kean far from New York's social gossip.

In truth, she liked the place. The views were

magnificent while the grounds were surrounded on three sides by forest. She frequently swam in the ocean, trying hard to ignore the flotilla of ex-navy seals who bobbed around in diving gear or high-powered inflatables. On the estate, ex-Delta men patrolled the woods and hid in the shrubbery when she strolled through the grounds. The only place outside in which she had privacy was an enclosed courtyard containing the pool. To rebel against those beyond the wall she had taken to swimming naked, waving if any patrolling helicopters infringed her air space. She enjoyed the sense of wickedness in deliberately exposing herself to those who guarded her vulnerability. Lisa scolded her, but Juliet just pouted and encouraged her to do likewise. At least Humarock provided a measure of freedom and peace to organise herself. She had space to research, to write her thesis and more important, escape the tension smothering her father and Walsh Towers, tension emanating from Jake Hammerton and his Draconian security. She kept the rules, stayed obedient under the dark memories of her mother's death and saw no reason why Jake Hammerton should send her to England. The cat began to purr and Juliet switched on the radio, searching the stations until she found a Mozart concerto.

"Love seeketh not to please, nor for itself to bare, but in another give its ease, and build a heaven in hell's despair," she quoted to the cat.

"What? You say something?" Lisa asked.

"William Blake; I was quoting a poem," she said.

Lisa activated a hands-free mobile over the dashboard then eased the Mercedes off the expressway to a state highway. "This is J one," she called base. "We're heading route one hundred, twenty-three, towards Green Bush junction and ocean, ETA thirty minutes."

"Would you please ask them to ready some milk and a little supper for Lucas." Juliet stroked the cat, which purred in contented lethargy, its eyes closed, its body snuggled between arm and lap.

Lisa grinned final forgiveness. "You're some blossom, Sweetpea. Medensky," she called back over the mobile. "We picked up a casualty. Ask the kitchen to rustle up some milk and fish paste for our return."

Juliet twisted in her seat as Lisa checked the rear-view mirror. From the darkness of the open countryside the screech of sirens and flashing lights gave shrill and urgent demand to their right of way. Lisa slowed and pulled over, allowing three police cars and an ambulance to pass in a tight-packed convoy.

"Must be a bad one," Juliet said, calming the cat which had tensed its body.

"The way they're driving they're going to cause a bad one," Lisa said, returning the car to its former speed. She leant to switch on the mobile. "Medensky, give me a situation status, highway one, twenty-three."

"Nothing on that. Want me to check with County Sheriff?"

"Do that."

Juliet fidgeted, waiting to speak, feeling she could delay no longer. "Lisa, we're buddies, we're close." She briefly touched Lisa's hand. "I got to tell you what I've planned, because you might be upset. I've rented a cottage up in Vermont. When I next see Lucas I'm going to ask him to spend three days there with me, alone."

"Baby," Lisa looked across and shook her head. "You can't do that. Do you know the problems that would cause?"

"Less problems than if I married without doing it. I want him to fuck the hell out of me, see if there's good sex, then move on to see if there's friendship and love."

"Juliet, how do we deal with security?"

"I'll make him wear a condom. And you can snuggle up outside with his bodyguard. The two of you, deep cover."

"Sweetpea, that cat will fly before your Papa lets you do

that."

"I won't tell him. I ain't going to England, Lisa. I'm going to show Lucas what I expect of him. My question is, do you want in?"

"I'd follow you to the end of the earth, you know that."

"Thanks." Juliet lingered with her touch. "I want Lucas to do the same."

Lisa slowed the Mercedes as it approached the flashing lights of a patrol car and a line of stationary traffic. She reached for her mobile.

"Medensky, where's that situation report?"

"I've cleared you with County Office." Medensky's voice came back.

"Cleared us for what? God dammit."

"Hope no one is hurt." Juliet leaned forward, caressing the feline warmth of her new pet.

From out of the shadow a uniformed officer flickered a floodlight over the Mercedes' licence plate and came round to Lisa, kneeling as she lowered the window.

"Miss Walsh?" he enquired.

"Who's asking?" Lisa's hand lay on the butt of her Glock automatic.

"Officer Mattlock. Been a bad smash ahead. Road won't be cleared for an hour but we have a patrol car on the other side waiting to take you home."

"Why us?" Juliet asked. "Other people are waiting."

"Orders down from the County Sheriff's office. You got powerful friends, Miss Walsh."

Lisa hesitated on her call over the mobile. "What about the Mercedes?"

"We'll look after it – deliver it back when the road's open. Mind if I get in, show you forward?"

Lisa shook her head. "You mind handing me your gun?"

"I can't do that, Ma'am."

"Then you walk in front. Keep a distance, nice and steady so I don't get nervous and run you over."

For seconds the officer's intended reply was plain on his face. Instead, he breathed deep and said. "Just follow me, Ma'am."

Juliet clicked her tongue. "Now you've upset the nice policeman. Better be careful with your speeding." She watched the officer move forward and start to pace with the unhurried gait of a funeral director.

Lisa kept the car a couple of metres behind.

"Rules for girls, big and small. Never take sweeties from a stranger and never let a stranger into your car. No matter what he's dressed like." She went back to the mobile. "Medensky, who did you speak with at County Sheriff's?"

"Some guy up top named Driscoll."

"You arranged some clearance with them?"

"No, they arranged it with me."

"Medensky, stay on immediate response." Lisa reached out and switched off the mobile. "Juliet, baby, put down the pussy cat and hold your call alarm. I'm hiking this situation to code red."

"Oh, Lisa." Juliet rolled her eyes. "They're the police. People are hurt."

"Do as nanny says, or nanny will get cross."

Juliet winced in despair but hoisted the cat to her left shoulder, leaving her right hand free to grasp the gold alarm pull around her neck.

"Lisa, you're over-reacting."

"Over-reacting, nothing. I just saw a flea jump off that mangy creature. For Christ's sakes, Juliet, until we're clear, get smart and concentrate."

Juliet looked from the safe luxury of the limousine to the lights of the stationary vehicles and their frustrated occupants. Once past the police car blocking the lead vehicle, the Mercedes traversed a blind bend and stayed in darkness until turning a second. Ahead, emergency vehicles and patrol cars formed a barrier beneath a single, portable floodlight. Beyond, an ambulance stood in readiness, its doors open, its interior a gleam of brilliant light. Lisa halted the Mercedes beside the officer. Juliet saw hunched figures, police or paramedics. The officer tapped her window, indicating for Lisa to release the central locking.

"You have to walk from here, ladies. Car's on the other side." He opened the door for Juliet. Lucas squirmed in her grasp, forcing her to let go the alarm while she tried to calm him. She saw Lisa lift the mobile from the dash and un-holster her Glock, holding the weapon at full drop as she left the Mercedes.

The close proximity of the car bonnets forced them to single file, squeezing them one by one through the gap, the officer first, Juliet behind and Lisa at the rear. The area had emptied of people. Juliet sensed the cat bristle, its nervous agitation triggering her own uncertainty. The tighter she held, the more the animal twisted until the slipperiness of its feline fur shot from her fingers. Momentarily, its paws touched onto a car bonnet, then it leapt through light for darkness beyond. At the apex of its leap, the explosive impact of a single shot pulped its body into a slick of flesh, blood and torn fur, the rear legs extended in flight before it fell to the roadside.

"Lucas." Juliet's voice screeched in her own ears, her chest tight with horror. She twisted back to Lisa and heard her friend's muffled shout as two men rammed a sack over Lisa's head and shoulders; a third forced down her gun arm so the neck of the shroud was drawn tight about her waist. Juliet's second scream was solitary.

Hooded figures appeared from nowhere, crossing the light like animated shadows. The next instant she was thrown bodily onto the ambulance floor, spinning round on her knees as a second shot racked open the night. Before the door slammed shut, she saw Lisa's body on the highway, her shrouded head in a pool of blood.

When a pair of arms circled and lifted from behind, Juliet reacted as taught. Allowing her body to go limp she let both arms upwards, slipping in her attacker's grip, forcing him to bend and change his hold. In those brief seconds, her hand snatched at the gold cylinder secured around her neck. She knew the miniature transmitter sent an instant, but powerful signal to the house at Humarock and Walsh Towers in New York, then changed to a pulsed tracker transmission. The initial signal would be picked up by a dozen different receivers, activating computers which gave a combined cross-reading to locate her position to within three metres.

Juliet squirmed, kicked, punched and clawed as she was lifted onto a stretcher, arching and writhing her torso to prevent strong hands from strapping her down. Her screams were drowned by the wail of sirens while the ambulance turned in the road, its lights flashing past waiting traffic towards the freeway.

Sitting in the lead helicopter, Jake hit the immediate action button and sent fifteen ex-Delta Force scrambling for two military Black Hawks. As they clambered aboard clutching assorted weapons, Jake's luxurious Sikorsky S-76C was already skimming the rooftop of the Humarock beach house.

Jake sensed the surge of adrenalin which caused the glory-bound excitement he had discovered when a a mere captain in Iraq. Direct persuasion, he liked that term. Old man Walsh would have been informed of his daughter's situation immediately and a helicopter would now be transporting him from Philadelphia to Walsh Towers in New York.

"General, this is Navro." The man spoke over air transmission. "I just flew past attack point. No accident, no police, no ambulance."

"I read you, Navro. Trace now passing under the freeway and skirting South Weymouth airstrip. They're heading for the woods. My guess is, they got a chopper somewhere. Take highway five three. I have a wager we retrieve within fifteen minutes."

"What's the situation, Jake?" Wat Walsh's voice cut in on the general's headphones.

"Sweetpea now on red six minutes, forty-five seconds. Tracker beam gives a moving target. We have three choppers in the air and closing."

"Is this code red for real? What the hell's happening, Jake?"

"It's for real, sir. It's the only way my men play."

Juliet had lost her scream and was losing her strength as she struggled between two women. A third cut the gold chain from her neck.

The bedlam of noise from sirens and the shouted commands of her attackers were joined by the hacking thump of approaching helicopters. Juliet jabbed a bare heel into the stomach of one assailant, causing the woman to stagger. The others began pulling at the tracker bracelet.

With the under-slung searchlights of three helicopters on full-beam, Jake gave orders for each machine to fly parallel either side of the road, ensuring their quarry had no way to escape, holding the ambulance in a cone of moving light. Highway five three had taken them deep into open country. He saw no other traffic; no lights.

"Navro, go forward and use your beam to block the road. The moment they stop, we hit."

"On my way, General."

Jake watched the S-76C lift higher and swing forward in a wide, sweeping arc. A mile ahead it hovered feet over the road, both searchlights directed onto a single blinding cone centre of the highway.

* * *

Beyond the windscreen Juliet saw the road become a dazzling circle of brilliant whiteness. The driver was screaming out his panic, jabbing the brakes, toppling Juliet into a jumbled heap of sprawling bodies. Moments later she felt the ambulance bounce off the road, its nearside wheels furrowing downwards as it tipped over.

Looking up through the windows from where she lay, she saw the night sky change to an incandescent glow of multi-coloured lights as men abseiled from hovering machines. Within seconds, the ambulance door crashed open and she was dragged out with the others, all of them thrown spread-eagled in the dirt. The noise of machines and shouts rammed into her head, obliterating any rational thought. Hands searched over her body, which was then lifted and bundled between a crush of men who hurried in close order from the ambulance and her abductors. She had no idea if she was saved or caught by others; to live or to die. Everyone was shouting; no one listened to her protests. She could distinguish nobody's face or make sense of what they did. Against her will she began to cry. Didn't they realise Lisa was dead? Away from the helicopter they placed her on the ground and left her on hands and knees while the squad of men returned to darkness.

"Hostage secure, sir," someone shouted behind.

"Twelve minutes, twenty-two seconds. Well done, Juliet." General Hammerton came out of the shadows and offered his hand. "No need to cry, you're safe now. My God, you did well. Your papa will be proud."

"They killed Lisa. They put a sack over her head and shot her."

"Navro," the General called on his handset. "Get your ass down here. You got a passenger for New York." General Hammerton clasped her arm, leading her towards the S-76C as it settled on the road, the downbeat thrashing at her skirt and hair, whipping road dust to sting her face.

"Lucas, what about Lucas?" Juliet pleaded, wiping her eyes.

"Don't worry, Miss Juliet. We'll tell Mr Lucas you're safe."

Juliet wanted to explain but stopped as the helicopter door slid open. In the flutter of light there was no mistaking the lithe figure who leapt from the interior, running towards her with arms wide.

"Baby, oh my baby. What have they done to you?" Lisa swept her into a hug.

Juliet buried her head against the warm and comforting body, pressing her face and her tears. "I thought you were dead; I thought they'd killed you."

"No, babe, no, just stunned. Come on, let me get you out of here."

Arms around her shoulders, Juliet allowed herself led to the helicopter. "Who were they?" she asked. "What did they want?"

"Just don't worry, Sweetpea. You're safe now."

CHAPTER 3

Wat Walsh sat in the lavish comfort of his executive Bell helicopter, the sprawl of suburban New York passing three thousand feet beneath. Wat concealed his slight body in a carefully tailored suit and projected his presence with sharp, intelligent eyes. Always he kept his expression calm and took pride others found him inscrutable, never realising the dark pressures which sometimes threatened to crush his life. In an act of self-comfort he stroked the tight, grey curl of his beard and considered the present dangers, particularly those dangers which threatened Juliet. For eight years he had allowed security to dominate his life, allowed the claw of bitterness to haunt his conscience and give justification for Jake Hammerton's military methods. As always when black memories pricked through his brain, he saw the image of his wife, her decapitated body. He had failed her, but the vision gave determination. He would not fail Juliet. America was at war, its soil too frequently in the field of combat, his empire a part of America's defence. Like it or not, that made Juliet a target, as it had her mother. Wat lifted his iPhone and dialled Hammerton.

"How is she, Jake?"

"You bred a tough one, Wat. Two females from the opposition have severe bruising and she kept her main tracking device."

Wat felt guilt and shuffled in his seat. "You said a surprise exercise. I didn't realise they could take it that far."

"Rough and real, sir. It's the only way. Times are mean and training must reflect the situation. But there was no physical damage."

For a moment Wat held his words. Jake would never realise the confusion of a young girl's mind. There were occasions when this man stretched all tolerance, but the Pentagon trusted him and his presence kept intrusive military interference out of Walsh Towers.

"I assume this is part of your direct persuasion, to get her over to England?"

"Due to the current situation with Raider, it's imperative we change Juliet's schedules frequently and preferably put her into deep cover. Change of country will frustrate and confuse possible enemy intentions. She needs to realise living a regular lifestyle makes her an easy snatch. Unfortunately she took Lisa's simulated killing hard, cried like a kid."

"She is a kid, General, let's not forget it."

"Yes, sir!" The general's voice came back, crisp, respectful. "But maybe now she's a kid more willing to listen."

"It's difficult for her without a mother and a father who's hardly there. She's a young woman who's developed her own mind. I'll get Lucas in on this. His persuasion might clinch it. I know his week ahead is busy, leaving no time for socialising with her but a few phone calls from him could persuade her."

"Talking of Lucas, sir, I have reliable feedback she's grown soft on him."

"She has?" Wat eased his face to a smile.

"When she was snatched, she shouted Lucas' name. Like he would leap from the night to save her. Then after the rescue she mentioned him again."

Wat looked at the wedding ring on his left hand and braced his fingers. Ahead of him Walsh Towers poked its glass-speckled nose above rivals. "Then I'll definitely get him in. OK, General, stand down. I'll be in touch." Wat turned to Betty, his secretary of thirty years. "What's Sweetpea's favourite restaurant?"

"Currently, Harry's Piano Bar. One of those designer places full of celebrities."

"Book her lunch there tomorrow. A table for six. Lisa,

of course, and four others. What friends do we have on duty? I want ones who'll steer her marriage-wise."

Betty checked her notebook. "We cleared two girls she met at Avionics last week, very friendly. Jo-Jo and Annabel from Communications. Jo-Jo is just married and I can schedule another two chums recently engaged."

"They'll do. Let's keep romance and marriage to the fore. Could be Lucas is winning the day. Politics needs money, Betty and money needs politics. Money's no good unless you use it."

"You should know, Mr Walsh. You own most of it."

"And get Sweetpea some flowers. In fact, fill her apartment with flowers. When we meet, she might be a touch tetchy."

At 1.30 a.m. Juliet nodded to the sentry and entered her father's apartment on top of Walsh Towers. Her tears had dried but she knew they still lay close behind her anger. When she stepped into her father's study he came from his chair, smiling, arms open. Was this her father she thought, or the emperor of Walsh Industries? For seconds she was tempted to capitulate, to hug him, instead she lifted one of his prize porcelain pots and let go her rage as it hurtled to the floor. The tears came then, welling up through frustration.

"How dare you? Do you know what they did? I was shit scared. I thought Lisa was dead."

"Realism is essential. You have to understand what you face. It's a cruel world, Sweetpea."

"Don't call me Sweetpea. I'm twenty-two years old, a grown woman. That was my momma's name for me. I want my momma, why isn't my momma here?"

"Juliet, Juliet my child."

He stepped up and gave her the comfort of his arms as he had done when she was little. She sagged against him and felt her wet cheek on his, felt her strength and anger cave as he whispered in her ear. "Your mother would never have forgiven me if I allowed you to be harmed."

"Then let me go free. I want to please you, Papa but I have to breathe, I have to be my own person."

"And so you shall, Juliet. Just give it a little more time, a little more understanding. We are both captives in this empire. Captives by the need to serve our country. Being my daughter places you amongst the targets for terrorism. But when Raider is handed over my importance will diminish and with it any threat from terror groups. They murdered your mother and I am to blame. I could not bear the thought that any harm might come to you."

"It wasn't your fault, Papa." Juliet stood back and saw his fragility and sorrow. "They took her; they killed her because you were unable to give in. You did all you could." His eyes closed and she rubbed his shoulders trying to pass over her love.

"To prevent such an occurrence again, the exercise imposed upon you was hard but necessary for all involved. I am responsible for hundreds of thousands of employees. It is not easy being emperor, it is not easy being an emperor's daughter. I need your strength, Juliet, your kindness and understanding but most of all your smile."

Juliet touched his cheek. "To give you strength, Papa, I must build my own. I have mother's spirit and your tenacity, so let it blossom, please." She kissed his cheek.

"Then make my life easier, go to England. Stay hidden until Raider is handed over. Jake has it all arranged."

Juliet stood back and felt the flush of instant resentment. Did her father love her or manipulate her? "If you want me as First Lady, I must learn the pressures of being a target. I must also learn the pleasures of the man I'm meant to love. If you want me to marry Lucas, I must know the man I get into bed with."

She saw the hurt on his face and suddenly felt shame over what she had said, but now she had started she saw no point in stopping. "History is littered with political mis-marriages, I'm aware of the importance you place in mine. Black and white, the two united in marriage and America but there has to be a human side. Next week I intend to take Lucas to the woods. I want to see him without his trappings. I want to know his weaknesses, I want to know his strengths. I want to see him as a man capable of love and passion. You have to give me some small chance in this, Papa."

His face changed, becoming formal like a minister who had heard something improper. "Perhaps in the morning you should call him and explain your proposition."

"I will. Goodnight, Papa."

Juliet left her father's penthouse apartment and walked within the glass corridor that protected her from the buffeting winds. She circumnavigated the helicopter pads and reached her own apartment on the opposite side. In the process, she passed six armed and uniformed guards. Each man saluted her with the precision and discipline gained from enlistment in the Marines. With her father's encouragement, General Hammerton had developed Walsh Security into a formidable force, with its own boot camp and training ground. It seemed to Juliet that they employed half the US veterans from Special Forces; men who protected his buildings, his property, his plant, his aircraft, his daughter, his empire.

In the sanctuary of her apartment she leant against the bombproof door and let go a long, plaintive sigh. Only here did she feel the privilege of having her own space. No one entered without her permission. No hidden eyes and ears watched or listened through bugs or surveillance cameras.

Her watch read 2 a.m. but Eva, her maid, sat waiting. The living room was filled with dozens of flowering bouquets, their bright colours and scentless petals creating a sense of surreal intrusion.

"They're from Papa and Lucas." Eva stood. "They must have given you a rough time."

"No harder than was necessary."

"You've been crying, child." She came across and eased Juliet out of her jacket. "Look at you. Mud on your face, dirt in your hair. It's like you've been scrapping in the playground."

"One of the General's soldier games."

"You want I run a tub?" She lifted the torn hem of Juliet's skirt. "You got knees grubbier than an urchin."

"Really, Eva, I'm OK." Juliet smiled impatience. "I promise I'll take a shower and go straight to bed."

"Mind you do." The old woman eyed her in stern benevolence. "And don't let that Lucas too close either," she said, leaving for her own room. "You just stand your ground. You're too young for going with a grown man like that."

"Yes, Eva." Juliet smiled as she departed, thankful for the comfort of genuine motherly concern.

When finally alone in her bedroom, she stripped off her clothes and so as not to disappoint Eva, left them where they fell. She showered quickly ensuring the cleanliness of her knees, dried, put on pyjamas and climbed into bed. For a while she lay staring into darkness, determined for revenge. They had killed her cat and that was murder. She would not forgive or forget. Somehow, somewhere she would escape.

Wat entered his office by 0700 hours, a massive bombproof glass cubicle which divided the tower block floor and held a working replica of GR4's flight deck. The glass divided him from where Betty and other secretaries laboured over computers, their office walls covered in rows of CCTV and monitors, each showing various floors of Walsh Towers along with offices and factories from China to Mexico. Activity in many of the American factories had already commenced. By 0730 hours local time, Wat expected everybody at their workplaces. Wat gave commitment and demanded the same from his employees.

Behind a mahogany desk banked with communication equipment he settled his mind on the immediate problem – security. If Perry had lifted information it was inconceivable he acted alone. That meant likely accomplices in technical or security departments. If in the higher levels of security, they would also have access to personnel movements, including Juliet's. He considered it imperative she go to ground. He was aware the military saw Juliet as only a minor concern over Raider's security but then the military who roamed his building had never viewed the headless body of a wife. He lifted the phone for Lucas Kean.

"I have reliable information Juliet's gone soft on you, Lucas. The future is looking good."

"Makes me a privileged man, sir."

"But burdens you with a problem. She's young, headstrong and her values are ... modern," he paused and let Lucas assess the loaded description.

"Marriage will give her a sense of old fashioned values and hopefully take the bite out of her."

Wat nodded his head and hummed agreement. "Until then, you might just have to manoeuvre a little, show encouragement. She's got some notion of taking you into the mountains during the next two weeks. I've seen that determination in her before, I saw it in her mother. Once she's made up her mind about something, ain't nothing going to budge her. She wants you, boy. Upset her and you could land a vixen." Again he listened while Lucas picked over his words and felt satisfaction with the younger man's response.

"Let's talk openly, Wat. I have the greatest respect for you and Juliet. And she's one hell of an attractive girl with fire to burn. But a white presidential candidate trying to bond black and white through marriage and family cannot afford any indiscretion on the way. Satisfaction of a young female's demands included. Besides, next couple of weeks my schedule is tight."

"As I expected, Lucas. So let's circle this to advantage. Next ten days while Raider's handed over, I want Juliet safely hidden away in England. Now she won't go or give up the mountains unless she thinks you'll go there too. Of course, once she's gone, your busy schedule may well cancel your own departure, but she'll get over it."

"I read you, Wat. Leave it with me."

"I appreciate that, Lucas." Wat swivelled his chair and looked beyond heavy glass windows to the New York skyline. "My Gulf Stream's parked up a few days. If you need to fly interstate, it's yours."

"That's real generous of you, Mr Walsh."

"My pleasure, Lucas. Be in touch."

Wat hung up and climbed steps onto Raider's replica flight deck where he sat in the pilot's seat, his favourite place. The whole set-up had cost him thirty million dollars and at one time was the main control and aviation centre for Raider's unmanned flight from Whitman Air Base. After 9/11 they had built a second replica six floors below ground and left this as standby. Because it was shielded by bombproof glass and remained the second most secure room in the building, Jake had insisted Wat move in. He agreed because it gave access to the ultimate executive toy. He loved this place and ran expert fingers over the switches and controls, knowing from here he could fly the machine via substation or satellite over any hostile country. This was his dream, an unmanned missile deployment system capable of circumnavigating the world beyond the reach of any enemy. In eight days he would give GR4, Global Raider to the nation, next year he hoped to give his daughter for First Lady. Both had to be perfect. He felt these moments should be his happiest, everything on line, everything going as planned, except for the dark spectre which haunted his mind, a spectre inside the firewall. He prayed to God it wasn't Bin Qasem. The intercom's buzzing interrupted further thought.

"Your 8.00 a.m. appointment, sir." Betty spoke from the outer office.

Wat climbed from the flight deck and pressed the door release on his desk so a heavy glass panel slid open. He waved Jake and Max Crawley to sit and paid no heed to formalities.

"We had a theft, Max. Can you explain?"

Max shifted in the chair. "Perry was vetted for A1 security. I don't know who got at him or why. I've been up all night, I stripped his computer, checked all files. Nothing but information he was meant to have, though I admit, as chief exec, that was most everything. The reason I put Raider's data into a loop system was so no one could take out anything other than what they worked on, and once logged out, it was monitored all the time until logged back in. Failure to do so would bring immediate action from security." He looked to Jake. "No information from the loop can be transported to another computer or be printed. All line links and cell phones are monitored. Hell, Fort Knox ain't safer."

"So how come Perry walked New York with a briefcase of classified documents?"

Max shuffled again. "He copied them from the screen, maybe memorised them."

"The man was clever but not a fucking genius."

"Which means the leak had severe limitations." Max's face brightened as if he offered some redeeming revelation.

"I don't see the purpose. Who would pay for chicken shit?"

"It's possible Perry's death was a genuine accident," Jake said. "Truck and driver have not been found. That was a multi-wheeled vehicle. It's possible the driver never realised he'd run over Perry's head. Alternatively, Perry could have been set up as a patsy, deliberately hit to put him in the open. If it ever came out that unknown amounts of information have been passed to an enemy, GR4 would be permanently compromised. Heaven would harbour concern over the bomber's ability as America's foremost weapons system. If the craft was shot down they would think Perry's security breach was a possible cause. The GR4 missile deployment system would be prematurely flawed."

"So it's better all knowledge of the incident is contained," Max said.

Wat shifted in his seat, feeling reservations. The idea was too neat. It allowed immediate damage limitation by deceit. He trusted these men, but he was also aware that to join concealment of facts incriminated him, which then gave both men the power to threaten revelation at a later date.

"The police and FBI agent who handed in the briefcase, did they realise the contents?" Wat asked.

Jake shook his head. "Unlikely. The documents were in sealed envelopes. The FBI was called because Perry carried Walsh Avionics and Government ID. The briefcase was handed to my chief exec, Henry Taylor. He opened it and came straight to me. No-one else knows."

"Keep it that way." He watched Crawley glance to Jake, then at the floor, his eyes shadowed. Wat pulled at the grey curl of his beard. "The three of us are lined up as principal code holders for Raider's final tests. If the military discover a security breach, they'd take that privilege away. That would play havoc with our schedule. I got a five billion dollar fortune riding here and we all got reputations. If any outside agencies become involved, they'll make hay and turn the whole incident into a fiasco. We bury it, okay?"

He watched Max nod then show a lame smile. Jake lifted his hooknose.

"With due respect to Max and his department, I want

everyone down there under 24/7. I also want Max under house wrap."

"I don't need that." Max drew back his neck and shoulders and looked between them.

"Trust no-one, Max. I don't."

"Jake's right. You're too important and your department is compromised. Jake will take care of arrangements. Eight days and we can all relax." Wat pressed the door release to end the meeting. "Jake, I need to talk about Juliet." He shook Max's hand and watched him leave before the door slid closed again. "What's the truth, Jake?"

"Someone must have helped Perry hand copy that information from screen. My guess, we got enemy in the compound. We can't take chances. We don't know what information has been leaked or for how long. I don't want to paint a black picture, Wat but let's look at dark scenarios. Max Crawley designed Raider from scratch. He invented the loop security system and made it foolproof, or so we thought. He even designed the tracking bracelets worn by top personnel, your daughter included. Raider is his, and after its inaugural flight he'll be acclaimed amongst the greatest flight engineers in history. He'll walk off with applause, you'll walk off with five billion, plus. Get the scene?"

"Come on, Jake." Wat sat back and stared at the friend he'd known since Iraq. "Max is a scientist, justifiably accredited with great respect. He may not own billions but he plays with other people's billions all the time. I don't even get to play with my own money."

"Seemingly above reproach," Jake said, one thick finger stabbing at the table. "He made the loop, he made the code system. Sure as hell I bet he can bypass both. If found out, no one would think to question him. He could lift the whole GR4 project, store it until he's on GR5 then sell GR4 to the Chinese, the Russians, whoever pays. He gets glory and money."

"You've no proof."

Jake shook his head. "He was never a soldier but he is a faggot. Perry was a faggot. Christ knows what they do across the mattress. They did have a relationship. My guess, that's why Perry got the job, one of the boys in the Pink Club." He lifted a forefinger and leant back in his chair. "That's the blackest picture but it's my job to look at all possibilities. As I said, we have enemy in the compound."

"I can't touch Max. Without him Raider don't fly."

"I don't advise we touch him. He may not be part of it but he could be innocently drawn in, blackmail, trickery. What I do advise is trust no one and covertly place internal security to code red. Vigilance will catch the spy. We watch, we wait."

Wat felt the dark pressures slither over his mind and visualised the decapitated body of his wife. They never found her head. "Let's get real. In this building we have Army, Navy and Air Force uniforms everywhere, but how many other agencies do we have in here under cover? How many secretaries, cooks and bottle washers are really CIA, FBI, counter-intelligence and God knows who else, including al-Qaeda? We are in a security nightmare but above all, we still perform and produce. Code red and vigilance I go with but no dramatic interference with procedures, Jake. And no harassing Max Crawley unless there is irrefutable proof of his involvement in this affair."

Jake nodded his head and stared across the desk. "Code red means Juliet in deep cover whether she likes it or not. Enemy coming through the back door via abduction is a real threat."

Wat closed his eyes and contained a shudder. "The English trip, I'm working on it. What's the set up? I might need to sell it to her."

"She's booked in as one Holly Johnson for a two week seminar on English Literature at Cambridge University. We got a flat arranged in the town plus a Brit setup called

CAT, the Combined Agency Taskforce, to watch over her with Lisa. CAT is meant to be the British Special Forces elite."

Wat nodded. "Sounds good."

"I checked these guys out, everyone of them is handpicked and in this situation we need the best. Soldiers who are proven men, who will never let you down. Only a few members of the immediate security team will know who Holly Johnson really is. On top of that we have decoys, plus a bolt-hole known only to Henry. He arranged it."

Juliet drew the sheet up to her eyes and watched Eva slide back the curtains on a bright blue sky. The old maid put hands to hips then muttered words as she picked Juliet's discarded clothes from the floor.

"The day's a-wasting, Miss Lazy Bones."

"I had a hard night, Eva. Be kind to me."

"Young lady, when I was your age, come dawn ..."

"I was working in the fields," Juliet finished for her and pushed up on the pillows. "Eva, you know I'm just a spoilt brat."

"Then it's a good job I'm here to keep you in line. What you wearing this morning?"

"What's Lisa wearing?"

"Armani jeans, pink polo shirt."

Juliet considered, absently twisting the tracker bracelet on her wrist. She disliked matching with Lisa, disliked to feel she followed her friend's dress sense.

"I'll go for those new black stretch pants and blue top, you know, with the square neckline."

Eva turned to the cupboard and Juliet slipped from the bed to the bathroom. Behind closed doors she stood stripped off and before the mirror began to exercise with two dumb-bells, appeasing her slender nakedness as she did so. She figured her breasts OK, small, but proudly

43

held, her bum neatly curved and compact. The rest of her she judged too skinny. She tried to imagine Lucas watching from behind, smiling as he came to caress her neck and shoulders, his hands running over her breasts, over her hips and thighs. She closed her eyes, opened them again and imagined Lisa there instead of Lucas. Neither image set her mind at ease, which seemed to make it all the more imperative she became certain of herself. She felt incapable of making a life commitment which her inner spirit would never accept. Because once married there could be no other man or woman. She stopped exercising and looked herself over. More than one person had said the innocence retained in her eyes made her appear younger than her twenty-two years. Her features appeared more European than African and her dark honey-coloured skin gave no hint as to what part of that continent her ancestors hailed from. She figured more Sudan and Ethiopia than central, with God knows how many races stirred in between.

Showered and dried she returned to the empty bedroom where Eva had straightened the quilt and laid out her clothes. From a drawer she picked black underwear, a string and matching bra. Before the dressing table she combed long, luxurious hair and thought of asking Lisa to come help dry it. She liked Lisa to fuss over her, to touch. For seconds she stared into the mirror, eyes narrow.

"Dammit," she said aloud, snatched up the mobile and dialled Lucas on his personal mobile.

"Juliet, my dear," he answered, knowing the caller before she spoke. She sensed instant deflation, then patronised as he continued in a honey sweet voice. "I hear you've had something of an ordeal but came out with every praise, even from Jake Hammerton."

"These things are necessary." She looked down at her pink toenails and imagined him in a stuffy black suit. "But I sure was scared."

"Heard you called my name when they fired the starter

44

rounds. Got to admit, Juliet, that kind of touched me."

Juliet drew breath and took anger from the cat's shattered body. "I want you to make love to me. I'm not a virgin. I want us to go some place remote, without bodyguards and trappings, just two normal lovers. Three or four days. I want you to roll me in the hay and I want it now. This week. I want certainty of a compatible union." She listened to the gag of his voice then his silence. "Lucas?"

"My dear, I'm overwhelmed."

"You don't have to say anything. Your eyes will say it, your touch, your passion. These things will show if we are making love or fucking each over. There's a difference."

"Such fire, such wanton need would be wonderful to consume. But the practicalities do not allow time, perhaps later in the year. I have a hunting lodge in Montana."

"With servants, bodyguards, ranch hands. Lucas, when I was at uni I had two boyfriends. I allowed both to fuck me. And that's what they did, fuck me. And it was good. I'm asking you to make love. You turning me down?"

"I have to be in England next week. I can't postpone."

"You do?" Juliet felt stunned and bit on her lips as she looked down at her pink toenails, curling them as she realised the possibilities. "If I came over, could we meet?"

"That is possible but secretly."

"Very secretly. And my proposition?"

"Fills me with desire and happiness."

Juliet felt her smile, felt the world lift. "I'll let you know my arrangements. Promise you won't let me down?"

"From my heart."

Juliet switched off and began to dry her hair. She had a thrill in her body which came from disbelief in saying what she had. Maybe he was OK after all.

Lisa sat in the kitchen, coffee and newspaper on the table.

"Hi babes." She looked up and Juliet kissed her cheek, receiving a raised eyebrow and smile in return.

"I feel good," Juliet said, putting arms round Eva's waist and dancing her in circles.

"I knew you'd go crazy, child." Eva shook her head, light on her feet as they circumnavigated the table. "All that bookwork and learning. No good for a girl."

"I changed my mind," Juliet said.

"Your prerogative, babes. We don't go to Harry's Piano Bar for lunch."

"No, we go to England. Soon as it can be arranged." She watched Lisa's eyes widen and saw the smile of relief. "Eva." Juliet swung wide. "How do I look?"

"Your cute little tom-boy self. But better in a dress." She sniffed.

"OK, Eva. Go pick me suitable attire. Something you would approve of."

Eva muttered as she left. Juliet pulled a chair beside Lisa and took hold of her hands. "If I go to England like Papa and Jake want, what's the set up?"

"You travel incognito under the alias of Holly Johnson. They have a place set up in Cambridge. You attend regular lectures on English Literature with other foreign students, all looking to take their PhDs. It's a bona fide course while the university is closed for summer recess. The whole object is Holly blends with the indigenous community. Concealment in the crowd is the most effective method of deep cover. But I can guarantee Jake will have a bolt-hole somewhere if needed."

"Sounds perfect. Where's that?"

Lisa shrugged. "I don't know. Nothing is revealed except on a need to know basis. That's the rule."

"Just the two of us?"

"To my knowledge," Lisa nodded, clearly delighted. Juliet compressed her lips and renewed her hold on Lisa's hand. "For three days Holly Johnson is going to have a fling with the future President of the United States. That

OK with you?"

Lisa became very still, her face suddenly blank. "Jesus, Sweetpea, we tell no-one our location. That's the whole essence of deep cover."

"We can tell the future President. For Christ's sakes, Lisa, I'm going to be his wife." Juliet put a hand to her friend's cheek. "Sorry, Lisa but as princess of the empire I'm playing the brat. It's all arranged."

"Your happiness is my happiness, babe. But we won't be entirely alone. Jake will have backup in case I go down, Brits most probably. Most times you won't see them, but they'll be watching. Lucas will need a good pair of sneakers."

Juliet felt conspicuous in the dress, a cotton floral print with lace at neck and cuffs, something Eva might wear to church. Ideal for the image though. Papa was all smiles, Jake patronising. Juliet played at her little girl come home role, ignoring Lisa who sat in the corner with a smirk of cynical disbelief.

"After last night's exercise I lay thinking. Raider's final test and hand-over is big for Papa and everyone in Walsh Industries. Guess it's only fair I play my part and co-operate with security during this uncertain time." Juliet smiled what she hoped was candy while flashing her eyes at Jake. "Lisa explained what the tutorials at Cambridge were about and I thought, hey, they could really help the research for my doctorate. Top of that, I'd be safely out of the way like you guys want. So, better late than never, here I am." She tweaked her skirt and plucked at the neckline.

Jake looked down at her over the brow of his big hooked nose. The bastard who let someone kill my cat, she thought. She had the sense of being viewed as an insect, a jewelled beetle that was kept in a box and occasionally brought out for display.

"I appreciate your co-operation on this, Juliet. It's a responsible decision you've made. The cover works on simplicity. You travel under a false passport and identity provided by the CIA, one Holly Johnson. There will be two decoys. All three of you stay in different hotels and when we're sure no one follows, you switch to a safe house in Cambridge. The decoys continue with their tour while Holly Johnson the student occupies herself in her studies. No-one but a two-person close support team will know who or where you are. One of that team is Lisa. The other from Brit security, who will watch covertly and escort you when required. The very best. Naturally Walsh Security will keep discreet surveillance and backup over the whole op, ready to step in should it be needed."

"So very re-assuring." Juliet smiled and looked to Lisa with wide eyes.

"Lisa is already briefed. Flight is day after tomorrow. Outside of those immediately involved, your trip is secret. Henry Taylor also set up a bolt-hole just in case. But no one, other than Henry, knows where that is."

"Bolt-hole? What's that? Surely one hide is enough." Juliet crossed her knees, feeling the skirt hem at her calves.

"Moving you out of routine to different locations will wreck the plans of any would be abductors. Humarock, Walsh Towers, the hotel in London, then Cambridge, give four widespread destinations, the bolt-hole is for emergency."

"But where?"

"Somewhere in England. Location on need to know only. You'll have to ask Henry."

In shirtsleeves and braces, Jake completed fifty press-ups then swung his legs forwards before standing in a swift straight movement. Erect, he checked his pulse then nodded in satisfaction. Since retiring ten years previously he prided himself in never missing a day's exercise, of still running an eight minute mile and still keeping total control of his army.

Major Henry Taylor, retired, knocked before entering.

"Jake, you'll want to read this." He placed a four-sheet report on the desk. "Police and FBI put Perry's demise down to accidental death caused by unknown hit-and-run driver. They have no leads or information."

Jake shrugged into his jacket and felt a second of gratification. Shalk of the FBI had finally seen the light.

"You conduct an internal enquiry, Henry. Inform the FBI, ask for their assistance, but keep 'em outside. That should satisfy everyone. This also gives us licence to tighten up on Crawley, to dig shit on his private life."

"I assume that's metaphorically speaking, General?"

Jake paused as he straightened his tie and looked askew at his executive officer. "Henry, you have wit. But on consideration, it's not a bad idea. The more we have on Crawley, the more control we exercise. Now Perry's gone, get our nice boys active again, Tweedledum and Tweedledee. Crawley has a live-in faggot called Bernard. Let's see what games he likes to play."

"Any feedback from last night?"

"Roughing her a little worked a treat. Sweetpea's so pissed off she decided to escape, go to England." Jake grinned. "Direct persuasion, works every time."

"So I activate Holly Johnson, get the Brit over?"

"Do that. Also, get a decoy up to Humarock. This cottage she rented for screwing our future president, you know where it is?"

"The tap on her phone indicates she booked it through a letting agency in Miami. I can find the location."

"Send a couple of look-alikes up there with all the precautions, as if it was for real. The more decoys we have out, the safer Holly Johnson."

Henry pushed the bridge of his glasses back with a finger. "The Brits' Combined Agency Taskforce. I ran a routine check. They're good but very secretive and self-contained. We may have trouble getting close."

Jake holstered his old military .45 automatic and felt the

comforting weight. He knew this would be a problem, Henry never missed a thing. "Quality," Jake told him. "They're pros. Holly has Lisa so only needs one man close quarters. We just make sure we have another looking over his shoulder. I've operated with the Brits, they don't mess."

"If you say so, Jake."

"I say so. Get their man over here. I want Operation Candy Girl rolling and Sweetpea out of my hair within forty-eight hours."

CHAPTER 4

In the untidy clutter of a Westminster office, Seb looked across to Colonel Freddy Fox and tried to judge if he knew the truth. Seb doubted Anderson had spoken and other team members just assumed Seb had done his job. The extended debriefing had revealed nothing.

"Well," Fox said in a light Belfast accent while he shuffled papers. "I think congratulations are called for all round. You passed with all guns blazing. Not only are you now a member of the Combined Agency Taskforce, you have also proven your ability as a terminator and that takes hard edged determination." Fox smiled while nodding approval.

For a moment Seb stayed silent then shook his head. "No, sir. I didn't kill Al Razi, Anderson did. I kill in combat, I have no problem with that but when it comes to cold-bloodied execution I didn't have it in me. We had no time for hesitation, so Anderson shot him. Sorry, but I failed."

Fox stared at him, his eyes suddenly without light. "No need to be sorry. It shows you're human," he paused. "What if Anderson hadn't been there?"

"I don't know." Seb glanced to the floor. "For sake of mission, maybe."

"I appreciate your honesty Lieutenant, it shows you are an honourable man. It also changes the situation. I was intending to place you in a unit known as the Football Team. Frequently in the world there is someone who needs to be removed. So the Football Team goes out to play the opposition. They usually come back one goal to nil. Had the Americans listened to us, Saddam would have departed this world long before the need for a war. Hundreds of thousands of lives might have been saved. But the ability to execute is paramount."

"I understand, sir. So, is this return to unit? Do I also fail my selection into the Agency?"

Again Fox smiled. "Seb, I can find a dozen men able to kill in cold blood, but few who have the honour as a gentleman to speak the truth, particularly when they think it would harm them. We have various units in CAT requiring different types of individual. Some people work best in a team, some best on their own. You may well be suited to the Secret Operations Executive, more underground than warfare but it's essential to our security. So, welcome to the Combined Agency Taskforce, Lieutenant Havic." Fox stood and reached out his hand.

Seb felt the smile spread on his face and the relief flood his body. He had made it, euphoria coursed through his veins in the same manner it had done when he passed for the SAS.

"So, go see your folks, have a few beers. Give me a day or two and I'll be in touch."

Seb went straight to the Lamb and Flag in Covent Garden, a place with good beer and relaxed atmosphere. No television or music blasting on indifferent ears, just gentile conversation from men and women in suits. Pint in hand, Seb sat before the open window and watched the people pass outside.

Only now did it dawn on him that his whole life might change. From his youth at Welbeck College followed by Sandhurst and a brief sojourn with the Guards, his life had been army, army, all accomplished mainly to please his father, a man with single-minded ideals. Escape had been the SAS. Acceptance into the Regiment gave him an adrenalin surge never realised before. He enjoyed military life but realised he was there because health had prevented his father achieving the same ambitions. He loved his father, his only parent, but his father's ambitions were not Seb's. CAT seemed a compromise to unite the two and the Secret Operations Executive sounded James Bond enough to provide lots of opportunity.

Seb sipped at his pint and watched a pretty girl go by, the sunlight briefly turning the skirt of her dress into a diaphanous veil that revealed long slender legs. Seb smiled and sipped more beer. His last girlfriend had departed amicably into the arms of a banker with a Ferrari. Seb didn't blame her. The Regiment kept him busy on covert operations helping to take out Taliban groups in Afghanistan. He hardly ever saw Louise who had her own ambitions based round a large house and bank account. Seb found the civilian world and its inhabitants becoming remote, a place where house prices, fashion and wealth superseded any concern over the secret wars which went on in their name. He knew his life had been swallowed but saw no other way to do the things he considered important. He reasoned that people without knowledge or understanding, people who believed what they read in the newspapers had no desire to care beyond their small environment. Traffic congestion caused more anger than some cleric smuggling a flask of anthrax from the Eastern badlands of Yemen to Piccadilly tube station.

Seb ordered a second pint and reclaimed his window seat, switching his mind to the real reason he had left the Household Cavalry for the Guards Squadron SAS and consequently the SAS for CAT. Some might have judged it as upward ambition but Seb knew it stemmed from a fear of failure, fear of failing his father, the Regiment and himself.

During the previous night he had woken in a cold sweat, the visions of ragdoll bodies scattered over the desert vivid in his mind; not the enemy but his own men. For seconds panic had clawed him in full savagery. Not the dread of his own death but of causing the deaths of others; dread of giving the wrong order, not reading the battle situation, not calculating the time factor. Before he had the excuse of always being second in command. Now he wondered if others realised Desert Snatch had been his first command in close quarter combat. He wondered if any realised the remnants of his youth lay with the shattered skull of Al Razi, that the action had moulded him to maturity, made him understand he must never alienate himself from the existence of normal, everyday people. He wondered if he should seek another girlfriend and find solace in her arms. Someone warm and happy, someone of the real world. Maybe in the Secret Operations Executive he could operate alone, far from the open battle field and the responsibility of other men's lives. The brief fire fight in the desert now hovered as a violent but distant memory and he jollied himself by thinking he had won. All of his men returned home. Afterwards, three days of debriefing and serious piss ups with the lads had all seemed relevant. Only later did he realise the extent of his fear and only now understood its reasons. But one good thing had emerged, perhaps at twenty-six, he'd finally grown up.

Back in his hotel room he kicked off his shoes and shrugged from his jacket. When sleep came it devoured him, leaving him in restless dreams until the following morning

Two days later Fox phoned while Seb ate breakfast with his father.

"Got an op for you," Fox said. "Rather delicate and very, very secret. Be at my office 0900 hours tomorrow."

"Business," Seb said for his father who sat opposite. "Can't tell you but I think you'd be proud."

"I m proud, son and I know you'll do your duty for Queen and country."

Seb turned up the following day suited and booted but minus a tie. Fox positioned his bulk behind the desk while a second and larger man around forty, sat with the relaxed expression of one who is clearly in the know.

"I'd like to introduce Sean Fagan," Fox said as Fagan extended his hand. "Ex-detective inspector, ex officer in the Serious Organised Crime Agency. And for your information he's read your file and knows all about you."

"Not everything, I hope." Seb grinned.

"Enough to realise you're one dedicated and determined young man," Fagan said, giving a firm handshake.

"So, what's the op, jungle or desert?" Seb leaned back and tried to appear at ease even though his stomach felt in the tight grip of apprehension.

"Nothing so simple. Something for our American cousins. They have a VIP citizen arriving in the UK for two weeks and need us to give shadow surveillance. We intervene and protect only in emergency, our main job being to alert her own backup if safety is compromised."

"Her?" Seb raised eyebrows.

"They've named the operation Candy Girl. So we assume the client is female," Fagan said. "She might be a politician, a star witness in some Mafia trial but definitely someone they want to hide, no one is telling us why. They've given her the name Holly Johnson and she's in deep cover for two weeks."

"If they don't trust us with information, why trust us at all?" Seb looked between them.

"They probably don't but simply have no choice. Her hide is in Cambridge," Fox said. "Though the university has recessed for summer there are still plenty of students, foreign and otherwise using the facilities. A bunch of American secret service agents hanging out would appear like gorillas at an academic tea party. Whereas you would blend as a summer student, as no doubt she will also. If you befriend her no one would think twice."

"Except on that point you are advised to keep a discreet distance," Fagan said. "They're clearly touchy about this girl."

"So she's young." Seb smiled.

"By the code name we assume so. But we are informed she is accompanied by an older, very capable, female bodyguard who we assume will be armed."

"This Holly Johnson sounds a real important person."

Seb looked between them. "But they won't tell us who?" He raised his hands.

"Deep cover works best on a need to know basis," Fagan said. "I doubt we'll ever know her true identity or importance. All we do is watch over her. My guess, she's the daughter of some high ranking politician. Not the President, his family don't match."

"In the course of time I'll whittle it down," Fox cut in. "Meanwhile Sean has the full brief on contact procedure and addresses. Candy Girl starts on her arrival at Heathrow day after tomorrow. Her backup team are already here. Your job, Seb is lead eyeball and panic button if needed. But rest assured her American heavies will always be lurking somewhere."

"So when do I start?"

"Now. Sean will brief you." Fox stood and shook their hands. "Any problems come straight to me. I got a feeling there is more to this than our cousins are saying."

Seb followed Sean from the building and out into Whitehall.

"Fancy a drink?" Sean asked.

"I know a great pub about fifteen minutes walk."

"They sell good Guinness?"

"I guarantee it."

Seb let Fagan buy the round and waited in the sunshine outside on the cobbled road where no one could eavesdrop.

"Fox tells me you're ex SAS," Sean said, holding the Guinness so his shadow gave cover from the sun.

"Couple of years but I'm a new kid in this outfit. I've been undercover in Afghanistan but never in a home city."

"The secret is normal behaviour, that way you keep track of the target without drawing attention. Normality makes you invisible.

"Bit of piss by the sound of it."

"Don't believe it. I've frequently been undercover and if a situation occurs, not blowing that cover is difficult." He passed Seb a card. "Meet me at my place in Camden 10.00 hours tomorrow morning. I'll give you a full brief, then we plan our strategy."

Seb pocketed the card and sipped away at his beer, mulling over his next question. "You ever kill a man? I mean, like in cold blood?"

Sean furrowed his eyes waiting, maybe thinking before he answered.

"Yes," he said finally.

"How did it make you feel?"

"Sick. End of story."

In the light of London's dawn, Dr Jaber received the expected call and shuffled his feet in the public phone box off Bayswater Road. "Five billion dollars is a great deal of money, Octavius."

"Well it ain't coming no cheaper from no place else. My expenses are considerable. Ambition and politics cost."

"I do not have the authority to agree your demand. I must speak with Khalid bin Qasem."

"You do that, pal. But do it quick. Within seven days the American Air Force complete trials and accept this bird. Then you ain't got no chance. They'll take over the code system and remove its present weakness."

"I shall call within the hour." Dr Jaber replaced the handset and felt the pressure of anxiety etch his face. Qasem would be displeased by the man's greed. The sum was preposterous, more than even al-Qaeda could raise. They had prepared for almost three years, now everything appeared lost.

As light spread over the streets and brought new morning activity, Dr Jaber walked, hands behind back towards Kensington, his clothes rumpled, his posture slack. He adopted the image of a mild mannered academic more by instinct than effort. He had never considered himself a terrorist but a soldier fighting for the freedom of his Palestinian homeland. It occupied most of his thoughts and placed motivation into what he considered his useless life. Walking with unhurried steps, he gave careful consideration to the intricate details Bin Qasem had placed in his trust and to the dangers of that trust. His introduction to Bin Qasem had come through al-Qaeda. His recruitment had been immediate and total. Khalid bin Qasem, the most secret and revered of all Islamic leaders, had influence throughout the Muslim world. A man rarely seen, who disappeared for years to return with devastating effect; a lion among the fundamentalists who ate the flesh of Zionism and scourged the despicable Western Governments who gave them support. For Bin Qasem, he would die.

In Kensington High Street where telephone lines went through a different exchange from Bayswater, Dr Jaber pressed a twenty-pound pay card into the slot of another public telephone. His call connected to a central Parisian apartment. Equipment there activated a computer link which transferred him to a scrambled second line. This required the input of a ten-digit code linking him via satellite to an unknown destination. Jaber brushed sweat from his brow and waited for the line to open. He had no need to identify himself.

"His price is five billion dollars." Jaber waited on the silence that followed, surprised when Qasem finally spoke.

"Such a sum is not unexpected and my plans are structured so the operation is self-supporting. America will pay this money."

"But how? Khalid, it is impossible."

"My friend, until spent, money is but a collection of figures on paper. You have done well. Let our operation commence. Henceforth I deal with Octavius personally. You will implement our diversions and maintain your group in readiness. The package arrives within the next few days, you will be notified. Guard it carefully. It is worth more than five billion dollars. It is worth the might of America."

CHAPTER 5

When Seb arrived at Sean's flat the guy ushered him in and indicated a laptop screen.

"Change of plan," Sean said. "You leave for America to escort the lady in person. The flight's at 20.00 hours this evening." He handed Seb a ticket. "It seems our cousins wish to vet you before handing over their prize. So, no time to waste, sit down and listen in."

Max tried not to feel intimidated. Agreeing to accept that Perry memorised great swathes of data seemed feasible at the time, a logical way out of preventing Jake's full inquisition. Now he realised agreeing to the suggestion had only compromised his position and unwittingly drawn him into the man's power.

Max sat at Raider's flight deck above the control room on the sixth sub-floor of Walsh Towers. On the facing wall a giant screen showed the panoramic view from Raider's cockpit, a near satellite view of Northern Indian and surrounding countries. He considered this seat his domain. From here he could fly Raider to any place in the world and lecture over gathered politicians and military personnel in the adjoining auditorium. Save on this occasion, Jake Hammerton watched from the observation box. Max found the man's uninvited presence inhibiting and obtrusive. Two young men either side of Jake sat with bland expressions, but Max recognised their persuasion. They would dance at the Apple or Oscar clubs, wear velvet stretch jeans and sit on high stools drinking expensive cocktails bought by other men. He assumed their presence was one of Hammerton's ploys to further bully him under the guise of extra security; or perhaps a manoeuvre to annoy Bernard. Either way, he considered it an infringement of his privacy. Never had he brought any facet of his personal life to work, save for a brief association with Perry. A mistake Hammerton now seemed determined to exploit.

Flanked by assistants, Max looked over the subterranean auditorium where America's military elite had gathered with senior members of the Defense Department. All stared at the giant video screen displaying the slender shape of Global Raider filmed from an escort drone.

Max loved to set the military cockerels crowing, dangling his invention for approval, savouring the accolade. In the final trials and at hand-over he expected acclaim from the President down. GR4 was his aircraft and no one could deny him the right of absolute sovereignty.

Sitting in the full replica of Raider's flight deck, identical to the one in Wat's office and a dozen others which necklaced the world, he had the capability of overall strategic flight and mission control. Manoeuvring the joystick, he turned the aircraft to follow its escort drone, allowing the cameras to view head-on the ambiguous, flat surfaced shape which combined body and wings making any concept of definition difficult to distinguish. Such a view always impressed and he listened to the general murmur of approval.

"There you have it, ladies and gentlemen, the definitive strategic weapon current technology can supply, an invisible, missile transporter and dispersal craft. Its unique cenosphere coating makes it only 0.02 percent detectable by radar, plus it has additional capabilities of being invisible to thermal imaging. It can hide in the upper stratosphere deploying missiles with impunity, or glide undetected at hyper speed, circumnavigating the globe ready for low-level attack. The payload is fourteen cruise missiles with either nuclear or conventional warheads."

"It must have some weak point," a voice said from the auditorium. "When is it most vulnerable?"

Max looked at the digital screen showing the layout of

his audience and a flashing neon which indicated who had spoken.

"I'm afraid that's classified, General Mears, until trials are complete and GR4 accepted by the Air Force. But I can tell you, this craft has the capability to attack any given target as if from nowhere. An enemy would need its exact location and be extremely quick to retaliate. As it is undetectable on radar and is mainly deployed at an altitude beyond the range of current missiles, it can operate with impunity."

"What's the crew size? What if it was downed?" Mears asked.

"It has no crew, only ground staff. I control the aircraft from this flight console via ground and satellite links. We deliberately chose the centre of New York to demonstrate its versatility. I have ability to put her through every operational manoeuvre no matter what part of the world she flies in." He listened to the murmurs of amazement, then started his winding up speech. "Due to high altitude flying, much of the technology was developed by NASA in its space shuttle program. The team here incorporated that technology into a unique aircraft, an entirely different concept to anything flown before. A UCA or unmanned combat vehicle. You are looking at hardware which swallowed billions of dollars. The task for Walsh Avionics was to design the craft then implement control, attack and defence systems. It took ten years of research by many distinguished scientists, plus a dedicated team headed by Chief Executive, Dr Rawlings and myself." Max felt it prudent not to mention Perry. "Ladies and gentlemen, you witness the result - Global Raider."

"We already got Global Hawk. Ain't that good enough instead of spending all this money?" Mears asked.

Max curled his lip. "Global Hawk is primarily a URV, an unmanned reconnaissance vehicle modified to carry missiles and with limited strategic use. Global Raider is an unmanned combat vehicle with maximum strike capability to any location worldwide. An enemy won't see it, hear it or know it's there until it's in his face. It's worth every penny, General." Max waited for the murmur of chuckles to die. "OK, ladies and gentlemen, lunch will be served in the adjoining reception room where my team will answer further questions."

"What is your security on the electronic data for this programme?"a female voice interjected.

Max twitched and looked at the ID console. "Impenetrable, Miss Farlow. I designed the system myself. All information is contained in a fragmented loop circuit. Any research or test engineer seeking access is given a fluctuating code that allows an individual to enter only the section they require. It is impossible to download any information without alerting central security, neither is it possible for data to be transferred out of the loop."

"That may secure development information, but what happens when Raider flies?"

Max sensed relief, realising the speaker was not leading her questions to enquire about Perry. Hammerton had at least contained the incident. "Control of Raider is through a unique master switch with a sixteen-digit enigma code. The code is split to varying lengths, one section useless without the other. The segments are allocated to a number of designated personnel taken at random selection. On routine deployment, that's military and Pentagon officials. For practical reasons, during trials and test flights it's kept within this building. I designed it myself and for that privilege during tests I hold the first half of the code. The second half goes to in-house military, then it's General Hammerton, Wat Walsh and finally the President himself. I'm sure I need not remind you, ladies and gentlemen, of the sacrifices Mr Walsh has made regarding the security of this great nation." Max listened to the shuffle of feet followed by a tight, embarrassed silence. Now he had them beat.

"What about physical security? Every building is vulnerable. The information sheet says you have two separate control modules here. Where's the other?" Miss Farlow asked.

Max shook his head and looked to Rawlings in disbelief at the woman's stupid insistence. "After 9/11 a second flight deck was built here in the basement. Until handover, our two modules are the only ones which have full and total control ability. As a pre-requisite of the Air Force, the second module is always on standby in case of emergency. It is situated in Mr Walsh's inner office, the original test centre, a room that has security rating on par with this one. In fact I can tell you, ladies and gentlemen, Wat Walsh often acts as ground pilot. It's a privilege he claims as the force behind the technology. And with his long, distinguished flying career in the Air Force, he certainly has the necessary skills. As for physical protection, all our installations and employees are contained under the jurisdiction of General Hammerton. We feel safe."

"You mean Hammer head Jake," General Mears cut in. "Believe me, lady, this place will be cut tighter than a duck's ass."

Amidst polite laughter, Max indicated for the lights and handed control of GR4 to the pilot beside him. He felt a sense of tired relief, his performance was over and the remainder day promised to be less stressful. True, he faced thirty minutes of mingling with guests over a buffet luncheon and a long afternoon satisfying the bureaucracy of Air Force trials, but after, he had the theatre and Bernard to amuse him.

Outside the auditorium he helped himself from the buffet and mixed amiably with the military brass, confident in his ability amongst lesser mortals. At least until Jake Hammerton arrived with his two young men.

"Sorry about the intrusion, Dr Crawley," Hammerton said, displaying the cocksure smile of an agitator. "These two here are allocated to your house to ensure 24/7 personal protection."

"My life is busy. I don't have time to accommodate others."

"You should be so lucky, Max. But they stay until Raider is handed over. I'm afraid Perry was an arsehole plucker, it makes you kind of vulnerable."

"Reserve your language, General." Max sensed the rush of blood to his face, conscious those nearby might listen

"My apologies, words just came kind of natural. Hit and run makes for a suspicious death. Perry was your admin chief. If you read your contract, that puts you on code red. Sorry, Doc, but your household is under wraps."

Max put what malice he could into his smile and turned his back. He was immediately faced with the predatory eyes of Miss Jody Farlow, CIA.

"I've sent for the Brit who will be first watch on Miss Juliet," Jake said to Wat Walsh. "I'm assured he's good, Guards, SAS, the very best but I need to be certain. Freddy Fox, who I knew in Iraq and Afghanistan is team leader. A very capable man, someone who would only pick the best. Still," he shrugged, "no harm in playing safe. We're talking about the protection of a head-strong young woman."

"Close quarters is Lisa's department," Wat said, spreading his hands to dampen down irritation over his security chief making unnecessary waves. "You've already had Henry and CIA check them out. The Brits' Combined Agency Taskforce care for British Government and high profile foreign visitors, on occasions even royalty. They don't mess, Jake, and I wouldn't trust Juliet with anyone less than the best. But if you have doubts, let's look elsewhere."

Jake raised his nose and strode back and forth as if his

steps were boxed. Wat let him brood, knowing the man's prejudice was the absence of his own cover team in the frontline instead of British security. Wat saw no way out of the situation other than by persuasion. If for a moment Juliet thought Jake's boys were following her over, she'd refuse to go, whether Lucas played or not.

"You convinced me of this set up initially Jake, let's not detract. By the time she's in England, we'll have only three or four days to handover. Your men will be stretched and remember, these CAT guys were once Special Services like our Delta boys. They don't come better. I want Juliet with people I trust."

Jake brought his nose down, a sure sign of reconciliation to fact. "Well, I'm doubling her decoy cover. An extra one in the apartment, another in her mountain retreat. I'm also switching flight time at the last minute, changing hotels and have a further two decoys set up during transfer. I take no chances, Wat."

"I appreciate it, Jake, but don't rattle her. Let's keep her co-operative. And while we're about it, Max's been on the phone. Go easy on him. Whatever your opinion of his personal life, he's our star. He put this thing together."

"What do you think, Henry? Give me some logical input on this situation." Jake strolled with his chief executive through the open office that housed Intelligence and Logistics for Walsh Securities.

"You could send Navro as a tail," Henry said.

"Like a fire cracker. Holly Johnson is meant to be deep cover. The more who know, the less that cover is, although it's possible to put him on close standby. What's your second option?"

"Someone who could operate out of the Embassy and wouldn't be suspected if they made contact," Henry nodded his head. "Hell, the Embassy is going to be interested in Miss Walsh. Like it or not, she's a VIP."

"Ratner from CIA had a female in the building today. My guess he lifted her from Operations Directorate. I did ask for co-operation, maybe she's it," Jake said.

"If she's available, we can always keep her at heel."

"Better there than getting in our way. OK, home problems. Max and his boyfriend, Bernard. During your investigation of Perry, see if we can link these two shirt-lifters. If we find suspicion of a homosexual conspiracy, Crawley would be locked out, fast," Jake said and grimaced in pleasure.

Henry looked at him and pushed the glasses on the bridge of his nose as if he didn't understand but Jake knew he did.

"I have him under routine surveillance," Henry said. "Even had cleaning services collect samples from the sheets; Bernard's not HIV. Hell, what's the worst the guy can do? Bite Crawley's dick?"

Jake's laughter came spontaneously, turning all office eyes towards him. "Henry, you've still have humour." He leaned close and went into a whisper. "But you know well that if Crawley was proved to have a second lover with suspected enemy contact, our good doctor would lose code rating for Raider's flight. He'd be out the building. I want Ed Rawlings to take his place. He had two brothers killed in the towers. He's eager for Fireback."

"When Fireback does happen, the military will intervene, the President will use his code, you know that?"

Jake looked down at Henry and this time put real pleasure in his smile. "That would leave just Wat Walsh and myself with final code control. Raider couldn't be in safer hands. Crawley needs to go, Henry. His work is done."

Lounging in her bikini out on the roof terrace, Juliet felt far from the city below, a privileged alien held captive in the sky. The small ornamental fountain pushed its cascade of water down polished stones to tinkle melodious noise over the far distant roar of traffic. Other side of the drinks table Lisa lay on a sun bed, her body tanned and taut, her modesty barely concealed beneath the inadequate bikini that Juliet had loaned her. Juliet had found adolescent pleasure in cajoling her to sunbath, in causing her companion's near nakedness, it gave small, personal power over a world in which she felt helpless. Lisa lay with sunglasses perched on top of her head, one eye open as she watched Eva approach through the ornamental shrubbery.

She handed Lisa a large brown envelope. Juliet watched her bodyguard turn it, sniff and hold it up to the light.

"It came via security," Eva said and left.

"Has Henry Taylor's signature on the seal. My guess, it's the itinerary for England. Want me to open it?"

Juliet nodded. She felt the shimmer of excitement and imagined Lucas on some four-poster bed amidst the splendour of a Tudor mansion. What if he didn't respond? What if he didn't find her woman enough? What the hell would she do?

Lisa extracted several sheets of itinerary, passports and a digital photograph. She glanced at the photo and raised an eyebrow. "This dude could be fun." She passed the picture across.

It showed a young man dressed in field fatigues, his beret folded and tucked beneath the epaulettes on his shirt. He had a wild, swept look, more a surf dude than a soldier. Juliet guessed him a little older than herself. She liked his face, his smile, his tussled hair undergoing a permanent bad day. He looked the kind to have a regular girlfriend who slept with him.

"You know what they call British army officers?" Lisa sat up, her breasts nearly falling from the too small bikini top.

"Rupert." Juliet continued to stare at the picture.

"The soldiers call them Ruperts. He's got nice eyes. Wonder what his butt's like?" She looked to her friend expecting some jibe of derision.

"We'll be with honoured company. Entry to British Special Forces is only for the best."

"Do I sense respect?" Juliet smiled up as Lisa gathered the papers and stood beside her, hand on hip, long shapely legs like a protective wall. Silence lasted longer than it should and Juliet reached her hand to Lisa's thigh. "Tell me you don't mind about Lucas, that you understand?"

Lisa stroked her hair. "Got things to do, babe."

CHAPTER 6

Seb arrived at the Burlington International Hotel on 45th Street just after 10.30 p.m.. The single room booked by the Americans was comfortable and spacious. No message awaited him, no instruction as to where he should go or whom he should meet. He checked again at Reception then went to the hotel bar. He had been given no contact number so figured if they wanted him they'd better come and find him. At 12.30 a.m. he went to bed.

Jody Farlow slid into the booth opposite Jake Hammerton and smiled up into his disdainful glare. She needed the man's trust and co-operation but had only half-truths and rumours to secure it. She smiled a second time for Henry in the corner. Neither man acknowledged. She remained unruffled.

"You have a hard team, General," she said and unbuttoned her jacket. She found the café's interior warm, the glare of the two men opposite daunting.

"I know." Hammerton's words were clipped and uncompromising. "You work for Ratner?"

Jody shook her head. "Ratner's Science and Technology. I'm Operations Directorate. He borrowed me on the basis of mutual interest."

"Just what is that, Miss Farlow?"

"Khalid bin Qasem." She saw the momentary shift of Henry's eyes. Hammerton remained stone-faced. Jody leaned forward and kept her voice low. "I've been tracking him eight years without much success. Khalid hides in deep cover, but when he shows, something nasty happens. Rumour on the block say he's out of his hole."

"Get to the point, Miss Farlow."

"The next big event in this country is the unveiling of Global Raider."

"We've planned for it. Every eventuality is covered.

The aircraft is secure."

Jody straightened her back and folded her forearms along the edge of the table as she picked her words carefully. "My Director's concern is not with the aircraft, that's Ratner's department but with the plane's control and strike software held in Walsh Towers. Systems with remote access on a global scale such as warships, embassies etc, can be hijacked and controlled from sources outside of this country, hence my department's interest."

"Tell the Director to rest easy, we have a failsafe, it's been tested many times."

"That's when the Air Force move in. I'm talking about now, during the last days of trial." Jody leaned slightly forward and again tried a smile to beguile him. She failed. "You have a fragmented loop system making it impossible to access data; plus a split code system for control of the aircraft itself. A split code which during final tests includes only one outside person."

"You've been to the lectures, Miss Farlow. Tests are conducted by civilians at Walsh Towers because Crawley's department require absolute control. Military interference would be disastrous."

"But the last code used can override all others, even the President's. If he uses his code before, say you and Wat Walsh, you could effectively push him out. That wasn't in the lecture, General."

"So, you've been an inquisitive girl. It's a common but effective failsafe to facilitate our administration." He shrugged. "It's used by many agencies including NASA. Read it in the manuals."

She watched the slight twist of his lip and her dismissal. She knew then he was hooked. She leaned forward, closing with him for greater confidence. "But I didn't, General, I heard it on the wind."

"Cut the shit, Miss Farlow, what exactly is it you want?"

"If I heard it, so could Bin Qasem. Over the next four

days the Director has identified two potential dangers, Dr Crawley and Candy Girl. We believe Crawley's chief exec, Perry, was selling information. We assume his unfortunate accident," she deliberately lingered on the last word, "ceased this leakage."

"All is being investigated but I can state categorically there was no leak."

"Perry was gay, he was Crawley's occasional lover. Crawley also has another full time lover. It's the kind of situation Khalid would exploit."

The man kept his eyes rock solid on her. "Crawley is under close, personal protection and he is no longer imperative to GR4's inaugural flight. These are home affairs. I suggest you keep your interest abroad."

"You forget Raider circumnavigates the globe, flies right over Khalid's head. What happens here affects out there."

"We are experts in our business, Miss Farlow."

"So are we all, General. Which brings me to Candy Girl. She staying or going?"

"None of your business."

"If she steps off American soil it is. Remember what happened to her mother."

"She has Lisa Longford, a woman who would die in the performance of her duty. Even Navro would back off from crossing that woman."

"I don't doubt it. But in your last exercise, Longford was taken out in the first minutes. Afterwards she appeared too emotionally close. We believe that closeness is a danger." Her words stopped on awkward silence.

"You're talking riddles, lady."

"At twenty years old Lisa made Lieutenant in the Marines and graduated to Delta. She served two years then went to the Seals, then back to the Marines. By twenty-six she was one of the youngest females ever to make Major; that was four years ago. She was flying, then she dived."

"It's on record. She left after a shooting accident. A brilliant career dashed."

"I'll tell you what's not on record. The wound was superficial and no accident. She was sleeping with the wife of the officer who shot her, plus several enlisted girls." Jody watched the twitch of his lip. "How were you to know, General? I guess such things never happen in a man's army. Longford left with full military honours and half a million dollars in compensation, thus no scandal, no gossip. Army happy."

Hammerton shrugged. "So? All women who join the Army are dykes. It goes with the uniform. But she's still the best for her job and has my full confidence."

"Does Walsh know of her inclinations, does his potential son-in-law?" Jody edged forward again; she could smell his sweat and knew at this range he would smell her perfume.

"Are you trying to apply some unofficial influence here, Miss Farlow?"

"Listen to me, Jake. You're sending the daughter to deep cover in England. Hell, England's safe. All they got is the IRA, Islamic terrorists, Russian Mafia and psychopathic bomb-makers. Not to mention Khalid waiting in the shadows. We know of the Combined Agency Taskforce, know it's good. Over the years we've occasionally employed them ourselves. Save the minder they've sent over don't look dry behind the ears and will have more interest in Juliet and Lisa's ass than their safety. With Longford's emotional involvement that don't make for a hard team. You need help and I'm offering to shadow the shadow. It's why you encouraged me here in the first place, isn't it, because you're worried about Khalid and feel a second backup would be prudent."

When his eyes dipped Jody smiled triumphantly. Jake looked to Henry then back again. "The guy from CAT is simply the panic button to bring in our own boys who would be too conspicuous as first shadow. So what's your boss's plan, that you follow too?"

"The Government has a lot of political hope and money on Raider. I understand the White House is anxious. This meeting is a way of squaring it with you before we move."

"Lisa will spot you a mile off and if Sweetpea gets wind, she'll start yelling at Papa. He has power enough to complain to the President direct. Your boss would be out on his ass."

"But his ass, General, not yours. You'll get extra Embassy co-operation and frequent situation reports."

"Tempting, Jody, tempting."

She watched his smile but saw no mirth. "Unofficially, of course," she added in persuasion.

Henry leaned his head and whispered to Hammerton, loud enough for her to hear. "If we inadvertently passed the tracking code for Miss Juliet's bracelet, then Miss Farlow could find and follow her target without our help or knowledge."

"That still leaves Lisa. If Lisa thinks she's not trusted, her back will go up. I've seen it. She can be one bitch."

"It takes a bitch to deal with a bitch, General," Jody said. "As for the young man they've sent, the CIA has a favour system with MI6. Through it I secured a full dossier on Lieutenant Havic's military career. It contains every operation in which he has taken part including those with the SAS, every country he's been to, plus personal assessments. He's a good soldier but like all Brit soldiers, there's a weakness for drink. That aside, he's A1 and with my knowledge I can make him an old friend."

"There's still Lisa, she's not stupid."

Jody smiled up at him with pure guile. "I was Marines too, Jake. Lisa won't see me, I'll be too close."

Jake watched her go and waited until she closed the café door.

"What the fuck are women doing in this business, anyway? Smart-arsed bitch."

"It's new age politics, Jake. But she did offer a safeguard we can't afford to ignore. God forbid but if ever an enquiry came, this will show us as good compassionate souls, doing our best to protect Juliet from every angle in a difficult situation." Jake stood and Henry followed him between tables and out to the street.

"So, do we trust her?" Henry asked.

Jake stayed momentarily in thought. This was not going as he had planned.

"She made no mention of Fireback. Ratner's stayed quiet which is good. But the CIA are devious bastards. My guess is, they may know something about Khalid we don't. OK, play her along but just in case better put Navro in behind her shadow as a secondary strike force."

"What about ordnance?"

"Get what vehicles and helicopters he thinks necessary. As for weapons, I'm sure you'll find a means."

"I have my man. Do we tell Wat?"

"No, Candy Girl is meant to be deep cover. We're taking additional precautions. If he thought Juliet's life seriously threatened I don't know what he might do but it could disrupt the GR4 Program, Fireback with it." Both men stopped at a road crossing and waited for the lights to change.

"Let's cause a distraction by dumping Max for Rawlings immediately after the penultimate test flight and before the final handover flight," Henry said. The light showed "Walk" and both men crossed together.

"That's kind of callous, Henry," Jake smirked.

"Logical. Fireback is revenge for 9/11. That calls for sacrifice. I prefer Max's sacrifice to that of Candy Girl's."

After breakfast Seb had sat for two hours in his hotel room expecting a contact. When none came he figured they were waiting on him to leave the hotel where any approach could be disguised as chance. In which case, Seb figured, sightseeing might make their life easier. Collecting a map from Reception he joined the people of New York. Twice in the first hour instinct had caused him to look behind. He had no positive gut feeling, just a sense of unease. People milled around him, traffic flowed, the noise, the smells, the colours all colluded to create hyper city life. Yet within this environment he had a sense of hostile forces. He knew his concerns were unwarranted, he did not feel threatened, even worried, just a loose notion to take care.

"Sebastian! Sebastian Havic. How are you? And what are you doing here?"

Seb stopped on the pavement beneath the Empire State Building. The woman who called was trim, early thirties, dressed in a neat business suit which did not sober her attractive figure. She shifted spectacles on her nose. "Shame on you, you don't remember me, do you?"

Seb stood baffled. He had met few American women, all of whom were service personnel. Her smile appeared genuine which eased his mistrust.

"You must excuse me, jetlag is not good for the brain."

"I know your excuse. Put 'em in uniform, they all look the same. Germany, three years back. NATO, combined forces escape and evasion exercise. You were Guards SAS, I was with Delta, one of the interrogation team. We caught you, remember?"

"Good Lord, you have a sound memory." Seb thought back, still unable to place her. He scratched his head. "Your lot gave a party when the exercise was over. A big barbecue - in a field. We must have met there."

"Sure did." She strutted her hip, head to one side. "You gave me your photograph. I still have it."

Seb became flustered. The party had been wild, a meeting of Special Forces on a mission to get drunk. "I remember there were girls in uniform. We were dancing.

Jack Daniels has a lot to answer for."

"Certainly does, you proposed to me four times."

"I did?" Seb felt the flush of heat on his face.

"You looked so cute lying in the grass butt naked."

"Oh my God."

"Don't worry, we didn't." Her eyes smiled over the gold-rimmed spectacles. "You fell asleep."

The heat in Seb's cheeks became acute. "Could we put it down to tempestuous youth and start again? Maybe I could buy you a drink?"

"Maybe, if you can remember my name." She folded her arms, observing him with her head on one side. Her smile was now wicked. "You certainly had it in a safe place. Except I didn't write it where you asked me to, I wrote it over your navel instead."

"Oh ground, please swallow me up." Seb looked to the sky, thinking if this was the expected contact they sure knew how to do it while laying a guy low.

"Not till you buy me that drink. The name's Jody, remember? Jody Farlow, ex-captain, Delta Force."

CHAPTER 7

Lisa entered Juliet's bedroom and watched while Eva zipped the back of young madam's dress. Her babe was looking good, cute and sexy with it. She liked that, liked to see her charge desirable, untouchable to all, except herself.

"Performance time, baby. The annual bash." Lisa came behind to look over Juliet's shoulder into the mirror. "You have three hours of handing out medals to Jake's army, shaking hands and congratulating them on keeping you and the empire safe."

"They don't keep me safe, they keep Papa's property safe. I'm just a shapely bit of ass who's one of the assets." Juliet flicked her hair and began to gather it into a ponytail, a black velvet band over her wrist in readiness.

Lisa recognised the tone, this was tantrum or tear time. She glanced at Eva who raised her eyebrows, gathered clothes and escaped the room. Tantrum time, Lisa thought. "Well, you look a million dollars, that little black dress is perfect." She smoothed the lapels of her own satin veteran's suit, the sleeves and front ablaze with emblems and medals denoting the places and Special Forces group in which she had served. Normally, this was time for mutual compliments but the girl said nothing instead turning her head to ensure every strand of hair was captured in the band.

"I like your perfume." Lisa leant to her shoulder while placing long, firm fingers round Juliet's tiny waist. "Relax sweetheart. Tomorrow you're heading for England, out of the circus and the cage. Just the two of us, free as the wind."

"Not out of the circus. They have some guy called Rupert sniffing around." Juliet stared into her eyes via the mirror. "I don't want Rupert. It's your job to look after me. Get rid of him."

"Can't do, babe but I'll keep him uptight. His orders are to watch our backs when moving between secure accommodation, to keep long-range cover and to do as I tell him. You won't see him most times, won't even know he's there. But he's necessary backup."

Juliet bent to the mirror and began to apply lipstick. "Does that mean he'll be looking through the bedroom window?"

"Only if he wants my knee in his crutch. Besides, Brit officers are gentlemen." Lisa kept her fingers resting on Juliet's hips, thumbs massaging the small of her back as she tried to establish intimacy. Something was coming, she knew it. This was not Juliet's time of month, her day had been relaxed. The reason was deeper.

"Lucas is definitely coming over. I phoned an hour ago. We'll meet in Cambridge for three days."

Lisa felt the knot in her stomach and her thumbs stopped their motion. "Is that wise, honey?"

Juliet shrugged, pursed her lips and snapped the lipstick closed. "It's essential for my future. The only reason I'm going to England is because Lucas agreed to join me."

"I know I said maybe, but please consider the consequences."

Juliet pushed her hands away and turned with arms folded. "If you have any feelings for me, if you really are my friend, then you'll help."

"Deep cover is nobody knowing where you are, nobody able to let slip information to people who might harm you. What's the point of getting rid of your circus if Lucas arrives with his?"

"He's coming alone."

"Don't believe it." She watched Juliet's eyes narrow and saw the gathering of moisture. She resisted holding and comforting the girl.

"He says he loves me. Well for three days he's going to do so physically. I want to see the hot-blooded man, not the future president. I'll learn more in those three days than I would in three years the way he's going. Any friend would support me."

"Babe, I'm a professional entrusted with your life, please don't make my situation impossible."

"Don't babe me. You're only jealous." Juliet pushed past and snatched her day purse from the bed. "Lucas is coming to dinner and I'm telling him our arrangements."

Lisa waited, counting slowly as she stood alone before the mirror, smoothing the jacket over her breasts, allowing past military conquest to give sanctuary. She saw a long turbulent day ahead. She felt both sympathy and sadness over Juliet's dictated future. At the same time her own love, love of the girl, became torn between duty and the desire to please. Worse, what she had hidden was now in the open. Jealousy did exist.

Seb sat in the booth slightly bemused by the bubbly woman opposite. He remembered the party, he remembered getting drunk along with everyone else. He remembered the girls, he remembered waking up in the corner of some field, but fully dressed. Just the time with Jody remained blank, though he did have some inkling of smudged felt-tip across his stomach.

"Are you the contact?" he asked her after an hour.

"Contact," she frowned.

"I'm on an op, so secret I don't really know what it's about or who's involved. You Americans sure work in mysterious ways." He looked at her as he sipped wine then nibbled on a cheese straw. Sounds of the busy bar churned in the background as he recognised the sly smile of a woman caught out.

"Not quite," she answered. "I'm a security advisor with the American Diplomatic Mission currently attached to London." The tip of her tongue slipped snake like between lips. "Due to our past meeting," she shifted shoulders on the words, "I was sent to vet your ID. This is a hot one, Seb."

"Jody, you're one hell of an attractive woman but I

have a feeling your heart lies with another. So let's not play act, let's get on with our business."

"You're cute, Seb." She touched his hand. "Maybe when this is over we can meet up in England, then I can really tell you what happened in that field."

"Am I ever going to live it down?"

"No," she pouted and took out her mobile. Moments after she switched off a giant of a man slid into the booth beside her. "This is Navro," she said. "He'll brief you."

Seb shook hands. The guy appeared like some star from a Hollywood blockbuster, his hair black and thick, his handsome features tanned.

"So when do I get to meet the team?" Seb asked.

"You don't. But they get to meet you. You also get plenty time to see and familiarise yourself with the client's identity. You won't meet her backup team so you won't be able to give them away if you bump them. But as I said, all her close protection will know exactly who you are. That way if you're constantly too close they won't accidently shoot you."

"How reassuring." Seb raised his eyebrows. "But what if I mistakenly shoot one of them?"

"Don't worry, pal," Navro shook his large head. "You won't even see them. Your sole purpose is to press the panic button in the event of hostile action. The likelihood of that is zero. We will have a minimum of ten decoys out. The client will travel under an alias without apparent need for protection. No one outside of the immediate security will know who she is or where she is. That's how deep cover works."

"So when do we start?" Seb looked between them.

"Now. Client is handing out veteran citations followed by an informal party. You're invited, so let's go."

"I'll catch up with you later." Jody looked across at him and winked.

"See you in England," he smiled for her and followed the giant from the bar.

* * *

After passing through the grand entrance hall of Walsh Towers, Navro led Seb into an empty office where two austere booted and suited men observed him with cold detachment. One held a tailored blazer with the winged dagger of the SAS embroidered on the pocket.

"May I?" one said and removed Seb's suit jacket. The other helped him into the blazer.

"Measurements were a little guessed at but it seems to fit."

Seb flicked the cuff, noting a lapel pin for the Guards SAS Squadron above the buttonhole. "I don't understand. Why the advert?"

"Because you're going to a shindig for American Special Forces veterans," Navro said while placing an ID tag and ribbon over Seb's head. "An outsider wouldn't get through the door, never mind anyone talking to him. Also, this way, all those who need to know will be able to clearly identify you. You spend an hour or so there then return to your hotel."

"Understood," Seb nodded and pointed to his suit jacket which had cost him over £200.

"Don't worry, that will be left hanging in your hotel wardrobe."

Seb followed Navro to the lift. "You're on your own from here," the man said, pressing the button. "May see you in England." He turned and strode away.

"Fine," Seb muttered after him then rode up to the eighteenth floor. When he emerged he saw a reception desk with a stern faced woman behind. "I have an invitation," Seb told her, showing his ID tag.

She took details and tapped keys on a computer.

"Lieutenant Havic, you are expected. But we have a request you see Major Taylor first." She beckoned a uniformed guard. "Security will escort you." She stamped and initialled a pass before sliding it over the counter. "Keep that with you at all times and welcome to

Walsh Towers."

Seb followed his escort, intrigued by the man's precise ceremonial movements and his immaculate uniform which sprouted enough gold braid to satisfy two generals. Only when they entered a second lift did the man speak.

"Sir, I am required to inform you that, at this precise moment, your face is being matched with photographic ID and your body scanned for concealed weapons, sir. It is impossible to move between floors without coded keys or personal escort, sir. At all times you will be under the scrutiny of surveillance cameras. These security conditions apply to all visitors, sir."

Seb was lost for an appropriate reply. The lift door slid open and he stepped into a plush corridor. A second guard, identical to the first, pivoted as if by automatic control and led him to a palatial office where numerous secretaries worked at computers. One, plump and pretty, led him towards an inner sanctum cut from view by a corner. As he walked he passed banks of flat monitors displaying a variety of buildings and manufacturing plants, the design and weather conditions indicating numerous international locations. The largest screen was filled by the image of a young black girl standing centre stage as she passed out awards to a line of veterans. To her right, a hooked nose man scowled over the proceedings. Behind them a tall, blonde woman with enough emblems on her jacket to make gift wrapping, handed over trophies. Seb crossed the room with his eyes on the monitor, thinking the black girl stunning. Beyond the corner, heavy glass doors screened a second office of equal dimensions. To the side of this vast inner sanctum stood the full-scale alloy frame of a flight deck replica. The glass doors slid back on Seb's approach and a small black man with bright eyes held out his hand.

"My daughter," the man said, glancing to the screen. "Demanding, intelligent and headstrong. Not an easy client, Lieutenant Havic. I'm Wat Walsh. This is Major

Taylor." He indicated a thin, bespectacled man who stood beside a huge mahogany desk, most of its surface inlaid with electronic controls and communication equipment. Seb shook hands with both men, conscious that Wat scrutinised him with slow deliberation.

"I congratulate you, sir. Your daughter is most becoming." Wat raised an eyebrow and Seb immediately sensed his words too familiar.

"I'd like you to repeat that, Lieutenant, when you bring her back in two weeks. The looks come from her mother. She was Afro-Asian with a grace and beauty surpassed by none. But daughter like mother, Juliet not only has her looks, she also has her dedication and spirit." He peered over spectacles. "I hope you understand what I'm saying."

"That she can be a trite difficult on occasions." Seb smiled.

"What I'm saying is, do your job but keep your distance. Like any young woman, she don't like being under observation. Do I make myself absolutely clear on that point, Sebastian?"

"Absolutely, sir. You can rest assured that your daughter's safety and integrity will be paramount at all times," Seb said, thinking integrity meant no chat-up lines, no hands on. Pity.

"I knew I could rely on you, boy." Wat moved to the business side of his desk. "How are you enjoying New York?"

"Brilliant, sir. It's a city that lives."

"Myself, I don't get to the pavements no more, security don't like it. So I watch life pass beneath the helicopter. I was near forty when Juliet was born but I can still remember what it's like to be young, to feel the vibrancy, the need to live. That's what Juliet's feeling right now. She wants to leap from the palace walls and find her way. But in truth, she's never left home or academic society. She's still an innocent, a grown child, you understand? And to give added incentive I've put a quarter million-dollar bonus on this assignment. Just bring my Juliet home, safe." He offered his hand again.

"Thank you for your generosity, sir." Seb felt pressure in the handclasp.

"OK, Lieutenant. Now go with Major Taylor. He'll show you the ropes." Seb followed Taylor to the outer office, glancing back to see his new employer press buttons so heavy glass doors slid back over the opening, sealing him inside.

"Bomb-proof," Henry said. "The General's and State Department's idea. No-one can touch him in there, yet from that console, he has contact and control throughout the world."

"Is Walsh Industries that big?" Seb asked, keeping stride with the major.

"Where you been, son? This company is bigger than anything worldwide. From space to below earth. America, Europe, Asia; software, manufacturing, real-estate, but aircraft design and systems controls are the main items here. Hence our heavy involvement in Global Raider."

"Global Hawk saved our bacon on my last mission against al-Qaeda. Two Hellfire missiles like bolts from heaven. Bang – enemy gone."

Henry stopped and looked at him before pushing spectacles with a finger. "You seen enemy action?"

Seb did not wish to elaborate; all operations remained secret. "Yes and recently."

"I'll let Jake know, he'll appreciate that. So will Wat Walsh." Henry began to walk again. "Love of daughter, love of nation, love of aircraft. They're the man's concerns in order of priority. Consequently, the reference to Miss Juliet's moral integrity. She's princess of the empire, Lieutenant, and lined up to be America's First Lady. You'd better be sharper than a samurai sword in protecting that one. Where Juliet's concerned, you either get her smile or walk on thin ice."

Seb remained undaunted. "I'll be like a shadow, there but unnoticed."

Henry extracted an envelope from his jacket and passed it over. "Air ticket, petty cash for expenses, rules of behaviour and etiquette. They get given to all employees guarding Sweetpea. Read tonight. Don't deviate and don't let the envelope off your person. You carry a weapon?"

"It's against the law in Britain."

"If you need anything, let me know. Strictly off record, but we have a source for ordnance in most major countries." Henry ushered Seb into a lift and pressed for the 27th floor. "Ever hear of a guy called Khalid bin Qasem?"

"Islamic terrorist."

"Associate of al-Qaeda but his own man. Responsible for bombings and hijackings worldwide. Though you probably know, he was also involved in 9/11 plus three of our embassies being blown. Eight years ago in an attempt to gain vital information on the early GR4 program, he abducted Juliet's mother and tried to blackmail Wat. Neither gave in. I'm told she was a beautiful woman, charismatic, courteous. Qasem cut her head off. Juliet's beautiful too. Keep you eyes on the job, not her arse. Might be you have a bogey looking over your shoulder."

"Thanks for the warning. Am I right to assume when Candy Girl goes deep cover, only the ladies and myself will be in the centre group?"

"Correct, but you're in the shadow, except if Lisa calls. Then you do what she asks. Neither will you be quite alone. Both Miss Juliet and Lisa wear transmission bracelets hooked into a satellite link. We can locate either of them twenty-four hours, within three metres. Sitting the other side of your shoulder will also be a backup team. You're basically their eyes. Shout and they'll come running."

"Reassuring, but I also report to my commander at the

Combined Agency Taskforce in London. I need to keep them informed at all times."

"Fine, but just inform us first."

The lift stopped and the door slid open allowing Seb to look over a banqueting hall. Several hundred ex-soldiers in bomber jackets and jeans clustered before a stage, all cheering and whistling the girl in front.

"Welcome to Juliet's world," Henry said. "If by chance you get close, go for Lisa, find out if she really is a dyke. First General Hammerton would like a word. "

Seb came down steps from the entrance and onto the main floor. Resplendent in blazer and grey trousers, he felt a touch overdressed, not unlike a Public school boy at a Hells Angels gathering. He walked slowly to an open space by the buffet tables, conscious of looks and whispers as he passed. Up on stage he saw Juliet watching while she talked. The tall, good-looking woman behind he guessed was Lisa, the man striding towards him, Jake Hammerton.

"It's a good job these boys are off duty. I thought you Brits blended with the jungle?"

"Sebastian Havic," he held out his hand. "General Hammerton, I presume?"

The General looked down at him then grinned without reflecting it in his eyes, as if unsure there had been humour. "I've heard a lot about you SAS boys. Sure you can handle this?" Hammerton was looking at him, stone-faced, eyes hard. Seb saw no quarter. This man would cut his throat.

"Absolutely, sir. I've even guarded Her Majesty the Queen at Buckingham Palace."

"Grab yourself a beer, Lieutenant, join the boys. I'll bring the girls passed when they leave."

Hammerton turned on his heel and Seb let go his breath. He was accepted.

At the buffet table he eased through the cluster of men and collected a bottle of Budweiser. When he turned to edge his way back it was into a group of ex-marines, all clutching beers, all grinning like he was the turkey.

"You Brit?" one asked.

"Through and through. You Yank?"

"Cherokee."

"Seb Havic." He held out his hand and shook with those who reached. "Jake Hammerton looks a tough boss," he said, in the hope of information.

"It's his way but he's a good commander. The guys here will follow any place."

"You guard the building?"

"We're out at Humarock. Looking after Sweetpea. Least from the perimeters. No one is allowed close."

"She OK? I mean, no problems?"

"It's a joy, particularly if you fly over in the chopper. Half the day she walks around butt naked and makes Longford do the same. Some sight." The Marine shook his fingers while blowing through pursed lips.

"Must be tempting."

"No chance. They're both dykes. Why, I've seen them at each other like cats on heat. But no one gets close quarter. No man touches there. Least not unless your potential president of the United States."

In the background Juliet finished her presentations amidst a flurry of applause. Seb watched Hammerton escort her from the stage to walk with her and Lisa towards him. Juliet was waving and throwing kisses, greeting men left and right as she gradually came closer. Seb liked her sparkle, liked the generous way she gave her physical presence, as if her inner self belonged to every man. He felt guilt that he had been party to scurrilous gossip. Her ambiance was magnetic but it was her aura of innocence which made it so attractive.

Hammerton pushed between them and the Marines straightened. "Lieutenant Havic." He ushered the two women into the cleared space, their female presence overpowering the male enclave. "May I introduce Miss Juliet Walsh and Lisa Longford?"

"Pleased to make your acquaintance." Seb took Juliet's small hand and bowed slightly as he spoke. Her eyes were large and inquisitive, her smile gorgeous as she stared at him.

"I hear you come from the elite, Lieutenant Havic," she said, puffing out her chest. "What do you think boys? Should we give Mr Rupert a chance?" she asked across her shoulder, eyes still on his, her slight grip remaining cool against his skin.

"Sure thing, Miss Juliet." The Marines voiced agreement, their grins wide.

Seb felt heat on his face. The next second she had slipped her hand and gone.

"Report tomorrow," Hammerton said. "You're two rows behind them on the aircraft and next to them in the hotel. Your boss will be waiting at Heathrow."

Seb watched them go then looked to the Marines who were staring slack jawed. "You getting into her hotel?" one asked. "With a name like Rupert."

"Personal protection, close quarter, 24/7. Now excuse me, gentlemen, I'm on a mission."

Jake Hammerton left them by the lift. Lisa pressed buttons and stayed silent until they were inside. She knew Juliet would start on Lucas again so tried to divert as the lift carried them upwards.

"You were showing Rupert your petticoat, sweetheart. Rule one, keep male bodyguards in place, otherwise he'll be mooning around your feet."

"Like you."

Lisa closed her eyes. "That was uncalled for. I do my best for you. You know for me this is more than a job, you know I … " The final two words failed her. She said instead, "You know I would do anything you asked, except risk your life."

"The only risk I face is from Jake Hammerton's

excesses. If you don't help, I'll get Rupert too. I saw his look. I could twist him around my little finger. The address in Cambridge was on the itinerary, I've already given it to Lucas."

The lift stopped and the door slid open on West Penthouse. Lisa folded her arms and looked down at her wayward charge. "What you did was irresponsible. I won't tell Jake but you phone Lucas, tell him you are otherwise engaged and your location must remain his secret."

"No. It's my life, I want him and I intend to have him. So help or keep out of my way."

"You do as told young lady, or my God I'll … " Lisa drew back, knowing she had overstepped the mark. The girl had her head on one side, her smile teasing,

"What's that Lisa? What would you do to me, chastise my sweet, little bottom?"

"The precautions we take are for your own safety."

Juliet shook her head. "The precautions you take are to pacify my father's guilt for allowing my mother to die. I maybe the victim of it but I still intend to have a life. Don't wait up." She turned and walked away, strutting as she did so.

Lisa snorted and stabbed at the lift button.

The banqueting hall was still busy, more relaxed now the star had gone and the beer flowed. Lisa saw no sign of Rupert. She picked up a Budweiser, flipped off the top and drank from the bottle. Halfway along the bar she chose a space next to the man she wanted, then leant back on her elbows, waiting thirty seconds before Navro spoke.

"Chill out, lady."

"It shows that bad?" She swigged from the bottle. "It would help if I gave a certain young madam a damn good spanking."

"Mind if I watch?"

"Navro, you got an immature mind." She looked down at her beer. "Wanna play top dog?"

For the first time Navro smiled. "If I recall, last time you didn't do so good. Took a month before you talked to me again."

"A woman has to rebuild her pride. But tonight it will be different, tonight I'm feeling real mean."

"You're on."

"Exec gym, twenty minutes." Lisa put down her beer and pushed from the bar. Across the far side she saw Jake Hammerton lecturing Rupert.

On the 22nd floor, Lisa pulled four mats into the centre of the deserted executive gymnasium then capped the security cameras before removing her clothes. When Navro arrived, she locked the door behind him.

"Don't be shy, Navro, let's see what new muscles you've developed." She watched him walk round the mats, take off his sunglasses and begin to divest his clothes.

"You're looking good, Lisa. Wearing a bigger bra?"

"You look all you want, just keep your hands off 'em."

"Till I've beat ya." Navro removed his shorts and tossed them aside. "Three strikes or a submission," he said, "and no sneaky stuff."

She watched him step onto the mat, his penis rigid. "Kind of taking things for granted ain't you Navro?" She began to circle, her hands held flat.

"Just watch me in the clinches, little gal you could be in for a shock."

"You got to catch me first."

Navro came with a faster speed than expected, sending her side stepping, striking his forearms and biceps with the flattened edge of her palms. Expertly, she shuffled steps, knowing if he took hold of her, his superior strength would be overpowering. She adopted the strategy of attack and retreat, each time searching his defence. On the fourth sortie he grabbed for her waist but was too slow to stop her springing left, allowing her to pivot half circle before bringing the heel of her foot hard into his back.

"Strike!"

Navro went sprawling face to mat and lay for a second. "You're getting lucky, little lady."

"Luck, my ass. You're just whinging 'cause it hurt, jarring your prick and all."

"See this, gal?" He pointed down as he came back to his feet. "Now it wants revenge."

"It can want, but it ain't going no place." Lisa's confidence soared; she had never floored him before. He came in a flurry of blows which she parried with both forearms, feigned retreat, then counter-attacked with a single blow under his kidneys.

"Strike!"

Navro backed away, hands clutching his side while trying to regain dented pride. She began to circle, deliberately goading him, dancing foot to foot, her breasts jiggling. She wanted him riled, one more mistake and he was hers. She beckoned him.

"Your one-eyed demon is losing, Navro. You're going to end up lapping pussy milk."

Never," he said and lunged. She ducked left, then leaped for a neck blow, not realising he had grabbed for her leg. Momentum and swing lifted her horizontally, throwing her face to ground. Immediately he was down on her back, his arm around her waist, lifting her from behind before holding her head downwards, buttocks up as he probed with his penis.

"You bastard. That's against the rules. Don't you dare!"

"All's fair in love and war, sweetheart."

In outrage, she straightened a leg, pushing to twist them both over sideways. Immediately his left leg forced up between hers, parting her thighs. One arm still around her middle, he applied pressure to her neck, forcing her head down to waist, all the time jabbing to enter her body. In desperation she grasped hold of his testicles.

"Bitch! That's cheating."

"All's fair in love and war, Navro. Submit or squeal."

"Never!"

"You know I can pop an orange out of its skin with one hand," she said, teeth clenched, steadily increasing pressure as he drew her against him. On the point of penetration she twisted her wrist and jerked, feeling gender satisfaction at his high-pitched shriek.

"OK! I submit." He released his hold.

Lisa untangled their bodies and stood over him. "Why, Navro, that submission brought tears to your eyes."

"It ain't fair. You play dirty."

"You were about to take advantage of my compromised position. What do you expect of a lady? Now stop whinging. You lost." She stepped over his torso, a leg either side. "Stay on your back, Navro, and keep that little pecker handy. I like to warm to my pleasure, then take it slow and easy."

"I demand a rematch. Next week, in England."

His news made her stop. How did he know? "They sending you too? It's meant to be deep cover"

"Just in case. Didn't they tell you? We got choppers and a full backup team."

"Sure they told me," she lied naturally. "I just didn't get the full briefing."

"I can fill you in now if you want."

She saw him creep for escape, seeking to divert her.

"Later." She pushed him back with the sole of her foot. "Next half hour, your tongue gonna be too busy for any talking."

Seb kicked off his shoes and lay back on the hotel bed while opening the envelope Henry had given him. He extracted folded sheets plus an economy class airline ticket. Details of etiquette and conduct in the presence of Miss Walsh ran to twelve pages, all of which he skipped. His interest lay in the final close quarter operations brief. Under requirements decided by Lisa Longford, he was to shadow any outing beyond their secure accommodation or facilities, to give additional backup on demand and provide assistance in any situation deemed necessary by her or Miss Walsh. On Miss Longford's instruction, to carry out forward reconnaissance and ensure security in areas Miss Walsh chose to visit. His interpretation was that this made him Lisa's dog's body. It's what he expected and had no problem with that, knowing Sean Fagan would also be hovering. There would be little sleep. He shrugged, what were two weeks? Walsh Securities seemed an organisation steeped in bullshit; well he could bullshit too, and bullshit always baffled bullshit. His final instruction was to report at 0800 hours West Penthouse, Walsh Towers.

He rolled from the bed and helped himself to a beer out of the mini bar. It was 8 p.m. and New York was looking good. Changed into jeans and sweatshirt, he was checking dollars in his wallet when the phone rang.

"Seb, this is Jody Farlow. Can I buy you a drink?"

"If you let me buy you dinner."

"Strictly buddies. No asking me to see your etchings afterwards."

"But I've brought my very best."

He listened to her pause. "Right now I'm fondling a long stemmed glass of Chablis, Hatchings Winery, 42nd Street, middle bar."

"Give me fifteen minutes."

"So finally I get to the head boy. Money sure speaks, Khalid."

"Time is pressing, Octavius. What of our

programme?"

"Sweetpea is out of the cage tomorrow. I have flight details and arrangements from there on. Time to arrange payment."

"Only at point of execution."

"Well, just to know we understand each other, I want point of payment instantly prior to that. Don't want you disappearing on me."

"Trust, Octavius, is essential."

"Well I trust you, Khalid, just as you trust me. Go to hotmail Spaceman185cc.com. You will be faced with a coded page. User name Coffee, password Tomcat. Beyond you will find depository codes for twenty-five bank accounts. I want you to set up an automatic and immediate deposit arrangement for a substantial amount in dollars. This payment, when it happens, will be electronically transferred and divided between all twenty-five accounts, instantly, at the touch of your computer key. I want you to do this immediately, then transfer one dollar to each account as a trial. Needless to say, when the main payment is made, I got drop down facilities for immediate transfers to other accounts, so forget about any snatch backs. The ball's in your court, Khalid, only when I see these arrangements in place does your operation go to phase two."

CHAPTER 8

Seb left his hotel and entered the bright morning carrying his small bag of clothes and a mild hangover. He had talked with Jody until two in the morning, encouraging her to share three bottles of Chablis. In the hotel room an exchange of kisses and caresses warmed their passion and removed most of their clothing. But when Seb commenced his final approach, Jody apologetically excused herself for the bathroom. Tucked in bed and pondering the ceiling he had waited and listened, wondering why Americans always showered before, instead of after love. Two time zones and little sleep over forty-eight hours weighed heavily on his eyes. He fantasised Jody's naked figure leaning over him, fantasised kissing and touching her breasts, fantasised the embrace of her body, until his 6.30 a.m. alarm call brought back reality. Her note by the phone was brief. Hope you had sweet dreams. See you in London.

"Oh fuck, not again!"

After countless checks and barriers Seb finally showed his pass to the armed guard outside the West Penthouse and was led in by Henry Taylor. At 0800 hours the atmosphere in the main lounge felt like a doctor's waiting room, people tense, not talking. Two pretty girls looking much like Juliet sat on a sofa, one dressed in an expensive outfit, the other more casual. Two female bodyguards with short blonde hair and features like Lisa's, stood behind. Seb smiled his greetings and received acknowledgement from some a little wave from Juliet who lounged in a corner chatting on her mobile. As if his entrance signalled start of proceedings, Lisa checked her watch and moved centre floor.

"OK, operation commences. Holly Johnson one, code name Queen Bee, time for your departure. You take the limo, first class seats and most of our luggage." She nodded to the smartly dressed girl who stood and linked arms with her female bodyguard. "Second decoy, Holly Johnson two, code name Field Mouse, goes via a back elevator. Juliet travels as Holly three, code name Candy Girl. You have confirmation all systems go at your end?" Lisa asked Seb.

"A team will be at the airport to meet Queen Bee. She gets our best car. No one but myself knows Candy Girl's ID."

"Candy Girl will carry minimal luggage for convenience and speed. She's a student checking out coursework for her PhD. So, one case and a backpack. Speaking of baggage," Lisa reached under the jacket of her trouser suit and extracted a Walther P88 pistol. She handed it to Henry. "England's got some weird rules regarding guns," she said.

"Got to give the bad guys a chance," Seb smiled. "But if you need a weapon, I'm sure it could be arranged."

"We stay within UK law," Henry said and handed Lisa an envelope. "Last orders plus location of bolt-hole. Open only when in the UK."

"I get the info also?" Seb asked.

"Unfortunately, Candy Girl is on need to know only. I'm sure you understand, Lieutenant."

"Sure." Seb made a pretence of smiling but realised he was excluded from the inner circle. To feel mistrust at start of mission was a bad omen. His mood brightened when Juliet came over. Dressed in jeans and blue cotton shirt, she appeared the most relaxed in the room, more a college girl eager for a field trip than some rich kid avoiding terrorist abduction.

"Please to meet you again, Rupert." She offered her hand.

"Sebastian," he said. "Seb for short." He clasped her fingers and felt their small pressure. Her smile seemed open, full of genuine warmth and for seconds he sensed temptation to sow seeds but instead took warning from the sober faces overlooking them.

"Sebastian is too formal and Rupert so cute," she said. "So, as this trip is all secret and stuff, let's code name you Rupert. I like Rupert." She released his hand, her smile lingering to the last.

Henry pushed spectacles with a forefinger and grunted a cough from the back of his throat. "We're ninety seconds behind schedule, Miss Juliet."

"I'll just say goodbye to Eva," Juliet said. "But the reason I came over is because you mentioned the bolt-hole. I tell you, Henry. I'm not playing another of Jakes stupid games. And I ain't hiding in no box."

"No worries, Miss Juliet, the location I chose is a beautiful setting at the very heart of research for your thesis. There's swimming too. I promise you'll love it, if you ever get to use it, which is very unlikely."

While Queen Bee used the main elevator and Field Mouse a back one, Seb and party reached the basement via a service elevator. All climbed into a laundry van and Henry tapped the sides, sending them up the ramp to the busy street. Both girls lugged rucksacks and trolley cases, both looked like mid-American senior students on a culture trip. Close up he could see their clothes were brand new and straight out of the supermart. Neither girl wore makeup. Such detail for blending with the crowd gave him confidence. If this was Lisa's doing, she was at least professional. The drive to JFK Airport was mostly in silence with the girls occasionally talking between themselves about trip details. For the first time Seb also realised a tension, mainly from Lisa. He dismissed it as job pressure. He had never worked with a woman before but took account of the warning that this one could be queer cattle. He hoped Sean Fagan had a good line-up at Heathrow. A suitable first impression was essential for client confidence, Lisa's included, not to mention the quarter million dollars bonus which rode on a successful result. Outside of remote threats from the likes of Qasem, he saw no real problems. South East England was a crowded place and the more crowded the place, the easier to hide. Compared to snatching anthrax from the middle of the desert, this would be a doddle. A fortnight's baby minding two quiet American girls, no problem.

As ordered, he split at the airport and checked in for Flight AA 148 with a group of homebound British tourists. Queen Bee and co made their own check-in causing suitable attraction in the process, Field Mouse took a different flight. Candy Girl just slotted into the crowd. Waiting for departure, he kept close shadow, watching while the girls shopped, had coffee and a sandwich. They never acted other than as friends and by boarding time he believed both the Marines and Henry pushed out unfounded gossip over their lesbian relationship. It also made Juliet's smile more dangerous. To banish temptation he considered his chances with Lisa, perhaps taking her to dinner. She had something about her he found compelling.

Throughout the flight he maintained his distance, sitting behind them on the opposite side of the aisle, just three individuals lost in a jumbo full of tourists. During the five hours flight he heard their voices only once, Lisa with an emphatic, no! Then both faded to heated whisper. Friends' squabble, he hoped.

Heathrow Airport was at maximum capacity. Seb lingered behind, ready to cover if needed. He saw Sean Fagan amongst the group of Asian taxi drivers gathered at the exit barrier, all clutching placards to identify their passengers. On the far right, first class emerged in a less pressurised queue, Queen Bee, alias Holly Johnson one and her bodyguard both struggling with two over laden trolleys. Seb recognised Colonel Freddy Fox and another suited man go to their assistance. All appeared organised and controlled. A black Bently would take Queen Bee to the Plaza Suite in a swanky hotel. Juliet and Lisa would share a double economy room in some hostel. Whilst normality amongst the herd gave perfect cover from would be abductors, it also meant the client became vulnerable if things went wrong. Seb stood deep watch with responsibility to give warning. Easy though this job appeared, he sensed his need for total commitment. As a member of CAT you either did, or you did not.

Dr Jaber stood a little to one side of the taxi drivers and watched passengers from flight AA148 shuffle towards the barriers. As described, he saw the rich American girl with her bodyguard in close attendance, both manoeuvring heavily laden trolleys.

Jaber called on his mobile and instructed the three key figures of his seven strong group into place. The exit gate provided a perfect covert opportunity for close identification, where they might observe both women without either being aware. He considered it imperative that his key members knew the facial identity of their target.

"Tanisha, go to left position," Jaber spoke quietly into his mobile phone as the first passengers started to exit. He watched his head of unit glide with the natural grace of a highborn Somali, a cell phone to her ear, a long skirt hitched delicately in her fingertips. Mild in his own manner and physical strength, Jaber found Tanisha's strong abilities reassuring. Her recommendation by al-Qaeda guaranteed her credentials.

"I have target contact," her velvet voice whispered back into his ear.

Jaber watched her stop by the barrier, one hand to her mobile, the other wrapped to her waist as the American girl was approached by two, dark-suited heavies. The female bodyguard was quick to intervene. Tanisha stood no more than a few metres distance as the four exchanged words. Jaber redialled on his mobile.

"Amin, have you ID'd our target yet?"

"I am moving slowly as instructed," Amin answered.

"Then move faster," Jaber ordered, not hiding his irritation over the twenty-four-year-old's Palestinian's impertinence. "Lena, she is with you?"

"Of course, as you instructed. Clinging as always to my strength like a little vine. Crowds frighten her."

Jaber heard the girl's dismissive laugh. He knew well who had the real strength. If orders were given for one to kill the other, he did not rate the chances of Amin. "Do you have the target in sight?" Jaber asked.

"We see the beautiful black American girl talking with her servants. I could kill all four, right now."

"No! We are here only to observe." To show his presence and authority Jaber relocated to the fringe of people now separating to allow passengers through. Amin and Lena stood opposite, the boy with his arm around the girl's waist, both behaving like middle class students, she in a mini skirt, he in a leather jacket. Neither gave a hint of the ruthless executioners he had employed. Only Bin Qasem's word that they had independently murdered over sixty-two Israelis made them viable. For his own liking, Amin was too intense, too self-opinionated.

He watched as the two dark-suited heavies relieved the women of their trolleys and pushed for the terminal exit along with the main flow of passengers. Through the passing bodies he made eye contact with Tanisha.

"Here she comes," he whispered into the phone. She was as Octavius had described, small and pretty, in blue shirt and jeans. "Candy Girl is directly in front of you, now," he said to Amin, watching to see that Tanisha had identified the girl also. "The tall one with blonde hair is her bodyguard. There is another, a young male with light hair. Be careful, he is skilled and dangerous."

Seb kept his eyes on the crowd as he moved to the exit. A

hundred pairs of eyes looked back from faces bored or expectant, mainly chauffeurs and taxi drivers holding name placards, a few welcome home parents for backpackers and a dozen business people. None appeared any threat.

Juliet and Lisa walked straight to Sean Fagan who held a card identifying him as City Connect. Seb maintained his distance, keeping vigil over the two women as they followed Sean from the terminal to the multi-storey car park. Other people headed in the same direction, groups and individuals going this way and that. Occasionally he looked behind. A young couple had trailed at some distance but they appeared more interested in each other than their surroundings, the boy with a mobile to his ear, the girl trying to stop his hand from going under her tee shirt.

Across the stretch of cluttered car park, Sean opened the door of an aging Mercedes and helped his passengers inside. Seb slipped between vehicles and concrete pillars, stopping by the slip road as Sean drew the Merc beside him. The young couple had gone. Probably groping in some corner, he thought. Climbing into the front passenger seat, he smiled at the girls behind.

"Welcome to England." His smile was returned by Juliet, warm and beautiful. Lisa scowled.

"Is this car bullet proof?" she asked. "Like the contract states?"

"No, Miss Longford." Sean glanced over his shoulder. "But it's rustproof, mechanically sound and has an MOT. I should warn you, all our vehicles are similar. Large expensive limos attract the attention of Romanian gypsies, street gangs and neo-fascist football hooligans. We run a swift, covert operation that moves our clients unseen through the city streets. The Royal Family frequently travel in similar circumstances," Sean said, his tongue rubbing inside his cheek. He put the Merc into drive and headed for the airport tunnel. Once out and cruising the motorway towards London he switched on a short-wave radio and spoke so everyone could hear.

"Fagan to Queen Bee, sit rep."

"No visible tail. Taking circular route to hotel," a voice cracked over the amplifier.

"Roger that, over and out." He put down the mike. "No sign of enemy. We're clear," he said, over his shoulder.

"That's fine for Queen Bee, but how do you know a car ain't following us?" Lisa asked.

"There is, but it's one of ours, and a second following that. We'd soon know if we had a tail," Sean said.

"For your sake, I hope so."

The following silence lay heavy and Seb wondered over the truth of Sean's words. The Combined Agency Taskforce did not have spare manpower for such double protection. To lighten the atmosphere he twisted around in his seat.

"What's the subject of your PhD, Miss Juliet?"

"Drop the miss, Rupert. I ain't no old maid. Miss is my formal defence against Jake's boys."

"I'll drop the miss, if you drop Rupert."

She smiled again, the same big, beautiful smile that ate right into him. He felt the stirrings and ignored the warnings. "My friends call me Seb."

"OK, Seb, it's a deal. And I'm studying the effects of myth and truth in literature. Those aspects of history which our culture believes in but are unsupported by factual evidence. My main thesis is the Arthurian legends, Camelot and such."

"The dream stuff of every English schoolchild. I know it well. Tintagel in Cornwall, I used to visit when I was a kid."

"Tintagel, right. You got it. Looks like I got help with research " She smiled again and Seb smiled back. Visual contact lingered until Lisa's mobile rang.

"Hello, Henry. Yeah, entry made. Transferring to hotel, backup in position. You got a fix on our tracker bracelets yet?"

Seb watched as Juliet unconsciously touched the electronic band circling her wrist. Lisa nodded on the reply from the American and switched off.

"They have contact," she said. "But it's weak. When we reach Cambridge we set up a portable relay station. It allows easier tracking from the States."

"Like tagged animals in the jungle. We can't even go to the john without Jake knowing." Juliet's smile grew thin as she stared from the window.

Freddy Fox hovered in the foyer of the Linster International Hotel, central London, while Queen Bee as Holly Johnson one, went through her grand entrance. Satisfied the whole hotel had realised a VIP arrived, he escorted them to room 105. Inside two female operatives from CAT introduced themselves. Fox left immediately for Bayswater, checking on the way that Field Mouse, Holly Johnson two, had caught her flight OK.

Abigail's guesthouse in Bayswater cost £60 a night per person, including breakfast. Seb watched the girls go up to their room then called Sean in the car outside.

"Candy Girl installed, job done," he said over the mobile.

"Rooms either side are occupied by CAT operatives. Your room is directly across the passage. All rooms have been swept for devices. We have a ten man patrol keeping surveillance over the area. If any bad guy is watching or waiting we will soon know. The whole point of the London sleepover is to ensure Candy Girl's cover has not been compromised."

"OK," Seb nodded. "Early night then."

"Just keep your eyes and ears focussed. I'll be somewhere outside. Oh, and Seb, if for one moment you grow suspicious, ring 333444 on your mobile. It will connect you to a microphone clipper under Candy Girl's bed."

Seb grinned. Sneaky. He took his case and went up to his room. It had views of the backs of other buildings, was for single occupancy but bright, neat and clean.

He threw his case on the bed then knocked on Candy Girl's door. Lisa answered, opening the door only a crack while standing to block any view inside. Still he caught a fleeting glimpse of Juliet as she entered the bathroom in her bra and pants.

"OK?" Lisa questioned.

"I'm in the room opposite," Seb told her. "And we got guys either side. Yell if you need anything."

Lisa checked her watch. "Some food and a drink about 7.00 this evening. Pizzas, coffee, whatever you can get."

"OK, no problem," Seb said and watched the door close. "I know who's the handyman," he muttered.

Lisa read and re-read the last orders Henry had passed before exit from the penthouse. It was code red, for receiver only. She crossed the room and sat on the edge of Juliet's bed. "Honey, we got ourselves a problem. Instructions read, ditch our bracelets and stay hidden here an extra two days while Rupert checks out Cambridge. Seems we have a mole at the heart of Walsh Securities with possible access to the tracking system. It's the main reason they wanted you out of America. If nothing happens within seventy-two hours, then we go forward as planned."

Juliet screwed up her nose and put her book to one side. "If this is some ruse to prevent me meeting with Lucas, forget it. Tomorrow he'll be in England. Don't matter where we hide, I'll tell him."

"Please, babe, give me a chance. I've told no one what you intend. I just hope you won't. Now these instructions are reading serious. Henry has real concern."

"I'm not going to play their games, Lisa."

Lisa looked down at her young charge, the girl's eyes were glowing, her lips tight set. She figured devious diplomacy the best option. "Let's play cool, we get Rupert to pick up Lucas, bring him wherever you are and take him back afterwards. No one else to know, ever." Lisa tried to cover her guilt over what she was really thinking. But for now it was the best lie she could offer. She just hoped Rupert would play along by refusing to break Juliet's cover, refuse to compromise. The alternative was to get rid of him all together which she considered the best option. But then others might take his place. Better maybe to just have him on their side. Baby minding was out of his military environment which made him gullible. Sean Fagan appeared a more serious problem. But by feeding Seb maybe she could influence his boss. She gave Juliet a sigh of capitulation and in result the girl sat up and took hold of Lisa's hand before pressing it to her cheek. "I just love you for this. I have to discover Lucas, I have to develop some sense out of a whole jumble of feelings. Call it confused and frustrated innocence if you like."

Lisa lifted strands of fallen hair over Juliet's ear. "I understand but you must realise during the next seventy-two hours Raider will be handed to the Air Force. That's what this is all about. Jake spreading his own confusion." She reached for the dresser and face cream to rub a dab onto Juliet's wrist. "OK, let's slip these trackers off, let's be free."

"Maybe this is your chance to cuddle up with Rupert," Juliet said, as Lisa removed her bracelet before starting on her own.

"His eyes are for you, babe, another one of your puppy dogs."

"I saw him watching us at JFK, not me but you, Lisa. You beckon, I bet he'd come tail wagging. He's sure got a cute butt."

"So long as he does as he's told."

CHAPTER 9

The early June sun had already pushed temperatures high enough to layer the rush hour traffic in heat and exhaust fumes. At 0745 hours Seb walked round the back of the hotel where he had parked his own Jaguar car. All appeared secure, but he checked beneath, then the doors, boot and bonnet before feeding the meter for a three hour stay. Old hands from Northern Ireland had taught him never to trust an unattended vehicle, never assume a car safe while an enemy was hunting.

He had seen no sign of the girls at breakfast but was reassured by the murmur of voices from their room. In the hotel lobby he eased between groups of Japanese and American backpackers and used an internal phone to call Lisa. Ten minutes later she came down carrying a briefcase.

"Change of plan, Seb. Juliet's unwell, doesn't want to travel."

Seb felt immediate unease. "If we divert from our itinerary, I'm supposed to report. Shall I email Jake?"

"No, I'll do that. If he interferes, Juliet will get her temper up and make life difficult. It's women's problems, you understand. She just wants quiet for a day. Let's keep Jake out of it."

Faced with the great enigma of female anatomy, Seb felt pressured to back down. He nodded uncertain compliance. "OK, so I'll hang out down here."

"No, I need you to take this to Cambridge." She handed him the briefcase. "It contains the transmitter which relays our tag bracelets via satellite to Walsh Securities, New York. Check the Cambridge flats are secure and plug the transmitter into a telephone socket, then I can test we got auto-tracking to base. Wait till we come up, later today, maybe tomorrow."

"I'll call Sean Fagan in, he can take it." Seb watched the spread of a patronising smile and realised his words would go nowhere.

"Seb," Lisa gripped his arm and guided him further across the lobby as if to confide in friendly trust. "We girls periodically have feminine difficulties. That's why Juliet has a same gender bodyguard. In other words, she don't want men around. What's important is, you establish security transmission from base. Those bracelets pinpoint our exact location but they can't do it accurately without a satellite link. It's essential that link is established in Cambridge ASAP. I'll stay in touch."

Seb still hesitated. "You'd never notice me if I …"

"Somewhere close Jake will have a team ready to pounce. Plus we have mobile contact." She shrugged, as if reluctant to confide. "I confess Juliet and I occasionally play outside of Jake's rules. Sometimes just to breathe, sometimes like now, because I know it's the best thing to do. But we have Lisa's Law and that's pretty strict. OK? Now, I know men don't like direct orders from a woman, but I'm giving one." She passed him a card. "We'll contact every four hours by cell phone. The number's there and this hotel's a safe place. Her daddy owns it."

He left feeling like the hired help but rationalised it could also be his bewilderment over the complexity of women. Part was Juliet's smile beckoning him to disaster; part because he felt excluded from Lisa's trust. That irritated. Ultimately she was ground commander whose orders he was obliged to obey. But trust had to work both ways.

Navro's team had travelled in pairs, split between four flights, all masquerading as business executives for Walsh Industries. Jake spared no expense. On arrival each pair was provided with a hired 5 Series BMW. Base was set up near Cambridge at Hardwick Grange, a manor house and grounds with helipads. Hired without staff for a two-week conference, Navro found the place secluded and large enough for scramble training with a company-owned Bell Kiowa helicopter.

His immediate concern became hardware and ammunition. Told that the Brits objected to people bringing in weapons, he asked Henry to use CIA and company influence so that specialist machine parts were delivered to a Walsh distribution depot in Birmingham. Parts which he hoped would give enough clout for any close quarter combat.

Navro went through procedures under a regimented sequence of priorities, checking incoming ordnance, sending men to Birmingham for the hardware and establishing a communications room. Slater, his techie, quickly had contact between base and New York over a secure satellite link. Both men unpacked the tracking equipment, Navro watching while Slater plugged in leads for power, computers and telephones. Within minutes he had located both bracelets.

"They're on top of each other, figuratively speaking of course." Slater smirked. "And as I locate them, on freeway M11, travelling north, I would say in the same car."

"Right on schedule." Navro checked his watch at 1000 hours. "Can you tell if they're really in the same car?"

"Bracelets have to be apart at least three metres for it to show, so unless they were jockeying each other in a highly dangerous manner, I'd say they're definitely together. Want me to phone Lisa, check their ETA?"

"We're not meant to be here. If Sweetpea finds out, she'll go ape shit. Orders are from Jake himself. Providing everything goes sweet, there is to be no contact. We stay in shadow watching the guy who's watching the princess."

In a small room at the back of the American Embassy in Grosvenor Square, Jody Farlow sat close to Al Domeco,

Assistant Shift Officer for Communications. A small, bespectacled man, he had that know-all certainty of one who does nothing which might incur failure. "This is most irregular, Miss Farlow. You CIA guys are considered bogey men."

Jody smiled with warm, sensual lips, opened her jacket and expertly hitched it wide with a hand to her waist. She swivelled to face him. "I shall consider your involvement a personal favour, Al. Someone to keep watch while I go about my external duties. Just a few days, look in every hour and give me a call on the situation."

She watched his eyes dart down over her blouse and pert nipples beneath as he made a pretence of adjusting the disk aerial. "Where did you get this anyway? S'not standard issue."

She lent forward to whisper. "From Walsh Securities, Jake Hammerton, Global Raider. Need I say more?"

"You're telling me this is classified?" He began to falter.

"And some," she said. "That's why I've brought in a guy like you, someone I can trust. Al, this is strictly inner circle and between us two. It's a personal favour I'm asking."

"You are?" He looked to her blouse again.

"For your country, and my gratitude." She inhaled voluptuously.

"Yes, ma'am."

Away from the Embassy, Jody dialled on her mobile. "This is momma, you got Candy Girl in residence?"

"Tracker shows her on the outskirts of Cambridge," Navro answered. "You got cross-reference?"

"No, but I now have them monitored from the Embassy via a contact."

"Didn't think they'd let a spook like you through the door."

"Navro, being in the CIA's Special Activities Directorate, don't mean you tell people about it. I'm a roving security officer checking on Embassy access procedures. That gets me through most doors. My credentials are cool, OK? So are you on the ground up there?"

"Fully rigid. Where are your agents, you sent anyone?"

"I have you, Navro. What more could a girl want? Keep house for me. Right now I got fingers in something sinister. If Jake is right and Qasem does have contact inside Walsh Towers, then the dangers to Candy Girl and GR4 are real. If it happens, they'll come hard and from nowhere. I've got bad feelings over this."

"You want to tell me about it?"

"When I know for sure. Till then, keep reporting to Jake … and to momma."

At 1100 hours, the temperature in Cambridge hovered towards 30°C licensing the beautiful and not so beautiful to parade in skimpy clothes. Seb drove his Jaguar to an address off Andrew Street and collected keys from the letting agent while leaving others behind as spares. In an outer suburb the keys opened a Victorian house converted into two flats, both sharing a common entrance and garden. It was obvious to him Sean had picked the building for ease of security rather than proximity to city centre. The guy knew his priorities. Seb parked on the gravel drive behind a hired BMW left by Sean for client use. The floor allocated to the girls was spacious and bright with high ceilings and period furniture giving the ambiance from days when middle England had servants and empire. In a back bedroom he found an unused telephone jack with adjacent power socket. Kneeling beside the briefcase he lifted the transmitter onto the floor, leaving inside a padded envelope he assumed contained spare parts. He plugged in both leads and watched two rows of diodes flicker into life. The transformer within began to hum, recharging batteries and transmitting signals. Seb unfolded the antenna dish and raised it on a short, telescopic stalk which he stood on a windowsill. When satisfied the device worked, he went down to install himself in the flat below.

A brew up was first priority. While the kettle boiled he phoned Sean Fagan.

"Slight change of plan," Seb told him. "I've been sent ahead to set up a satellite disk for their tracker bracelets. Lisa's orders. Juliet's unwell, coming up later."

Sean laughed. "Don't the SAS teach you anything about women? The decoy has worked. They're relaxed. I can guarantee they plan to go shopping. The first thing any woman does when she hits a new city is go look at the clothes."

"Oh shit, she sounded so convincing. Would they do that to me?"

"SAS, bloody golden boys. I'm surprised you can find your way to the pub. Best thing is to sit tight till they reappear. Just keep them in contact."

Seb grunted disillusion. "You coming up today?"

"Tomorrow. I'm outside their hotel. If they go out I'll need to keep track. Also need to keep up the decoy cover."

Seb switched off and contemplated his position while the tea brewed. If Lisa had lied he was out of her rules and into his own. That meant anything he wanted. He felt angry over his gullibility and disappointed by her deceit; or was Fagan just winding him up? Bloody civvies were a pain in the arse. He tried Lisa's mobile and got voicemail, so left a message saying the transmitter was active. Next came waiting and the suppression of impatience with every passing minute. The weather forecast predicted a three-day heat wave climaxing in thunderstorms. The humidity was climbing with temperatures recording the hottest June in thirty years. It did nothing for his mood. By late afternoon four calls to Lisa's mobile had received the same negative response. By five his patience evaporated.

To keep the building secure and create the illusion of occupation, he drew curtains in back and front bedrooms, then put on lights and a TV. He did the same in the flat below. For minutes he paced the floor, unsure if he was now involved in female deception or a situation more serious. Fagan answered his cell phone on the second ring.

"Lisa's not responding to calls," Seb told him. "Illicit shopping or not, that's hardly professional."

"I haven't seen them leave the hotel, unless they've somehow sneaked past our man at the back. Try New York. Maybe they can give a location on the tracker bracelets."

"You forget, I'm supposed to be physically eyeballing them. I didn't want panic or to drop anyone in the shit over nothing – especially the Combined Agency Taskforce. But right now, I'm worried."

"Don't sweat, I'm told Lisa's the best. If there's a problem she would hit code red. I'll check Reception, if they have done a bunk I'll ask Walsh Securities to do a trial test on the bracelets. At worst if they're not shopping they'll be on their way to Cambridge," he paused. "Hang on I've got a call coming over my CAT link."

Seb listened to the passing silence then heard it broken by a single expletive.

"Bollocks."

"What's up?"

"Field Mouse has been hit, taken, her bodyguard shot."

"Shit." Seb dropped on the bed realising his world was about to implode. "If they knew of Field Mouse then it's probable they know of Queen Bee and Candy Girl. The decoys didn't work."

"The opposite, they hit the wrong girl, but I ain't taking chances."

Seb heard Fagan switch the closed circuit microphone in his car then heard him shouting instructions over the clunk of slamming car doors.

"All units stand to for imminent enemy action. Adopt close quarter protection, now."

The call terminated leaving Seb to sit motionless, his hand tight around the mobile, his throat dry. "For fuck's sake Lisa, be there," he whispered. Minutes dragged into oppressive silence while he stared at the digital flow of his watch clocking the passing of time. When the wait became intolerable he again punched numbers on his mobile.

"They've gone," Fagan answered. "Reception saw nothing. Queen Bee also got hit same time as Field Mouse but they escaped. Freddy Fox got both in lockdown."

Seb shunted breath in relief. "That means they don't really know which decoy is Juliet. They're guessing. The instant Lisa heard she would have her girl out of it."

"Possibly" Fagan said. "Or they got taken very quietly. I've checked their room and found no evidence of a struggle, except their backpacks are gone. But even if they did escape, Field Mouse would have been interrogated by now. Bin Qasem will know the whole decoy plot. If he didn't take them he'll be out searching."

Seb closed his eyes and suppressed a shudder while thinking of the pain and sexual degradation Field Mouse would have suffered while undergoing interrogation by Bin Qasem's followers. The poor girl probably lay dead by now.

"What you want me to do?" he asked quietly.

"Stay put, they could show any moment. Then you'll be a hero."

"And if they don't?"

"Then we're in deep shit but nowhere near the depth you'll be. The fact Bin Qasem knows of the decoys shows a leak in Walsh Securities or CAT. Our side is small, select and without motive. Hammerton will know the leak is his side so will blame us." His voice dropped a tone. "And when I say us, I principally mean you. Believe an ex-policeman, I know how devious the guilty can be."

"Thanks a million."

"It comes with the job. Colonel Fox will be in contact, till then sit tight and pray. Over and out."

Seb remained listening to silence slowly replaced by traffic noise from outside. He wished, oh how he wished, to be back in the Army. Spread on what would have been Lisa's bed he lay for an hour, then another, until realising they were not coming. Lifting his mobile he pressed the keys watching the numbers appear beneath her name. Again Lisa's phone rang and rang then voicemail answered.

"Bitch," he said and tried texting. Immediate contact imperative. Next was to try Fagan's solution. It could drop him completely into the mire, or just maybe give a lead. All depended on the American situation and Jake Hammerton. Seb rolled himself from the bed and lifted the landline unit slotted beside it. From now on the rules would have to be his own because only his own initiative could haul him from the jaws waiting to snap. He dialled Walsh Securities in New York and asked for Henry Taylor.

"Major, I'm doing a double check on bracelet transmission, making sure everything is working. You have a fix on us OK?"

"It's fine," Henry answered. "Looks like our ploy worked but with both decoys out of it you're now frontline. Everything OK your end?"

"Sure, just running through procedures, making certain you have an accurate pin point. After what happened I'm taking no chances."

"Wait, let me switch on my monitor. We have the penultimate test going through on GR4 at the moment, everyone's involved." He left the phone and Seb sweated until he returned. "Yep," Henry said finally. "We have them together. Same place as last time, their mobiles indicating the same. They watching TV?"

"Relaxing after the trip." The lie came easily and without thought. "Just ratifying as instructed. Cheers, Henry." Seb hung up and looked at the transmitter then the two bubble-wrap envelopes in the briefcase. Inside one he found both bracelets and in the other their switched off mobiles. For seconds he clenched teeth realising he was trapped between his own deceit and Lisa's lies. To create some sort of credibility to his own lie, he carried one bracelet to each bedroom and laid them on the pillows.

Back in the living room he closed the curtains and opened a front window against the stale heat before switching on Lisa's mobile. After dialling he listened to it ring then switched off again. No wonder she didn't answer. He thought of Juliet's charismatic smile, her huge, dark eyes. Was this set up her deceit or Lisa's? What game did they play? Or had they also been taken?

While he stood trying to make sense of their motives, he admitted inwardly his own commonsense and trust had been duped by gullibility over a pretty face. These two were clearly no angels. Maybe they had planned to ditch him all along. If Qasem didn't have them, then he sure as hell scared them badly, hence their runner. All Lisa had to do was stay hidden and wait for help. Presumably that meant the bolt-hole. Seb figured all he had to do was find it. He remembered Henry's conversation, the place being good for her research, good for swimming. He remembered Juliet's conversation on the drive from the airport regarding the Arthurian legend. Tintagel. He stretched out on a couch and thought about it. Had Juliet told him? Deliberately told him in case of separation. Her eye contact had lingered, Lisa's expression had been disapproving. It was a wild shot but his only chance. He lay until absolutely certain they were not travelling between London and Cambridge. If that was the case they should have arrived hours ago.

His iPhone showed a drive of two hundred and fifty miles, foot down the Jaguar would get him there just after dawn. It was a long shot but Tintagel Castle gave the only common ground, his only chance. For moments he thought of informing Fagan then decided against it. If ordered back to base he was finished. Passing through the quiet streets he checked for any tail, then confident no one followed he headed for the motorway and Cornwall.

Mid evening Navro lounged back on the couch, the floor around him littered with boxes of takeaway pizzas. He sat with four of his men watching TV. When his mobile rang he flipped it from a shirt pocket and caught it in his left hand.

"Yo."

"Navro, this is Henry Taylor. We got a test on GR4 and Jake's down at Whiteman Air Base. So I'm up here in charge. Wouldn't want to bother you but I just had Mr Rupert phone from Cambridge wanting to test both bracelets again. Kind of weird phone call, like he didn't know what he was doing."

"I have a surveillance team couple of hundred yards down the road," Navro said. "There's a hire car which was there when we arrived. Then the Brits came in a Jaguar. Fraid we missed how many of them Could have been one or could have been more. The Jag was reported leaving fifteen minutes ago. One Brit driving. Could be they're changing shifts or maybe Lisa sent him out for food. Sweetpea is studying. She's got college tomorrow. Lisa's probably reading, both having a quiet night. You want I should check them out?"

"Do that. After what happened to the decoys we can't trust the Brits."

"Will do, Henry." Navro hung up and headed for his car, calling his two-man watch on the way, warning them he was going in. He parked fifty metres from the house and walked unhurriedly down the road, turning into the driveway as if an expected visitor. Away from the streetlight he sidestepped into moon shadow from a bordering hedge. The hire car still sat on the drive. A garage blocked off the back garden on the left side so he skirted to the right and found a locked gateway. Again he stood listening. Lights from downstairs and the upper rear windows spread over both lawns. He heard his own breathing, cars in the town and the bark of a distant dog, then barely audible female voices and music, possibly from a TV. A front window stood open. He had expected a patrolling sentry, or at least a passive infrared beam connected to lights. He had no doubt someone kept watch at the rear and for this reason did not climb the gate, worried the Brit would see him and get ratty. After ten minutes he returned to the surveillance car.

"They're watching TV," he said through the open window. "Sounds like the girls are upstairs. Sweetpea starts college at 0930 hours tomorrow, so I guess they'll leave by nine. Stay vigilant. These Brits are as useless as their pizzas."

CHAPTER 10

General John Chambers and Major Frank Marriot of the 509th Bomber Wing, Whiteman, Missouri, sat in a Global Raider GR4 flight module and took the latest of America's strategic weapons to its maximum ceiling of one hundred thousand feet. Remote control of the drone was also shared by ground teams on Midway Island, the aircraft carrier USS Abraham Lincoln sailing the Indian Ocean plus stations in Turkey and the UK. Overall control came through Walsh Avionics, New York. Six floors below ground, Max Crawley and Ed Rawlings used flight computers linked to satellites and Walsh Avionics global positioning systems. Following a pre-designated flight plan, Raider was kept to positions within a ten-metre tolerance. From their control module they had the ability to send GR4 around the globe, attacking fourteen targets en route before landing at point of take off.

General Chambers' voice was heard at all ground stations. "GR4 level at one hundred, that's Raider at one, zero, zero. We are hypersonic and in blind alley. Initiating stealth glide. OK you guys we are now bogey. All stations commence radar search. Come find us men."

"They've gone applejack, Raider now enemy aircraft. All tracking stations to search." Max's voice went round the world. Simultaneously, American Air Force and naval radar stations at home, on sea and in allied countries worldwide started to search for a machine that gave a radar image no larger than a football. Midway Island, Central Pacific station one of flight control, made laser contact and synchronised with Walsh Towers.

"Midway Island, we have lock-on and read transfer codes. Bird descending, Raider now at one, nine, nine, eight, zero feet. Heading for carrier beacon. Thank you Whiteman, Missouri, we have the baby in our power."

Wat Walsh listened over a secure transmission that linked all participating factors to the full-scale control module in his office. This machine in the outer stratosphere was of his making and deep inside he felt enormous pride. Ten years and eight billion dollars of his own and Government money had brought Global Raider from the abandoned B2 Stealth Bomber and created a new class of unmanned combat vehicle, a strike craft capable of trans-global attack. No country and no place or person in it were immune. Inside the hold, fourteen missiles of varying strike capacity hung waiting to destroy the most impregnable targets. Wat saw GR4 as the end of ground wars, the end of carpet-bombing and civilian casualties. This weapon had the capability of a precise strike; missiles arrived as if from nowhere without chance of enemy retaliation. Within seventy-two hours Raider would again circumnavigate the globe, undergoing final acceptance by demonstrating its ability to attack any target fed into its deployment system. Only then would Wat hand over his baby to the nation; this gift for his life and extraordinary wealth. Only then could he look to his second baby and his next ambition; Juliet as First Lady.

Behind the bombproof glass of his inner office he sat in the full-scale cockpit, watching the simulated view from Raider's flight deck. Simultaneously, codes governing the switch of control between ground stations were displayed on a screen to his left. Although these systems were considered unbreachable without input of master digits held jointly between five independent individuals, Wat still considered covert hacking into the aircraft's database its principal weakness. Crawley, the man who invented it, had privately hinted he had ways but the laser lock system had been incorporated on Defense Department instructions, a necessity to mission fulfilment should the immediate participating control unit be wiped out. Providing a single flight unit remained operable, once airborne GR4 was unstoppable. Satisfied all was on schedule and happy with the plane in dead flight over the Pacific, Wat left his module and went down to see Crawley in mission control.

Crawley and Ed Rawlings acknowledged his entrance as they hunched before banks of screens. Eighty-five systems and flight engineers gave backup.

"Any problems?" Wat asked.

"Behaves like a darling," Crawley answered, sitting back to twiddle a pencil between fingers. "Blind alley descent bottoms out in ten hours, by then USS Abraham Lincoln will have laser lock-on. Next test comes on the Saudi run. We'll have dropped to sixty thousand and be ready for re-boost. That means producing infrared. With Iran so close, they might just get lucky. No question, we'll be on sweat time."

"Have faith, Max. Our own people can't find us and they know where we are."

"Wish that idiot Hammerton thought likewise. He has me so surrounded by security I can't even fart without a response team turning up."

Hands thrust into pockets, Wat tried to sound sympathetic. He disapproved of Crawley's morals. Gay or straight, the man was sleeping around and that gave Security bad dreams. "I know how you feel," he said. "Most of the time he has me locked in a glass tank. You're our top man, Max and everybody that's anybody in this company is under tight wraps. Even Juliet has the SAS guarding her."

Ten hours later in the electronic warfare suite of aircraft carrier Abraham Lincoln, Commander Gary Baker sat in the darkened Ops room. On every wall and surface, radar, communication and computer equipment hummed and flickered amongst banks of diodes, screens and switches. As senior systems control officer, Commander Baker watched twin laser beams emitted from his own and a sister ship, converge with the directional beam from Midway Island, each crossing on the exact reference fed from the computers in Walsh Towers. Amidst the glow of red night-lights the Commander's voice sounded low and resonant.

"Midway Island, the Lincoln has locked on. The bird is ours for delivery."

"Lincoln, Dark Alley slide now bottoming out at six, zero K. I repeat, sixty thousand feet. Raider is yours; control passed on your click. Good luck, Abe."

"Thank you, Midway." Baker watched the second beam switch off and his own laser track the aircraft across the radar screen, unseen and unknown to anyone without precise co-ordinates. With the beam locked, Baker manoeuvred the aircraft and relayed simultaneous control to New York. Sixty thousand feet above him, Raider crossed over the Oman coast heading towards Saudi Arabia.

" Lincoln to New York, prepare to increase and monitor fuel burn. Burner and dispersal shield closing. Engine contact, after-burn concealed, we have ascent."

"Fuel increase forty percent and rising." Crawley answered from New York. "All tracking stations, this is your big chance. Find the birdie and prove me wrong."

Baker increased power to maximum on the GR4's General Electric engines, enabling each to develop a thirty eight thousand pound thrust, sending the aircraft back to the stratosphere and a speed of Mach 2.

"Fuel consumption at fifty percent. Prepare to decelerate on required altitude," Crawley said.

Baker recognised Crawley's stress and imagined him biting at his manicured fingernails as the aircraft climbed, fuel burning by the ton. Without enough spare fuel GR4 would not accomplish its simulated low-level attack over home base. Failure would mean cancellation of the armed run in three days.

"Ascend at eight, zero. Out of missile range," Baker said. "Come in Turkey. Blind Alley glide in ten minutes forty seconds."

" Lincoln, this is Turkey. We have laser lock-on.

Ready for control on your click."

High over Saudi Arabia, Global Raider's massive engines thrust it to maximum height of one hundred thousand feet, its guidance systems levelling the craft towards the earth's curvature and Raider's long, hypersonic glide to America's East Coast.

"Turkey, this is Lincoln, we click control, you have the bird." Baker felt immense relief in passing command. For seconds he listened to silence before Turkey came back, the operative's voice screeching.

" Lincoln, we have an intercept, I repeat, we have an intercept. For Christ's sakes, a bogey is blocking control."

"Fuck!" Crawley sat forward in his seat. " Lincoln, re-establish lock-on. Cut engines! Close all after-burn ports. I want minimal infrared. Pilots, immediate evasive action. Drop five thousand to second corridor and spray chaff."

Lincoln came back. "Lock-on ineffective. Source of interceptor's beam, unidentified."

Crawley gasped and half stood from his chair. Around him the whole flight room in Walsh Towers became a frantic scramble of activity with people shouting situation reports and responses. Containing panic, Crawley hit an emergency communication button linking him direct to Wat. He did the same for Jake Hammerton. Wat's response was immediate.

Crawley shouted. "For fuck's sake, we have enemy lock-on during transfer. Your code, we have to change codes. How can God do this to me?"

"Calm down, Max. Code, two, three, five, zero, Juliet, Zulu, Alpha."

Jake's response was equally fast, his voice over the headphones spitting out a combination of numbers and letters.

As the words came to him, Crawley stabbed digits on his keyboard which transferred to the screen. Within seconds, the aircraft's electronics, evasion and defence avionics changed the body's acoustic, electro-magnetic and radar signatures to a different pattern, simultaneously re-setting codes to govern control and flight systems. Ten seconds later the raider's interception beam faltered then vanished, allowing the pilots on Lincoln to lock-on and level to a second, pre-set course. Crawley shouted and punched one fist into the air. "Lost you! Counter surveillance activated. Raider is free. Do you have a clear window, Lincoln?"

"New York, this is Lincoln. The bogey has gone. Do we reinstate control procedures with Turkey?"

"Yes," Crawley said trying to resume calm, his mind in turmoil. Was this Perry's doing? No one should have been able to intercept without pre-knowledge of transmission codes or flight path. His only consolation came through the effective demonstration of GR4's security systems. Of one thing he was certain, the attack had not been a design failure. Perry was dead but someone else was still feeding information.

Turkey came back on air. "We have established lock-on. Relinquish control, Lincoln." Crawley waited, conscious of pain as he clamped teeth over knuckles.

"The bird is yours."

"Thank you, Lincoln. Raider gliding Blind Alley, altitude nine, five k. Target, America."

"Any fix on our bogey's beam?" Crawley asked all listeners.

"Negative," Turkey answered.

"We had one fix, but base not confirmed. Possibly Yemen," Baker answered. Crawley looked for ways out. If he did not give a solution to the raider he would face an enquiry plus a protracted delay in handover to the Air Force. The cost to his systems and equipment would be millions in cross-checking. The Perry incident would be dragged out in the open. An enquiry would expose their affair, maybe implicate Bernard. He could see the headlines, Gay Spy Ring. Global Raider was his design, his gateway to glory, he could not allow any doubt of its ability. The lie came easily, carried on the instinct of dutiful self-preservation.

"Ladies and gentlemen I congratulate your efforts over the rogue interceptor. Reaction time to throw the enemy was only two minutes twenty-eight seconds. That's twenty percent faster than Air Force requirements. Our stealth procedures have shown no after-burn, body reflection or sound transmission. That guy's now trying to relocate a needle in space. But I think it only fair to tell you, this was an unspecified test to demonstrate conclusively the ability of Raider's defence and evasion systems. The enemy was one of our own mobile land stations in Oman. Ladies and gentlemen, as a team, we threw that bogey out the window." He turned to Ed Rawlings who was mouthing disbelief. "Once again our bird is gliding Blind Alley. No one can see her, no one can touch her. ETA Mediterranean seaboard four hours. Spain, you fly Raider up the Med and Missouri can bring her home." Crawley switched off. "Take over, Ed. I have to see Wat." He smiled for the rapturous applause which came from every member of the mission team; every member but Ed Rawlings.

"We never rigged a test interception." Ed looked at him, his eyebrows raised.

"So we got ships in the Gulf, ground stations in Oman. Some asshole got lucky. Are we going to jeopardise this test for one lousy incident?"

"Max," Ed raised his hands. "We're supposed to be invisible."

"Ed, we got a blip. It's no great deal."

"Two minutes and twenty seconds during hand over is long enough to lock into our software."

"So we changed codes."

"But the software of the whole infrastructure remains the same. In two minutes twenty seconds, you can hack out a lot of data."

"But not enough. And now we have new codes. The system worked, Ed. Be happy. Don't make a problem. Maybe I do have a land station in Oman."

Crawley left his chief executive in charge and five minutes later entered Wat's inner office, waiting for the glass to close before he spoke. "Is this box soundproof?" Crawley looked to the office personnel outside.

Wat pressed a switch on his desk. "Is now. How come we had a bogey find us? What went wrong?"

"Nothing. That's why I'm worried. We have a bogey right here in this building. Someone with access to our most secret files."

"Had to be Perry."

"Maybe for equipment that could lock-on, but flight coordinates were only known after Perry's death. Everyone with access is cleared by us and the Defense Department, and I mean, A1 clearance. Yet right in the middle of that core, we find a second leak." Crawley clasped and unclasped his fingers before running them through his hair. "I made up crap. We have no mobile ground station in Oman. So we'd better materialise one fast. This bogey has stolen or made equipment to match our own. He's sophisticated, he has money."

Wat leaned forward, hands on desk and from the look on his face, Crawley knew his question.

"How about a design flaw?"

"No, and that answer is not through self-defence. It's scientific logic."

"Then let's look from a different viewpoint. We don't deal in radar, other than in procedures to avoid it; and we avoided it. If someone has hoisted radar technologies, then they did so from the Air Force, not us. As for knowing our flight plan …" He leaned back in his seat. "People can get lock-on but it would still do them no good. No enemy has air strike capability exceeding sixty thousand feet."

"The point I'm making is, someone locked on when we passed control, that's our Achilles heel, a raider would have ability to interpret software systems. To hit us at that precise moment is unlikely to be luck, coincidence or even an act of God. That raider knew exactly what he was doing."

"Possible." Wat reclined in his chair and shrugged dismissively, though Max knew that wouldn't be so. "Russia and China are looking over our shoulders all the time," Wat said. "Within this building there are people among us we don't know from where. The Defense Department, the State Department, the CIA, the FBI, and God knows who else. Jake looks after our physical side, bodies and buildings." Wat leant forward as if to confide. "Listen, Max, one more test and the Government can look after the whole damn lot. As for the flight plan, many people outside our jurisdiction would have that information. That's people scattered halfway round the world receiving transmissions. More important, we have ability to backtrack any lock-on and discover the precise source. If Raider had been armed, we could have stuffed a missile down someone's throat."

Max raised both hands. "You think I'm over-reacting and maybe I am but I never transmit details of Raider flight path until she's airborne."

"I'll investigate, Max. But in my view, somewhere, some place, a radar jockey is telling his boss of intercepting an alien spacecraft. Then to his amazement, it bogged off into the Universe. I'll speak with Jake, see what we can fix."

Max did not wait long. Jake Hammerton stood by the lift and stepped in with him as the door closed. His size alone was intimidating. Max felt both fear and resentment. This man could destroy him but also help him.

"What if it happens again, Max?" Jake spoke, not looking at him.

"It won't. It was the luck of some rogue, that's all."

"Bullshit and you know it. You're knee deep in it, Max but luckily I can get you out. The Marines have a specialist group in Oman, the CIA have the equipment on hand. Your mythical ground station will be operative within the hour."

Max felt no sense of relief, Hammerton's manner and presence was too oppressive. Neither did gratitude come easy. "Thank you, Jake. The whole team will appreciate your fast action over this."

"It's not the team that's in trouble, Max, it's you. The next time Raider flies, she'll be armed with fourteen missiles, ten of them cruise missiles with a two kilo ton capacity. I suspect the guy who locked on today was Bin Qasem."

"That's not possible."

The lift stopped but Hammerton held the door closed. "Perry made it possible. The next time Qasem locks on, you let him stay locked till we have a back reading on his ground position. Then you fire two, three missiles into his face."

"I can't do that." Max sensed a creeping tightness over his skin. "It might be Russia, China."

"So what? You do it or I'll get someone else who will."

"Preposterous!"

"If you don't Max, everything will come out. Raider will be grounded. Wat will lose billions and the media will crucify you. Particularly as you entrusted classified documents to Perry." Hammerton let the door slide open. "Off you go, Max, and have a nice day."

When Max left, Wat looked at the silver-framed portrait of

Juliet and her mother kept on his desk. By British time, he figured Juliet tucked up in her bed. He understood her frustrations. He suffered the same sense of claustrophobic tension caused by his own security. After the abduction and murder of his wife, Juliet's safety had become an obsession and in guilt he subjected himself to the same rules. Rules he found oppressive and tiresome. He hated working in his bullet-proof box or being unable to walk alone, buy a paper or take a beer with people who did not have security clearance. Every aspect of his life was governed by safety and he felt it wearing him down into an old man. But the foiled abduction in England gave clear demonstration of how essential security was. It also showed Max was right. Someone was selling information on Raider, and now, Juliet. This was the nightmare he had dreaded. Bin Qasem was out of the shadows.

Wat rubbed the grey stubble of curl over his chin, weary of the years it had taken to get GR4 to completion. The political and military arguments, the technical nightmares, the financial manipulation of funds needed within his empire, the responsibility for hundreds of sub-contractors and thousands of staff. He felt the weight of it all, felt it crush his spirit. He did not want Max's anxieties. He wanted rid of Global Raider, the threat of Qasem and the pressure of a thousand worries. Until then he needed vigilance, someone close was deceiving him. He touched the portrait on the desk, comparing Juliet's smile to that of her mother. His one consolation was Qasem now believed Juliet under close guard in hospital. Wherever she hid with Lisa, she was at least safe. Deep cover had worked. Once again Jake had been right. He hated to suffocate her life but out of this present hell would come a wonderful dream. Why shouldn't she marry the future President? Her mother would have wanted it.

Wat sat forward on his seat, lacing his fingers and tensing the knuckles, realising he had used his daughter for temporary distraction from what was at hand, the questioning of trust. It gave sorrow that he should doubt old friends and loyalties. He started a list of all personnel, official or not, who might have access to classified information on Raider's test flights or Operation Holly Johnson. He placed his own name at the top, followed by Crawley, Rawlings, Hammerton and Betty, his secretary. Beneath he made a separate list of Henry Taylor, Navro, Lisa and Colonel Freddy Fox. He then went back to the first list and added Crawley's senior assistants. It quickly became apparent the names could be endless. Better, he thought, to eliminate those around Juliet. Jake could fill in the rest. He phoned Walsh Corporation's senior accountant, Matt Corrello and told him to use the best and most discreet agency to check employees' bank accounts for abnormal payments, to discover undeclared accounts held by people on the list. Enemy in the compound, Jake had warned. Thank Christ Juliet was outside, safe in hiding.

CHAPTER 11

"You sure scare the shit out of people, Khalid."

"The incident at the hotel was staged to delude. Candy Girl and her escort now believe themselves safe and free from danger. They are relaxed in the bolt-hole, which was my intention. Better still her British bodyguards have no idea where she is. She will be taken within the first hour of GB4's inaugural flight. I congratulate you on your precise information."

"I give value for money and arranged it so your little intervention over the desert came out as friendly radar from a station in the Oman desert. On the surface, no one is taking it too seriously, but underneath there's a lot of doubt. You got less than seventy-two hours to be ready."

"My intervention in Candy Girl is meticulously planned, Octavius. Precision is my speciality."

"So let's just test your precision, Khalid, along with your ability to spread dollars. Our last little test went fine, one dollar apiece ended in twenty-five accounts. But that doesn't satisfy my Swiss bankers. So let's raise the stakes. Twenty-five million in Saudi riyals, same process but in my email you'll find one new account with multi-currency drop down facilities in Panama. I've earmarked it so you don't make a mistake. I want you to credit that particular account with four million riyals. Is that clear?"

"It will take time."

"You have one hour. At 0300 hours I want to see twenty-four million of Arab money flying over the network."

"You must be patient."

"Precision, Khalid, is my speciality also. Having Candy Girl is no good without Raider's next flight plan. Let's see you deal, my friend, because the next and final payment will be serious."

* * *

131

"What time did Rupert leave?" Navro asked.

The driver checked his clipboard. "Around 0200 hours. We figured it was a shift change."

Navro leaned back against the BMW and called Hardwick Grange. "You got movement yet?" he asked the operator on the tracking device.

"Not since they went to bed last night," came the reply. "They ain't even been to the bathroom and they should have been in college twenty minutes ago."

"OK," Navro said. "I'm heading for the door to ring the bell. If there's no response, we're going in."

In the heat of the early morning, Navro began to sweat. He kept his mobile connected to base and prayed he wasn't going to fuck up. He could imagine Sweetpea screaming her head off, imagine Jake kicking his arse out of a job if they were hurt. Whatever happened, in the next ten minutes he was set to lose.

He rang the ground floor first and listened to the bell for a good minute before speaking into his mobile. "OK, immediate action. Slater, take the front entrance, rest follow me round back." Leaving his mobile connected, Navro ran to the side gate and ripped away the bolt with a single kick. At the rear of the house he glanced briefly into the empty kitchen then smashed a window. By the time he reached the communal hall his men were in the drive. Navro raced upstairs and hammered on the door of the upper flat, kicking the wood in frustration until Slater came with a jemmy. Two minutes later, the doorstop split and they were both inside. Navro went straight to the bedrooms and collected a bracelet from each before throwing them to the floor.

"Pair of fucking bitches, what the hell's going on? Get Jake. This is code red, my God, we're going to eat shit."

Jaber had found the cottage six months previously during a walking holiday on Bodmin Moor. His wife had moaned constantly over the rain and to Jaber's relief, she spent the last four days refusing to leave their hotel. During this time he checked and double checked the two most suitable places he had found. Cleg Cottage was isolated in every direction by a least a mile. Bordered by a wood on three sides, it gave views over the Camel valley and was no more than eight miles drive from Port Isaac. The entrance track from the road had potholes deep enough to put off tourists and gates that declared private grounds.

Unsure of timing, Jaber had rented the place from mid-June to mid-July and stocked the cupboards with food and bedding for a month. The previous day he had sent his wife to visit her mother in Palestine, so removing any complaints over his absence from home. The four Chechnyans had arrived in a separate car with automatic weapons, ammunition and carpentry tools. Once Jaber had decided where to hold the prisoners, they immediately set about screwing down the windows and fixing anchor points to the walls. To each of these they fastened three metre length chains. Jaber would have preferred these restraints to reach the lavatory but this would have allowed prisoners into each other's rooms. Leaving the Chechnyans at work, he went in search of chamber pots.

It was an hour after dawn when Seb drove his Jaguar into the village of Tintagel. Morning mist from moor and hill still drifted ghost trails down to the houses, hushing his drive along deserted streets as he headed for the castle. A hundred metres inland, the crash of Atlantic breakers rolling their perpetual force against barren cliffs became a constant background sound. Before him, thirty acres of craggy headland heralded the once majestic seat of Dumnoia monarchs, a place where legend wove the tale of King Arthur and Merlin.

After hiding his car, Seb clipped field glasses to his belt and shoved a crumpled packet of motorway pizza into the pocket of his waxed jacket. During his climb to the castle entrance, seagulls pitched raucous cries and dived from the blue sky to wheel and screech defiance at his lone intrusion. As he expected, gates giving access to the narrow footbridge, which traversed the gorge between land and castle, were locked. Not wishing to damage property he clambered round the edge and moved along the outside railing, shuffling himself across a hundred-foot drop. On the opposite side he climbed the rock face until above the safety barrier, then leaped downwards to the path and started walking between walls erected in the 12th and 13th centuries. Gulls continued to circle, their cries and the sound of sea permanently on the wind. At the highest point he spread his coat in a small dip squared by ancient stones laid in the time of Celtic Britain. The position gave clear views of the castle entrance and the fork of a path circumnavigating the headland. The Atlantic swell rolled in its restless pounding of the cliffs, racing an undertow of currents around rocky headlands, passing small coves where lesser waves gave a pretence of tranquil water. In these small, hidden places, a bather might swim in safety or test his nerve amidst the open sea twenty metres beyond. From childhood memory, Seb knew only the strongest swimmers, the surfboarders and the foolish gave challenge to these coastal waters.

By 0630 hours the sun was already heading for another hot day. Cushioned by his coat, Seb leant back against a rock. The gulls had accepted his presence, satisfied to a degree by the distribution of inedible pizza. The gates did not open until 1030 hours and with time to spare, he set the alarm on his watch, praying to God he was not wasting time. He left a text message for Fagan and with little else to do but wait, fell asleep.

Juliet woke early and took comfort in the swaddling of her duvet. From the bed opposite, Lisa's faint, rhythmic breathing gave sound to her deep sleep. Juliet turned a little and looked to where sunlight spilled beneath the bedroom curtains. She saw the back of Lisa's head, a tuft of blonde hair and one white shoulder banded by the ribbon strap of her nightdress. In sleep she appeared as vulnerable as any woman and Juliet was tempted to move in behind, cuddle up and share feminine tenderness in thanks for the protective haven Lisa always placed around her.

Juliet had enjoyed their shopping trip, helping each other choose outfits, buying little presents. When they returned to the hotel with their backpacks full of clothes, something dramatic was clearly going on. Lisa had insisted they take no chances and without being seen they had sneaked off. Lisa's mobile became full of messages from Rupert but she refused to answer. As of now she decided their best bet was to go deep cover. Lisa had hired a car and they left immediately. Juliet had complained but Lisa insisted. London was looking dangerous. They were going to the bolt-hole, just the two of them. Once in the car Lisa had phoned Henry on her second mobile then suddenly relaxed. They were safe now, she said, safer than sitting on top of Walsh Towers. Juliet had sulked a bit but then swallowed her anger and frustration, happy they were at least clear of the circus. She felt mean over duping Rupert, mean of her secret call to Lucas arranging to meet up with him. She hated to deceive Lisa but this cottage sounded perfectly situated without anyone to disturb the peace. All she had to do was give Lucas the address. She wondered how she would persuade Lisa to leave them. Juliet was determined. Lisa herself had said once there, they were a hundred percent safe. Lucas planned to arrive in London that night. By tomorrow lunchtime they could be together, him in her arms, in her body. He only needed the address.

* * *

At first light Juliet slipped from bed and out of the room. She paused to collect the new iPhone Lisa had provided as they're old ones were traceable, then left the cottage to stand on the grass. Below her the garden lay bordered by fields, the far edge hedged by cliff top and sea. Gulls circled, their voices adding to the constant sound of surf. The breeze stirred her negligee and brushed her cheeks as she held the iPhone in the palm of her hand to carefully scroll the digits. She sensed exhilaration at this, the start of her great adventure. For once she had taken the initiative and was controlling instead of being controlled. She waited a full minute before Lucas answered.

"Hi, honey." She smiled for him while pushing back her hair with a free hand. "This place is beautiful, can't wait to get you down. We'll have four days, just the two of us, no one else."

"Juliet, I'm in Boston and it's two o'clock in the morning. I can't get over. A change of plan, business," he said. No face, no warmth, just a gruff voice over the instrument.

"But you promised. Yesterday you promised you'd catch the night flight."

"Politics is a hard life. Look, when you come back we'll fix a few dates. I have several house parties scheduled for Philadelphia. Lots of people, they'll be fun."

"I don't want lots of people. I want you. Don't you want me?"

"Sure I do and I promise I'll make it up. I'm off to Washington this morning. Phone me as soon as you're back. We'll have dinner."

Juliet listened to him switch off so she had only the sound of the gulls and the sea. "He lied," she whispered to herself. When she turned Lisa stood close, the breeze sculpturing her nightdress over the shape her body. To Juliet she appeared as an angel, beautiful, strong. "He lied to me. He said he was coming to love me but he lied."

Lisa walked across and put arms around Juliet's

shoulders, holding her, kissing her brow. "All men lie, babes."

"Even the future president?"

Lisa gently stroked her hair and shoulders. "All men lie to women. Did you tell him our location?"

"No. All he wants is to take me to parties and display me like a jewelled beetle." In the strength and warmth of their embrace, Juliet let her hand run gently down Lisa's body feeling its firmness and the narrow curve of her waist. She hated men. She leaned back and looked up. The kiss came so naturally and full of tenderness, their tongues touching gently, one against the other. It gave awareness of Lisa's soft strength and new sensations found against the mould of her body. Juliet's hand slid down to Lisa's buttocks and for a second she pulled them both together. "I'm sorry," she said, suddenly ashamed as she drew back.

"Don't be. It's very natural to feel for another woman what some men could never feel. It's very natural to be close. Come on, baby." She took her hand. "Just the two of us now. Let's get dressed, let's go enjoy ourselves, vacation time. We're out of the cage. Ain't no-one looking for us no more, no one to bother us, no electronic devices to find us. Jake and Henry know but they won't tell nobody till Global Raider is handed over."

CHAPTER 12

Seb shielded his eyes from the sun, then raised his field glasses. Concealed by the dip he focused first on Juliet then Lisa, studying each as they passed through the castle turnstile. Both wore shorts and skimpy T-shirts, Lisa carrying a pink rucksack on her shoulder. Seb waited until they were well clear of the entrance and other visitors before slowly descending the hillock and closing from behind.

Lisa turned first, Seb guessed because of her natural and instinctive sense of someone following. He expected a surprised reaction but in the first seconds her expression showed hostility, then annoyance.

"Can't you take a hint? This outing is girls only."

"Sometimes the girls need protection. Only doing my job." Seb looked between them. "If you wanted to be on your own, you could have told me the truth. I would have stayed out your way. I respect people's privacy but I also expect trust."

"Deep cover means just that. I'm afraid you were another decoy. I was ordered to skip the cage and come down here. The hotel fracas hurried it."

"Except no one told me. My orders are to stay in your shadow. So I'm here."

"Your orders are to do as I tell you. So, who gave the location?"

"I figured it myself. Henry said it was good for Juliet's research, also swimming. Juliet said she was writing about Tintagel. It didn't take much to connect."

"You tell anyone? Anyone follow you?"

"No." He looked to Juliet who was watching him with that big, wide smile of hers. He smiled back.

Lisa frowned and her eyes narrowed. "Listen carefully. No-one but Jake and Henry will guess where we are. One peep and Qasem will be on our track. And that means you say nothing, not to your boss, your team, no-one. If in the next days we are in anyway compromised I'll know who to blame. So go back to Cambridge. We got no room for you here."

"He could sleep on the couch," Juliet said.

"We don't need him."

Seb looked between them, then took out his mobile. He hadn't come all this way just to leave again. "I'll phone your boss at Walsh Securities. If they say go, I go."

"No! Don't you understand, the whole reason we skipped is because we have a leak back home. You phone, everyone will know exactly where we are."

"Then I stay."

"There is a box room," Juliet added.

"Shit." Lisa put fists on hips.

"Come on," Juliet nudged against her. "Lighten up for baby. Maybe he can cook pizza."

"I'm even better at lamb curry." Seb tried his nice guy smile, a quarter of a million dollar bonus hung on it. "Or I could take you both to dinner."

"This guy's not for real." Lisa shook her head.

Juliet was definitely on his side. She leaned to her friend and put an arm around her shoulder. "It's vacation time, your words. And if Sebastian is here, he can take duty, you can relax. You said yourself the threat is gone."

Lisa sighed before putting a reciprocal arm to Juliet's waist. "OK, in the box room. But one foot wrong and you'll be in the hedge. You stay only so I can keep an eye on you, is that understood, Sebastian?"

"Settled then. So let's give research a miss." Juliet waved her arm to the castle and winked at him. "Now you two guys are buddies, we'll celebrate instead. I saw a neat little pub on the way here which overlooks the sea. Let's try some English beer. Maybe have a swim. Come on you guys, smile for Juliet."

The Merlin Arms stood on a cliff top above a sandy inlet. While the girls chose a table outside, Seb bought a pint and two halves of bitter and carried them to the garden.

"It's a good spot," he said, sitting opposite the pair, the air noisy with gulls soaring overhead, the heat laced with a salted sea breeze.

"So why are there so few people?" Juliet asked.

"Give it another four weeks when the schools break for holidays, Cornwall will be packed."

"Then we picked the right time. I just love this place. Beer's good," she said, taking a long swallow. "Do they have a restaurant here?"

"Small one maybe." He looked at Lisa who seemed more relaxed now his presence was accepted.

"I'll book a table for tonight," Juliet said. "Is that OK with you guys?"

"Fine," Lisa said and closed her eyes, her face raised to the sun. Juliet stood and walked back to the bar through the garden.

"She OK on her own?" Seb asked.

"She's a big girl. Don't crowd her."

Seb sipped on his beer, wondering how he could win friendship and trust. "Sorry if I spoilt things by coming here. You should have made contact."

"Sorry you were set up but Henry knows we're safe, even if he thought we were in Cambridge. Informing you was not priority. Also I know Juliet and sometimes I can best handle her on my own. These last months she's been edgy over Lucas. Papa wants them married but Juliet's not ready, least not till she's certain of herself." Lisa lapsed back into soporific stillness.

Seb felt grateful for the information, it was a start. "You know the hotel raids were by Bin Qasem, that one decoy was taken, a guard hit."

"Henry told me, it's why we're in hiding. But don't tell Juliet. She'll get real upset if she knows people were hurt, maybe killed. Promise me?" She opened one eye.

Seb nodded. The protected easily took on guilt if someone was hurt on their behalf. "OK," he said, realising Lisa guarded mentally as much as physically.

She kept her eyes closed until Juliet returned. "You OK, babes?" Lisa asked.

"Nine p.m. It's late but the only time they could give a table for three."

"You'll be hungry."

"I'll make us ice-cream and strawberries when we get back. It's holiday time, let's piggy ourselves." She drank more beer. "I didn't see this beach when we passed. It was all surf and water, I'd like to take a swim."

"Tide's fast and high," Seb told her. "When the tide's in, the beach disappears, but when it goes out you have lots of little inlets and sandy coves under the cliffs. It's the charm of the place but watch you don't get cut off. You a good swimmer, Juliet?"

"Like a fish."

"Be careful. The currents are strong."

"I swim in the same sea on the other side. Go surfing too. Come on, Lisa time to get your bathing suit wet." She took hold of Lisa's hand and encouraged her up.

"Juliet baby, you're too full of energy for such a hot day."

Seb watched her weak protest as she was encouraged up and led down the path onto the beach. He finished his beer than followed at a distance, skirting a scattering of large boulders which had slipped from the cliff face. In an innocent gesture of affection, or an indication of their illicit relationship, both women removed their sandals and held hands. The small, naked footprints side by side in the wet sand seemed to bear testimony to their bond. Was this why Lisa wanted Juliet alone? For the first time Seb sensed sexual implications which he had previously dismissed, at the same time wondering if his suspicions were possibly the result of exclusion. As if to tease him further, Lisa glanced briefly over her shoulder and placed an arm around Juliet's waist, receiving the girl's own arm in a reciprocal squeeze of affection. As they started around the headland and into the next cove, Lisa's hand slipped down and patted Juliet's buttocks. The movement was a simple gesture easily misconstrued with fanciful interpretation but left alone to follow their footprints, Seb had to admit a twinge of jealousy. They were the couple, he the intruder.

They remained out of sight over two minutes until he rounded rocks and found their clothes in a discarded pile. Both women in miniscule bikinis were jogging towards the sea. Seb dutifully pushed their shorts and tops into the pink rucksack then took pleasure in voyeurism. He decided Juliet more slender and her figure more streamlined. But best was macho revenge in salacious consideration of Lisa's less compact posterior. It did not help to realise how immature and adolescent his thinking but it satisfied male honour.

Juliet shrieked childish delight and dived headlong into the surf. Beneath the blazing sun and feeling like the hired help, Seb shouldered the bag and sauntered to the rear of their secluded cove. To obtain a better view, he climbed the sloping side of a high, flat rock beneath the cliff and sat facing the sea. Gulls, disturbed by his arrival flew out across the sand then glided back to their perches, waiting as he did for the turn of the tide. From this vantage point he watched for the safety of both girls as they belly-surfed the waves, squealing in excitement.

What the hell, he thought, consoling himself. He had no right to even think himself part of their scene. His job was protection. The fact they both attracted him and were possibly lesbians was irrelevant to his professional duty. In a few days they would be gone and he could go back to soldiering instead of running round like some skivvy. He leaned against the cliff, hands behind head and gave full attention back to the girls thinking maybe he could be in for a seaside holiday Together they swam back to the shallows then lay in the surf before splashing like kids as they raced up and down the cove, chasing each other in and out of the waves, shouting and screeching without care. Seb kept himself in the shade and watched for over an hour before deciding he had landed the best job in the world. They sure were a gorgeous sight, all limbs and shapely bodies sheened by water, both jiggling beautifully in the right places. It certainly beat humping battle kit through the Yemen desert. Every so often they would embrace and put their heads together, sometimes one of them looking back to him as if he was the subject of conversation. Seb did not know what to read. He saw two girls having fun, the occasional cuddle. He wouldn't mind either of them cuddling him.

Juliet took Lisa's hand and both raced back into the water. Around them Atlantic breakers started to roll white surf a full twenty metres from the shore. For moments they were held high on a crest, then plummeted from view into the trough behind. When the first of these breakers reached the beach, its foam made higher inroads over the flat sand and Seb knew the tide had turned. To his relief both girls started belly surfing shoreward, Juliet first, Lisa behind. Once clear of the drag pulling around her legs, Juliet began running over the hot sand, her skin glistening wet and golden in the sun. Seb sighed and stood, waiting to help her climb the rock. When he looked down into a precariously perched bikini top, her smile and the manner in which she held his hand for unnecessary balance provided an open invitation to admire. Again his thoughts became clouded with temptation. Instinct prompted him to make some small gesture of approach but caution over the possible consequences of misjudgement held him back as she hitched up the minuscule top.

"Must be chilly," he said, with polite concern, unconsciously looking at Lisa's pert nipples when she finally climbed up beside them.

Her smile held sufficient patronisation for him to realise he had been misunderstood. "It has that effect." She brushed fingers through wet hair in a provocative stance. "But it's not that cold, you should try it, see if you shrivel to pea size."

"No squabbling you guys. Seems you need a cool drink," Juliet said bending for her shorts. Seb glanced over the thin bikini bottoms spread taut and discovered the close proximity of two virtually naked women was having a physical and embarrassing effect.

"There's a beach shop by the car park, I'll buy." He leapt downward before Juliet could offer him money. "Watch out for the tide, it's on the turn and it comes in fast." He began to jog across the sand. He looked back once before rounding the headland. The girls lay side-by-side, their knees bent and, he guessed, holding hands. He stopped jogging and began to walk. He felt less concerned about leaving them alone. Qasem had fucked up and that made life easier but he knew from past experience never to get sloppy over vigilance.

The small cabin sold seaside paraphernalia, ice cream and soft drinks. The whole place bristled with stock ready for the school holidays and a million tourists. Seb bought three cans of lemonade and opened one immediately. A few older people were around, none adventurous enough to leave the proximity of the car park. The place was almost deserted, a paradise in expectation of the holiday hordes. He returned slowly and met the two women as they rounded the headland. Both had pulled on shorts and tops but remained bare-footed as they paddled through the incoming water.

"Another thirty minutes and there'll be six foot waves over our heads," he said, passing the drinks and walking alongside. "What now?"

"Now we go back to Port Isaac for strawberries and ice cream," Juliet said.

Seb nodded and smiled for them both. Even Lisa smiled back. They strolled without hurry. No one around but OAPs and a young couple who were necking on the top of some boulders, their faces turned to each other, the guy's hand under the girl's tee shirt.

Seb followed in the Jag to Port Isaac and carried his bag into the rented cottage. Juliet insisted she shop immediately so Seb accompanied her leaving Lisa to take a shower.

"You like ice cream?" Juliet asked when they walked down the hill. "Lisa just loves it, 'cept she's putting on weight. But as this is now holiday, I'm going to make her a huge bowl with strawberries then she can enjoy without feeling guilty." She grinned at him.

"You're very close, you and Lisa," he said.

"After eight years you get to be special friends. But she sure is bossy at times."

Juliet went first to the supermarket then the chemist. "We're running short," she said, emerging with two bags, one containing lavatory rolls.

When they returned Lisa was in her dressing gown. She helped place the strawberries and cream into the fridge then sent Juliet for her shower. Seb had a gut feeling she was preparing herself to give a lecture on professional ethics so he escaped to the box room and a mattress allocated as his sleeping space.

"Jody, this is Navro. God, do I need help."

"Tell momma, Navro and momma will do her best."

"Lisa and Juliet have removed their bracelets and bunked. The Brit's gone too, so it's probably collusion but we can't be sure. Jake's rolling thunder. But with the final test on Raider coming up he can't get over. He's put it on my plate. Jesus, Jody what am I gonna do?"

"Calm down, just listen to momma. If they deliberately skipped, most likely it's to the bolt-hole. All we need is to find where. You phoned Henry?"

"He says they might be en route. And he's not

divulging location in case. But there's more to it. I went to Rupert's office at the Combined Agency Task Force. It's shabby, like they got no money. I pretended I was US Embassy on protection business. A guy called Colonel Freddy Fox asked if I knew where Rupert was. I said "You're supposed to tell me." He said his man was under orders from a Walsh Security agent so what was happening. It's like no-one knows who is where and what's going on. I'm at the hotel. Found out the girls hired a car yesterday. But they sure didn't go to Cambridge. They're out there somewhere and so is Qasem. We got to find Candy Girl, and quick."

"Give me Fox's number. These guys can help and we got to use them." She reached for a pen in her handbag then began to scribble while Navro read the number. "You have a team here?"

"Fully armed and ready."

"For God's sake, Navro. The Brits don't like guns. You're our senior CIA agent in Walsh Securities. If you get into a fire fight because of Hammerhead Jake, you better have a good story for the judge. My advice is dump the hardware."

"Jody, you're asking me to walk naked."

"Later, Navro. Just for now, don't carry weapons."

She hung up and dialled the number given by Navro. "Colonel Fox, please." She waited a moment. "Colonel," she said to the man who answered. "My name is Jody Farlow, CIA. We have a mutual interest in a guy called Sebastian Havic. Can we meet somewhere discreet?"

From Colonel Fox's description Jody found the men half way along the crowded bar. Both were large and menacing, Fagan in a suit, Fox in a wax jacket and cords. He had a brooding sinister air which she considered a possible front for a sharper man beneath. Conversely, Fagan appeared as if he consumed every word and action.

For her own role she decided to play female rather than Secret Service. Unbuttoning her jacket she ran a thumb around the waistband of her skirt so tightening her blouse. Even the most serious men could be coerced.

"The Maiden's Head. You sure this place is respectable, Inspector?" Jody looked around the panelled walls and glass partitions of the pub, conscious both men were eyes on.

"Maiden refers to Queen Elizabeth I. It is respectable," Fox said. "May I introduce Sean Fagan, Operation Co-ordinator."

"Please call me Jody." She smiled for them and showed her ID card. Fagan examined it in detail, produced his mobile and keyed in her service number before texting it somewhere.

"Right," he said, giving back the card. "May we buy you a drink, Jody?"

"So kind, I'll take mineral water with ice."

"A seat." Fox ushered her to a corner booth. She sat opposite and smiled for him again.

"So Jody, what can the Combined Agency Task Force do for the CIA?"

"I need to find Sebastian Havic."

"And why would the CIA be interested in our Lieutenant?"

"Because of Walsh Securities, Candy Girl. I'm fully briefed." She waited till Fagan placed their drinks on the table then watched him sit beside his boss.

"You must understand our work is classified. We are not at liberty to discuss any part of it, CIA or not." His following smile came tight, more patient than friendly.

"Havic's on contract via your outfit as a bodyguard for Holly Johnson. Holly Johnson is currently missing. One of three Hollys. One captured, one in hospital. The third, hopefully under the protection of Havic. We were never given information as to any of these girls. So let's say Holly three is very precious. Walsh Avionics have important contracts for the US Government so we kind of keep an eye on things." She glanced between them. Nothing showed but bland, enigmatic faces.

"You think this Holly is in danger, possibly from Havic?" Fagan asked.

"On the contrary. If he's there, Holly is with two very able people but she's not where she's meant to be. That's worrying." She leaned forward as if to whisper. "I can tell you a whole lot, gentlemen. But you guys will need to level with me, first, help me find Lieutenant Havic. A deal?"

"I'm sure we can come to some amicable arrangement," Fox said with a dead face expression.

"Ever hear of a guy called Khalid Bin Qasem?"

She watched both men nod. "Eight years ago, the founder of Walsh Industries lost his wife to terrorists. She was abducted and held to ransom for military secrets. Wat Walsh followed the Government line and refused to concede. She was murdered, beheaded. The person leading that particular terror group was Qasem. He's capable, organised and bad news on anybody's patch."

"He attacked the hotels, caught two decoys but the third escaped, common knowledge."

"But did Havic go with them?" She glanced between them the same time Fagan pulled out his phone and examined the screen.

"OK, you're verified," he said and put away the phone before placing his large hands together while staring into her eyes as he leaned forward. "Seb Havic was ordered by a female Walsh Security operative to take a tracking device to Cambridge. What he did not know was their tracing bracelets were also inside. Meanwhile both women vanished. I have confirmation Havic has gone searching for them but I don't currently know his location."

"They are probably in a bolt-hole but I don't know where that is. Walsh Securities have a leak so they're saying nothing. Too scared in case it comes out. The situation is Qasem will also be hunting. If he finds them we could be in for a high body count. We got to get active."

"We?" Fox raised an eyebrow.

"Eight years ago, my old boss went hunting for Qasem. When he retired, I took over. Between assignments I've been on the case ever since. Qasem goes deep cover, re-emerging every five or six years. He's out now, probably with financial backing from al-Qaeda. Got a team in London, hence the attempted abduction at the hotel. He's also got someone high ranking in Walsh Industries. Uncle Sam's got billions of dollars flying in the sky and Holly Johnson is in danger of becoming a key player." Jody sat straight shouldered, hands on hips. "Now, if you want to prevent a blood bath, you need me, gentlemen. And I need you, so do we get something going between us?"

"Specially for you, Lisa." Juliet carried a tray with three bowls of strawberries and ice cream into the garden. "You got one too, Seb," she called back to the living room.

Seb looked up from where he had taken refuge behind a newspaper and momentarily caught sight of her silhouetted beneath a cotton dressing gown as she paused in the doorway, smiling over her shoulder.

"God give me strength," he muttered and went out to join them in the garden. Lisa sat filing her nails.

"I can't eat all that," she protested. "I have my figure to consider."

"So have I." Juliet pushed the bowl in front of her. "You love ice cream, it's holiday and you won't get anything till dinner. Eat for Juliet or I'll cry."

Seb took a seat opposite. "You Americans don't mess. You could feed the Regiment on this." He scooped a spoonful. "Delicious."

"If we want something, we go for it. All's fair in love and war, ain't that so, Lisa?"

"I've heard that before." She smiled for him before sampling a taste, her tongue sliding over lips. "It's beautiful. What's the background flavour?"

"Sugar, vanilla and brandy."

"You spoil us, baby." Lisa began to eat.

When Seb had showered and changed his shirt, he went back to the garden. Lisa sat looking pale-faced and unhappy.

"You okay?" he asked.

"No, dammit." She leaped from her seat and ran for the bathroom. Seb stood hands in pockets, staring at the sky and the gulls which cried and circled in the hot evening sky. When she returned, Juliet was consoling her. Both women were ready for their outing, Lisa in a trouser suit, Juliet in a miniscule cotton slip some designer had sold as a dress.

"Bad gut," Juliet informed giving Lisa a hug. "Maybe it's the water."

"I can't think what. I'll be OK. God, I've never been sick on the job."

"You want we don't go?"

"No, I'll be fine." Lisa picked up her bag. "Dammit!" She ran back to the bathroom.

"She's going no place tonight," Juliet shook her head.

"Maybe we should stay home and cook," Seb suggested.

"I prefer to go out." She looked to him, her lips puckered. "Promise I'll be good."

Seb looked back and imagined her on the beach, imagined her naked, imagined Wat Walsh tearing up a quarter million dollar cheque. They sat for ten minutes until Lisa re-emerged, her face ashen.

"I'll stay if you really want me to," Juliet said placing a hand over Lisa's. "I was just kind of looking forward to …" She shrugged shoulders, as if not willing to voice her wish.

Lisa was looking at her, eyes narrow, lips aligned in a grimace. "The danger's passed, that's for sure but I don't know." She glanced at Seb. "SAS are meant to be hot."

"The best."

"OK, Sebastian, you're on duty. Phone in every hour, be home by midnight or immediately that place closes."

"Lisa, I'm twenty-two, a grown woman," Juliet protested.

Seb glanced to Lisa and read exactly what she was thinking. "I'll look after her, don't worry."

Juliet kissed her cheek. "Just tuck up in bed and rest."

CHAPTER 13

Due to the hot, still night, tables at the restaurant had been set outside. Seb sat admiring Juliet, the blackness of ocean behind her and the waves occasionally highlighted by the mingling of moonlight over surf. He made small talk, uncertain how far he should go. He felt enraptured by the sheen of her hair, the reflection of candlelight in her eyes and a sense of being with the loveliest girl on earth. It did not help that alone and face to face she had grown shy, almost nervous of his company. It became clear how much she relied on Lisa. His inclination was to touch her, to reassure her. Instead he kept his fingers firmly interlocked and away from fire.

She declined a dessert, professing overindulgence, asking instead for coffee. Seb contented himself with finishing the wine.

"I love your Jaguar car," she said, after a pause. "I'll get Papa to buy me one when I'm home."

"Mine's a classic, Series 3, XJ6. It's thirty years old. But it still does 0 to 60 in ten seconds. I've spent a fortune rebuilding it." He lifted his hands with enthusiasm for what he explained then lay them on the table in front of his place setting.

"I bet the girls love it. I mean, you must have lots of girls to ride with you."

"One or two, on rallies."

She also rested her hands on the table, her fingers splayed towards him. "I'd love to go rallying."

"I could arrange it, if you came over again."

"Are the rallies two or three days?"

"Sometimes."

"Do you get to sleep over?"

"Sometimes."

"I think I'd like that." She touched his fingers with the tips of her own. The flame was instant and he looked to immediate evasive action.

"Juliet, I promised your dad I'd treat you as a sister."

She drew back in her seat. "Papa! He's always sitting on my shoulder. You his man too?"

Against better judgement he lifted her hand. "No, I'm an officer of the Queen. It might sound old fashioned but I'm meant to have honour."

She leaned back towards him. "A lady has honour too. And in this age, she also has the right of freedom, the right of self-determination. If you have honour, respect mine, respect my independence."

"If it helps, I find you very attractive."

"It does. You know, it's two years since a guy took me to dinner alone, said sweet things and held my hand. I go with the girls, I go with groups, I go with Lucas, President intent but I never get to go with a good looking guy who's got a cute ass and a nice smile."

"If that's me, thank you."

"It's you. But I need sweet-talking too. Sometimes a girl needs a boost to her confidence. The only compliments I ever get are from a bunch of ex-Vets ogling my butt. You know what they say about Lisa and me?"

"We live in a modern world."

"So diplomatic but in answer to the unspoken question, we're like any two women locked in a harem. She's someone who gives comfort and I sometimes treat her shamefully but I also love her dearly. We're close, close as any two women in such a relationship. To Lisa, I'm baby and yes she loves me in a way she won't admit. Satisfied?"

"Her affection for you is unquestionable." He returned her hand to the table and felt the pressure of her fingers, wondering if she also had love she would not admit.

"That's why I feel so mean." She lowered her eyes.

"Why?"

"Because I mixed a whole six pack of laxative powder with her strawberries and cream."

"You did what?" He sat back, unable to stop his snigger. "Jesus, poor woman. No wonder she had the

153

runs."

"I wanted you on my own. I wanted to be out on my own."

"You're a real Tinkerbell. That's naughty."

"You going to spank me?" The big smile came back.

"I think that's Lisa's prerogative."

He saw disappointment. "Come on." She rose from the table. "I want to go for a walk."

"Phone Lisa first." He handed her his mobile. "Tell her you're safe."

"If you insist." She pushed back the chair and walked to the edge of darkness, tapping on the mobile before holding it to her ear. Seb paid the bill then joined her on the path.

"She's OK." Juliet handed back the phone. "She's watching TV. Said don't be late."

"You want to walk to the car?" He asked.

"No, I want a walk on the beach."

"But the tide's nearly in," he said, following her down the path and into the still, velvet night.

"Don't matter, there's enough room for what I need." In the darkness made navigable by moon and stars, Juliet stepped onto the sand and removed her shoes, throwing each in turn behind her. "Catch."

Seb took them in mid air and followed to where surf crashed moon glow over the silver sand. Close to the water's edge she slipped off her dress, then her knickers, the only underwear she wore.

"Catch." She tossed both towards him then stood with feet in the wet, rippling sand. Seb looked at her back, at her tiny waist and the round curve of her hips. In turmoil he bundled her clothes between fists as desire and disaster became interlocked. She turned to face him.

"Am I still attractive?"

"More so."

She kept her distance, hands by her side as she spoke. "I'll be honest. I'm on a quest to discover. It was meant to be Lucas who'd help me. Help me find who and what I am, help me understand my sexuality. I've let guys make love to me but I never made love to them. I want to do that. I want to know if I'm spiritually able to be in union with a man as I know I can be with a woman. You understand what I'm asking, Seb? I'm asking for your help."

Seb gazed at her moon shrouded body, mind, desire, duty and promise all pulling in different directions. If he took her there, between sea and sand, would it be the two of them doing what both wanted? Or would she grow scared and turn on him with horrendous consequences. Seconds passed.

When he did not respond immediately she knew she had lost, that she was not woman enough, that he was Papa's man and scared of her, scared like all the others. She turned into the surf. "I'm going for a swim," she said. "Alone."

"Hold on, Juliet. There're big waves out there and currents. Stay well inside the cove."

"I swam here once so I'll do it again. Watch out for me and keep my clothes dry." She ran into the waves. It was colder than expected and rougher too but she didn't care. He had made her feel like the jewelled beetle everyone admired but nobody dared touch. She was an object for Lucas to display at parties, for Papa to barter with, for men to stare at. She had been rejected as a person so better to be alone and free, no bodyguard, no bracelet, no lover, naked and at one with the elements. She swam with strong, defiant strokes, gliding herself from wave to wave, conscious of the sea's caress upon her nudity, its cold and restless force stimulating the depth of her frustration. When she could stand it no longer, she flipped on her back to look up at a thousand stars shimmering in the black sky. In this surreal and isolated world she placed a hand between her legs, pressing her fingers for the exhilaration of her own body, giving herself to the force of nature, whispering her pleasure to heaven. For the first time in her life she felt free of oppression, of men, money and convention.

For glorious minutes she floated, cradled by the rhythmic passing of sea beneath her, then sensed herself unexpectedly lifted higher and higher. In the next instant she was tossed helpless over the back of a massive wave and tipped headlong into a swirling mass of churning forces. For long, desperate seconds, she thrashed back to the surface until finally able to gasp for breath. Gripped by panic and terror she stared into a dark, towering wall of water until it lifted her to its pinnacle. There she searched fruitlessly for the shadow of headland and cliff until she was once more dipped down into the following trough. On the next rising roll of black Atlantic she saw nothing but ocean.

Seb watched her stand in the surf, the slender form of her back and waist, the shape of her limbs, all became irresistible. He took a step towards her, then she was gone, the water rising to thighs then hips before taking her completely. Unease immediately crept over him. Running to the scattering of cliff boulders, he climbed for a better view of the bay. Her clothes at his feet, he searched the dark ocean, regretting his hesitation in not taking her. Better to love and risk the consequences than chance her being carried out to sea. When the full moon came from behind clouds he saw her as a tiny shadow on the surface. She swam with confidence, untroubled and in control, then turned on her back, her skin glistened by moonlight. At any moment Seb expected her to turn but she continued to drift, moving further and further towards the headland, seemingly content to rest on the waves. Seb began to remove his clothes, dropping them on hers, never taking his eyes from the shadow of her body. Naked, he held his luminous wristwatch at chest level and took a compass bearing on her position. When she suddenly vanished from view, anxiety turned to fear. He leapt to the beach and sprinted for the surf.

He swam with all the strength he possessed, sometimes under, sometimes over waves, always keeping the cliff face twenty metres to his left. On a peak of water he looked back to the dark shadow of rock on which he had stood, lining himself up to take a rough back bearing. Near the headland he started to shout her name, conscious of an undertow pulling at his feet. Waves higher than any within the sheltered cove began to lift and buffet him. He knew then he was beyond land and in open sea. Caught in the current sweeping down coast, he stopped swimming and began to shout. On the fourth call her voice answered, small, frightened and far away, driving him to a hard, frantic crawl in what he hoped was the right direction. Periodically he shouted and sometimes heard her reply, never seeming any closer. He prayed clouds would not drift and obscure the moon, knowing that without light she was lost. After five long minutes her head rose on a parallel wave and for seconds they looked to each other, their voices intermingled. Then she was gone again. Swimming under the wave's crest and down into the valley of water, Seb kicked out until he emerged almost beside her, snatching her outstretched hand in his. Her panic was near hysteria as her arms went around his neck. He clutched her waist, drawing her to cling onto his body.

"God, I'm scared, Seb ... I'm sorry ... I'm so scared," she shouted, her words broken by splashing foam.

"You're OK. We're safe now." He kicked to keep them buoyant. "Hold my shoulder and stay floating," he said, waiting for the next lifting swell before snatching an approximate check on his compass. "There's an undertow and it's dragging us off shore. Flip on your back, get your legs out of the current. When we go up with a wave, kick out to stay with the crest for a long as possible. We're being carried round the headland but if we get further in, there'll be breakers to body surf into the next cove. We can do this, Juliet. Be calm and together we have the strength." To his surprise she kissed him.

"Forgive me, Seb. Please, please forgive me."

"Let's swim." He returned her kiss then spun her round clutching under her arms so her back lay on his chest. Kicking with his legs he edged them over the next crest feeling Juliet thrust with her own legs. Amidst the turmoil of noise and sea, Seb gradually guided and pulled her shoreward, periodically checking progress and direction. After twenty minutes a surging wave tumbled them below the surface, tearing them apart amidst powerful swelling forces. When he resurfaced she was ten feet away, thrashing water in drowning panic until he again clutched and lifted her against him. Behind him and to his left he saw the dark shadow of headland. "We're there," he shouted. "Link my arm and belly surf. A few more waves and we can walk." They surfed for fifteen waves before his feet touched bottom. Even then they were drawn back by the fierce under-pull. Scrabbling and kicking against the water, he held around her waist, her arm over his shoulder as he stumbled towards the cliff base and the high flat rock he had sat on that morning.

"Climb," he told her, putting her hand into a crevice and pushing beneath until she started up the sloping surface. Battered by waves, he guided her feet then followed behind, pushing and encouraging until clear of the ragged foam. When at last she rolled over the high ledge above he hoisted himself until finally collapsing beside her.

For minutes he lay motionless, listening to the pounding surf strike below them, flecking them with spray while his heart hammered blood through muscle. When strength returned he sat and touched her shoulder, only to have her burst into tears. "It's OK," he said. "We're safe."

She came to her knees, clasping him with the desperation of a terrified child. "I'm so cold," she said. "So cold, so stupid. Forgive me."

"There's nothing to forgive."

"You saved my life and nearly drowned. God forgive me for what I put you through."

Seb put his head against hers and cradled the shivers that ran over her body. "The sea is cold but the night will soon warm you," he whispered. "It was my fault you went in, because I'm an idiot. You looked so beautiful in the moonlight and I wanted so much to love you. It is you who must forgive me, please."

Her face turned upwards and her shivers became a tremble as she kissed him. "Then love me, Sebastian. You are the only man who will ever have the right," she said. "Love me, make me a woman, for I am yours."

CHAPTER 14

Wat Walsh sat in his glass cage and re-read details of the financial investigation he'd ordered. It included bank accounts of all prominent and close employees. Only one was brought to his attention, a Panamanian account in the name of Lisa Longford. Declared at the start of her contract then probably forgotten, it had lain dormant for eight years. Two days previously an unknown offshore account had electronically credited it with one dollar. Yesterday the account had been credited again. Even with the air conditioning Wat began to sweat in cold and clammy dread. On a scrambled phone he called Whiteman Air Force Base, Missouri. "Jake, we have a serious problem. Get Navro in Cambridge to look after Juliet, bring Lisa back here. We need to have a talk with her." He listened to long silence before Jake replied.

"She's not in Cambridge, Wat. After the hotel incident they took off. Maybe to the bolt-hole, no one knows. I didn't tell you because of the pressure with Raider and the probability of their imminent return. I expect the all clear any moment."

Wat rested his head on one hand, his eyes closed, his mind jagged. "This goes to priority, Jake. From sources unknown, someone just paid Lisa four million Saudi riyals, that's over a million dollars."

"Still cold?" Seb asked. At his insistence Juliet lay partially on his body with his arms wrapped round her, a position he hoped where she would gain some small comfort from both rock and chilled air.

"Not too bad." She snuggled in closer, her face pressed to his neck.

"Dawn's coming, tide should be out enough for us to wade round the headland."

"I'd rather wait till we can walk. I don't want sea

anymore." She lifted slightly and kissed him. "You know, three days ago when you walked into the Vets' party I never guessed I'd make love with you."

"Three days ago I never guessed I'd even be alone with you."

"Was it good, our love making?"

"Magic."

She shifted to lie completely on top. "Sebastian, let's do it again. For us, for the joy of living. Such moments as these will never be forgotten. Such men like you may never pass again."

He felt her hand go down between his legs but there was no need, her mere suggestion carried him. He rolled and she lay backwards, parting herself in offering as he entered her. Amidst the constant sound of surf and the morning cry of gulls, he listened to her soft voice of pleasure, ignoring the rock digging at his elbows and knees. He kissed her deeply, entwining their tongues before drawing to the fullness of her lips. He thought her wonderful, the most fantastic woman he had ever loved. With the passing of heavenly time, somewhere inside she shuddered her total capitulation, her cry joining that of the gulls as he allowed himself to follow, sensing that away from their sensual euphoria, a deeper union had germinated.

When they ceased, when the chill of new day caused them both to shiver, they drew apart. "We need our clothes," he said. "Tide's out, people will be coming."

She stood and rubbed the flesh of her buttocks. "I wish we could stay all day." She touched his chest. "Believe me, I wish we could." She turned and began to climb down the sloping rock.

They walked hand in hand where hours before they had swam, each leaving sharp prints in the soft, wet sand. To his relief the first cove remained deserted, the shop and pub closed, the car park empty save for his Jaguar. Their clothes lay intermingled where left and they dressed in silence, Juliet with speed, turning her back as if suddenly inhibited and shy. Having more items, Seb took longer, then watched her start for the car before his laces were tied. "You OK?" he asked, hurrying behind.

Her expression had become resigned. "There'll be a row," she answered. "Real time's back again."

"Lisa. Oh yes, I'd forgotten Lisa." He opened the car allowing her to slid in before going to his own side. "So tell her the truth, what harm?" He looked to her tight smile.

"That we made love! You any idea what my father would say if he knew I did it with an unapproved white boy? Oh Seb," she touched his shoulder. "I thought I was the innocent."

"She would tell him?"

"She wouldn't do anything to hurt me but she'll sure as hell be jealous. If she did let slip, my father would see our love as an act of betrayal. No one crosses Papa, not even me."

"I don't understand. I thought we all lived in a brave new world."

"You do. I live in a medieval empire. Let me spell it out as Papa would see it. I'm princess of the empire. I'm going to marry a president and make our family the most powerful black family in the world. You fucked me."

"Is that cold reality?"

"Yes. It's why my life is so miserable and confused. It's why I grab moments of freedom." She leant and kissed his cheek then put her hand to his arm. "Sorry if I sound harsh. Our lovemaking was beautiful. You saved my life and when I gave myself to you, I meant it. You are the first man with whom I feel at one. For that you will always be in my heart. I wish we could continue, build on what we found but I'm not free and you are not safe unless Lisa keeps our secret. I will do anything to ensure she does."

Seb shook his head. "You said she loved you."

She smiled and touched his cheek. "Men are so naïve. Yes, she does love me and when we get home she'll go ape shit. She'll throw you out. Please go. I don't want you to be there. Let me take care of her alone."

Lisa stood waiting at the cottage window and had the door opened before they were on the path. "What happened? I've been going crazy, been down to that car park four times. I was about to call Jake. Are you all right, baby?" She guided Juliet down the hallway to the lounge.

Seb closed the door and followed. "She's fine," he said with his best, reassuring smile.

"Fine." Lisa turned her lips in a snarl so fierce he believed she might bite him. "She's been out all night. She looks like a drowned rat, she's got no shoes. There's sand in her hair, there's sand on her dress." She lifted the skirt, yanking it to Juliet's waist, indifferent to her protest. "There's sand in her goddam knickers and you tell me she's fine. What have you been doing to her, Mr SAS bodyguard?"

"We got stranded by the tide, unable to return till now."

"Don't give me shit! You had me worried sick. You know what I've been through tearing my hair while you've been out there humping her on some beach all night?"

"Not true." Juliet pulled away. "It wasn't his fault, I went swimming, it was my doing."

"Swimming! Who thought that one up?" She looked between the two of them. "I can see it in your faces exactly what you've been doing. Get the fuck out of this house, Mr." She pointed to the door. "Get up to Cambridge and make sure it's safe because we're gonna be right behind you. This party's over. As for you, you damn little whore …" She pushed Juliet towards the bedroom. "Get in there, get washed and decent, then I'm going to take a strap to your backside so you won't sit for a week. And tomorrow you're going into isolation." She pointed to Seb. "You, get out of this house and get to work." She marched Juliet to the bedroom and slammed the door.

Seb raised his arms, letting go his breath as he listened to the row continue.

"You got no thought for me, for my job, for my concern. I'm going to whip you good and sound you damn little bitch."

"You're only jealous, that's all," Juliet shouted. "You're jealous because I let him make love to me, instead of letting you do it." Seb heard the sharp slap of hand on cheek. "Don't you dare hit me, you fucking dyke!"

For seconds the house fell silent. "Baby, I'm sorry. I didn't mean to hurt you. I was worried sick. Forgive me, baby. Please, I love you so." Lisa began to cry and Juliet followed.

"I wanted the guy, I wanted a man to love me. He saved my life. Please don't cry, I love you too."

"It's OK, baby. I'll look after you. You're safe now. That's it baby, let me hold you."

"Lisa, I'm sorry. Forgive me?"

Seb listened to their anguish fade to incoherent murmurs, then whispers. He heard the squeak of a bed, then Juliet's small voice.

"Bollocks." He walked to his car and drove out of Port Isaac. Orders said to follow their instructions and if this is what they wanted, so be it. Qasem believed his target was in London. Both women were safe and apparently content in the comfort of each other's arms. He swung the Jaguar out of the lanes and onto the dual carriageway, increasing speed way past the limit, conscious of his grinding jaw. His first tentative experience of encapsulation by female love felt kicked, yet the memory of Juliet's small voice still remained as if a song. Something wonderful had happened, something given a voice by those soft utterances of sound, sound that had pierced deep inside of him. Sound no doubt now heard by Lisa. Bloody women. There was nothing he could do for either. Al-Qaeda and Razi had been easier to deal with.

CHAPTER 15

Henry watched Bernard step out of the palatial entrance to Crawley's apartment block and stop to exchange words with the doorman before heading towards his work place on East 28th. A slim burgundy document case was tucked beneath his arm. Seconds later two men from Walsh Securities also left the apartment, specially selected men, nice boys; Tweedledum and Tweedledee. Both maintained a ten-foot gap behind Bernard. Henry maintained equal distance, a folded newspaper under his arm, an identical document case to Bernard's tucked inside the newspaper. The expensive leather had been crafted with exacting care, all copied from photographs and measurements provided by Tweedledee. Henry appreciated Bernard's attention to detail, his obsession with tidiness, his ordered and regulated lifestyle. He never went wild or faltered from his daily routine. The perfect patsy for surveillance.

At 0913 hours Bernard entered Toby's Coffee Shop and headed for his usual window seat. Tweedledum and Tweedledee paused momentarily by the door, idling until Henry had passed Tweedledee the second document case still wrapped in the newspaper. He watched both men enter then crossed the road. Bernard now sat on a high stool fronted by the window, his legs neatly crossed, his own document case resting squarely on the counter beside him. Henry watched from behind cover given by the flow of people on the opposite pavement. Tweedledum and Tweedledee balancing coffee and cake pushed in behind Bernard, until Tweedledum spilt coffee down the guy.

Bernard leapt from the seat, gesticulating in frantic outrage. Tweedledee carried out the switch. Slick, Henry thought. Both operatives fussed around, mopping Bernard with handkerchiefs. A waiter joined in. Henry re-crossed the road to arrive as Bernard stormed onto the pavement, his shouted opinion of Tweedledum and Tweedledee unfavourable. Both men followed him,

Tweedledee passing Henry the newspaper with Bernard's document case inside.

Henry trailed at twenty paces to the apartment watching Shalk and two FBI agents slide from a car and approach Bernard. Mission accomplished, Henry thought and crossed the street. On the pavement he recognised two boys from Jake's hit team. He frowned not understanding why they were here.

"Captain Taylor, sir. General asks you attend an urgent meeting."

Wat Walsh sat across the desk from Jake Hammerton and Ed Rawlings. "How can this be happening, Jake?" Wat clenched fists and felt the suppression of rage swell in his chest. "Max Crawley invented this bird. He could not possibly be selling secrets."

"The FBI caught his boyfriend with a case full of documents. First Perry, now Bernard, except Bernard had vital information regarding tomorrow's inaugural flight. That could only come from Crawley. He must be suspended pending a full enquiry."

"How can I suspend our top scientist?"

"No man is indispensable. Dr Rawlings can take his place. The flight team is on standby and ready to roll. The absence of one man changes nothing. You OK to handle this, Ed?" Hammerton asked.

Rawlings raised his palm. "Sure. We practised a thousand times. But if I'm going to fly Raider, I'll need control code clearance. The Air Force run this show but supreme control is through the basement module or this office module." He waved to the flight deck opposite. "I also have to know who the other code holders are." He shrugged while looking between them. "Just in case, you understand."

Wat sat back and tapped the desk with one finger. "In case the building is attacked and we're all held to ransom?"

"It's a Pentagon stipulation. To commence flight they hold joint codes with mission control. In the event of an incident, then emergency code control goes in ascension to three others, that's guys on the ground, guys in the building. If something did happen I'd need to know who to contact."

"In case of lock-on by any unknown intruder," Jake said. "Like Crawley's radar station in the Oman desert?"

Wat saw the weariness in Jake's eyes as his security chief visibly sagged. "For the inaugural flight, code control is held jointly, first by you and the military, second by Jake and myself, thirdly by the President alone. His code is a one hit and overrides all others." Wat let go a sour smile. "My inclusion is money privilege. I got a good share of eight billion dollars on this. I insisted."

"Happy?" Jake turned to Rawlings.

"I can handle that," Rawlings answered, a smile creeping in as if he suddenly realised his new importance.

"OK, gentlemen," Wat said while looking between them. "Until this crisis is over and Raider's inaugural flight is complete, I'm staying in the building. I would advise we all do the same. OK with you, Ed?"

"I'll inform the wife. Now, if you'll excuse me gentlemen, I need to brief the team and start winding up. During flight we have fourteen armed missiles on board heading for individual targets. Besides Raider, that's a lot of Naval and Air Force co-ordination to align."

"I appreciate your efforts, Ed." Wat pressed a button to open the glass partition of the inner office.

When the scientist had gone, Jake leaned on the desk and lowered his voice. "It gets worse. The FBI were tipped on Bernard from where I don't know. They've been on to me, they're going to pull Crawley next." Jake twisted in his seat and brushed a hand over his chin. "I have a good working relationship with Shalk, the man in charge. Maybe I can contain damage by putting this over as Crawley's stupid disregard for security, coupled with an opportune theft by Bernard. Then the matter can be dealt with internally and all concerned dismissed. If not ...." Jake raised his hands. "I've told Henry to start a full investigation."

"What news of Juliet?"

"We sent Navro down to the bolt-hole. Don't worry, if Lisa's turned bad, I'm told Havic will give her serious grief."

"Get Juliet out of there, now!" Wat let suppressed horror into his mind, allowing him to see the decapitated body of his wife stretched on the mortuary slab. "How can this happen? I trusted these people," he said unable to control the trembling which shuddered through his body.

Jake reached across the desk and placed a reassuring hand to his shoulder. "Steady old friend. Navro's good. He has a full team and helicopter. He's probably lifting Juliet now. I have the CIA involved and they've kicked butt with the British authorities. It's still low key and away from the media. Though Lisa has turned, it doesn't mean Juliet is harmed."

"I don't understand. Lisa loves Juliet like a sister."

"Not quite like a sister ..." He trailed off and shrugged. "But she sure as hell had our trust." Jake covered his face. "I've known the woman eight years. God forgive me if I've failed you."

"Get Juliet back, nothing else matters."

The patrol car followed Seb for two minutes before drawing in front to stop him. The policewoman who approached had a big blouse of a uniform and an officious expression.

"Your car, sir?" She did not lean to the open window.

"It is." Seb allowed her a non-committal smile, the type he reserved for tiresome people. Another speeding ticket, another three points on his licence. For what? He watched her male colleague leave the squad car and stroll to the bonnet talking over his radio. He nodded to her.

"Mind stepping out of the car, sir?"

Seb did as requested, his polite smile difficult to maintain. "Do we have a problem? I wasn't going that fast."

"The sergeant will explain at the station. Could you get into the squad car please?"

Juliet lifted cases into the car boot and slammed the lid, moving to the passenger side as Lisa locked the cottage then pushed the agent's keys back through the letterbox. Against heat and the long drive, Juliet had chosen to wear shorts and singlet, Lisa a white cotton top with matching skirt, the material flowing around her legs. Juliet thought the outfit unusually feminine for Lisa, almost a statement to soften her anger of early morning. They were friends again but Juliet realised it would never be the same. In the turmoil of emotions both had gone to the boundary and both had stepped over. Once Juliet realised their kissing had become sexual and their embrace no longer plutonic, she felt shocked, then scared at her willingness to allow what was happening. To her relief later morning had seen Lisa return to character without any comment regarding their physical union. Juliet felt grateful for that, still deeply uncertain of where she was physically and mentally. She sensed both had touched the stone, then reclosed the veil. To know Sapphic love existed was enough. Past uncertainties had been removed but only to allow new ones. She held no desire for a binding commitment and viewed Lisa's retreat from comment as a measure of the other woman's understanding and protective love. Because of it Juliet felt their bond now stronger than ever.

She waited until Lisa climbed into the car beside her before speaking. "Lisa, promise you won't tell anyone about Rupert."

"He saved your life. No man has ever saved my life.

Guess he'd have my gratitude if he did."

"I didn't mean it to happen. It just did, like it was the most natural thing."

"It was the most natural thing. Learn from it but as of now, your boy stays in the shadow. No more meetings. Understood?"

Juliet nodded. "If you say so."

"I say so. Now it's back to the cage. Can't trust Rupert not to contact his side and give away our position. Jake has a second bolt hole known only to him and Henry. I'm afraid it's lockdown time, babes. Three days in the dark, then you're free." Lisa extracted a gold necklace alarm from out of her handbag and passed it across. She took another minute cylindrical object and dropped it into her side pocket before swapping both their mobiles for two no bigger than credit cards. The old ones she tossed out of the window. "Soon as you make the first call security will be able to track so don't use it unless there's an emergency," she said.

Juliet slipped the necklace over her head and placed the new phone in her pocket realising the cage door had firmly closed again. Such sweet freedom with such a wonderful guy. For moments she sat in silence staring out of the car windscreen as Lisa drove down a long, forested lane then turned onto a main road. She felt relaxed, as if she had been through some great adventure, sharing it with real people who had entwined her body and soul for what she was, not the jewelled beetle favoured by her father and Lucas.

After a mile Lisa hissed a protracted, agonised sigh and slowed the car for a young policewoman who stepped into the road ahead, her patrol car across the carriageway, blue lights flashing. A white van was turning to come back as if the road was blocked.

"What now?" Lisa said and wound down the window. The policewoman leaned to them and smiled.

"Sorry ladies but a tractor has shed its load. You'd be

better to turn round and take an alternate route."

"We want the main road," Lisa said.

"If you follow the white van, there's a forestry track on the left about half a mile back. It cuts across country to a B road which links with this one passed the blockage. It's the quickest way out."

While she spoke she stared at Juliet. Juliet thought maybe because of her black skin, perhaps that was unusual in Cornwall. But then the policewoman was young and slim with a perfect olive complexion. Juliet thought that unusual for a policewoman anywhere.

"Thanks," Lisa said and began to turn. Juliet twisted in her seat to watch the policewoman go to the next car that stopped. The elderly driver also began to turn.

"No code red then?" Juliet said.

"How do you mean?"

"Last time the police blocked the road you hiked to code red."

"That was night time America with big, bad Jake in the bushes. This is England on a summer's day and nobody knows we're here, except Henry ... and Rupert." She followed the van off the road and on to a track. The car behind also turned, all heading towards a pine forest, its sharp green edges towering either side.

As they entered the woods Juliet looked back and saw the police car two hundred metres behind. She felt slight apprehension, more so when she looked to Lisa's face which was now screwed with uncertainty. The white van slowed and stopped, leaving both vehicles hemmed in by trees.

"Now this is code red." Lisa pushed down on the door lock.

"Maybe he's stuck."

Lisa drew the tiny cylindrical device from her pocket, lifted her skirt and pushed it under the elastic of her knickers. For moments she closed her eyes while fiddling with unseen fingers, shifting slightly in her seat. Seemingly satisfied with her efforts, she produced the credit card sized phone and also pushed that down into her knickers, turning the instrument until it was held tight against her pubic mound by elasticated lace. "Probably harmless but take hold of your alarm pull and give me your phone."

Juliet did as instructed, shifting in her seat as the following cars pulled up behind. Lisa began to press buttons on Juliet's cell phone the same time the policewoman and the older man left their cars. The next instant both van doors burst wide and four Balaclava clad men with Uzi sub machine guns leapt out.

"Pull the alarm!" Lisa shouted and yanked Juliet's head to her lap, laying across her in protection. Amidst the shouts from outside, Lisa was yelling into the cell phone. "Code red, code red, Port Isaac."

A sledgehammer battered on the side window splintering glass everywhere. Next instant the car door went wide on its hinges. Looking up between the crook of Lisa's arm, Juliet saw the barrel of a gun pressed against her head.

"Out, out," male voices were shouting while hands dragged them both from the car to throw them to the ground. Juliet screamed and heard Lisa curse as someone stamped on her wrist. Another twisted the mobile from her hand. Wriggling like an eel Lisa entangled her feet between ankles, toppling one guy before regaining her knees to punch hard into another man's groin. Moments later a rifle butt struck solidly into the back of her head sprawling her forward. She made no sound then. Juliet was conscious of the dank forest smell. Someone pulled her arms, clamping and fastening her wrist. She screamed, then drew breath to scream again until a backhand swung heavily across her face. She had no chance to recover, unable to stop her body being lifted and thrown into the van. Seconds later, Lisa landed on top of her. Men and boots were everywhere, yanking her legs high as they rolled her over by the ankles. She tasted blood in her mouth and felt it hot on her head as she was gagged. When finally she could look up, the policewoman was looking down, pointing a small automatic. It never wavered when the van moved off down the track.

Al Domeco entered a basement room in the American Embassy and checked the receiver left in his care. Two of the diodes were flashing red. Unsure what had happened, he picked up the phone and dialled for Jody Farlow.

Lisa twisted and a foot pressed hard into her back.

"You stay still, woman," a female voice shouted. Lisa did as she was told but from her new position she could see across to Juliet.

"You OK, babes?" She spoke reassuringly, hoping to assess her condition.

"Shut up," the voice came from above and a heel jabbed her spine.

Lisa winced and tried to stay calm for her baby. She judged their journey time about twenty minutes, mostly up and down hill and not fast. When the van turned off the road again, it laboriously started along a track obviously full of potholes. After five minutes it stopped. The barrel of the Uzi pressed into Lisa's neck.

"Listen, woman. You got no value. You cause trouble, we beat you. You cause trouble again, we kill you." A loose carrier bag was jammed over Lisa's head. The same time strong arms lifted her from either side, dragging her to the tail end of the van until her feet dropped to the ground. She heard Juliet placed beside her. Looking from under the bottom of the carrier she glimpsed the girl's bright pink trainers, huge compared to her dark and slender calves. Led by the arm, she moved over hard compacted rubble mixed with dried earth, a place not used too often by cars. She smelt the evergreen of forest, the scent of pine and realised they were back in woods.

Moments later, she stepped over a threshold and into a house. Blood stuck the carrier bag to her cheek and she shook her head, attempting to keep the plastic from her mouth, all the time hoping her blouse and skirt hung loose over the mini mobile thrust inside her pants.

"Remove the hood," a voice instructed, its tone deep and cultured, possibly East Mediterranean.

Stood against a wall beside Juliet, Lisa was hemmed in by five armed men and two women, the younger woman in police uniform, the rest in boiler suits. The older woman, tall, maybe East African, removed Lisa's gag. The fact they showed their faces indicated their indifference to future identification. They believed in the success of their objectives or sudden death. These people were clearly fanatics. The room was small, cottage-like, somewhere, she guessed, in the middle of nowhere.

"Who am I talking to?" she asked.

"Khalid bin Qasem."

"You, the infamous Bin Qasem?" She smiled disbelievingly at the short, portly figure but new fear now knotted her stomach.

"I am Jaber, his spokesman, but Wat Walsh will know of Khalid and his acquaintance with Mrs Walsh."

Juliet sucked sudden breath in terror and pushed close. Lisa suppressed a shudder and momentarily wondered if this man had been the one who decapitated the girl's mother. She also realised the only person they considered of value was Juliet. Her own presence had no purpose other than to pacify Juliet into obedience. When it came to first hostage killed, she knew who was prime candidate.

"OK, Mr Jaber," she said. "Allow me to speak for Miss Walsh. I'm her guardian, so let's resolve this situation with safety on all sides."

"A most helpful attitude, Miss Longford."

"OK, what do you want?"

"That is not for either of you to know. Enough to emphasize your safety and wellbeing depend entirely on your co-operation."

Lisa looked to Juliet and saw the fear generated by her mother's death. "OK, baby. We'll come through, don't worry."

The woman in police uniform produced a recording machine and held it to Juliet. "Talk to your father."

"What do I say?"

"Tell him you'll be home soon," Lisa coaxed her.

"Tell him you have been on a long car journey," the woman said. She switched on the tape and looked between them.

"Papa, they want me to talk. I don't know what's happening. Lisa's here, we're both tied. They hit us. Seb's gone. So we're on our own." The woman nudged her. "We've been driving, driving for hours. I love you, Papa." The tape was switched off.

"Excellent," Jaber said. "Now take them upstairs. Dress their wounds and change their clothes. Ensure they conceal nothing. I'm afraid, ladies, you must be separated and restrained but I assure you this is only temporary and will be less arduous if you co-operate."

"Do as they say, babes," Lisa instructed Juliet. "Remember your training, mind above situation. And remember also, we are not alone. People, the police, everyone will be looking."

"They won't hurt us, will they?" Juliet said, her voice quavering.

"No, baby, they won't. Just stay cool," she said, surprised at the calm in her own voice.

Grabbed by the shoulder she was forced upstairs to a corridor. Juliet was pushed to the first room, Lisa to the second. "Play it easy, babes. Do as they tell you," she shouted last encouragement before being thrust into the bedroom by the African woman and a thick, robust man of obvious strength. He threw a blue tracksuit at her feet and stood back, his expression clearly anticipating what would follow.

"Put them on," the woman said. While the man covered with an Uzi, she undid the bonds to Lisa's wrists, then stood away, levelling her own weapon. "Listen, woman, my name is Tanisha, I am your guard. This is Sarj. You do anything stupid, you get beaten or shot. You enjoyed your swim yesterday, we watch you. You want to take Juliet swimming again, you do as you are told. Now take off your clothes. Naked."

Lisa slipped off her shoes and started to unbutton her blouse, staring defiantly at the smirking male. Dropping the top, she unhooked her bra. "Can I retain my modesty?" She asked. "Can I turn my back?" When neither answered she allowed the bra to fall away and lifted the tracksuit top before shrugging it over her head. She unzipped her skirt, knowing the moment she let it fall they would see the mobile held in the apex of her groin. Without asking she turned away. The man immediately grabbed her shoulders, attempting to twist her around.

"I'm having my period," she lied. "I want to keep my pants on."

"Sarj," the woman's voice stopped him. "Leave her. Keep your underpants, woman. But face us."

Still with her back to them, Lisa let the loose fitting skirt pool on the floor, instantly slipping her feet into the tracksuit bottoms, only turning as she pulled them up. "Satisfied?" she asked. "Now I want to speak to your boss. I want to know the situation. If you want to negotiate, I can help. But I warn you, no harm must come to Miss Walsh."

Sarj grinned at her. "I think you're very cute, Lisa. You got a good body, strong like Kosovo girls I rape." He levelled the Uzi, indicating she should move to the bed. Tanisha lifted a length of chain from the floor, one end of which was anchored to the wall. Lisa resigned herself and allowed the loose end of chain to be padlocked around her neck.

"Good woman," Tanisha said. "But you think you fool

us?" She thrust her hand down Lisa's tracksuit bottoms and into her pants, clutching the tiny mobile hidden inside, ripping it upwards with a handful of pubic hair.

Lisa screamed in pain as she was bodily lifted and thrown back on the bed. "Bitch."

"And how. You want I should whip you? Let them rape you? You have no more chances women." Tanisha pointed her finger. "Next time you will suffer. Stay good and I look after you. Keep away Sarj and his Chechnyans. In corner you have pot to piss in. When we eat, I bring you food. Now, you lie on bed and stay quiet."

Lisa complied, remaining still until they both left the room locking the door behind them. Then she smiled. "You OK, babe?" she shouted, half turning to the adjoining room.

"They took my clothes and locked me up," Juliet's voice replied through the wall. "I heard a scream, they hurt you?"

"No, I'm fine. They left you decent?"

"They left you decent?"

"Got a tracksuit, nothing else."

"You shut up," Tanisha's voice came from nowhere. Lisa looked around the room and for the first time saw the eye of a video camera above the solitary cupboard, a speaker beside it.

Undaunted, she turned to the curtain covered window which overlooked the front garden. Rising from the bed she pulled on her chain, reaching with outstretched hands but finding herself inches short. Tanisha laughed and Lisa pretending resignation, flopping back onto the mattress where she curled into an embryonic position. For ten minutes she listened to the house, hearing people leave and cars starting. Then came Tanisha's voice giving orders but now all sounds came from below left. Men's voices mainly, she figured maybe three, then Tanisha's again followed by the clinking of plates. Then silence, a few murmurs and she guessed they were eating. She stood, carefully looped her chain then played it out silently until it pulled taut at her neck. Lifting her right leg in balletic pose, arms outstretched she hooked her big toe to the curtain edge, shifting it sideways until able to look out over woods and valley. The day was clear, hot and bright and some five hundred metres distance down amongst trees she saw the glint of water. On the hillside beyond and just visible amidst forest rose the stonewalls and slate roof of a large house. She could gain no other distinguishing feature, no villages or steeples, just forest, hills and moorland. She let go the curtain and returned to the bed. Her back to the camera, she again hunched into the embryonic position and eased out the tiny cylindrical object from the crevice of her vagina, holding it hidden while she extended its length to reveal the transmission switch. Having previously input three recipients she now sent a satnav location of her position to each. The first went to Seb who she figured the closest, the next to Navro and finally to Walsh Towers, New York. Only Seb's message would transmit. She tried the other destinations four times before switching off to push the device back inside her vagina, anxious to save the battery for later.

Jake stood mid way at a conference table adjacent to Wat Walsh's office. Wat Walsh slumped in a chair opposite, his eyes downcast and without light. Jake placed the small digital recorder on the table and looked to the gathering, members of the State Department, the Defense Department, the FBI and the CIA. How many, he wondered were party to the inner circle of rightwing bigots, how many were hooded crows waiting to pluck eyes?

"Two hours ago we received this message sent via a public phone box in London." He pressed the recorder and Juliet's small voice filled the room. When the message was finished, a man's voice came on. "My name is Jaber,

Operational Director for Khalid bin Qasem. Your daughter is safe, Mr Walsh and will remain so providing you do as instructed. Do not seek us, we will be in contact."

"Gentlemen," Jake leaned forward, his hands clasped. "If you are aware of past events, you will know that eight years ago Mrs Walsh was abducted and murdered by an international terrorist named Khalid bin Qasem. Through information from the CIA, we confirm Jaber is part of his terror group. I'm sure I need not explain the fear this causes. Eight years ago Bin Qasem wanted classified information which would have jeopardized our whole unmanned bomber program. He did not gain that information. In result Mrs Walsh was executed." Jake halted on his words and looked to the crows. What the hell do they care, he thought. They want revenge for 9/11. Who gives a shit over one college kid and a dyke? Enemy blood is what counted. "GR4 will commence its inaugural flight tomorrow. We can only surmise the abduction of Miss Walsh is directly connected. Due to past experience no one person is in a position to individually pass information or open files. Bin Qasem will know that."

"But Walsh Avionics does have overall control of flight mission," a member of the Defense Department reminded.

"That was a precondition of the military to centralise emergency procedures in the event of systems failure," Jake said. "But final control is in the hands of this building. First level codes are held by our Chief Flight Director and a top Air Force executive. Second level codes to override are held jointly by Mr Walsh and myself. Final code is held solely by the President. This means if required, he can give mission back to the Air Force. But these codes only control the aircraft during flight, they give no technical data."

"Has Qasem made a demand?" The voice came from Ratner, CIA.

"Nothing. But our first instinct must be for the safety of Miss Walsh." Jake looked round the table and knew what each was thinking. Raider was their priority, Juliet Walsh could go the same way as her mother. "There will be an update briefing in this room every hour. At this stage the press have little detail and we do not want their intrusive interference. Secrecy is priority. Ladies and gentlemen," he nodded to finish.

Wat Walsh spoke only when the room had emptied. "I'm not going to sacrifice Juliet. No one has the right to ask me, not after my wife."

"Government policy is no surrender." Jake stood slowly and shuffled papers which he placed into his briefcase. "We have to get her back. Navro's there now, plus the CIA. The British police have lifted Havic, useless piece of shit."

"Don't make sense. How did they know?"

"Lisa. Why else was she paid a million dollars? Worse, we must also consider Henry. Only he and Lisa knew about the location," Jake said. "The FBI have taken Henry for questioning. Nothing I could do about that." Jake looked to Wat and shook his head. "My God, if he's involved I'll …"

"No rough stuff, Jake."

"In the old days we used to shoot 'em."

When Jake returned to his own office on the twenty-second floor, Dalvarral, Ratner and Shalk waited in the outer lobby.

"What the hell are we going to do? Once the guy gets lock-on, unless we fire, he could destroy the plane."

Jake moved behind his desk to sit with his palms flat on the top, the three crows jabbering on the outer fringes.

"So we fire as planned. We have fourteen cruise missiles aboard plus an assortment of smaller ones. We only need two missiles, that's all it will take."

"He'll kill the girl."

Jake raised his hands. "Maybe I can reach her first. Go

chivvy Rawlings. Make sure he knows his patriotic duty. He had two brothers die in the twin towers. Go flame his revenge."

"You ready to answer Wat Walsh when we contribute to the murder of his daughter?"

Jake hunched shoulders. "It's a dangerous world we live in and this country is at war, that makes every citizen a soldier."

Dressed in jeans and tee shirt, Navro stood in the cottage garden talking on his mobile. Four of his six man team lounged against cars parked outside the gate.

"The bolt-hole's deserted. Agent had a call to collect the keys three hours ago. That figures with Juliet's alarm."

"Get your boys to check the site." Jody's voice came back. "Tracks, witnesses, anything. We got to move on this, Navro, 'cos I think it's going to get bad real fast. And Navro," she paused, "I remind you again, the Brits get touchy if you're hoisting shooters."

"Yes, Ma'am, I'm listening, Ma'am. Got it all stashed in the chopper on a local airstrip, place called Mawgan."

"I'll arrive in two hours." Jody switched off.

Pleased he now had something positive to report, Navro immediately dialled Jake. "Bolt-hole deserted, General. Going to check the location where Sweetpea was lifted."

"Navro," Jake's voice held caution. "Listen in, what I say is highly confidential. I find we've been double-crossed by Lisa Longford. The bitch is shooting for the opposition. She's not on our side. I repeat, she is enemy and not on our side. Do I make myself clear?"

"Lisa! She wouldn't do that!"

"She sold us out for a million dollar bribe. Don't tell the men, it's bad for morale. And no need for me to say, in this outfit there is only one punishment for desertion to the enemy. First contact, kill her I'm relying on you." He switched off.

Navro took the mobile from his ear. "Lisa, you cocksucking idiot. What the hell are you doing?"

After the long drive, Jody pulled the blouse from her perspiring back and entered the Bodmin Way public house. Her two favourite Brits stood propped at the bar. She made no effort over tact and went straight to the point. "You have our boy?"

"In the local nick. Rightly refuses to tell the police anything. Due to the nature of his training and the current situation the only people he'll talk to are ourselves in private. Care for a drink?" Fox asked.

"Mineral water with ice and lemon thank you," she said to the hovering bar man. "That sure is a long drive, I hope it's worth my visit."

"What are you after?"

"Sebastian Havic's info and your assistance."

"For that we'll need a full briefing from Walsh Securities. But so far they seem reluctant to trust us with anything."

Jody accepted her drink. "Kind of hot in here," she said, fanning with one hand. "Mind if we sit outside?" Without waiting for a reply she walked to the French doors. The two men followed. "Walls have ears," she said choosing and sitting at a small, round wrought iron garden table away from others. Deliberating she positioned herself so both men had full view of her legs.

"You going to tell us who Candy Girl really is?" Fox asked her.

Jody hitched her skirt for comfort and crossed her thighs. "Strictly between us and no-one else. Candy Girl is Juliet Walsh. Since our last meeting she's been abducted by Khalid bin Qasem. Juliet's female bodyguard is accused of conspiracy. No doubt there'll soon be a warrant for her arrest. But it's bullshit," she said and sat under the full silent stare of Freddy Fox, his face giving no expression to his thoughts.

"So why do you still want Havic?" he finally asked.

"I'm CIA, Inspector. We work covertly with any available material." She re-crossed her legs but neither men glanced down. Now she really had their interest. "If he's found the bolt-hole then he's a clever and highly capable operator. I want him on our side. Maybe he could give us numbers to track their mobiles. Juliet's alarm pull gave the abduction spot. Lisa is too shrewd to rely on only one device though as yet we've picked up nothing. Maybe, just maybe, Seb has a means of contact."

"We're on our way to talk with him now. Come too."

"Thanks guys, I appreciate that." She re-crossed her legs and absently tucked down her blouse. "In which case I'll tell you we are faced with an act of terror so serious it will have world repercussions."

"That's out of my jurisdiction," Fox said. "You want MI5 and 6."

"That's what I'm trying to avoid. MI5 are already pushing in and causing distraction." Jody glanced to Fagan as he was about to speak, then hitched her skirt a little higher, minutely parting her thighs. "We don't want to get bogged in cross-departmental bureaucracy," she cut in on him. "Valuable time and decisions will be lost. Juliet Walsh may end up dead and America will suffer a catastrophe. Walsh Securities are already here, headed by one of our own CIA people. It's almost certain when Juliet is located, Jake will send them in. Anyway you look at it, that will make one hell of an operational and diplomatic mess."

"You said you wanted Havic."

"No matter what is said about him, he's innocent. He's also a serving army officer with the SAS. That gives us a lead edge. You guys are like us, you work covertly. If Havic is free and involved, his presence could give cover to CIA and Walsh Securities, particularly if CAT additionally threw some of their own boys in. The press know nothing yet and afterwards you could invent whatever story you want."

Fox leant back and laughed. "Even if I agree, which I don't, no way can I sanction your request. Only MI5 can set up that sort of operation. Chat with the Home Office, the Defence Department."

Leaning on the table with one elbow Jody rested fist against cheek, her eyes unblinking. "Colonel, MI5 will certainly not sanction involvement of Jake's boys so I'm trying to avoid that tangle. But what if you applied to a much higher power? What if you told the Home Secretary the situation required covert involvement of the Combined Agency Task Force who just so happened to have men on the ground?"

"Listen Jody, my men on the ground in live action could only be authorised from senior Cabinet levels. We're an intelligence gathering force who occasionally pop some baddie. We don't do heavy action."

"We have terrorists who are highly dangerous, trained and armed. You've got one SAS man already here with intimate knowledge of the hostages. We probably need, say, another ten. I've done my homework on you guys. CAT have some of the most highly trained and capable men out of Special Forces. We need Seb and one of your teams on this, and we need them fast before interference from other agencies."

"No chance."

"Your country would avoid an international disaster, plus you might save the lives of Juliet Walsh and Lisa Longford, leaving Wat Walsh forever grateful."

"I can do nothing without authority," Fox said, shaking his head. "Abduction of two foreign nationals does not warrant such procedures."

"I'll flex muscle, you flex muscle. We can do this."

Jody took out her mobile, smiling between the two men as she called her boss, then on his sanction, the Director of the CIA. He called Hal Johnson, the Secretary of State who in turn called the British Home Secretary on a scrambled line. Waiting twenty minutes for an answer Jody spent her time explaining the background of Global Raider and the abduction of Mrs Walsh to Fox and Fagan; then her boss called her back.

"Keep everything under wraps," he said. "This is unofficial but tell your man to make his request."

Jody switched off. "You have lift-off anytime you want, unofficially of course. Now do I get Sebastian and action?"

Fox remained non-committal. "I'll phone Headquarters. If they give the nod we go. That is if Havic knows where to send us."

Jody slowly re-crossed her legs and beamed for them both. "Pray he does."

Seb became increasingly bored and frustrated by enforced inactivity. Stretched on a rubber mattress in a cell at Padstow police station he tried to think how the whole operation had gone so wrong. The police who questioned him made no sense, saying only that he was wanted by the National Crime Agency regarding an abduction. Seb figured the whole thing had to be Bin Qasem, which made Juliet's cover paramount. He could say nothing until he talked to Sean Fagan or Colonel Fox.

"Fancy a cup of tea?" A policewoman looked through the cell grid, her manner inexplicably cheerful.

"Please." Seb stood from the mattress. "And my mobile. Surely there's no reason to confiscate my mobile?"

"Suppose not. Considering your release is imminent. There must have been a dozen calls over you." She left and Seb waited ten frustrating minutes before her return with tea and his cell phone.

Her male colleague stood by the door while the policewoman placed a brimming mug on the table. "I've got all your documents ready," she said, handing over his cell phone. "Just waiting on your solicitor. We've had calls from the Assistant Chief Constable. That's big wheels in Padstow. Surprised they know we exist."

Seb hardly heard as he tapped keys on the phone to find Lisa's mobile switched off. He left a message for her to ring immediately, and just in case, checked his text messages. "Jesus," he said aloud staring at the screen. "Red alert. Satnav reference 976321."

He stood when the cell door re-opened.

"Your solicitor," the policewoman stood aside. Colonel Freddy Fox stepped past her and beckoned with one finger.

"Oh shit! I should have been there. I should have stayed." Seb stared from the Range Rover to the grey sea. "The situation became heated, both wanted me gone. Lisa ordered I go check out Cambridge. Like everyone else I believed them safe, so I left."

"You get close to Juliet?" Jody asked.

"Close as any man can get in one night."

"What about Lisa?"

He smiled and shook his head. "From the way she reacted this morning, I'm lucky to be alive."

"I've got tales that she was in on the snatch."

"Never. You know the rumours concerning their relationship? I think Lisa's a lot more than a simple bodyguard. She's devoted to the girl. In truth, I think there is something between them."

Jody leant back against the car door and folded her arms, her head to one side, her smile patronising. "Men's talk," she said, looking to the three men who stared back. "You need to understand women. They can become very close, they can even cross sexual boundaries forbidden to men, yet still walk away with opposite gender preference intact. They can also be very possessive, particularly if in love."

Seb smiled, visualising the sea and the dawn light on Juliet's brown, naked skin. He stayed silent for a few moments then extracted his mobile. "I think Juliet's very lonely, I think she relies on Lisa and I think Lisa offers all the love she dare give within the confines of their relationship. Does that make sense?"

"Makes sense to a woman."

Seb switched on the mobile and scrolled for the alert. "Lisa would die protecting Juliet. She's sharp and cool. Sometime this morning she sent this. Did you get one, anyone gone in yet?" He handed the mobile to his boss.

Fox read the message. "Why the hell didn't you tell us? For Christ's sake this could be their locations."

"I thought you had it already, she wouldn't send just to me." Seb raised his hands.

"If she believed there was a Qasem mole in Walsh Securities that's exactly what she would have done," Jody said. "Or maybe she only had time for one message. But it proves she still trusts you."

"So let's go find them." Seb turned to his boss who was now speaking urgently over his mobile.

"Roger that," he said into the phone and switched off. "OK, we're on. Get the team down here, Sean. This lady sure got influence."

"Thank you, Colonel Fox." She raised eyebrows for him. "Now let me fill you in on the current political thinking. Putting Global Raider aside, we have two situations here. Juliet as a hostage and Qasem as public enemy number one. Qasem has to go. If not, he'll keep bouncing into America's face. We have two links. Events here, plus an unknown spectre within the Walsh organisation. Though I can't prove it, I have grave suspicion who that someone is. If we beat the bushes here and communicate with New York what we intend, that spectre might show himself by informing the enemy, then maybe we can use him to draw Qasem out. That, whether

I want it or not, will be the long-term strategy of my department. I'm sorry, guys but everyone in this game is an expendable player, Juliet and myself included. At the moment, Juliet is safe, she's too valuable a hostage to shoot for vengeance or temper. Qasem wants her to somehow get influence over Global Raider. That allows a short time to play the situation for advantage and hopefully, rattle Qasem enough to get careless. Then maybe you and I can do something here. Helicopters make noise, they frighten people and if they move Juliet we have a better chance of finding her. We have two lives. OK, Juliet is baby, she comes first, that's our job. But Lisa is one of us. Sure she deserves a fighting chance and that's where you guys come in when hitting the location. Navro goes for Juliet, you take the others. Help me do it my way. If that doesn't work, we do it yours."

Seb watched as she unfolded arms and drew a small, embroidered hankie from the cuff of her sleeve. She dabbed at the perspiration which moistened her upper lip, then looked back, her expression half wistful, half resigned to forces beyond her control.

"I doubt there will be second chance," Sean Fagan said.

"Then let's roll. We have limited time and licence. I've stirred a hornets' nest and across the sea my masters will be going for the kill. It's why they pressured the Defense Secretary to persuade your Government to help. That's a rapid reaction team from the Combined Agency Task Force. We're breaking the rules, so the moment the press find out the politicians will think only of covering their own backs. That means we are to extract Juliet before she's used in some way to terminate Global Raider and we need to do that in the next twenty-four hours."

"And Lisa?" Seb asked.

She tucked the hankie back into her cuff. "Lisa's alive because threat of her execution will keep Juliet obedient. Unless she is a collaborator and I don't think she is, Lisa has no other use. And even if she did betray us, the chances are they'd kill her anyway. I understand your concern that she's a fellow soldier and a good one too but she ain't coming out of this alive gentlemen," Jody paused. "And she knows it."

Twenty minutes later Seb spread an ordnance survey map on the floor of Jody's hotel bedroom, placing his mobile showing Lisa's co-ordinance on top. Colonel Fox and Sean Fagan knelt either side while Jody squatted opposite with a pencilled copy of Lisa's satnav location.

"OK," she said, looking at the map's grid reference. "According to this reading they are right here in this isolated cottage."

"So first we need to do some careful reconnaissance," Fox said. "We need to know approaches, exits and the building's layout."

"I can do that," Seb volunteered. "Then brief the team soon as they arrive."

"Stealth is essential. We need to be in the house before they even know we are there."

"What about Navro?" Jody knelt up.

"He follows. When action commences. Sorry, there is no other way."

"Listen, US forces have to be the ones who rescue our girl. Otherwise the political bureaucrats will go mad. Of course with Brit help." Jody looked between them.

"Tell the press what you want. But you're on UK soil so it's my shout. That means we go in quietly, discreetly, no helicopters."

Jody knelt back on her haunches. "I'll tell Navro but you got to understand he and his boys are ex-Delta, Special Ops. I don't know their chain of command."

"That's fine so long as they're quiet and do as I tell them."

"I'm sure they'll be like obedient ghosts."

Lisa twitched as the tiny device concealed in her vagina

gave a brief vibration. For seconds she clutched herself and closed her eyes. She was no longer alone. From the kitchen came spasmodic chat plus noise of a television or radio. Occasionally she heard Juliet move in the adjoining room, the squeak of a mattress, the slither of metal chain trailing over a bed frame. OK, she thought, she had to prepare herself. Whoever had sent the return signal could strike any time. She prayed they wouldn't mess up, otherwise both she and Juliet were dead.

CHAPTER 16

Wat made the conference room adjoining his outer office the strategic headquarters and equipped it with all necessary communications linking between his own office and the outside world. He saw the room quickly filled with a variety of military personnel, secret service agents, psychologists and a full Government team specialising in hostage negotiations. He spent his time between there and the glass booth, either finalising Raider's test mission or worrying over Juliet. Navro had arrived in Cornwall and was investigating the snatch point, his entire team armed with temporary diplomatic status. Both British and American Governments had been one hundred percent co-operative, the Brits providing a special ops unit called CAT. White House staff kept the President personally informed and everyone involved made sure no-one from the press heard anything. Now he waited on the call from Bin Qasem. When it came, Wat stood at the head of the conference table either side crowded his advisers.

"Welcome, Mr Walsh, to the world of the oppressed, where people exist in fear, enslaved by America's greed and its machines of war and destruction," Bin Qasem's voice filled the room.

"Where is my daughter?" Wat asked, looking to the many faces of the men and women who listened on every word.

"Safe. Safer than the children who die in the Palestinian refugee camps, who struggle for survival in Syria or Somalia, safer than those who suffer under the dictatorial regimes of your western allies."

"My daughter is an innocent person in this world. Let her go. You've already murdered her mother. She has paid enough."

"The death of your wife was entirely your own responsibility. Had you co-operated with simple demands, she would be alive today."

"I could not meet your demands, Qasem. And I still can't. It is impossible for me to extract information from our database." In the silent room he heard the sound of his own heart, of his breathing, of the blood flowing through his body.

"The American Government could have helped, it did not. Consequently you and they sanctioned the execution of Mrs Walsh. But this time it is different."

"Just what is it you want?"

"Five billion dollars deposited in Saudi riyals within the next twenty-four hours. For this transaction you will affiliate the assistance of the Bank of Dubai. The depository will have the facilities to electronically transfer to a named account at the press of a button in your office. That account number will only be given to you on the imminent release of your daughter. Needless to tell those who listen, the account will have drop down facilities to disperse into other currencies and depositaries which in turn will have similar drop down facilities. Your five billion dollars will evaporate into the system."

Wat listened as those around the table broke their silence. He heard words like, smart bastard, cute, but his mind was already considering how to overcome the enormity of such a demand. "Qasem, I am amongst the richest in America but my money is in assets, there is no way I can produce five billion dollars cash at such short notice."

"Go to your bank, Mr Walsh. Go to your American President. See how America loves you. Or use the cunning and lies on which you built your fortune. When the money is ready to place, your bank will notify Dubai and a time set to transact the exchange. Five billion or your daughter will be decapitated as was your wife."

The phone clicked and Wat covered his face, trying to control the trembling which again threatened his body. When finally he looked up, every person in the room stared at him. He turned first to Matt Corrello, his chief

192

accountant. The man answered with a slight shake of the head.

Jake leaned forward and whispered. "American policy is non capitulation. Don't even think of it, Wat."

"I have to try. I have to set it up at least. If I don't prepare he will know. To hell with money, Juliet must have a chance. Any trace on the call?"

"Paris," someone answered. "But as yet we have no address."

"Work on it."

Jake took a message from an aide behind him. "Got a report from Jody Farlow," he relayed to the table. "Seems there's a message received from Lisa Longford providing an indication of where they might be. As some might know, Longford is under suspicion of helping these terrorists so it could be a deception. We have our own team there investigating and ready to act." He turned to Wat again and spoke quietly. "I got Henry downstairs. The FBI have released him without charge. It's time to find out his true colours. We can use the man, feed false and real information. See what goes to the enemy."

"I leave it with you, Jake. I got to talk with the accountants and the White House."

Wat sat staring at the phone before him. He had booked the call fifteen minutes earlier and when Betty buzzed the internal line, he picked up the receiver to wait thirty seconds for final connection. He had one last chance to save his empire.

"It's good of you to give me the time, Mr President."

"We're old friends, Wat. I know of your situation. How can I help?"

"I'm putting together five billion dollars to save my daughter's life. Is that OK with you?"

"You know this nation's position. We don't give in to terrorists, no matter what circumstances."

"It's money, just money, and my money at that. I have to put it together. I have no choice."

"I've been given the transcript of your call. I sympathise, Wat. But the Federal Reserve Bank will not allow your bank to transfer such a sum out of this country for payment to terrorists. A court injunction to prevent such payment is already in place."

"You're signing Juliet's death warrant." Wat closed his eyes and rested fingers to his forehead while listening to the other man's silence.

"I have no choice. Hard as that may seem, if I give in, somewhere another father, another Juliet will soon take your places. The line of victims will never cease."

"I already sacrificed my wife for this country but I will not sacrifice my child. I am not Abraham and you are not God. Your court might make me a criminal but not an infanticidal murderer."

"Listen to me, Wat, hold back. I give my solemn promise to do everything within the power of my office and this nation to save your daughter. But you must stand with me. No capitulation."

Wat tightened on the shudder which coursed his body and drew hard breath to regain control. "I'll wait on developments but I still have to raise the ransom and put everything in place. He would know if I didn't."

"I appreciate that and as a father myself I understand your pain. The moment this call is over I'm going to contact the British Prime Minister and have the situation escalated. We'll get Sweetpea out of this or so help us we're not a nation who cares."

The receiver went dead in his hands and he wondered who had briefed the President on his daughter's nickname, wondered who was giving advice, chancing Juliet's life for political firmness, wondered if Wat Walsh was already regarded as a has-been.

* * *

"This better be serious, Octavius. Communication silence is imperative to security."

"Khalid, you're getting sloppy. One woman still has a mobile."

Khalid paused. "It shall be dealt with."

"Money. You have everything arranged?"

"It requires only the press of a button."

"Then I tell you something for free. Not long now and people will be closing in on you. If you want to stay on top, you'd better shift Candy Girl. And remember, you get nothing more till I get my money."

Lisa listened to the rush of feet on the stairs and only had time to sit before the door burst open. Four men and two women entered. She had no chance to protect herself. Hauled head backwards over the bed, her tracksuit top was yanked upwards until jammed under her chin while her arms were held outstretched. She felt her trousers and pants ripped down and pulled over her feet then screamed when rough fingers probed insider her body, pulling her painfully apart to hook out the small electronic device. Held spread-eagled she was pinned without modesty or defence.

"You pay, woman." Tanisha's eyes bulged as she slammed her fist into the hollowness of Lisa's stomach. She could only scream while three more blows landed in quick succession.

"You tricked me, woman. Now I give you to the Chechnyans, they fuck you then kill you. Lena, tie her."

"You're making a mistake. There was no communication." Lisa tried twisting and thrashing as the four men stretched out her limbs to the edge of the single bed, fighting to hold her until Tanisha knelt on her chest.

"Keep still or they kill you now."

Lisa ceased her struggles, allowing the younger woman who had been in the police uniform to use plastic ties, binding her wrists and ankles to the metal frame. Jaber stood watching from the doorway and Lisa tried pleading direct. "Jaber, the device has no signal from here, nothing was sent. Don't hurt the girl. For God's sake, Jaber, don't hurt her." Lisa lifted her head to stare at him. "Jaber, you hurt the girl, your mission will fail. Wat Walsh will hunt you down no matter where you are."

"Once our objectives are achieved, my future existence is immaterial, Miss Longford, as is your own." He moved further into the room. "Nevertheless, it pains me to see a woman in such a distressful and degrading situation as you find yourself. We have tried to treat you in a civilised manner but you have betrayed our trust and kindness."

"Your trust and kindness, Jaber does not live up to civilised expectations."

"You think not, Miss Longford? Then let me demonstrate an uncivilised alternative. Bring the girl." She watched Tanisha and Amin leave the room.

"Don't lay a finger on her, you bastards."

"Temper, Miss Longford is not to your advantage."

The four Chechnyans stood back against the wall, their eyes on her body, their expressions full of leering expectation. The younger woman Lena, folded her arms and stared to a corner of the room, seemingly disassociating herself from the situation.

Juliet was thrust forcibly through the door, Tanisha holding her shoulder.

The shock of what she saw brought her immediate retaliation. Holding her left hand to cup the fist of her right, she jabbed back with her elbow as Lisa had taught her, catching Tanisha in the side so the woman doubled in pain and let go. Juliet immediately snatched up Lisa's tracksuit bottoms and flung them onto her naked body. Nobody attempted to stop her as she pulled down Lisa's top and held her cheek to cheek.

"What have they done to you?"

"S'OK, baby. They haven't hurt me. Don't fight them

or they'll hit you. I love you, baby."

"Love you too."

"Enough," Jaber said. "Teach the young lady her lesson."

"Don't hurt her!" Lisa shouted while watching Juliet dragged back by two of the Chechnyans. Juliet kicked and lashed, her screams full-throated until Tanisha punched her stomach. The room went suddenly silent as Juliet doubled her body up.

"Bitch," Tanisha said. "Next time you get a real hiding."

"No next time," Jaber said. "Amin, shoot the woman."

"No!" Juliet screamed. "Please, don't."

Amin took a Browning automatic from his waistband and walked across to the bed while cocking the breech to hold the barrel inches from Lisa's temple.

"No," Juliet sobbed. "No, please, I'll do anything you want. Don't kill her, please."

Seb had parked his CAT Land Rover on the outskirts of Dunmere village and with Jock Anderson climbed a sheep fence into woods. Once under cover he made contact with base over a UHF set, then both moved swiftly and silently through trees before running two hundred metres along the Camel riverbank. At an exact distance they turned uphill into forest, moving from tree to tree. Fifty metres down from a track which led to an isolated cottage they went belly to ground, then moved only under each other's forward vision.

The single screech stopped them both. Crouched amidst the brambles and undergrowth straggling the forest floor, Seb listened over the wind while trying to distinguish if the sounds they heard were natural, a child's voice, or the shriek of a woman. The crack of a pistol shot was unmistakable.

"That's for real," Seb spoke over his body set to

Anderson. "About two hundred metres, eleven o'clock. Move up but gently does it." He called base and Sean Fagan on the open transmission. "We may have positive contact, heard sound of gunfire. Going forward to confirm. Can you get people on the move?"

"No-one within twenty minutes unless Navro can use his helicopter."

"Too noisy, too risky. We don't know the situation. But you can get him in the air. Keep him at five kilometres distance."

"Seb," Jody's voice cut in over the air, pausing, clearly finding difficulty in choosing her words, knowing his unit control and others listened. "I've just received a warrant for the arrest of Lisa Longford over her involvement in the abduction of Juliet Walsh and activities at the hotel. Evidence is supposedly substantiated by Walsh Securities, that's Jake."

"This is no time for some copper to be pushing his weight. Tell him to fuck off."

"I tried but he's insistent. If you get her out then keep her secure, understand?"

Juliet screamed, her eyes closed. The deafening report of the pistol in the confined room vibrated the air, leaving her head as if encased with lead, her scream trapped within. The air smelled of cordite and bodies. She sensed the smell of her own fear, her dread, but when she opened her eyes, Lisa stared back, her face ashen, lips tight. "'S Okay baby, they're playing with us."

"Missed," Amin grinned. "Shall I try again?"

"That depends on the young lady. If she behaves herself, if she does exactly as told, then Miss Longford will live. Do I make myself clear?"

"Yes," Juliet whispered.

"Not convincing enough," Jaber said. "Amin, the knee." Amin moved from the head of the bed and placed the pistol barrel against Lisa's knee.

"I promise, I promise!" Juliet reached with both hands, imploring. Lisa had jammed her eyes shut.

"I accept your promise. Amin, Lena, take the girl to base 2. Tanisha, the responsibility for anyone finding this place rests with you. If they do so, you will hold against all forces. If they concentrate their efforts here, the final phase of Candy Girl will have less hindrance."

"Lisa," Juliet said, feeling the awesome realisation of imminent separation.

"Just do as they tell you, baby. We'll get out of it. Papa will come."

Juliet's wrists were bound by Lena who pushed and shoved her from the room, down the stairs and out of the cottage. Juliet had no thought of escape, only of complying, only of saving Lisa's life. When ordered into the boot of a red Peugeot she obeyed without protest. Others climbed into the front and the car moved away.

Progressing slowly up the hill, Seb still saw no sign of the cottage. The spasmodic screams had ceased. They could have been from a child in tantrum, or a group of them playing. The gun shot may have been fired by a lone hunter, he had no firm idea, only a hope they were closing on their target. When the sound of an engine came from the slope above and to his left, he clambered to the lower branches of a tree. Unable to identify the car clearly, he saw only the movement of red metal behind foliage bordering a track. He called Jody. "I have a red vehicle leaving. How far is Navro?"

"Five kilometres and getting bored."

"Give him this location, see if he can pick up on the vehicle and follow it. Not close, but at a distance."

"Ask the impossible, pal and you get it, possibly."

"Continuing my approach." Seb climbed from the tree and signalled to Anderson. One at a time they resumed moving forward.

Lisa lay with eyes closed, wondering how in hell she had got herself into this situation, how long Seb would search before he found her, whether he had already brought in Walsh Securities and CAT. She had heard no sound of helicopters, the noise a sure sign of Navro being in the locality. Jaber and his group were obviously well trained and under intelligent command so were unlikely to kill Juliet except as a last resort. Wat Walsh would give everything for his daughter's safe return. It was still possible Juliet would come out alive. She was less certain of her own fate. The humiliation of her position demonstrated the small regard they gave her. She was an expendable item, useful only for bargaining and if the Chechnyans had their way, available for sex.

Every few minutes she clenched her fists, moving her body as best she could to help circulation, careful not to disturb the tracksuit bottoms thrown strategically over her stomach. Such near and precarious nudity filled her with ridicule and compounded her sense of stupidity. If Navro walked in, he would ask what the hell she was doing on her back, waiting for the Marines? But he would untie her, lift her and carry her to safety, telling how many wrestling games she must forfeit against her rescue. She prayed desperately he would walk in. Sarj came instead.

He closed the door quietly and crossed the room on tiptoes, clearly intent on keeping his presence from those below. Lisa calmed immediate panic, thinking desperately of ways to turn the situation. For seconds he stood staring at her, then removed a knife from his pocket. The mattress compressed as he sat and threw away the tracksuit bottoms.

"You want free?" he whispered, flicking open the knife, leaning over her body and unzipping the tracksuit top to fondle her breasts.

Lisa tried not to shudder. She kept her eyes on his face and felt the knife placed on her stomach. "Cut me loose, then I can do things for you." She smiled.

"Sure, if you are good girl," he said, moving his hand down over her pubic mound. "But you make sound and you are dead woman."

She began to sense panic. "Wat Walsh will pay you a million dollars." She twisted, pressing back against the mattress. "You do anything to me and they'll hunt you, kill you." She winced as he pulled a tuft of pubic hair between thumb and forefinger.

"The whole of NATO tried to kill me. I ruled villages in Kosovo where all women were mine. If they were good, I let them go back to their mothers and husbands. If they were stupid, they went to their graves. Do not be stupid." He ripped hair and held it high, blowing with a soft puff of air.

The moment he returned his hand and attempted to forage into her with two fingers she snapped and screamed. "Fuck off you bastard!"

Tanisha's voice came over the speaker. "What are you doing? Get off her." Moments later she was rushing through the doorway. Sarj had stood, his hands spread in innocent protest.

"She offered sex if I let her loose."

Pointing an automatic, Tanisha crossed over to Lisa and placed the barrel against her forehead. "You trouble, woman. I kill you now but I am told to wait. I give you choice. You stay quiet, you stay calm, I shoot you one bullet. You give me nuisance, then these fellows, they fuck you, then cut you to pieces like they did Serb women. I don't save you again, understand?"

Lisa nodded. "Please, one woman to another, cover me, please."

"No, woman. I want you ready for them."

* * *

The scream was loud, the expletives holding a positive American accent clearly recognisable as Lisa's. Seb lay in dense bush five metres from the cottage garden.

"Jody, I confirm positive contact. Hostage under duress. Lisa's voice recognised. I want immediate action."

"Hold back, Seb. Do not go in. I repeat, do not go in. Negotiations in Walsh Towers are at a critical stage and release of both hostages is the primary concern. We must assess the situation."

Seb knew she spoke truth and checked his impulse to act by instinct. Chances were if they went now both he and Anderson would end up dead and the hostages killed in bloody-minded retaliation. He figured Lisa a tough lady, whatever her current duress she would eventually overcome it. Juliet was a different matter.

"Roger that," he said finally. "Colonel Fox, could you get our lads here pronto. This is an isolated cottage approximately three hundred metres from our start point on the road. RV fifty metres downhill to the front. Need to be fully kitted to storm the building. And Jody … better inform the emergency services and police. When this is over we'll need them."

"Don't worry, Seb. Someone's got half the goddamn British Police Force mobilised on roadblocks."

"Did Navro find the vehicle which left here?"

"Found a red car and followed it onto the A30 going east but without getting close couldn't be sure. Lost it in traffic towards Liskeard, the police are now searching every red vehicle they find. And Seb, when Navro hits he won't play footsie. He and his boys are right behind if not in front. Juliet's their meal ticket and Holy Grail. Don't count them out."

"Shit!"

While his team came forward Seb did a close target recce, circling the bushes at the back. Before him was an open garden laid mostly to lawn. Not a place to cross unless under a diversion at the front. All windows had drawn curtains except the kitchen. A black woman was running water from an unseen tap, staring as she did so towards the trees. To get a terrorist team housed and in place would have needed prior knowledge of Candy Girl's movements. On the surface that could only have come from Lisa or Henry. Now he understood the reason for her arrest warrant, though he had no belief in its validity. Having watched both girls on the beach and listened briefly to the result of their row that morning, he realised Lisa's devotion was total. That left Henry.

The central top window, he figured, was the landing, the curtained rooms to each side the bedrooms; one for each hostage. He sensed unease at considering both in such an alien terrain. Twelve hours ago he had made love to one and felt jealousy from the other. Hostages gave a remote, clinical sound, a word used in reports and training manuals, not a description of warm bodies associated with passionate emotions.

Moving deeper into the tree line, Seb climbed branches directly in line with one bedroom window hoping to get a silhouette between front and rear. He saw no movement, nothing. When he returned to Anderson, Sergeant Pete Shaffer and a close quarter assault team lay in readiness, all kitted and armed. Seb exchanged greetings and began to fit his own belt kit. Ordnance was as he expected, Heckler and Koch MP5K sub machine guns, flash bangs and smoke grenades, enough in a confined room to scare the shit out of anyone. He dared not use real grenades. Shrapnel blast and fire in a small cottage would prove disastrous for friends and foe alike. He just hoped the enemy realised that. For entrance, Shaffer had made up two cutting charges using a quarter kilo of plastic explosives, primers and electronic timed detonators, sufficient to take off the strongest door. With kit checked, Seb started final briefing.

"No action till we get go. But here's the score." Seb spread an ordnance map with a sheet of A4 paper in the middle. On it he had drawn a rough sketch of what he guessed was the cottage interior. "Jock, go round the back and clobber whoever comes out. Watch for blue on blue in case someone's chasing. The rest with me, Pete, Mick and Titch, from the right, Dave, Bob, Joe and myself from the left. I'll blow the door. Number of players is unknown. Some must have gone in the car but I would guess about five or sex remain. I reason a hostage in each of the two bedrooms but in case one went in the car, we need prisoners to find out where they took her. Difficult I know, but give it a try. If we have female players, without being sexist, save 'em for the questioning after. The rest take their chances. Mick, Pete, have the kitchen, Dave, Bob, the living room. When the door blows, take out the windows and lob in flash bangs. Anyone goes for a weapon, whack 'em. Joe and I will head upstairs left and right for the hostages. Titch, check the lavatories. When you've dealt with the players, secure a safe passage. Priority is to get the hostages out alive. Any questions?" He looked to each man.

"Sound," Anderson said.

"OK, take positions, gas masks to pull on call for immediate action." He began to fold the map. "See you in paradise, gentlemen."

"No way," Bob said. "We'll piss this."

CHAPTER 17

Jake dismissed the guard and sat opposite Henry in the windowless cell. Henry's eyes were narrow and his mouth set hard. Jake tried the shadow of a smile but saw his insincerity dismissed. "Did you tell them anything about the briefcase switch or Fireback?" he asked.

"Course not." Henry leaned towards him. "But I'm sure getting screwed up on this. What the hell is going on? I was questioned for six damn hours before anyone would believe me. Where were you?"

"This is none of my doing, Henry. That was Shalk covering his ass in case Fireback has repercussions. I could have intervened earlier but it was better to let it blow away naturally on account you were the only one who knew the bolt-hole."

Henry stabbed the table with a finger and leant forward almost eye to eye. "Lisa knew." Jake guessed his next words but the man hesitated, leaning back as if changing his mind. "On Fireback I was obeying orders and to my knowledge, those orders came from the highest office."

"Unofficial and deniable." Jake never faltered in his return gaze. "That's the problem with conspiracies, Henry. Everyone wants cream out of it but nobody wants the shit if caught. I admire your resilience."

"Then get me out of here."

"You're already back online, Henry. Since you've been out lunching with the FBI, Sweetpea's got herself abducted. Lisa Longford has sold out to Khalid. There's proof and a warrant for her arrest."

Henry frowned. "Lisa. She's been on the team eight years, been screened a dozen times."

"She's a dyke, Henry. Those women get bitter as they get old and ugly. They get worried about security on account of not having a man."

Henry shook his head. "Never Lisa."

"Look at it like a witches' ducking stool. If she was

innocent, she'd have got herself killed saving Juliet. The fact she's still alive means she's double-crossed us. Arab money in her account is second proof. Wat wants to negotiate but the Government will do everything in its power to stop him capitulating. The best way we can help is to say nothing, then take out Khalid with Fireback. It's the only way."

"They'll kill Juliet."

"Not if Navro gets there first. I want you to man a clandestine listening station on negotiations. Feed me information I can feed to Navro. Jody Farlow reports good co-operation from the Brits and a defined search area near the bolt-hole. They had some location message from Lisa but that could mean nothing other than the enemy using her mobile for delaying tactics. The Brits have supplied a team of Special Ops to back Navro for surveillance then hard extraction. Police have roadblocks on all routes. If Juliet's there, Navro will find her. You get down to our old listening centre. I've set it up to cover all lines and rooms passing information on Qasem. Go to work, Henry, let's waste the bastard."

Wat sat in his glass booth with Jake Hammerton and Matt Corrello on the opposite side of his desk.

"The package we have put together is complicated but the only one acceptable to the banks. Unfortunately it will cost you everything," Corrello said. "The Federal Bank has blocked any capital transfer out of the country. Your assets abroad won't raise five billion but our own bank has done a deal with their associate banks in Europe. Jointly they'll deposit the five billion dollars worth of Saudi riyals in Dubai but they'll do this only in exchange for your total assets worldwide. There will be no dollar transaction, only assets. The Federal Bank won't have time or power to interfere."

Wat felt his shoulders sag, not a conscious action but

one in resignation of defeat and sadness. The banks he associated with, all their presidents who had wined and dined him, treated him like a king to gain access to his money, now turned their backs while drawing knives to divide the corpse. "Makes no difference," he said. "My daughter's safety is paramount, all else's irrelevant."

"What about Raider?"

"The money's spent, the plane is proven technology and within twenty-four hours I hand it to the nation. It's theirs."

Corrello shifted uneasily. "Once you sign those papers, you'll have no redress. You'll have nothing."

"I'll have my daughter."

The accountant stared at the floor. "We don't know that. We have no guarantees. This might not work."

"I have no choice. If I meet Qasem's demands, he has no reason to hold or harm her."

"Excuse me," Jake said, taking out a vibrating cell phone before turning away to listen on the incoming call.

"I have to say this straight, Wat," the accountant said finally lifting his eyes. "You have assets of around fifteen billion dollars. The banks are robbing you blind over this. For five billion cash they take your entire empire."

"Give me an alternative?" Wat looked into the man's gaze. "I saw the headless body of my wife on the mortuary slab. I don't wish to see my daughter in the same way. You're a father, Matt. What would you do?"

Corrello sat back in his chair making as if to speak but instead fell silent. Jake folded the mobile and looked to both of them. "We have a positive contact."

"Where?"

"Close to the vicinity of the abduction. Longford's voice was recognised, which confirms my suspicions. She and Henry were the only two with prior knowledge of the bolt-hole. If they've used a house close by, that house must have been secured before the kidnap. Damn bitch, she sure fooled us."

The accountant leaned forward. "Wat, this is fantastic news, we can save everything."

"No sudden risks. We have British specialist on the ground. Let them assess the situation before any action."

"Waiting is not an option, Wat. Get them out, now," Corrello said. "We have a tight schedule over this deal. Collating and placing such a sum of money ready for electronic posting is going to take time. It's possible you may have to sign an irrevocable agreement within the next thirty minutes. By then you could have Juliet safe."

Jake stood and leant both fists on the table. "Navro's there, equipped and ready to move. His boys are good. Why wait on the Brits? Let's hit these bastards now."

"Gentlemen, last time I messed up." Wat paused. "Last time I crossed these people they murdered my wife. We wait."

Jake and Matt Corrello travelled in Wat's private elevator down to their respective floors. "You know I have Wat's full confidence in all matters," Jake said to the accountant. "So give me the absolute bottom line."

"The bank will clean him out, break up the empire and sell off individual assets. They'll make a fortune. It's the end of Wat. And General, it's the end of our employment here."

"Unless we have Sweetpea in thirty minutes."

"One hour most."

"Will you tell me when the bank people enter the building? I think this situation calls for a little unscheduled military action."

Jake returned to the conference room and started to brief his team but within ten minutes Matt Correll phoned. "The bank team is on its way."

Jake input a new number and turned his back on the crowded table, speaking quietly as he moved with the cell phone towards the window. "Navro." He waited for the man's reply. "You ready?"

"Yo."

"Go."

Seb heard the radio bleep in his ear as simultaneously he picked up the distant thump of rotor blades. "Seb," Jody's voice came tight and urgent. "Navro's been ordered in, guns blazing. If you have a plan, execute it now."

"Roger that." Seb pulled down his gas mask and adjusted his throat mike. "All positions, immediate action." He waited for their call sign acknowledgements. "Go." Seb came to his feet in unison with his men, the silhouetted profiles of their gas masks giving an alien appearance. He knew Anderson would be closing from the back, positioning himself in case hostile players tried to escape.

Moving as planned, they approached the cottage from left and right, Seb, Pete and Joe moving under the living room window to position themselves either side of the front door. Seb stuck the charge over the lock using sticky pads and Velcro, then pulled the pin and waited on the eight-second fuse.

The blast blew door and frame half way down the hallway. Seb flicked the safety on his Heckler and went in at a crouch, Joe immediately behind. One player at the end of the passage had been thrown down under pressure from the blast but now started lifting himself in preparation to fire. Seb aimed towards the man's body mass and let loose a rapid burst. The smash of glass and thump of shockwaves caused by flash bangs exploded either side in quick succession trembling the whole building and dropping plaster from the ceilings. Seb was running upstairs amid frantic shouts and screams, all mixed with the clatter of small arms fire and the roaring rattle of a helicopter as it swooped into hover. Throwing open the first bedroom door, he allowed Joe to duck in beside him. Seeing no one, he turned and went immediately for the next target.

"Room clear," Joe shouted, amidst the deafening noise of the helicopter and snatched, chatter of machine gun fire from below.

A woman's voice grew increasingly louder, her frantic screeching a mixture of abuse and orders over the bedlam both inside and out. Then the whole building shivered in a contained implosion. Seb could hear men crashing into the hallway, adding to the noise and chaos. Amidst the smell of cordite and clouds of white plaster dust, they charged through the ground floor and up the stairs.

Joe threw open the second bedroom door and Seb slipped inside, covering first left then right with his Heckler. From below came a prolonged burst of fire then a shout.

"Building clear."

"Room …" Seb stopped his words on seeing the single occupant. Both men lifted their gas masks and lowered their weapons.

"Fucking hell," Joe said, crossing to the bed. Seconds later, Navro and six men burst in on top of them, each trying to shout down the next until they also stopped speechless. Gathering round the bed they stood open-mouthed.

"I hope you guys bought tickets for this show." Lisa looked to each of them.

"Clear the room, gentlemen. I'll look after the lady." Navro pulled a bayonet from his belt kit and handed his Heckler to one of the men. "Get these weapons and the chopper out of here, we don't want no cops on our backs." He turned to Seb and Joe. "Gentlemen, thank you for your help but she's one of our nationals."

"Enough said." Seb nodded to Joe and both left the room.

* * *

Lisa smiled for him. This dream was real. Navro sat on the bed. "Lisa Longford, you should be ashamed, not one single blush."

"I been saving them for you top dog. You going to take advantage of me?"

"Wouldn't be the same unless I had you beat fair with your rump in the air." He began to cut her ties.

Lisa waited until the deafening clatter of the helicopter lifted up and away. "They took Sweetpea. I don't know where."

"We'll find her. Don't like to admit it but these Brits are good. Anyone hurt you? I mean, kind of the way you're tied and all."

"No," she said, feeling the flush on her face and the first sense of shame. When he had her second arm free she sat and zipped up the tracksuit. "The black woman controlled them, she may know where they took Sweetpea."

"She's a dead woman, Lisa. All dead. Kind of difficult to keep 'em alive on account they were shooting." He threw the tracksuit bottoms to her. "Lisa, I have to ask. You crossed the line?"

"What the hell do you mean?"

"There's a warrant for your arrest. Says you collaborated with the terrorists in setting up Juliet's abduction. Says you took a big payoff. There's serious money in one of your accounts."

Lisa felt as if she'd been slapped. For moments she sat in stunned silence. "What the hell is this shit? Who could accuse me of such a thing?" When her legs were free, she remained sitting, clutching the trousers against her stomach. "I can't believe what you say. Who's accusing me?"

Navro bent down and scooped up her knickers, holding them out like some delicate offering in the big ham of his fist. "Jake Hammerton for one."

"That bastard never liked me."

"Get dressed, babe." He pushed the knife blade into the padlock chaining her neck, keeping it carefully away from her skin as he levered.

She heard the distinct tear of metal as it gave under his strength. "I got to sort this out. I got to talk to Wat. He put Juliet into my trust, my care. I love her." Lisa swallowed hard and held the onset of tears. "You honestly think I would harm my baby? My Juliet?"

"No, I believe you. Come on babe cover yourself I got to get you out of here."

Lisa pulled the pants over her feet, hoisting them as she stood. The tracksuit trousers followed. "Who the hell put money in my account?"

"That's for you to answer when the time comes."

"I need to get on the phone to sort this out. Then I got to go looking for Juliet."

"Lisa, till you're in the clear, ain't no one going to listen. Jake told me to kill you. And to save you, I told him I would."

Seb looked at the torn bodies sprawled around the cottage floor and shuddered under the rank stench of exposed entrails. The place appeared like an abattoir and ingrained in him the reality of death, the reality of soldiering, that part of his profession he found impossible to accept. Worse, these scattered bundles of torn flesh were not on some desert floor but in his beloved England, his home.

"Seb," Anderson came into the room behind him. "Just had a message from operation HQ, says they've been instructed to hold Miss Longford for the police."

"No way, she's on our side and the only one who has knowledge of Juliet." He left Anderson in the hall and went upstairs, calling to make his approach known.

"Come in, Seb." Lisa sat at the foot of the bed lacing her shoes, Navro stood beside her.

"We have to shift and fast." Seb looked between them.

212

"The police are coming for you. Someone wants you banged up and out of it."

"You got wheels, Navro?" Lisa asked.

"Not here but close." He held out his hand. "Glad to meet you, Seb. My boss spoke highly of you. Jody Farlow, CIA. She's a girl with muscle you wouldn't believe."

"You're CIA?" Lisa stood and placed hands on her hips. "Why didn't you say?"

"You never asked. But I tell you the situation. The dealing is in New York and Sweetpea is the shuffling ace in a complicated pack. Sooner or later I'll have to report to Jake the raid failed to secure her. That will complicate matters even more. I'm putting off that call. For now we better get out of here." He led them from the room, answering his mobile while clattering down stairs. "Law's coming through the gate," he shouted back.

"Jock," Seb ran out of the house and passed him the Heckler and his remaining ammunition. "Hand this in for me. Don't want any problems with the Colonel. We're disappearing, OK?" He turned to his men. "Listen guys, if anyone asks for Lisa Longford, say you think she's dead, tangled with what's inside. I'll contact later." Seb went back through the hall following Navro and Lisa across the rear garden into the tree line. Leaping bracken and brambles they scrambled downhill towards the river. "Navro," Seb came behind him. "If Jody has muscle, then get her to communicate it. Get the police out of the area and off our backs. Get her to bring pressure on the politicians. If the White House can influence our Home Office then she can at least swing my bosses to our advantage."

Navro continued running, answering over his shoulder. "Got a car coming. If we sneak past the cops I can get you out onto the moors. Jody's looking for an RV point east of here, then we make plans. No way we're going to find Sweetpea by chance but Khalid has to come back online to give instructions. With all these roadblocks, Jody figures they're still somewhere close. So we wait till contact then move in to snatch back if things go wrong. I know we're in England but it's Wat Walsh who's calling the play on this and he'll take no chances."

Still within the tree line they turned along the riverbank and ran in single file to the road. While Seb and Lisa lay hidden, Navro climbed over, resting casually as he spoke over his phone. Listening from his position, Seb heard a dozen cars go by before the crunch of gravel and a throbbing motor indicated one had stopped.

"Seb," Navro spoke over his shoulder. "Go for the trunk. Lisa, curl up in the back foot well, we'll cover you with a sheet." He waited until two more cars had passed. "OK, move it."

Seb leapt the low stonewall the same time as Lisa. A moment later the boot lid closed over his head. From the distance came the low, downward throb of an approaching police helicopter.

CHAPTER 18

General John Chambers and Major Frank Marriot sat in their ground-based flight deck and lifted the grey, elongated shape of Global Raider off the runway, heading for a ceiling of one hundred thousand feet. Inside its bomb bay, fourteen cruise missiles, each with a two kilo-tonne payload and a range of two thousand miles, lay ready for launch at various world targets. Under its flight path, five secondary mission control centres waited for laser lock-on and remote guidance during Raider's passage over their specified zone.

Sitting in Max's old seat, Ed Rawlings typed in a mission code given by the military, then a second from Walsh Avionics. Once the two codes were aligned he had power to assume overall flight control. A second set of codes was automatically sent to Wat Walsh and Jake Hammerton, each capable of replacing the original codes should there be an emergency. Only the presidential code could supersede.

"Whiteman Base, this is Walsh Towers. How do you read? Over."

"Loud and clear, Walsh Towers. Raider still climbing at twenty-eight thousand feet. Fuel at zero, four. It's looking good."

"Midway Island, prepare laser and signal lock-on. Ceiling at forty minutes."

"Roger, Walsh Towers. All systems to go."

Ed Rawlings tried to relax back in his seat. This was the big one, the inaugural flight. This was the final test thousands had worked to achieve. This was also Fireback, revenge for his brothers, for the twin towers, revenge for America. This was stuffing a missile up al-Qaeda's arse. Ed Rawlings did not feel relaxed, he felt anger.

Forty minutes later he listened to General John Chambers at Whiteman Air Base and watched the movement of controls as the pilot adjusted the remote bomber for altitude.

"GR4 level at one, zero, zero. We are hypersonic and ready for blind alley. Initiating stealth glide," Chambers said. "Fuel at seven point seven. We have a saving of three percent. All systems to go. Raider is gliding. OK, my friends, come find us."

Ed grinned nervous satisfaction over Raider's ascent. With a fuel saving of three points, it was enough to extend her glide by a thousand miles. When rogue lock-on came, it would allow valuable seconds to back check coordinates for a missile strike. The area to search would be vast, from Afghanistan to North Africa but somewhere out there, Khalid would be waiting, waiting to die. Ed switched his mike button. "Midway Island, how do you read? Over."

"Midway Island, we copy loud and clear. Ready for lock-on in two hours, six minutes, forty seconds."

"Sit down, Henry." Wat indicated the seat while trying to judge from the man's expression if he held hostility.

"If you're going to fire me, don't bother. Once this situation is resolved, you'll have my resignation."

"You don't get away so easily."

"I'm not trusted, I'm no use to you."

"Wrong. If you want to lift suspicion, you're of great use. You were arrested by the FBI in a situation which has grown bitter. You think you've been treated unjustly, then look at the world from my position. In twenty-four hours I'll have nothing. Maybe, not even my daughter. Raider is eighteen percent over budget, at my cost. I'm told we have a bogey in the woodpile. So I checked. The accountants used Mondec Investigations. They're the world's best for looking into fraud and hidden assets."

"So they pull me out the hat. I haven't even paid off my mortgage."

"Maybe you just haven't collected yet. The situation is

never as it seems. To make money you have to be a cunning, sneaky son of a bitch like me. When people are expecting one thing, you do another. There were two thousand, three hundred sub-contractors working to put Raider together, some with very lucrative deals. Mondec discovered Max Crawley owned seven of those companies. He's creamed off millions."

"Why are you telling me? I'm wondering why I was even called back."

Wat leaned forward on his desk. "Only you and Lisa knew where the bolt-hole was. The finger points at Lisa on account she received a sum of money. But would Qasem rest his whole plan on Lisa's betrayal? When you're playing for five billion dollars, a million pay-off is chicken feed. Lisa would get nearly that in her pension. Qasem wouldn't risk bribery on peanuts. Lisa was set up by someone too careful with money. So unless you prove otherwise, justly or not, you're heading to be main suspect, Henry."

"Why don't you blame Crawley along with it?"

"Because with the money Crawley's making, he wants Raider a success. He wouldn't jeopardise anything. Something's going on, Henry. You want to tell me about it?"

Henry pushed the spectacles on his nose. "Nothing to tell. I'm just doing my job."

"So why are you down in the cellar with a listening station on hostage negotiations?" He watched Henry redden.

"A precaution, you understand?"

"Jake's idea?"

"The station's always been there. I always had the key."

"We currently got the nation's best monitoring every communication in and out of this building. Every cell phone, every landline, they twigged you the instant you switched on. You can go one of two ways, Henry. You can go to the slammer for the rest of your life, or you can extend your listening station to include a few other people. Report to Jake only what I tell you. Report everything else to me."

The New York sun reflected from solar glass panels that helped power Walsh Towers, all placed at great expense to satisfy environmentalists. Wat had never felt so lonely. The five dark-suited bankers who sat opposite reminded him of jackals ready to feed. During their first meeting they had licked and savoured the carcass, now they waited to sink their teeth in. On the desktop lay an array of temporary communications which gave multiple open and closed lines to the outside world. In his mind, love of nation and love of Juliet tore him apart. To capitulate would earn him the anger of his fellow citizens, the alternative was to sacrifice his child. For what? To satisfy Government policy over one terrorist incident? Did the Israelis give up their children so coldly? He sweated, sensing a tremor in his hands which he knew would sound in his voice when he spoke. He thought of his wife, so tragically wasted. And now for a second time they were asking him to repeat the same tragedy with his daughter.

"Thirty seconds, Mr Walsh," the chief technician said over an intercom. "Keep him talking long as possible, that way we narrow the search."

Wat stared at the telephone and remained doing so until it rang at 1300 hours precisely, the ring cutting into silence. Lifting the handset he knew the whole conference room listened to every word.

"Wat Walsh speaking."

"Your daughter is safe and well," Qasem answered.

"I wish to talk with her."

"Presently. You have arranged the requested funds?"

"Yes."

"Then transfer them to the Bank of Dubai account

indicated in our previous transmission. As you have no doubt checked, that account is in your name. Do this immediately. I shall know when the transaction has taken place."

One of the bankers pushed the legal agreement across the desk and Wat signed away fifteen billion dollars of assets. A second banker switched on his mobile and began to speak.

Wat waited a full minute before the man finally closed his phone and spoke.

"Five billion has been transferred from Europe to that account number, Mr Walsh. All exchanged to Saudi riyals but it's still yours, still in your name."

Qasem's voice sounded in the room again. "Should you move the funds other than by my instruction your daughter will die. The gold alarm cord worn around her neck now contains the ingredients of a small, remotely controlled bomb, enough to disintegrate her neck. Do you understand the vulnerability of her position if you move against us?"

"You've made your point, Qasem. Now give me the handover location."

"Ordnance survey, Bodmin, grid reference 71472721. The place is an old mining complex. The point, a lone exposed telegraph pole set on the high embankment of a dismantled rail track. That is where we hand Juliet over. The track runs in a straight line for over a kilometre. To the west, at the furthest end, you may place a representative who must remain in view and stationary until Juliet reaches him. The necklace bomb may then be removed. Juliet will be released onto the track directly east of this point at 0630 GMT precisely. She will walk half a kilometre distance to the pole, there she will wait while the money is transferred. At all times, two marksmen will cover her with .50 high calibre sniper rifles. No need to tell you the effect of such high calibre on a human body. Her head would explode like a melon. I have other men in the area who watch, at no time must any helicopters or service personnel be in the vicinity of a twenty mile radius. Any trickery will mean your daughter's instant death. My followers do not expect to escape. They expect to die. Do you fully understand my instructions? Both you and the others who are no doubt listening."

"We do," Wat answered. "Now let me speak with my daughter."

"Wait." Qasem left him to a series of electronic switching sounds.

When the line reopened, Juliet's voice came uncertain and frightened. "Papa, are you there?"

Wat shuddered, how could anyone possibly think of sacrificing her? "They treating you OK, Sweetpea?"

"I guess so but I'm scared."

"Everything is going to be fine. All the arrangements are made to bring you home. You just do as they say. Come morning, you're going to walk along a track but there'll be someone to meet you the other end."

"Is Lisa OK? They grabbed her too, told me they'd kill her if I didn't play ball."

"Yes, I hear she's fine." Wat closed his eyes.

"Don't blame anyone. It was my fault. I made Lisa and Seb row."

"Don't even bother with it, baby. We're going to get you home."

Before she could answer a female voice interjected. "Enough," it said. The line went dead.

Wat switched off and waited for the phone technician to call.

"Central Paris again," his voice said. We're checking now with French Telecom for the address."

"He won't be there."

"We'll check anyway, sir. There'll be something, even if it's only a relay station."

Wat rose and shook hands with the bankers. Immediately on closing the glass door he called down to

Ed Rawlings. "Where's Raider at 0630 hours GMT?"

"On USS Abraham Lincoln's watch before starting her climb over Saudi."

"That's where he intercepted before. He's not in Paris, he's in the two thousand mile lock-on radius of Lincoln." Wat left for the conference room where he found Jake shuffling his feet. The others looked intimidated. "What's wrong?"

"We hit the cottage, had no choice. The Brits went in so forced us to give backup," Jake said.

"Who the hell gave authority to risk her life?" Wat hammered both fists on the desk feeling the burn of rage on his face. "I've just been talking to these people. Where's Juliet? What happened?"

"Juliet was moved. Lisa's dead, along with the terrorists. She was one of them."

"Then she had information we needed. Why the hell did you kill her?"

"When people are shooting, you shoot back. Come on, Wat, you know the score. You've been under fire. It's my belief Lisa sent a message to fool us. Draw our attention while they hid Juliet somewhere else. If she'd got out alive, she could claim to be a hero; but it went wrong on her. She got what she deserved."

"Damn you, now we're back to square one. Get out of here, all of you." Wat slumped in his seat.

Jake stayed and leant knuckles down on the desk. "I only have Navro's initial reports but we know Juliet was there, and then moved. Why? Because someone told them we were going in. I hate to say this because I put him back online but it has to be Henry." Jake breathed deeply and stood straight. "There's no one else."

"The FBI cleared him."

"Henry was trained by Delta to withstand interrogation. He'd laugh at the FBI. If Crawley passed information, Henry or Lisa would be the perfect conduits to get it out the building, feeding it to Perry or Bernard.

Who would think to search them? Henry, Lisa, Crawley, all conspired together. Crawley will talk, it will all come out."

"My only interest is Juliet. If what you say is true, arresting Henry won't help. Let's continue to feed Qasem information. Let Henry know I'm meeting all demands. Keeping Qasem confident will keep Juliet safe."

"This is Midway Island, we have lock-on and read transfer codes. Raider descending, one, three, zero feet. Thank you Whiteman Air Base, we have the baby in our power and flying blind alley."

"Lincoln, all systems await you." Ed Rawling's voice transmitted to every station.

In the interior of the USS Abraham Lincoln ops room, Jez Baker switched on his mike. "This is Lincoln, ready and waiting. Lock-on calculated at eight hours forty-seven minutes, twenty-two seconds. First target mid Arabian Sea, second target Saudi desert. Walsh Towers to verify target. Ready on contact."

"Target areas fed to computer. OK gentlemen, let Raider have her wings," Rawlings said and finally relaxed in his seat, grinning at his assistants. "Stand down guys, this baby will now fly herself."

CHAPTER 19

"They don't mess about, do they?" Sean Fagan wrinkled his nose at the crumpled, blood-splattered body in the hallway. When he looked into the living room he found the back wall blown out, the floor a tangle of upturned furniture, legs, arms, torsos and gore.

Colonel Fox grimaced and turned away. "Explosives don't leave much to bury."

"Where do you start?" Fagan pressed a handkerchief to his mouth. "It'll take hours to sort out what belongs to whom, male or female."

"Leave it to the police, our job is Longford."

Fox left the house and Fagan followed him back into clean air. No Americans remained but CAT's small team of Special Ops lounged against trees or sat on the ground, weapons and gas masks held in casual disuse.

"Does anyone know the whereabouts of Lieutenant Havic and Lisa Longford?" Fagan asked, seeing each man shake his head in non-committal silence.

"Know anything?" He turned to Anderson.

"There's a woman's body inside," Anderson said. "Plus a lot of scattered white flesh. You want to ID it, you're welcome. Seb went with the Americans."

"Armed?" Fox asked.

"No." Anderson held up the Heckler. "He gave me this. I think the Yanks wanted him in case he has info on the girl."

The BMW travelled fast for thirty minutes, then slowed. Huddled in the trunk Seb guessed from the shudder of the suspension they had turned onto an unmade road, lurching round hairpin bends, continually heading for higher ground. Inside the confined space the air grew hot and humid, sticking the shirt to his back with sweat. He shifted his belt kit still worn from the raid, easing the ammo pouch to dig less painfully against his side.

Occasionally the drawl of American voices drifted through the rear seat, then Lisa's in a one sided conversation. She spoke of clothes size, footwear and equipment, probably over a mobile. Forty minutes later the car stopped and the boot was opened.

"Sorry about the delay," Navro said. "But we had to bypass a couple of police roadblocks."

"Where are we?" Seb asked, clambering out into bleak and hilly countryside. On higher ground the hot, sultry day had grown heavy with humidity and the threat of thunder.

"Bodmin Moor. The road onwards becomes a dead end. If by chance you're seen you can pass as moorland hikers, no one should give you a problem. It's a good place to hide. If the red car I followed held Sweetpea they came in this direction. They're here somewhere, within ten, fifteen miles. I just don't see how they could have moved further with so much police activity." He indicated the landscape then checked his watch. "Jody should be here any minute, she'll have your equipment."

"To hold a prisoner they'll need cover," Seb said. "I've been here before. Getting round on foot takes time and fitness. On top of that, they'll get wet." He looked to the sky, then the road as Jody's Range Rover came over the brow and stopped behind the BMW.

"Hi you guys," she said, going immediately to kiss Lisa's cheek. "Welcome back, hun. Sorry you got such a rough ride."

"You Americans seem one big happy club." Seb looked between them.

"From long back, army days." Jody smiled, her hand sliding from Lisa's waist to open the rear door of her car. She hauled out two Bergens. "You got clothes in there, hun." She passed one to Lisa. "Hiking boots and some food. Seb, yours is a two-man bivouac, torch, maps, ammo and a whole heap of other gear I thought you might need."

"Ammo?" Seb repeated the one item, realising for the first time they placed him outside his Government's authority.

"We guess there were seven players," Jody said. "Three down, four to go. From what I've seen, they won't mess. They'll kill. You need weapons." She lifted a blanket from the floor of the vehicle to reveal a small arsenal of Heckler SMGs plus two M16s with telescopic sights. "Best I could do at short notice. And I tell you now, these firearms are kind of illegal. But with the co-operation currently going on between the two governments and all security services, when the war's over and the flags are waving, ain't no one going to ask too many questions." She handed a Heckler to Lisa and another to Seb. "The way I see it, you guys will be in the frontline. I'm sorry to say, Seb, your own boys are stood down."

Seb shrugged. "They would have no choice."

She smiled for him but not quite the same open, inviting smile she had given in New York. "Makes you one of us now, so listen in. Communications," she said, showing a small UHF belt pack radio with hands free mike. She flicked the control switch as she explained. "You have two channels. First channel is general communication, open to operations HQ and relayed to both sides of the Atlantic. Channel two is for communication strictly between ourselves, excluding everyone else. Stay on channel two unless told otherwise, particularly you Lisa. You're supposed to be dead. And none of you can disobey direct orders to pull out if you ain't been given any. Understand my meaning, Seb?"

"So when's the call?" Navro asked.

"GR4 is flying. It's my belief Khalid wants more than five billion dollars for Juliet. He wants that drone. How or for what, I don't know. But we got to be right there on the ground to deal with it. That smart arse Arab is playing poker with us, Juliet against billions of dollars and Raider. Except the White House won't give in. We're Juliet's only hope."

"Any info on possible location?" Seb asked.

Jody shrugged. "Brit cops got a circle of roadblocks on all routes out of here plus patrols all over. Between taking Juliet and the raid, the abductors didn't have time to clear from the area. They're somewhere close." She reached into the glove compartment of the Range Rover and produced an ordnance survey map which she spread on the bonnet.

"We're here." Navro stabbed a large, blunt finger. "Going to station a car over on the A30, Bolventor, another at Bodmin and the last out at Lewannic, where I'll be. That way we have a patrol at all points. The chopper we put on standby."

"Where do I go?" Seb asked.

"You stay hidden with Lisa a mile or so off road. You're centre action. When the call comes, you move across country. If you're too far, the chopper will drop you closer or one of the cars will collect."

"OK, you guys." Jody checked her watch. "The time is now 1928 hours. Co-ordinate watches. Operation commences 1930. We have around two hours till nightfall. Leave one radio on for each patrol. I reckon this baby will blow in about eight hours so be ready to move around dawn."

"Why then?" Seb asked.

"Because Raider will be somewhere over Arab country and at her most vulnerable. Could be the bastard wants to shoot it down. OK, let's split."

Lisa lifted her Bergen and started off up the track as the cars turned round. Seb followed, his shirt soaked with sweat in the close, humid evening, a Bergen on his back, a Heckler hooked over one shoulder. Four steps ahead, Lisa unzipped her top and looked determined to stay in front. Every five minutes Seb glanced at the ordnance survey map and occasionally took a reading on his compass. They had left the road two miles behind, moved down into a valley and crossed a stream before climbing up the other side. As they reached higher ground it started to level with good places to lie up.

"Bear slightly to your left," he called to her. "Away from the flat ground and reeds, towards the hillock."

"Isn't that ridge exposed? We'd be on our bellies or seen."

"The whole moor's exposed and the more we look like walkers, the less notice people will take."

"I say we go round the ridge."

"This is sovereign territory, I'm in charge."

"Lieutenant Havic." She turned to him, hoisting her Bergen, uncaring about her expanse of exposed cleavage. "I'll have you know I made major in the US Marines. I outrank you. Also, this is a covert mission under control of the CIA, with British Government sanction. We go round the hill."

Seb shrugged. "Please yourself. You find a place to bivvy on the other side, away from reeds. I'll go to the top and scan for search parties."

"You're crazy. You think anyone would search for us out here?"

"The Army would." He walked over the rough moorland heather towards the hillock, slowing as the ground began to rise. Beneath him, Lisa started her first perilous steps through marshy bog, accumulated where water had shed and gathered to grow clusters of reeds. He grinned when she changed direction and looked away when she was forced to climb for higher ground amongst a swarm of midges. Below the summit he lay prone and used field glasses to peer over the hilltops to the far moor. He saw no living creature save for sheep. To his right, at three miles distance, the village of Minions showed rooftops tucked between trees. All else was barren. He orientated the map and took a back bearing on several prominent hills to mark his precise location. Even when darkness came he was now confident of finding his way. On the far horizon, dark clouds pressed the ground, shimmering the occasional flicker of lightning over a fading day. The steep, undulating hillsides would not be the easiest ground to cover in darkness but on the upside, he figured dawn would break around 0400 hours. Before then they needed to check their weapons, eat and maybe sleep. He grinned and moved down to the site Lisa had chosen to camp.

She had opened her Bergen and was sorting through the clothes which Jody had provided, laying them on a sleeping mat beside her Heckler. Her face looked red and bitten.

"I tell you one thing, Lieutenant. It's bleak up here but it sure is beautiful."

"Not for long. In half an hour it will be dark and before that, very wet." He opened his own Bergen to remove the bivouac, pulling it from its pack and rolling it out. He began to slot small aluminium poles to lift the latest in storm-proof material. Jody had spared no money, the tiny tent was a miracle of survival technology. He shuffled over the lining sheet and secured the back before sliding out to fasten the outer ties, spreading the front so it gaped a metre wide.

"Regular home from home," Lisa said, pushing her Bergen and other belongings inside.

While she bustled around on her knees pressing the grass tufts beneath the ground sheet, Seb spread out the canopy to give a small area for storage outside. Lisa switched on a torch and seconds later her shoes were placed by the door.

"No room service, and they'll get wet," Seb told her.

"I got new boots, best money and the CIA could buy."

"I suppose you're CIA too," he said, coming round to the front.

"No. I'm Major Lisa Longford, ex US Marine, ex Navy

228

Seals, ex … " Her words stopped as he made to crawl through the opening. In her hands she held a pair

of black, elasticated knickers taken from the cluster of new clothes. She stretched the waistband between fingers. "You don't come into a lady's bedroom, Mr, unless invited." She let go the elastic and drew up the bivvy zip.

Seb knelt in the gathering dusk, the air had grown moist and the temperature was dropping rapidly. "Bitch," he whispered and knelt back on his haunches. "Lisa, I'm going to get wet."

"I thought you were a tough guy, SAS," she said. He could hear her struggling inside as she removed clothes.

"Getting wet is not being tough. It's being wet. Soldiers fight better when dry." The first roll of thunder came out between clouds and from the east, a grey sheet of rain walled the sky.

"You knew there'd be bog on that side of the hill, ain't that so?" she said between the sounds of rustling clothes.

"It was a natural watershed. Why do you think I wanted to pass on higher ground?"

"And all those mosquito flies, you knew they'd be there too? You knew I'd get bitten."

"Mozzies and water go together."

The second roll of thunder drew over the hill. Seb felt the first stir of wind and looked to place the Heckler inside his Bergen, pulling out a light storm jacket provided by Jody.

"For Christ's sake," he protested. "I'm not going to try anything if that's what you're worried about."

"Pity, cause if you did, I'd snap it off."

He listened to her struggle with clothes again and watched the contortions of her shadow between torch and tent.

"Have it your way then," he said. "I'll kip further up the hill."

Lisa unzipped the bivvy, allowing a waft of perfume from under the canopy.

"Come on in, soldier. Just make sure you don't put your mucky hands on my nice clean clothes."

Seb crawled head first under the awning, jamming his Bergen into the storage cover before sitting with feet over the ground flap to unlace his boots. When he turned, Lisa laid Roman-style. She had removed the tracksuit and put on new underwear with a vest over the top. Her new trousers and shirt remained neatly folded beside her boots.

"Most becoming." He smiled appreciation.

"Jody knows what a woman wants." She put down the perfume spray. "And I sleep better this way. In the field, US Marines bunk together, no problem."

Seb zipped up the opening and shuffled round to lie stretched beside her. In the light of the torch she put sandwiches and soft drinks provided by Jody at the head of the bivvy. Lightning flashed its jagged arm into the valley below and the first huge drops of rain began to fall with the thump of marbles. Slowly at first, then with torrential violence, they beat mercilessly on the man-made haven.

"I hope this thing's waterproof." Seb twisted to unclip his belt pack.

"Cosy," she said. "Our first meal together."

"But hopefully not our last."

"You like me that much, after all the yelling I've done?" She bit into a sandwich.

"Not your fault," he said, hoping for genuine reconciliation. "You must have been worried but I was never given a choice. What do you do if your girl strips off naked and goes for a swim?"

"Watch."

"I did."

"You liked what you saw?"

Seb picked up a beef sandwich. "Very much."

"Did you make love to her, or did she start?"

The flush to his face came unexpectedly. "Don't think I should tell you," he said, raising his voice against the storm. One side of the tent had indented with the weight of wind and water, forcing him to turn on his side, his legs against hers.

"She told me you did," Lisa said, her eyebrows raised. "Told me you were real cute. Saving her from the sea and all, she felt obliged."

He bit on the sandwich, suddenly annoyed, chewing and swallowing before he spoke again. "She had no obligation, it was my job."

When he looked at her again, she was picking at the bread, her expression distant, lips pursed. He knew then she had tricked him. "Don't be jealous," he said. "Naked man and woman clinging for warmth. What do you expect?"

"Why would I be jealous?"

Seb felt the flush deepen. She was staring at him, still picking at the bread, her dark eyes unmoving. "I thought you had a sort of, relationship," he said. She smiled then quite openly, sweetly, he thought.

"Sure we do. She's my baby. I've been looking out for her eight years. She's got no momma. You get to be close. Close as two women can be. Navro's my baby too. But in a different way."

"You mean you're not …?"

"Not what?"

Her gaze remained locked to his and he wondered how far she was deliberately baiting him. He was conscious of her effect, the smell of her perfume, the close proximity and charge of her body.

"Navro seems a good guy," he said, looking for escape. He took a large bite of his sandwich and lay prone.

"Just a little pussy cat I play with. Tell me," she said. "Do you think it's unnatural for two women to make love?"

"Well, no." He turned to her. "How can any love be unnatural? I suppose it depends on just what you do."

"You trying to qualify what's unnatural?" The rain

231

ceased suddenly, leaving silence between them.

"No, I'm just Confused of the SAS. Jody said women could make love to each other and go home, love and sleep with their husbands."

"We're a very adaptable species."

"You're bi-sexual," he said. "You like both men and women?" He helped himself to another sandwich.

"Sure but I only love one."

Seb twisted to face her, his forearm cushioning the side of his head. He was able to look down at her legs and her slim muscular thighs. "I don't understand." He glanced up briefly; she had that open smile again. Once more he was uncertain what to believe.

"Men seldom do. Not even when they grow up, if ever."

"You have a nice smile," he said, feeling himself seriously harden.

"Eat your sandwich, Rupert and take your eyes off my panties. It's against regulations to fraternise with a senior officer."

"Boy, poor Navro." Seb looked upwards.

"You'd be surprised." She laughed and pulled over her belt radio, switching to channel two and closed circuit. "Time to call base," she said, holding the mike and earpiece close. "Come in momma, this is Lisa. Do you copy?" She repeated the question three times before Jody's voice came back, filling the tiny bivouac. Lisa adjusted the volume.

"I copy. You wet out there?"

"Snug as peas in a pod."

"Be ready to move 0445 hours."

"That's dawn." Seb volunteered the information.

"All patrols are in position. Roger and out."

Lisa placed the radio by her head and switched it to listen only. "There we go, Sebastian. Now we got nothing to do but lie here and maybe sleep."

"I fancy Jody," Seb said to dig back at her.

"Me too. Ever since we were in training together."

"I don't believe it."

"It's a great pity boys can't be like girls, then maybe we could snuggle up. Goodnight, Sebastian." She switched off the torch.

"Confused of the SAS. I'm going to write to the Times."

"I'd try Cosmopolitan."

In the darkness he could sense her smile.

CHAPTER 20

Jody's voice came loud and clear through the darkness of the bivouac. "All units, New York has negotiated a handover. We finally have a location."

In the confined space, Seb remained where sleep had rolled them, his hand on her thigh, her buttocks tucked into his stomach, his head against her shoulders. For an instant he had the pleasure of her body, her soft skin, her warm limbs and fragrance. In the next second she had sprung away as if stung.

Lisa switched the radio and snapped on a torch. "Jody I read you." Seb reached for a map and marker pen.

"Across country, you're the closest. This is a taped transmission. All units listen in and copy."

Over the turned up volume of Lisa's ear set, Seb listened to the recording between Wat, Qasem and Juliet. He marked the reference on the Perspex covering of his map and began plotting the location.

"About four miles, an old mine area," he said when the transmission stopped. "But it's across hill and valley, not easy."

"An hour?" Lisa suggested, pulling on her new camouflage trousers.

"Still twenty minutes to dawn, there's cloud over the moon." He looked for his boots. "Darkness will slow us. We have to go down valley, cross a stream and up the other side. Only half a mile but it could take thirty minutes." He placed the map between them, shining the torch to trace a line with his finger. "Then if we stick to high ground we should make good time but we still have to go back into a valley to traverse this farm, then up again to the mine works."

"Why not through the farm?" She twisted over, kneeling in contortion to put on her shirt.

"Dogs. They'll bark. That close to the location the sound will carry. The opposition might realise why. We could screw the whole thing. Better to go round. If we really push, you're looking ETA 0615 hours. Then we got to recce and take positions." He began to tie his boots. "Hope you can run, lady."

"Mr, I was a marine. You'll be following my footsteps."

"You want a bet?"

"Top dog."

"What's that?"

She ceased tucking in her shirt and touched his face. "I look forward to teaching you."

"Navro," Jody called over her radio's close circuit transmission. "Lisa will be coming in from the east and can look after Candy Girl. You take west side which gives higher ground to locate snipers. Bodmin, Bolventor patrols, you got the MI6s. Advance over the hill from the south and take out any gunmen giving long-range cover over the track. Seb, you want the man holding the remote detonator, probably chief player, a guy named Jaber. Also link with Navro in case you can take snipers at close quarters. No firing without my say so, use knives if possible. Get ready to roll, copy."

She listened to each unit answer her instruction. Lisa came last. "Copy and out," she replied and clicked off.

Navro came back. "Don't want blue on blue, Jody. What's your position?"

"Why Navro, I'm the lucky girl, I've been nominated to receive Candy Girl from the enemy. It's agreed no one but ourselves will move in until she's safe. Once the necklace is off, we duck, then you guys have free fire. Till that time I'm standing at the end of the track ready to get popped should anything go wrong. Prepare to depart." Jody switched off.

In the Range Rover she watched first light crack through darkness over the grey, sodden moor. With the silver sheen of dawn came the pump of her adrenaline and realisation this could be the last day of her life. When a teenaged marine she had squeaked past formalities to join Desert Storm. As a CIA agent she had worked covertly in Colombia, Iraq and Afghanistan but she had never stood on a firing range under aim from a high calibre rifle while a human bomb walked towards her. She had no illusions over the enemy's ruthlessness. The prize money would change hands electronically thousands of miles away. The ground players would then be left to dish death, to escape or die with belief of right on both sides. From Lisa's briefing, she knew the opposition were young and fanatical, led by a mature man with calm dedication. If they were killed, Allah would welcome them to heaven. If they were captured, they would have the world stage to shout political propaganda. Their total disregard for life gave an advantage only equalled by an opponent's fearless dedication. Jody just prayed she had enough to see her through. It was Juliet she felt most sorry for. She was too young with little understanding of what might happen to her.

Once the money went over, the chance of her survival was small. Jody did not believe the opposition had honour. They would blow that bomb to create a diversion. She just wondered if anyone would remember her own mission, to remove it from Juliet's neck. She cradled her handset back amongst the mass of signalling equipment crammed in the Range Rover, equipment capable of receiving, boosting and relaying her communications worldwide. Calm and resolute, she fitted a UHF radio to her belt, clipped the mike to a button on her shirt and a receiver plug to her ear. Her appearance came next. She had no intention of dying while looking a mess. She turned the interior mirror, combed her hair then renewed her lipstick before spraying perfume into the neck and wrists of her combat jacket. "OK," she reassured herself, then clicked on her UHF. "All units, this is momma. Let's roll." She started the engine.

"Roger that." Seb's clear-cut English came to her ear. "ETA one hour twenty minutes."

"Roger that!" Navro's voice came back in mimic. "Why baby, I'll roger that. Whizzo chaps, chocks away."

Jody grinned, allowing his voice to ease some of her tension. "No lights within two miles of target," she said. "And watch out for sheep and locals."

"Bodmin, roger that and rolling."

"Bolventor, roger that and rolling."

She listened to the droll tones of Navro's boys over her earpiece, hands spread on her lap beneath a small reading lamp. She felt annoyed her pearl pink nail polish was chipped on one finger.

Seb switched his belt radio to receive only and watched Lisa do the same. Once dawn had broken and found them on high ground, he felt happy for her to take lead position, providing she kept direction and pace. He had little doubt she would streak ahead in a road marathon but in cross-country her footing was uncertain and her stride without rhythm. Tucked three paces behind he watched the sway of her hips and the slight jiggle of her backside under tight combat trousers. In any condition, he thought, the basic instinct of women to attract would never change. With the rising sun and warmth, ground mist began creeping over fields and moorland and with the incline of descent into the next valley, visibility closed to twenty metres. He judged the farm they had circled to avoid any dogs lay around five hundred metres south, which left one more track to cross before they descended north of Minions village. Ahead lay a stone boundary wall and farm track indicating the start of cultivated fields. Lisa began to slow on approach. Seb vaulted the wall with one hand, his SMG in the other. He had covered ten paces before he looked back. She remained on the opposite side, red faced and panting, seeking toeholds in an attempt to climb.

"Here, give me your Heckler." He retraced his steps and offered his hand. The look he received would have stopped the entire SAS Regiment. She hitched the weapon to her back and seconds later stood beside him.

"OK, Lieutenant. You're best on uneven terrain, you lead. My turn to ogle your cute little butt."

Seb smiled. "My pleasure."

He checked for bearing on his compass and started downhill in a controlled loping stride, the Heckler held out for balance. He figured their ETA now went forward to 0600 hours. If Lisa could maintain pace ascending the opposite side of the valley, they would have both mist and time to take position amongst the old mine works that covered the viewable area of the far hill. If not, they would have to go belly down and that would cost time.

Juliet lay curled up on the ground in an embryonic position, her wrists handcuffed, her ankles hobbled. Twenty metres to her front, dawn silhouetted a man standing guard at the mineshaft entrance, sometimes there, sometimes disappearing, a shadow merging into semi-darkness as he paced back and forth.

Last night she had been guarded by four of them. Jaber, who now sat with a torch reading from a small leather book, had overseen all activities. The girl who paraded as a policewoman and a young man, Juliet guessed in his late twenties, had listened to Jaber with careful attention. Then in hushed whispers they had talked to each other while dismantling, cleaning and reassembling two large, high-power rifles. Occasionally they looked to her, the girl with standoff pity, the boy with contempt. From their conversation she learnt one was Amin, the girl Lena.

Sitting with her back against a rock, Juliet had drawn her legs to her body while lightning flashed over the hills and rain beat the ground outside. Across the tunnel they had parked the red Peugeot behind the white van used in her abduction. Occasionally they went to the back for food, blankets or equipment. By watching their activities, coupled with their off-hand disregard of her presence, her sense of dejection became that of some unworldly alien, a person held in prejudice by colour, creed and nationality. She felt utterly alone, without recognition even as a human being.

While rain fell in darkness outside, Jaber had set up lamps and torches and finally a small mobile generator with two floodlights on tripods. These he shone into the long, cavernous interior of the shaft, the light unable to reach the far, unfathomable depth stretching beneath the hill.

Amidst much laughter from Lena, Amin had fetched two footballs, then with a marker pen, drew a face on each, the eyes large and female, the lashes long and curled. With one in each hand he counted his steps into the far subterranean distance and placed both footballs so they appeared no more than tiny dots. He had sung on the way back, a moaning wail of some indeterminable Arab pop song. Juliet sat watching without comprehension, at least until Amin and Lena fitted ear protectors and lay behind their rifles. The barrels supported on tripods, they looked through integrated sighting systems aiming at the two balls. As the storm crackled over moor and hill, they fired one after the other, each time adjusting their sights, each time filling the cavern with a vibrant shock of contained explosion which spat fire into darkness. Each time Juliet shuddered. On the fourth shot, Lena leaped to her feet clapping and shouting. It required two more rounds from Amin before he achieved the same. Punching the air with his fist, he shouted, "Zero, zero" and ran into the cavern, returning to hand Lena a shred of leather ball. He brought his own to Juliet and knelt before her. The ball was punched and split in half, the outline of one eye still visible at the edge.

"Pop, pop." He tapped the side of her head with a finger.

Juliet shivered not wanting the implication of his meaning. She sensed her mind in turmoil. She didn't want to die, didn't want her head blown apart. Never in any dry run exercise thought up by Jake had anyone made to blow her head off. Her mother had been primitively decapitated by these people. Was this their high-tech version of the same thing? She felt her eyes brim and felt the start of silent tears. Lena also came to kneel before her, embracing the long and heavy rifle, the butt on the ground, the breech on her chest and barrel to her cheek as if she cradled a standing child.

"What you crying for? You're a rich black girl. You have everything. I have nothing. My family were killed by Americans who gave planes and bombs to the Jews. My home was bombed, my mother and father killed. My brothers killed, my sister killed. Why are you crying rich girl? You life was easy while your father made planes to kill my people. I hope I have to kill you rich girl. I want to kill you." The girl lifted Juliet's chin and spat into her face.

Juliet's tears ceased immediately. "I pity you," she said.

When the girl made to slap her, Jaber called. "Enough! We have work." He killed the floodlights and generator, leaving illumination only from the battery operated lamps.

Juliet withdrew, pressing herself against the rock, lifting her cuffed wrists to wipe spittle with a forearm. Amin and Lena crossed to the van where each wrapped their rifle in a blanket before carefully laying them side by side. Jaber spoke in Arabic and handed Juliet's gold alarm pull to Amin who then busied himself dragging a wooden toolbox from the van before placing it on the blanket which Lena had spread over the ground. Sitting cross-legged, she watched Amin remove the electrical innards from the pendant and replace them with items from the box, tiny cylindrical plugs with wires sunk into plastic compounds that in turn were pressed into the pendant. Lena continually questioned with the eagerness of a high school girl trying to impress her senior, waiting on his answers, leaning her body towards him.

At the far reaches of light, Juliet watched Jaber come towards her, kneel and place a handkerchief in her hand, then as if in consolation, a bar of chocolate. Juliet felt numb, unable to speak.

"Do not be afraid. If you do as you are told, if your father does as he is told, you won't die. These two young people do not understand your fear. Death to them is inevitable and will take away their hell on earth. Their families are dead, their lives bitter and destroyed; they welcome death. But you have known love and comfort. You want to live, so you have fear. To overcome that fear think bravely. You have defiance and the will to continue. Good qualities but you also need intelligence and control. Obey, Juliet and one day you will have a loving husband and children. Do not throw your life away, obey."

Juliet spat in retaliation. "You murdered my mother, you're animals. You make your lives an excuse to inflict your own bitterness and misery on others. I despise you."

Jaber took back the handkerchief and wiped his face. "Control, Juliet. Now eat your chocolate."

She did so for strength, for the creep of hunger and her resolve to remain above her jailers. After hours, when darkness obliterated the shaft entrance and the others stretched silently in sleeping bags, she shifted her aching body and lay prone on the blanket, eventually drifting between nightmares, anguish and sleep. She thought of her father, of Lisa. Both in their different ways wanting their love to possess her. She conjured up memories of her mother and wondered how that loving person had faced her own death. For her mother's memory she was determined to retain her dignity. She was black, she was pretty, she was clever and at this moment, her own woman. She was alone, as last night she had been alone in the sea. She thought of Seb, of his body, of his lovemaking. She wondered if he searched for her. She wanted to return his kindness and give him love. She wanted to share her feelings with him, touch him.

"You wake up." The Chechnyan shook her and threw a chocolate bar on the blanket. She lay watching while he walked back to the mine entrance, disappearing into a sheet of brilliant sunlight. Beyond she saw moorland and fields, the lower ground layered in a white, curling mist which shrouded the valley below. Jaber was alone, reading by torchlight.

"I need to pee," she said aloud.

Jaber looked up. "Go ahead." He returned to his book, uninterested.

Juliet knelt, pushing from knees to feet, the hobble allowing her only a twelve-inch step. Hands before her, she shuffled back into the mine and the borders of darkness. Close to the wall, she struggled to pull down the tracksuit before crouching to relieve herself. All the time she watched him; all the time her fingers worked at the knots binding her ankles; but the rope remained firm, unmoveable.

"They are sealed with super glue," Jaber said and glanced towards her. "You'd better come back and eat your breakfast."

Juliet rose and struggled to hitch up her pants, her hands and arms straining round each side of her body until the elastic slipped over her backside. Returning to the light she stood before him. "What's going to happen?" she asked. Again he glanced from the huddled refuge of his book, then briefly checked his watch.

"In thirty minutes you are going home," he said. "Myself and the others are going to die."

* * *

The mist held chill enough to cool Seb's soaking shirt. Twice the visibility dropped below twenty metres as they moved to lower ground and followed the curve of a track. To their right, the target hill rose steeply, peaking at three hundred and seventy feet. The surrounding ground was terraced and pock marked with the debris of excavations and slagheaps. When he glanced behind, Lisa had fallen back by fifteen paces, her eyes to the ground, her Heckler SMG held in both hands, her face red, the front of her shirt dark with sweat. The set expression on her face showed she had gone into mind lock, ignoring the exhaustion that gripped her body. She appeared determined and to Seb that was good but she also needed to be agile and mentally alert. She needed to look out for Juliet while he went after snipers. For the second time in five minutes he checked his map, placing them in dead reckoning a hundred metres west and two hundred feet below the grid reference given by Jody. His watch read 0558 hours when he switched his radio to speak. "Seb to momma, ETA ten minutes."

"Roger that," Jody answered. "All units report."

"Navro, have left the car and approaching over ground from east. Have good mist cover. ETA eleven minutes."

"Bolventor, now leaving the road south west side, ETA fifteen minutes."

"Bodmin, approaching hill and heading north, ETA fourteen minutes."

"All units, roger that. Momma ready to walk."

Seb left the track and cut across a stream before starting to climb, checking briefly that Lisa followed. She had removed her combat jacket and thrown it away. Seb knew to jettison kit was an act of desperation. He stopped to take a protracted orientation of their position, deliberately allowing her time to catch up.

"We're about a hundred metres downhill from the grid reference," he said as she huffed beside him. "When we reach the start of mine workings, I suggest we set up an OP and decide our plan of operation."

She was panting, head down, hands on knees. She nodded her sweat plastered head, then looked up at him. "Agreed," she said. "But I'm going in for Juliet. When we've decided ground location, I'll take a position on the track. You go and look for players."

"Fine." He pushed the map into his leg pocket. "You about to tell me what top dog is?"

She grinned. "Never, Mr. You might just win. Let's go." She started up the hill, leaving him to follow.

Above the Indian Ocean, Raider's course was altered by Midway Island, turning the craft over the Arabian Sea towards the carrier USS Abraham Lincoln. Seconds later Midway's flight director spoke over Commander Baker's headphones. "Lincoln, prepare to accept control. Count down beginning at ten. Watch your clock."

"Midway, this is Lincoln. We are ready for lock-on, all systems at go, signal strength, pulse one. Counting with you, four, three, two, one, zero. Midway Island, the bird is ours. Blind alley at eight, zero K. I repeat, eighty thousand feet."

"Lincoln, Midway relinquishes control. You're minding the baby, good luck."

Commander Baker watched the disappearance of Midway Island's laser beam which had bounced by satellite from Central Pacific. Only his own laser now defined and followed the drone's position. Via digital umbilical cord from New York, Lincoln was now hands-on with mission control, ready for their orders to guide Raider through the most testing time of the mission. In his own mind, this was the greatest challenge of his career. It also had the potential to become his greatest nightmare; a hostile lock-on at low altitude. Without the advanced, long-range control and radar equipment developed with Raider's programme, he knew such a probability was remote but chance was always possible and chance had a habit of screwing things up, an Oman ground station had demonstrated that. He made minute adjustments to Raider's flight path and reprogrammed her degree of descent to remain above sixty thousand feet, the maximum strike altitude for most advanced ground to air missiles. When she finally came out of blind alley and headed over Oman towards Saudi, her low level flight and missile deployment tests would take eight minutes; eight minutes in which she would drop progressively lower, eight minutes in which she sat on a duck shoot and relied on stealth. It would be the longest eight minutes of his life.

Cocooned in semi-darkness and the intensity of his own concentration, Baker found sanctuary from the military brass who clustered in the observation window above and behind him. He had never cared for an admiral looking over his shoulder, even less be-medalled and gold-braided members of the Pentagon. On either side, illuminated by an array of instrument lights, his team watched over individual computers and consoles, each man dedicated to his task; each man as anxious as the next. In his mind Baker was clear, precise and zeroed. He had given years of his life to this mission and this was his world moment.

"Lincoln to Walsh Towers, all systems stable. Raider's descent set at minimal, defence shields at lock, anti-missile systems to standby. All other systems as normal. Speed to subsonic. We have a silent run."

"Thank you, Lincoln." Ed Rawlings' voice sounded over fifty headphones and the ops room speakers. "Fuel at fifty three percent and looking good."

"Raider at 60K in one hour, thirty minutes precisely." Baker came back on air. "Activating run-up for test procedures and missile deployment. Arming missiles."

"Test procedures commence. Walsh Towers to standby for instant ascent on hostile engagement."

"Raider at seven, nine, five and falling. Anti-missile now to code red." Jez Baker looked to each side of him, to the rows of men and women, their silhouettes hunched over screens as they searched and waited for possible missile attack. "Blind alley ends in one hour, twenty-two minutes precisely."

Wat was surprised at the willpower which coursed his body. He had no wealth, no possessions. For the first time since commencing his business, he was a free man; free to fight for his child, free to search out the enemy within. Free to act without political or commercial restraint.

He did not call Henry because he did not trust any who maybe listening. Instead he went to see the man at his lone post in the building's old communications centre. Henry did not look happy.

"The phone call traced to Paris. Does Jake have a man investigating?" Wat asked him.

"It's an apartment on the Boulevard St Michel, real fancy," Henry said. "The French police have been kind of slow in getting entry on account it's rented by some Saudi prince. Jake's had our own man there, asked a few questions of the caretaker. Except for a cleaning firm, no one been near for a year. I have a techie on location who used to work for the phone company. He has the very latest for tapping and tracing calls. Jake said wait for the police."

"Jake, waiting!"

Henry looked at him, then looked away.

"Get your man to put a line in there, now. I want to know where Qasem's call originated." Wat kept his gaze on Henry and watched the man push glasses up on his nose. "And, don't tell Jake," Wat said. "I want this line strictly between us two and the techie."

"Yes, sir."

"Anything else going?"

"Nothing that hasn't been through channels. A few calls re Crawley. The guy's blowing steam; denies he conspired in a breach of security. His lawyers are working overtime to get him back into the building and in control of Raider. Seems there ain't no proof Crawley did anything. But Jake still ain't having it."

Wat nodded and stood up from his chair. "Keep me informed, Henry. It's your only means of salvation."

Ten minutes later, Wat was on the seventh floor entering the indoor shooting range used by security and members of the company pistol club. In a small outer office the duty guard stood from his desk while hurriedly pushing a girlie magazine from sight. "Mr Walsh, sir." He saluted.

"Hemming, is it not?"

"Hemming is my name, sir." The guard remained at attention.

"Stand easy, Hemming. I've come to collect one of my automatics. Due to the current situation, I'd feel happier with a side arm."

"Yes sir. Shall I assist, sir?" The guard unlocked the armoury door. "All weapons for security are loaded, sir. All sporting weapons are empty."

"I know and I can find my own way, thank you." Wat entered the inner armoury and closed the door.

Inside, racks of heavily bolted firearms lined the walls, weapons that predominantly used 9mm rounds. Selecting a key from his chain, Wat unlocked his personal gun cupboard and looked over the assortment of sporting and military pistols. He chose a favoured Colt 45 automatic from his service days, plus a compact SIG- Sauer P228 with safety cock and lock mechanism. To his surprise and concern, all 45 and 9mm rounds which he had left in the cupboard had been removed. Such a small but now significant detail only increased his sense of unease and suspicion. For moments he was flummoxed, then on inspiration, slipped a magazine from one of the house security's Walthers P88s. Thirteen of its fifteen 9mm rounds went to fill his own SIG-automatic. He returned all magazines, cocked a round into the breech of the SIG, then tucked it to the back of his belt concealed beneath his jacket. When the cupboard was re-locked, he snapped the key to jam the mechanism and carried the Colt to the outer office.

"I appear to have used all my ammunition." He placed the Colt on Hemming's desk. "Could you find some 45 shells and deliver the pistol personally to my office?"

"Yes sir, immediately, sir. Will seven rounds be enough, sir, or do you wish for spare, sir?" Hemming had stood back to attention.

"If I'm confronted by some crazed terrorist, I reckon seven slugs from a 45 will calm him sufficiently. And keep this to yourself, Hemming or half my execs will be down looking to arm themselves."

"Yes sir. Do you wish to sign the release book, sir?" With spread fingers he twisted the armoury record book towards Wat. "Just for one weapon, sir, Colt 45 and seven rounds, sir."

Wat signed. "That is correct."

Wat returned to his office, the SIG automatic concealed beneath his jacket. He waited fifteen minutes for delivery of the Colt. Weighing it in the palm of his hand, he knew it was loaded, but he was now so wracked by mistrust of everyone around him, he unclipped the magazine and looked inside. The cartridges were there, but the rounds held no heads. Hemming had filled the automatic with live blanks. Wat placed the pistol on the desk before him and in a mood of tense bleakness, waited for his phone to ring, waited for Qasem to start playing with Juliet's life. He knew in the conference room, government and security people did the same, as did Henry in the basement, as did those at his bank and in England.

CHAPTER 21

"It's time for you to go home," Jaber said, helping Juliet to her feet. "Someone from the American Government is waiting for you. But it is important you do as instructed or you will not see your father again." He placed the pendant around her neck and showed her a small, hand held transmitter. "If you disobey, the explosion inside will sever your neck. Amin and Lena are positioned outside overlooking where you walk. You have seen their rifles and know what damage they do. Please, please, Juliet, for your young life, do not be foolish. Promise?"

Juliet nodded, unable to hide her fear. He strapped a small radio to her waist and placed headphones with a stalk microphone over her hair, adjusting them into place. "Is Lisa all right?" she asked. "Will you let her go too?"

"Of course but only if you are good. When the sound goes on you will hear your father and other people. They all want you to live, Juliet. You must not disappoint them. You must be sensible."

"I will," she said.

"Let us proceed." He checked his watch then holding her arm walked to the mine entrance and bright sunshine. Ahead she saw a long, partially curved track which had once been a railway, its high banks falling to undulating ground as it followed the contours of a hill. Left of the track, a two hundred-metre shelf of industrial wasteland had been cut by steps into shallow terraces, the scared land scattered with intermittent scrub and fifty-foot slagheaps. Beyond lay open moorland and fields. It was hideously beautiful, a landscape which only heightened her dread.

Jaber led her to a point where several low mounds of rubble marked some past building and where the ground gave a better position to eliminate the curve of the old track against the hillside. Staring to the far haze, she saw the track disappear into wilderness, its only distinguishing feature a solitary telegraph pole at mid distance. She saw no one.

"What am I to do?" she asked.

He switched on the radio at her waist and his reply came over the headphones. "Walk along the track, stay in the middle and do not stop unless told. It is over a kilometre and with your restricted movements will take you a long time. At the end, someone will lift the bomb from your neck and drive you away. That is all you need do. Goodbye, Juliet, may Allah spare you."

Juliet began to walk towards the track, her hobbled ankles causing slow, uneasy steps. In the landscape around her nothing moved. She had the sense of being an insect waiting for some unseen hand to reach out and crush her.

Seb clambered the hillcrest and immediately dropped to his stomach. He looked down on acres of industrial wasteland, its surface scattered with shrub, derelict buildings and slagheaps. Lisa came beside him. Both produced field glasses.

"Disused copper mines," Seb told her. "Dozens of them around, all abandoned in the nineteenth century."

"It's like the Klondike," Lisa said, her breath harsh and heavy.

"You OK?" he asked.

"Sure I'm OK. I just let you lead because I'm a good sport. Where's this disused rail track?"

Seb slid the map onto the heather before them. "Here," he pointed with his finger. "It borders the hill from east to west linking various mines. The grid reference given is there, on this long straight bit."

Lisa searched with her glasses. "No sign of Juliet but I see the pole, the handover point. Could be an embankment on the other side and good for cover. Either way, on the track she's totally exposed. Whoever picked this spot knew what they were doing."

"Momma to all patrols," Jody's voice whispered over

the closed frequency. "Juliet has an explosive, remote controlled device around her neck. We have two players carting Barrett 82s with optic and possible laser sighting. No need to tell you guys, that's a .50 calibre with a hit capability of eighteen hundred metres."

"Oh my baby." Lisa pressed her face to the ground.

Seb squeezed her shoulder and had momentary visions of Al Razi with half his head. "Don't worry. We'll get her back. She'll be OK."

"Yo, Lisa," Navro's voice came over the earpiece.

"The team's with you, girl," Jody cut in. "We can do this. OK you guys, search out your players but no action till Juliet is handed over. I repeat, no action. I'm leaving the vehicle to approach the rail track." The radio lapsed into silence. Seb switched off his mike. Lisa still had her head down and he nudged her arm.

"If they have two marksmen, they must be this side of the track. A hide on the opposite hill would prevent clear sighting." He pointed down to his right. "See that slagheap over there, beside the derelict building?" he indicated. "That position would cover the whole central area for at least a kilometre, plus the shrubs on top give good camouflage. The house is probably just a shell. But I'll check it, clear the first slagheap then move on to the next."

"What about the second sniper?" Lisa wiped tears from her eyes.

"Maybe a hundred metres further back, on Navro's side. That far away you could have sightings which take out the curve of the hill."

"You'd need to be a good shot."

"The right weapon in the right hands, no problem. And they have the right weapons. You said there were a young man and woman. My guess is, they'll be the marksmen. The remaining Chechnyan's an outsider, he'll be the lookout and cannon fodder. Jaber will hold the detonator and stay under cover. But he's also the one to set Juliet off, so he'll remain at the start and watch her all the way."

"You seem very sure," Lisa sniffed and wiped her nose on a sleeve.

"I've done the training. OK, I'm going to the first slagheap, then the next. If I locate a player I'll position and wait to take him out."

"What about me?"

"You wait here."

"You're joking?" She stared at him with disbelief.

"No. You got the most dangerous job. When we get to go, if Jody is hit you have two hundred metres to cover without being seen, then you got to take the bomb from Juliet's neck and get her down."

"You think I'm going to leave my baby up there for that time, shit scared, not knowing if she's to die, waiting on some war to start? Lieutenant, you're way out."

"Lisa, just look at the probabilities. Once they have their prize, they'll be looking for escape. First a tactical withdrawal, then whatever plan they've devised. They won't kill Juliet because so long as she's alive they can use her. That's why they'll probably shoot Jody to prevent her removing the necklace. But if you're seen crossing the ground before handover, chances are they'll kill you both."

"You're a shit!"

"I'm a soldier." He gathered up the map and switched on his radio. "Seb to Navro. Possible location of one sniper, second slagheap your end of the track."

"Roger that," Navro replied. "Moving in."

"Lieutenant," Lisa twisted to face him. "You're doing this because I'm a woman, but I outrank you. When you go, I go."

"Then look at it this way, Major. Half the distance to cover is open ground. You'll be seen, you'll be dead before you make it. And you're too beautiful to die." He kissed her. "See you in paradise." Seb rolled away, belly down through the sodden heather, propelling himself with elbows and knees, Heckler clenched before him. Not until he was low enough on the ridge and in mist did he stand and run for the derelict building.

Jody walked with hands open and splayed by her side. She carried no visible weapon, only a Colt Python revolver concealed beneath her Barbour coat. It had little value in such open territory, but magnum bullets gave mental security. From her neck hung field glasses and in her coat pocket a radio boost linking her to the Range Rover and world communication.

Antiquities of industrial history stood either side of her path. The ragged brickwork of chimneys thrusting into the air at random intervals, engine houses and partial buildings without roofs or interiors. Where once four thousand souls had walked to early morning work, grass now grew, dipped and pitted with muddy shale, ash and weed shrouded coal dust. In parts the mist was heavy but once she had climbed the bank of the old railway she was able to see a kilometre and a half of curving track. The level surface was covered in a green blaze of moss and weed, the banks sometimes high, sometimes level with the undulating ground on ether side. To her right, shrubs and old earth diggings pockmarked thousands of acres.

Jody stood centre of the track, long denuded of its rails and sleepers and peered to the distance where a small, solitary figure moved towards her. She raised her glasses, zeroed their focus, then switched her radio to the open channel of frequency one. "Juliet," she said, into the mike. "We have contact."

The flash of red over the front optic of her glasses was brief but she knew its meaning and instantly lowered her hands. A red spot, millimetres in diameter followed down over her chest, stopping in the centre of her body. "Also enemy contact," she said. "A laser sight, probably five hundred metres at one o'clock. There's a slagheap that way. Mist now defusing beam, now gone. The morning atmosphere is making their laser sighting spasmodically ineffective. OK guys, let play commence."

Alone behind the glass of his office, Wat listened to Jody's words and waited for the phone to ring as he knew everyone in the building waited. When minutes later the call came, he lifted the receiver slowly.

"This is Khalid bin Qasem," the voice said. "Let us make no mistake, Mr Walsh and all those who listen, this game is played only by my rules. Transgression will be fatal for your daughter."

"OK, Qasem you have the floor. All demands are in place, your instructions carried out to the letter. Now, I want reassurance of my daughter's safety."

"You have an observer, she watches the girl at this very moment. Comply and your daughter will complete her journey in safety. You have a second, secure frequency as instructed?"

"I do."

"Open it on the number I am sending to your personal email. Keep it to yourself. My equipment will tell if you allow interception by any other persons to final negotiations."

"You led me to believe our negotiations were already complete," Wat said, clattering keys on his PC to open the mailbox. He read the message and entered the numbers into his cell phone.

"Almost, but not quite. Juliet has a long walk before reaching the handover point. She is alone, she is frightened, if you would like to reassure her speak into your mobile."

Wat lifted the instrument to his ear. "Juliet, honey, you OK?" He listened as her voice came back, echoing over the transmitter.

"Papa, is that you?"

"Just stay steady, Sweetpea, everything's gonna be OK."

"They put a bomb round my neck. I'm handcuffed and can hardly walk. I'm scared, Papa."

Wat stood and began to pace before his desk. "Stay strong, honey, stay strong for Papa. We all love you, you're coming home."

"Is Lisa OK?"

"Lisa is fine," he said.

"Enough." Qasem switched off the phone and went back on the open line. "Commence transfer of the ransom money to the named accounts I have given the Bank of Dubai."

Wat stood still and drew breath. "When she's safe. When the bomb is taken from her neck."

"You play a dangerous game. Do not cross me, pay now."

"When she is safe. If you kill her, you get nothing." He waited on the other man's silence, waited for what seemed an eternity.

"For your reassurance I allow fifteen minutes, no longer." The line switched off and Wat slumped in a chair. Inside he felt hollow dread. He had fifteen minutes to decide if his daughter lived or died, coupled with the uncertainty of why Bin Qasem had agreed so easily.

Twenty metres from the derelict building Seb went to ground, crawling between shrubs and earth banks until he found a ditch that had once drained water from the slagheap. Crouched in the muddy residue of last night's storm, he crawled until beside the building. As he had guessed, the structure was an open shell with neither roof nor floors, no hiding place for a sniper. Once through the nearest window he crossed the rubble-strewn interior, all the time switching point of aim, his Heckler ready for instant fire. By the main entrance he knelt and listened. A thirty-metre stretch of open ground lay before the steep, grassy mound of the slagheap. If there was a sniper on top his best position would be at the opposite side which gave a clear, panoramic view of the whole area. If instead he had chosen the near side of the tip for a quick get away, then it would be possible for him to see and hear Seb as he went forward. Until he had committed himself he had no way of knowing. He took deep breaths, centred his mind and ran.

The gradient of the tip was steeper than he calculated. He scrabbled on hands and knees, pulling on tufts of grass while pushing with his boots for toe-holes. The whole climb left him an open target.

Feet from the top he slowed and edged forward until able to peer over the brow. Before him the slagheap sloped down into a shallow dip dotted with shrub and undergrowth. Beyond, the whole sweep of track and mine works lay in open view. Three hundred metres to his front, Juliet shuffled towards the lone post. Five hundred metres left, Jody approached from the opposite way, two solitary figures in an empty landscape. Seb saw no sign of a sniper. Still and silent, he examined each bush, each patch of ground, looking for traces of a hide amongst the two thousand square metres of flattened top. He searched for minutes until finally sighting freshly dug earth pushed over a scuffed mound of grass. Whoever lay hidden was trained but careless. It took seconds for him to distinguish the bodyline and finally the squat, battle end of a heavy calibre rifle.

Seb slid partially back down the slope and whispered into his radio. "Seb to momma, we have enemy sighting, one player at thirty metres, Juliet, target at three hundred metres to immediate front."

"Momma, roger that. Standby. Laser sighting on me, calculated at five hundred metres southwest. Just where you are, soldier. Navro moving over hill towards far slagheap. No action, repeat, no action."

"Roger that." Seb switched off to reclimb the bank.

The sniper moved once to realign his sight then lay still again. At thirty metres distance, Seb reckoned one prolonged burst from the Heckler enough to see the guy out. Alternatively in the hope of gaining a prisoner, he would try to take him alive but if the fellow retaliated there would be no choice but to fire. While waiting, he removed field glasses from his belt kit, wiped the muddy lenses with the moistened end of his finger and began to scan back from where Juliet had walked. Somewhere hidden was a man with a remote detonating device.

He searched for several minutes before catching sight of movement. A single figure crouched behind an earth bank was shifting sideways to keep Juliet in sight as she rounded the slight curve of the track. To watch her all the way, he would need to move at least five metres from his present position, that meant occasionally breaking solid cover. Seb calculated the target at nine hundred metres, a chubby, dark-skinned man who appeared to be holding either a mobile or detonator. Even for a rifle, it was an impossible target. Seb eased down from the brow.

"Seb to momma. Player identified near entrance of mine at far end of track, possibly with remote detonator. Too far for me and out of visible range for Navro. Bring in Bolventor and Bodmin, maybe they can get a sight."

"Bolventor to momma, we are on the west side of the hill with Bodmin. Have single player with advantage position directly in front of us. We can whack him or stay hidden. If we move forward, he'll see us."

"Momma to Bolventor, no shooting. Bodmin, move back down the hill and try approaching from the side. But no contact till instructed. I repeat, no contact."

"Bolventor, roger that."

Seb returned to watch the sniper. For the time being they were boxed. Whoever held the remote detonator held Juliet's life. He just hoped Lisa stayed patient and those in New York knew what they were doing.

CHAPTER 22

Wat felt grateful for the glass wall, grateful he could isolate himself from the activity outside, the embarrassment of those who turned their eyes to conceal their pity. He could not escape the phone.

Dalvarral came on line. "The President has asked me to convey his congratulations on your firm stand against this terrorist. And let me assure you, Mr Walsh, that Juliet will come out of this safe. Steps are already in place."

"Steps?" He sat forward. "Is there something I don't know?"

"You're going to be proud of Raider, sir. Proud of the technology that's gone into this program."

The line switched off and Wat felt himself back in the darkness of fear; fear of what he knew, fear of what he did not, all blinded by mistrust of those who plotted around him. He felt totally without strength, having kidded himself he had influence when in reality he had none. He wondered to what extent he was being manoeuvred as a pawn, as Crawley, Henry and Lisa were probably manoeuvred, as Juliet was manoeuvred. He realised in cold reality if he, if Juliet, were to survive, he needed to pull out of the quagmire now and start to manipulate others as others had been manipulating him. In this he stood entirely alone.

The phone rang and Henry spoke. "Crawley's in the building surrounded by lawyers and court orders. The police are with him, so are senior military personnel."

"Where's Jake?"

"With Rawlings."

"The next minutes are crucial to me. Legally, Crawley is correct about his right of mission control. Go see him, Henry. Tell him if he co-operates with me he can have Raider, anything he wants. But I need fifteen minutes, I need Juliet out of there."

Henry hesitated. "No one else knows of this but our

Paris operator is recording all voices going through the flat used by Bin Qasem. We get it back within a few minutes. If we can do a voice match on those Qasem talks to we can expose his contacts."

Wat let silence lie between them for a moment. "I got maybe minutes to make the most important decision of my life. You got something to tell me?"

"I share as much guilt as any other man. And Juliet was not part of what we planned but it's too late now. God forgive me, Wat. I wish I could change it."

Jez Baker's voice came back on the sound system, filling the office and rooms beyond with his droll, easy-going commentary of operations aboard USS Abraham Lincoln. "Lincoln to Walsh Towers, Raider now at six K and out of blind alley."

Wat made to speak but Henry's line switched off. It was replaced by the beeping tone of the direct and private line to Qasem. Wat did not move, instead he listened to Jez Baker's calm report of procedures.

"Arming two missiles ready for action. Walsh Towers to download navigation course. Re-ascent, eight minutes. Raider now on low level attack. Launch countdown at zero, zero, six, zero. Test target situated East Saudi. Walsh Towers prepare to instruct missiles."

"Lincoln standby," Rawlings said.

Wat lifted the handset and listened to Qasem's transmission. All he heard was Juliet's voice. "Papa, what's happening? Papa, he said they were going to blow my head off. Papa, help me."

"You have minutes, Mr Walsh." Qasem's voice interceded as Juliet faded.

"Launch at zero, zero, five, zero. Altitude held, six K. Walsh Towers, download missile course. I repeat, imperative you download for target, now."

"The snipers have now been instructed to take aim, Mr Walsh."

Jez Baker's voice rose an octave. "Hold operation. We

have an interceptor. We have alien lock-on. Go to code red. I repeat, code red."

"Got you, mother fucker." Ed Rawling's voice was clearly audible as was the cheer from Jake Hammerton who must have been leaning over his shoulder. "We have a target reading from hostile lock-on," Rawlings said. "Programming missile to backtrack. Interceptor located in South Yemen. Transverse of Raider's flight giving multiple readings. Interceptor zeroed to ten square meters. Launch missile one."

"Missile launched," Jez Baker answered. "Navigation re-aligned as your instructions. South Yemen, I repeat, target is now located in South Yemen. Missile two ready for launch. Computers reading course. Course now loaded."

"No," Wat shouted as he stood, realising the implications. "They'll kill her, they'll kill my Juliet." No one answered him.

"Second missile at launch. Missile away." Baker's voice stayed calm. "Commence evasive action. Close after-burn ports, spray chaff. All systems to stealth mode."

"Missile strike two minutes. Counting down. Missile strike one minute forty-eight seconds," Rawlings said.

Wat lifted the Colt from his desk and stood in helpless despair. They were sacrificing his girl. For what purpose? Revenge. He wanted to shoot someone, Hammerton, Rawlings. They must have known. Henry had known, all conspired to deceive him. The bleep continued on Khalid's line and Wat placed the instrument to his ear. Only he and Henry heard the man speak, clearly unaware of his pending fate.

"The snipers have been instructed to take aim. Pay now, or she dies."

Wat saw the faintest glimmer of hope. "You'll give instructions for her instant release?"

"I have always kept my word. Remember your wife?"

Wat jabbed computer keys on the desk and sent coded signals to the auto exchange at the Dubai Bank. Five billion dollars in Saudi riyals dropped into fifty designated Saudi accounts, each in turn dropping into a further ten secondary accounts. Within seconds the total amount was exchanged into multiple currencies and spread over hundreds of electronic based transactions. Outside the jurisdiction of the US Federal Bank, the entire sum flowed through an electronic labyrinth before it was re-gathered in Iran.

"Now let my daughter go."

"The snipers are instructed to rest their weapons."

"Missile one at strike," Jez Baker informed.

"But first …" Wat listened to the line go dead.

"We have a kill." Ed Rawling's voice came amidst an eruption of cheers. "That is American technology."

"Kill, you bastards! You've killed my daughter."

"Alien lock-on is gone." Baker's voice came hushed, then rose with excitement. "Missile strike two, on target. Enemy is down, I repeat, enemy is down."

"Resuming tests," Ed Rawlings said. "Raider has struck her first blow for America. That's one for 9/11. One for my brothers, for all our brothers and sisters. I report Operation Fireback a success."

Wat listened to the words drowned by cheers then opened his own line to Jody. "Is Juliet alive?"

"She's standing on the track. What the hell's going on? I'm getting a lot of conflicting information."

"All of you are still in great danger. I'm asking you to go forward and take that bomb from my daughter's neck."

"Are negotiations over?"

"So I'm led to believe. But I don't know if that's been relayed to Qasem's men."

"I'm starting to walk, Mr Walsh, but it's a good three hundred metres. Pray for me."

* * *

"You have your five billion, Khalid. If you want Raider, pay now."

"An excellent performance in the Yemen, Octavius. I have reports my monitoring station is completely destroyed."

"That's American technology. Now pay."

"So you can repeat the same exercise? Credit me with intelligent, Octavius. My fortress is impenetrable but I do not take chances. The money will be transferred to the ten accounts you specified only when I have full control of GR4. This was our agreement."

"Then don't kill the girl. She's the chip we play with. Kill her before time and we both lose."

Wat was oblivious to those outside. He felt as an old man with nowhere to turn, with no motivation but deep, embittered anger. He let it smother his mind, let is generate deep within him while he listened to the celebration that gripped the building. Who the hell was thinking of Juliet or the woman who risked everything walking towards her? Henry's line activated and Wat lifted the handset, barely grunting acknowledgement.

"Paris called," Henry said. "Qasem's transmissions were not from South Yemen, but from a satellite link emanating from the southern Afghanistan-Iranian borders. Qasem is not dead."

"Damn them all." Wat rested head in hand.

"I need to tell you something else," Henry said. "I was in on Fireback. Too low to make a difference but I helped. Juliet was never part of the game plan. I don't know what went wrong but I'll do anything to help her out of this."

"Including the full truth?"

"That part is easy."

"Who instigated Fireback?"

"Supposedly came down from Heaven, the White

House, but no one is saying. Jake's centre core. I'm about to report Qasem still lives."

"Don't. Don't tell anyone anything, only me."

"Then you'll be interested to know we taped two calls from the French apartment. Someone calling himself Octavius, like in Henry the Eighth. The mobile they're using is company issue, supposedly mine. Someone is impersonating me. I'm running a voice match on all recorded transmissions but it will take time. Due to the uncertainty of who may listen in, when I get a result I'll send it up by hand."

"Thank you, Henry, for the truth." Wat began to pace his office. "Is Crawley prepared to help me?"

"For mission control, he's prepared to listen."

"You got men in the building you can trust? You only, not Jake's men."

"A few."

"Gather them quickly. Go to Crawley. Tell him I personally authorised his reinstatement and full control of Raider. Get him in and Rawlings out of there. If Jake interferes, tell him you are obeying direct orders from me. I know what Qasem wants and it's not money. When Crawley is operating make sure he has contact here on a highly secure line. In fact, save for the operations room, make sure all my lines are secure. Then get yourself back monitoring. Tell Jake nothing. Do that now."

Wat opened transmission to Jody, aware that on this line the whole conference room listened. "How far away are you?"

"Two hundred metres. Juliet's still standing there. Had a shot hit the ground in front of me. I ain't sure of this no more. Could have been a warning, could have been poor marksmanship. I need to know what's happening."

"Stop. Take cover, the game's changed. Don't risk anything and keep your people down until you hear from me." Wat gripped the phone. "You other people listening, Bin Qasem is alive, you fucked up. That's my daughter out there, from now on only I negotiate."

"This is hostage control centre." Wat heard an unfamiliar male voice. "We can't let go, sir. Not until we have direct orders from the White House, to our knowledge, Qasem is dead."

"He is not. Neither are his men on Bodmin Moor. I repeat, if anyone interferes with my orders I shall hold that person responsible for the death of my daughter."

"We have to take instructions on this, sir."

"Do that." Wat hung up, confident they would back down. By allowing him control the White House could dodge out of responsibility.

Qasem's call came over the closed line within minutes of Wat making his transmission.

"How unfortunate you broke our agreement, Mr Walsh."

"Not me, Khalid. But I have a feeling you knew of events before they took place. The situation has now changed. Any trade is directly between you and me. You have five billion. What else?"

"You must love your daughter very much."

"She and thousands like her are the future of America. You kill her, others will take her place, others will come after you. You will never win, cannot win. Your Islamic dream is not even Islamic. You wallow in self-delusion."

"America's weapons of mass destruction hold millions in poverty through world domination. Your people grow fat on wars and exploitation of others. Your words hold no morality. My terms are non-negotiable. Your daughter's life in exchange for GR4."

"Impossible. I alone do not have control and you do not have the equipment to fly her."

"My objective is to destroy. The aircraft or your daughter. The choice is yours. You have three minutes."

He listened to the line disconnect and held the silent

receiver in his hand while thoughts of Juliet thousands of miles away, alone and isolated like himself, clawed deep within his mind. Through the heavy glass door he saw Jake enter the outer office and storm towards him. Wat called down to mission control on a closed, hands free line via the terminal on his desk. Crawley answered in a voice indicating he was re-installed.

"Welcome back, Max but the game's not over."

"Thanks for your confidence in me," Crawley said. "But it ain't shared. I may have mission control but they've nullified my code. The military are flying from Whiteman Air Base. They used the President's code."

"You invented the damn system, can't you hack it? I mean, break in and pass flight control to me, to this module in my office?" Wat waited long seconds for Crawley's reply.

"Steal it back from the military? How tempting. But why? The consequences could be serious."

"More so if we leave it. We still got enemy in the camp, Juliet is still in danger. Qasem is still demanding. We have to be ready in case of emergency."

"What you ask could be deemed treasonable. You're safe up there in your glass box but I've had clear demonstrations of my own vulnerability."

Wat looked to where Jake stood on the other side of the partition, banging the glass with the flat of his hand.

"You're right about being vulnerable, Max. You creamed millions off this project as a subcontractor. That was against your terms of employment. You invented the Oman monitoring station not through company loyalty but to save your investment. I could push proceedings to cripple you, or I could not." Wat listened to Max's breathing and waited for his decision.

"What do you intend?"

"To play Qasem at his own game. No time to argue, Max. You want to go to jail or into the good side of American history? If the latter, say yes."

"It will take at least ten minutes, the process is complicated even for me. And I've no certainty of success."

"Go to it." Wat hung up and pressed buttons to allow Jake through the glass door.

"Why did you let that arsehole back in?" Jake strode across the room to lean on the desk.

"Bin Qasem is not dead." Wat told him. "And by luck, neither is Juliet, yet. Fireback did not work. Now I'm trying to save my girl. I want your code."

"You kidding? You're going to give him Raider? No way."

"He'll destroy the aircraft but my girl will live. Eight billion dollars of technology puffed up in smoke. What's that to a life when we can build another aircraft?"

"You're crazy. He'll take control of Raider."

"He does not have the equipment. There is nothing he can possibly do but destroy her."

"I'm sorry."

"I don't have time to argue, Jake. Give me the fucking code or I swear to God I'll blow your head off." Wat lifted the Colt from his desk and placed the barrel tip to Jake's forehead. "You sanctioned the destruction of my girl's life for revenge. It would give me pleasure to shoot you."

Jake sneered and Wat realised he knew the futility of his threat, Jake knew the weapon held only blanks. He moved back slightly and Wat slid off the safety.

"Eight, eight, six, four, two," Jake said finally. "You won't get away with this, I'm going to the President."

"See you in hell, General." The Colt still level, Wat stared into Jake's impassive eyes wondering why the man had capitulated under an empty threat. No time for speculation, he lifted the secure phone linking him to Qasem. He waited seconds for an answer.

"Time, Mr Walsh," Qasem said.

"My code is eighteen, twenty-four, thirty-one. Second

code is eight, eight, six, four, two. Now let my daughter go."

"Patience, Mr Walsh. Allow me to ensure I have control of American technology."

Jake turned and walked towards the glass doors. Wat let him through, knowing something was wrong, something Hammerton knew which he did not. Qasem's silence demanded an answer.

"No stalling, Qasem. I'm sending my agent to Juliet."

Jez Baker interrupted over the open communications speaker, his whispered voice of disbelief causing every person in the outer office to turn and listen.

"Code red. We have a second intruder. All systems to code red, I repeat, we have a second intruder."

Max spoke over the closed link terminal on Wat's desk. "For Christ's sake, he has the override code, he's taking flight control."

"Stay calm, Max. You can hack him out of it."

"It takes time. This is not straightforward."

"Lincoln to Walsh Towers, Raider is not responding. We have monitoring but all other systems are blanked," Baker said, his voice still soft. "The intruder is taking Raider. I repeat, the intruder has control of Raider's flight path."

Wat listened to the following silence and waited to hear of Raider's destructive descent. When nothing happened he pressed the switch for Max.

"Get back readings. He's on the Iran-Afghan border. Get Turkey to try lock-on, if they, you and Lincoln search for his signal as Raider flies, we'll get hundreds of cross-references and pin his location within metres. He can only crash Raider, nothing else. Even a steep dive will take ten minutes. Once Juliet is safe, if you have the code, we can regain the craft."

Wat switched back to Qasem. "OK, you have everything. I'm sending in our people."

"Move before I say and they all die."

"No more bluff, Qasem, no more time." Wat opened the line to Jody. "He has everything but is still not giving. Proceed forward with extreme caution."

"I'll do my best, sir."

"God bless." Wat closed the line. Max was yelling over the desk terminal. "He's arming cruise missiles."

Wat sat forward and felt the sudden slackness of his jaw. "How can he, without Raider's electronic warfare system, it's not possible."

"Because whoever leaked gave him a lot more than we believed. Gave the whole damn systems package. No other way."

"Maybe he's going to blow Raider with her own cargo."

"Maybe." Max's voice was hesitant. "But if I were the Navy I'd put Lincoln on immediate alert."

"Lincoln." Wat felt the shiver of sudden understanding, realisation of being played like a complete fool, driven by bitterness, goaded by anger and paternal love into the delusion of self-righteousness. Hammerton had used him like an idiot. Of all people, he had been the principal fall guy. "We must regain control. You must hack it."

"Five, six minutes."

"Where the hell is the President. Get his override command code."

"Whiteman Air Base already used it after Rawlings fired his missiles. It can't be used a second time. No one saw a reason for more than three backup codes. They're all gone."

"For Christ's sake, Max, forget everything else. Hack that code, switch Raider to fly from the module in my office. If we don't succeed, the consequences will kill millions."

CHAPTER 23

When Jody came within a hundred metres of Juliet, a single shot sent her diving for cover. Juliet squealed and in the following seconds, Seb caught the flicker of movement in a straggle of undergrowth between Lisa's position and the bank. Using field glasses, he searched, cursing when he found her moving forward at a crouch. Lisa was well camouflaged. Mud covered her hands and face but her impatience had not gone unnoticed. Ten metres to her front the undergrowth stopped, leaving a twenty-metre gap before more scrub gave cover to the bottom of the embankment. Directly above, Juliet stood in full view. Even as Seb watched, the sniper moved his weapon, shifting aim to a point where Lisa would emerge from cover.

Seb's reaction came more through instinct than conscious thought. In the next seconds Lisa and maybe Juliet would die. He had no time for communication or warning and if he opened fire, so might the second sniper. He came up over the hilltop at full tilt, running in long strides down the small incline, cushioning his footfall on heather, watching the sniper take up sight on the target. The man seemed oblivious to Seb's approach until the last moment but by then Seb was in full flight, covering the final two metres in one leap.

He came down through undergrowth, landing one heel on the sniper's back, the other stamping his head. The man went face into mud the same instant he jerked the trigger.

The single, high-calibre round shimmered its violent report over the industrial wasteland, echoing and re-echoing back from the hills until muffled by mist. Seb struck downwards with the folded, telescopic butt of his Heckler, then rolled to his right, dragging himself free of the vegetation. The sniper remained still but Seb took no chances. Yanking him backwards he straddled the body and smacked down hard with a closed fist. Only then did he realise the enemy was female. She lay crumpled in semi-consciousness, blood on her lips and jaw, whimpering to the mike around her neck. From her earphone came a frantic and excited jabbering in Arabic. Seb jerked both leads from the radio socket and dragged her from the hide before lifting her rifle to face the opposite direction. Lisa was now halfway across the open space, sprinting at full speed. Seb left her to do whatever she intended and positioned the rifle ready to fire. Through the sight he searched the far end of the bank and the mine entrance. It took long seconds before he found his target. The man lay crouched and partially hidden by bushes, straining to see beyond the curve of the track, mobile in one hand, detonator in the other. Even with the optic sights it was a difficult, almost impossible, target.

"Mr Walsh, he's arming more cruise missiles and programming their gyros." Crawley's voice came over the terminal in the hushed tones of both warning and disbelief.

"Who else knows?"

"The team here, Whiteman Air Base, Missouri, the Lincoln. Ain't no one can do a thing."

Wat paused, staring at the ceiling. "Max, we can save this but I need your absolute trust."

"You gave the aircraft to him, you created this situation."

"I never realised he had the electronic warfare system. But we can get this back. Hang in there, Max. Get the code, let me fly the aircraft."

"It's possible he'll launch missiles before then."

"I'll leave this terminal open, keep trying."

Wat dialled on his direct, secure link to the White House.

"Presidential office." The woman's voice was crisp. Wat gave his password and the line immediately connected.

"Mr President, the situation can be reversed."

"We're in a meeting on that right now, Wat. I hear you placed a gun to Hammerton's head."

"Put USS Abraham Lincoln on immediate alert for missile attack, very soon they'll have a two kilo-tonne blockbuster heading in their direction. And they may only be one of many targets."

"How the hell can he do that?"

"Because Raider is basically a transporter and missile deployment system. All missiles can be programmed and aimed from whatever ground centre has control. Any target within two thousand miles of Raider is vulnerable. Currently that's the whole Middle East and further as she flies onwards."

"My God, this is awesome. How? Why did you do it?"

"We have a traitor in the top level of Walsh administration. Someone who passed more information than anyone realised. Someone who started years ago. Why did I seemingly capitulate? To save my girl and I still can. I can also save Raider, save the situation."

"I'm putting Hammerton in total charge of Walsh Towers. I've ordered your immediate arrest."

"Do that and you will start another world war."

"I'm sorry, Wat. I have no choice."

"Don't go!" Wat gripped white-knuckled on the arm of his chair. "How do I make you believe me?" He listened to the prolonged silence. "Man has no greater love of nation than he lay down his life for his country but it's not my life, it's the life of my child. You already risked it once and lost. Now, give me a chance."

"I cannot give control to you or a member of your staff while Bin Qasem has power and influence over your decisions. I have issued orders for the Lincoln to launch strike craft and destroy Raider on contact."

"I'm afraid you can't do that, Mr President." Wat looked at the flight modulator in his office and watched the instruments come to life as Crawley switched on down below. The cockpit screen was suddenly alight with views over the Saudi desert but still no flight control. "Raider can accelerate to Mach 3. It is impossible for them to catch up and if she begins to climb, they cannot follow to maximum altitude. No conventional missile will touch her. You'd have to use a nuclear strike."

"While your daughter is a hostage you must consider Walsh Towers out of this program." The phone went dead.

Immediately Max's voice came over the terminal. "I heard what you said. But only this building can reinitiate full control. They don't understand but they soon will. Khalid has readied five missiles for launch. Destinations Jerusalem, Tel-Aviv, Damascus, Tehran and the Lincoln. We have a maximum of ten minutes."

"This is no Islamic fundamentalist, this is a man intent on world war."

"He has seven more missiles. If he goes back up blind alley he'll be in a position to bomb Europe and eventually America."

"Have you tracked him?"

"Area is down to approximately one square kilometre and closing. Henry is studying satellite pictures of locations now. Looks like it's on the Iranian side of the border and below ground level."

"Get Henry to warn the President. The target countries have to be told. What of the code?"

"I have six of our most powerful computers compiling override sequence. Time, it's just time.

"Khalid, you have your aircraft. The ultimate weapon."

"Indeed, Octavius, and you have your money."

"Enough to activate a strike force while the politicians dither. My boys will be coming out to get you, Khalid. You and your kind have no escape. Any place in the world you hide, we'll find you. Al-Qaeda better start running because my boys ain't governed by the UN. Ain't governed by anything but duty revenge."

"I look forward to our meeting."

"The first you'll know about it will be a bullet in your face. You can kill the girl now. She ain't no more use." Jake Hammerton switched off his mobile and took the slip of paper from his pocket, reading the message sent by secure messenger from Henry Taylor to Wat Walsh. Jake was not too concerned. In his time he had tampered with a great many electronic security devices, computers and recordings. He was an expert in manipulation. He phoned a senior aide who sat with Hemming in the armoury. "Take six men and detain Henry Taylor on a charge of passing information to the enemy. Destroy all data held on his computer and hold him in custody."

"Yes, sir. Right away, sir."

"And Lieutenant, when Taylor tries to run, have him trip downstairs. Preferably from the twentieth floor. Do I make myself clear?"

"Yes, sir."

Jake dropped the slip of paper into a shredder and headed back to the conference room. Now the President had given him control, he had no more worry. America's enemies home and abroad were going to die.

"All units, this is momma. Word from the White House. Immediate action. I'm going to work my way forward best I can. Let's go."

Seb squinted through the telescopic sight at the man's face, the only visible target area on view. Steadying his breath, he allowed the cross hair on the optical scope to move in vertical rise with each intake of air. On the third breath he froze the cross hairs centre of target as he took first pressure on the trigger, then squeezed. The crack of the weapon firing its heavy round put a shock over his eardrums, the same time discharged gases from the huge rifle pushed sideways through a muzzle exhaust to soften the recoil against his shoulder. With the thud of explosive sound, he instinctively closed his eyes. When he looked again his target had disappeared.

From the far distant hill came the clatter of small arms fire that Seb guessed was the Chechnyan, either taking or giving hits. Lisa was now scrambling up the bank, screaming wildly for Juliet to take off the bomb. Centre of the track the girl was half bent forward struggling with the restriction of cuffs and headphones in a vain attempt to force the necklace over her scalp.

While Seb searched a second rifle report came with a chunk of earth blasted away beside the spot where Juliet crouched. The near miss showed the sniper on the far tip hampered by mist or not adequately zeroed but if he were a pro, he would be clicking the rifle sight to make compensation. Depending on his skill, Juliet would now live or die. Seb had little option but to return his concentration to the bomber. The sniper might miss again but the bomb would not. Looking back to his target he found him crawling between bush and earth mounds near the mine entrance, risking his cover for a better view of the track.

Seb aimed fast and fired the round in snap reaction. The third round blew off the lower part of the fellow's leg and sent him sprawling face forward, the remote detonating device pitching ahead of him. Seb took aim for the kill as the man first reached towards his missing limb, then rolled, screaming, stretching belly down for the detonator.

The click of an automatic being cocked was a singular, distracting sound from Lisa's frantic shouts. Seb used his trigger hand to lash out. The girl was kneeling over him, the weapon pointed at his head while she fumbled with the safety. The blow tumbled her off balance, sending the shot skywards as he grabbed her gun wrist, unable to prevent a second shot scorching his side. On one knee he drove the full knuckled impact of fist against jaw, crumbling her to a motionless heap.

He rolled immediately back to firing position. The bomber had crawled forward and his arm was stretched to clasp the remote detonator. Lisa was now on the bank, covering Juliet from behind, ripping at her mike and headphones which snagged the bomb. Jody was in full sprint towards them. Seb took quick aim and fired in rapid succession, imploding the ground around his target the same instant the man's hand covered the detonator. Jody's squeal came clear through the air as she fell sideways amidst a shower of dirt kicked up by .50 calibre bullets. Lisa stayed crouched over Juliet, the bomb flying from her hand.

Seb's last shot came the instant two others were fired from the second sniper and fractions before the morning air rebounded under the thud of exploding Semtex. When Seb looked over his shoulder, the bank where Juliet had crouched now stood empty. A small residue of smoke drifted in the air as if from the aftermath of a spent firework but there were no bodies, just a discolouration of black and red over the grass. Through the sharp, morning air came a wail of grief, inhuman, unearthly. Seb shivered and squinted into his sights. His target now lay minus head and one shoulder.

"Seb to momma. Bomber dead. One player down. What's the situation?" He searched along the bank and saw her field glasses lying beside a shallow earth furrow in which she lay flat, strands of blonde hair rustled by the breeze. The same moment the ground exploded beside her, followed by the single crack of a gun shot echoing over the valley.

"I'm down, can't move," Jody's voice came over the radio, cracked with trauma. "He got them both. I saw them fall under impact."

"One of them could still be alive. I heard a voice. I

don't know whose. Lisa's radio is not responding. Stay put momma I'll call the cavalry. I've got a hole to patch, then I'm going after the next player. Navro, you roger that?"

"Yo," Navro's voice came loud, almost a bark. "But this one's mine. Stay out of it, Seb. ETA, five minutes."

Seb knelt and took off his belt kit. The whole of his left side was a mess of blood. Beneath his shirt muscle and skin lay spliced by a four inch groove where a 9mm round from the girl's automatic had cut his body surface. He felt as if brutally kicked but knew he was a lucky man. From the small medical pack on his kit he slid out tubes of antiseptic cream and pressed the contents over the wound, covering the area with a field dressing before winding the bandage around his midriff and sticking it with tape. He hurried the last, watching the girl start to move as she moaned back to consciousness.

Shuffling on his knees, he turned her face up and began to undo the buckle on her camouflage trousers.

"Lucky I don't put a bullet in your head." He yanked the belt from its loops, pulled down her zip and unfastened the waist before pulling the trousers over her hips and thighs. In a reflex of modesty, she began to protest, reaching to stop him. Seb gave no quarter, rolling her face over he jammed one knee into her back while working the trousers over her legs until able to wind and tie them around her ankles. He looped the belt round her wrist, tied it once, then again between her ankles. She was left with her arms stretched behind, her knees bent and legs secured over her back. "What I'd really like to do with that belt is far worse than I've done," he told her. "Think yourself lucky." He threw the rifle and 9mm automatic over the bank then slid down himself, Heckler in one hand, his descent balanced with the other.

At ground level he did not bother with cover but ran straight for the next slagheap where the second sniper continued to fire at Jody. It was clear the fellow did not realise his position or had such arrogance he did not care. If he suffered a death wish, Navro would undoubtedly grant it, unless Seb got there first. He grieved over what had happened and the anger in him was cold. He wanted to kill.

"Jody, is my daughter alive?" Wat sat, both hands clenched to fists on his desk, his breath sharp and shallow, the cold grip of dread in his chest.

"I'm under fire, Mr Walsh, trapped and can't get out." Wat listened to the pause in her voice, then a small, tight squeal as the crack of heavy gunfire came over the air. "I've got blood on me, I don't know if it's mine. The bomb went off when I was about ten feet away, the same time the sniper fired."

"Please, the truth, how is Juliet?" He heard her hesitation and knew the answer before it came.

"Probably dead, she and Lisa both. There's no response from either."

Wat sensed the whole of his being, all his strength, all his spirit collapse into nothing. It went down into the bitter depths of despair and rose in a long, piercing cry until he shouted in full rage. "They killed my child. Why did you make it so they had to kill my child? What in hell was the purpose, God? Why? Why? You bastard!" Amidst a stony silence his secretaries stood on the opposite side of the bombproof glass and cried. Only Baker spoke.

"Lincoln to Walsh Towers. He's dropped five missiles and is preparing engines for ascent. If we don't stop him now, he'll go to blind alley."

Wat slowly turned his rage into ice-cold determination as he spoke to Crawley. "Get that fucking code, I want that aircraft."

"A little longer," Crawley answered.

"Mission control." Jez Baker spoke again. "He's

changing course, heading towards Russia and Europe. Two more missiles are now at pre-launch."

"Move it, Max you have seconds."

"Missiles launched."

"I'm inputting a new code now. Alpha, echo, zero, six, six, three, eight, four, two, seven. Code online and accepted. Get into your module, Wat Walsh. Get ready to fly"

Wat grabbed his mobile link to Qasem and climbed steps to the pilot's seat. Immediately he opened all communication channels, then looked at the banks of digital instruments and computer controls which swept in a curved console around him. Directly in front a monitor gave full visual of Raider's flight path.

"We have lock-on, we have resumed control." Baker's voice came from speakers in Wat's seat.

"If you're listening, Mr President, don't interfere. We have no time for game play."

"Disarm the missiles if you can, no more." The President's voice instructed over the aircraft communication system. "Disarm and then return control to Whiteman Air Base."

"Max, hear that? You are now mission control," Wat said. "Show us what Raider can do. First, what's the maximum missile range for us to disarm?"

"Three hundred miles, but we already have missiles spread over three hundred and sixty. We're too late for the Lincoln."

"Pry they are ready. What about the others?"

"I'm working as we speak. Last missiles fired at Turkey are still within range, Turkey's missile disarmed." Max paused. "Turkey to self-destruct. The rest are on the boundary. We're too far north."

"Alter course two, zero degrees, increase speed to Mach 3." Wat saw the fuel consumption gauge flicker to maximum and watched the ground visibly shift beneath as half a globe away Raider accelerated to full speed. Over the aircraft's audio monitoring system a long muted roll sounded as Raider reached three times the speed of sound.

"I have Tel-Aviv missile now coming within control. Disarmed, missile to self-destruct."

"Impact on Lincoln, one minute thirty-two seconds." Commander Baker's voice was calm over the inter-communication channel. "Anti-missile, missile system now operating and launching. Our aircraft intercepting with additional missiles. Distance at five miles, this is going to be tight."

"You are too late, Walsh." Wat heard the triumph in Qasem's voice and lifted his mobile.

"Never."

"Russia has a radar alert on your incoming missile attack. Jordan and Iran are scrambling their fighters against invasion by Israeli air force and American stealth bombers. There is nothing you can do, war is inevitable."

"We have visual contact," Baker said. "Impact thirty seconds."

Wat listened in silence, then let go his breath when a cheer went up from the Lincoln's crew.

"Missile destroyed," Baker reported.

"Down to you, Max." Wat moved the mobile from his ear.

"Iranian missile, disarmed, missile to self-destruct. Jordan missile, Jerusalem missile, out of range."

"Can we catch them?"

"No. Not without altitude. This is a bomber, not a strike aircraft. We've lost them."

"Mr President," Wat said to anyone listening. "Better start negotiating."

"I already have," the President's voice came back. "Jordanian and Saudi air forces have radar contact with the missiles and are closing to intercept."

"To save Israel?"

"To save Jerusalem, to save peace."

"If you'll excuse me, Mr President, we have Russia to

deal with." Wat looked back to his instruments and began to turn the aircraft in a one hundred and thirty degree arc. "OK, we got a chase on, that means interception over Iran. Raise altitude. Full after-burn, open this baby up."

"We have a fuel reserve."

"Fuck the fuel. We have missiles to destroy."

"But to get out, we'll have to return over Iranian air space at low altitudes."

"Then let's hope the Ayatollahs are praying for us," Wat said, looking at his screen as he lifted the nose of the aircraft. "Did you find Qasem?"

"We have a target area of twenty-five square metres on a mountainside. From surveys of available satellite pictures, it's been identified as a cave on the Iran side of the Afghan border. We have no idea of its depth. Location data is already on your navigational computer.

"OK. When she reaches eighty K, I want maximum burn. Full fuel until we have those missiles in range. Let's see if we can get to Mach 4. Your job is to neutralise, I'll fly the bird. Give me absolute control, all systems."

"You'll be solo flying billions of dollars worth of aircraft, Mr Walsh."

"Don't I know it."

"Remember your fuel levels. You have the baby."

"Keep me informed of the situation. Raider now at eighty K and going into descent. Increasing speed, no holds barred Search for your missiles, Max." Wat picked up his mobile. "You killed my child, Qasem."

"Unfortunate but what is the life of one person compared to the establishment of justice?"

"I don't care for your interpretation of justice. It's time for retribution."

"Foolish old man, you cannot touch me. You cannot even find me. I am deep within the earth protected by a country you cannot even enter."

"Qasem, you ain't going to like this."

"I have contact with the Russian missile," Max said.

"Missiles disarmed, missiles to self-destruct … missiles down. Mission complete. We can turn back now."

"Give me missile control, Max." Wat looked to his screen. Far below lay the vastness of Iran and the far distant border of Afghanistan.

"You already have it. The command switch top of attack systems. Down is shared, up is standalone."

Wat flicked the switch forward and began tapping keys on the missile deployment system.

"If we don't turn now, fuel will become critical. Change course, please."

"Wat," the President cut in. "We have achieved our objectives, now let's get down onto friendly soil. Iran has been patient, let's not make a fatal diplomatic incident."

"Gentlemen," Wat said. "I'm sitting in New York, yet looking out of Raider's cockpit I could be sitting on top of the world. Save that world is now bitter and full of anger. It's my craft, Mr President, I made it. I paid for it, so I guess I'll fly it. If you want it when I'm finished, it's yours."

"You have four cruise missiles belonging to the American Government. You will return the aircraft and those missiles immediately."

"Sorry, Mr President, I'm going to visit Bin Qasem."

"You cannot do that. Such an event over Iran could be interpreted as an act of war. The repercussions will be serious."

"You should have thought of that before Fireback. You were tricked, so I'm finishing the job."

Activation of the missile deployment system brought a myriad of lights to the system's control console. Wat entered the grid co-ordinates given by Max and moments later four missile codes flicked down over the screen, each showing course, altitude and impact time.

Wat grimaced but felt only hatred as he input a strike pattern of twenty square metres.

"Mr Walsh, is this wise?" Max asked. "Target area is

on the Iranian side of the border."

"You said we had a fuel problem but if we drop our payload we lessen the problem, correct?"

"Correct."

"Stop it, Wat, for God sakes, stop now." The President's voice came clear and decisive. "Instigation of a missile strike could be taken as an act of aggression. Iran would have the right to retaliate in defence, would have a right to call in their allies including Russia and China."

"You'll have politicians shouting, Mr President but that's what you're all there for. All I'm going to do is alter a mountainside and the balance of justice. First missile away. Impact nine minutes. Second missile on belt, second missile ready for deployment." Wat looked at the screen as the list of missiles slowly clicked down.

"Wat, I have no choice, I'm sending Hammerton to place you under immediate close arrest." Before he had time to answer, a female voice spoke over the network. "It is reported that the Jordanian air force has shot down the Jerusalem cruise missile over the Dead Sea. Damascus missile also destroyed. The alert in that area is now over."

Wat listened to the cheers sounding from a dozen sources.

"Co-operation, Mr President, makes the world a safer place. Missile four on belt, missile four away. Impact six minutes. OK, Max. Let's turn her round." He began to input a new flight path, swinging Raider in a one hundred and eighty degree arc, taking the aircraft's G force to maximum stress.

"Altitude six, one K. Fuel burn at seventy percent ..." Max said, then paused. "Mr Walsh, you have incoming Iranian ground to air missiles. Advise immediate evasive action."

"I told you so," the President's voice was cold. "Now leave that seat, Wat. You're not in a fit condition."

"Go back to Mach 3, we can out run it."

"Only if we use the remaining fuel, that means no

chance of landing."

"Then close dispersal shields," Wat said. "Cut engine power. Adopt blind alley glide."

"At this height! For Christ's sake, we've never tried it."

"Do it."

"Spraying chaff. Closing heat sources for maximum stealth."

"We have no enemy lock-on, Max. This is machine against machine."

"It's your altitude, without burn, your descent will be too fast."

"Speed dropping to subsonic. Bird at six, zero K and falling, Iranian coastline three, zero, four miles."

"I must warn you sir, this could well mean we crash on Iranian territory."

"Wat," the President came back. "Global Raider must not fall into foreign hands. Self-destruct the aircraft."

"If required, Mr President, if required." Wat glanced to his right where Jake and six armed men stood on the other side of the glass, two of them with sledgehammers. Wat checked his watch and lifted the mobile.

"You still there, Qasem?"

"I'm waiting for the demise of your nation, Mr Walsh. Waiting on the self-destruction of American technology. By now, the Wailing Wall and the Holy Mosque will have gone. You may have regained control of your craft but the missiles I have deployed will raise the Arab nations in revenge."

"If I were you, pal I'd look out the window. I'd like you to see another side of American technology." Wat heard the transmitted thump of explosives followed by a second and third, then a startled shout from Qasem. On a fourth explosion the line went dead. In the ensuing silence came the crack of hammers on bombproof glass.

"Hostile missiles diverted," Max said. "Raider now at forty five k, descent increasing by fifteen degrees. Coast at one hundred and twenty miles. She's falling too fast, we need to fire engines."

"Wait, those missiles could still turn or others be fired. If we give heat we'll be shot out the sky." Wat looked to the men attacking his door and switched off all communications but one. "Henry, get me an open line to this control module. I want it so that when I pull plugs on other communications, this line remains open. Henry?" When he received no reply he switched back to Max. "Send someone to check out Henry."

"Listen to me," Max said. "We have Iranian fighters on GR4's radar, interception six minutes, ceiling now below forty k, coast sixty miles. We're a sitting duck."

"We still have stealth." Wat switched him off and re-opened the line to Lincoln. "Commander Baker. Do you have lock-on?"

"Affirmative, Mr Walsh."

"I'm going to hand you control immediately we're over international waters, but only if you put a listening watch on this airwave. I mean a keen listening watch, one heard over the complete network from the mikes I'm currently using. I want everyone to hear what's spoken in this room."

"No problem."

"Standby Lincoln." Wat switched back to open channel. "OK, Max. Fuel control to you. All systems maintain stealth, rear burners closed. Steady as she goes, continue silent glide."

"For fuck's sake, Wat," Max's voice came back. "Don't cut it so fine, we're dropping like a stone."

"If we fire engines, they'll fire more missiles. This craft is a stealth bomber, it's meant to hide. Have faith. Coastline eleven miles. Altitude eighteen k, hostile aircraft approaching, bearing zero, three, five, contact four minutes."

"Raider now visible from ground," Baker told them. "If they have any missiles or conventional artillery units down there, you're in for a rough ride."

"Crucial recovery from descent now imminent," Max said. "Another minute and we'll be too low to lift the nose."

"Enemy intercept imminent, altitude nine k and falling. We are now crossing the Iranian coast."

"Immediately out of territorial waters, fire engines," Wat instructed.

"We are now entering critical dive, eight k and falling, international borderline at half a mile."

"Walsh Towers, Raider under renewed missile attack. Impact thirty seconds," Baker said.

Wat pulled back on his controls and switched Raider's four massive engines to full thrust, increasing speed to Mach 3 as the craft power dived to earth, setting speed against descent to lift Raider's nose.

Max's voice rose an octave as he slowly counted each reading. "Six k, five, four, three, two. She's levelling out. One k, five hundred feet, nose up. We have lift. We are out running the missiles. Those little demons can't catch us."

"Ladies and gentlemen," Wat said. "I give you the ultimate weapon to guard global peace. I ask only that you remember the young lives she has cost." Wat stared to the vast blue sky before him and felt the coldness of grief overpower all other emotion. "Commander Baker, she's all yours. Take her for delivery."

"Walsh Towers, the bird is ours, we have control. Raider at fifteen hundred feet and rising," Baker paused. "Where're we delivering? She's only got four percent fuel."

Jake stood pistol in hand, banging the glass with his fist, his angry voice unable to penetrate the soundproof partition.

"Try Saudi, Kuwait, you'd even make Turkey," Wat said. "All you need is a three thousand metre runway. You Navy boys are always smart, you figure it out. And Commander, stay listening."

Wat turned the volume on his mike to maximum and stood reluctantly from the seat. His game was over, the rest was bitterness. Jake watched him through the glass the whole time he walked to the desk and switched the intercom button. "You seem anxious for a meeting, Jake. You clearly have a problem." Wat pressed for the door to open. "Keep your men outside, General. I ain't going no place and I prefer our conversation in private," Wat said, shutting them in the room.

"By the authority of the President I am arresting you for misappropriation of military equipment and endangering national security." Jake stood before the desk, pistol in hand.

"Raider's back with the Navy."

"I'm talking about four cruise missiles. I'm talking about endangering the entire world."

"If you want to talk, Jake let's keep it between ourselves." Wat leaned towards the temporary communications board placed on his desk and ripped the leads from their sockets. "No one can hear us now, Jake. It's just you and me."

"From the President down, we're all sorry for the loss of your daughter but what you did is unforgivable. You endangered the lives of every American citizen."

"Bullshit. I blew up the side of a mountain along with public enemy number one. Maybe that's not diplomatically correct but it's nothing money won't brush over, nothing you didn't try with Fireback."

"You took unnecessary risks, both with national security and GR4."

"The aircraft is mine by right of sacrifice. Don't hedge, Jake, we're alone in the glass booth. No one's listening and in the end, only politicians and media will give a shit. Enemy in the compound, Jake. No wonder we could never find him."

"You're talking in riddles."

"You encouraged Juliet's British trip because you

thought the Brits Combined Agency Task Force weak. You thought Havic a pumped up kid and your misogyny blinded you against Lisa Longford's ability. The hotel attack was a ploy so Lisa would run for the bolt-hole in Cornwall, a place you knew about since Henry fixed it months back. A place away from Navro and help, a place where Lisa would believe Juliet safe."

"You got it wrong, Henry set her up."

"No, Jake you used Henry. You have security access to all computers in this building, including Henry's, including Perry's. You controlled security on the loop. You played Fireback as a ploy to delude. You even got the President on your side. The kind of information Qasem needed could only have been accessed by Crawley, Rawlings, Perry or you. You watched the other three but nobody watched you. You were in prime position. You said I was going to give him control of Raider. How did you know he had equipment to control if you hadn't given it to him? The setup in South Yemen was so I would think the White House betrayed me. That's why Qasem gave in so easily when I asked for extra time. His only interest was Raider and war. Yours was five billion dollars. Bitterness can do strange things to a man." Wat drew his Colt over the desktop. "You must have been overjoyed when I demanded that code from you. "

"You have no proof of this."

"Henry's doing a voice match of all the calls which passed through Paris. You needed to stay in contact with Qasem. That was your mistake."

"Henry ain't going to help you."

"Henry's in the basement listening to this conversation."

"Henry's dead, so is his equipment. You didn't have to pull the plugs, there's no line out of here. Sorry, Wat but this conversation really is private."

"Is that the closest you get to an admission, your use of conspiracy to place suspicion on others? You seemed to have planned everything in meticulous detail. But for who's gain, what purpose?"

"To beat terror, by terror. We must take action or new little shits like Saddam, Qasem and Bin Laden will be all over us. Ever since the first Gulf war, ever since the first time we let Saddam escape we were on a path to 9/11. Ever since then we needed strong covert action to fight the enemy both within and abroad. When Bin Laden put the war in our face, I knew my duty. Not through the UN and a bunch of wet politicians but through strong executive operations that don't hold back. Politicians dancing to world politics just gets us more terrorists. Our failure over Afghanistan is proof of it. The Taliban and Qasem don't go through law, why should we? Thanks to Walsh Securities I have my own specialist force. Thanks to Fireback, I got five billion dollars to fund it and you can bet the White House will soon be knocking on my door asking for my help. Qasem is dead; our first operational success, thanks to you. I depended on your skill as a pilot, Wat on your natural inbred bolshie attitude. Glad to say, you never faltered."

Wat put fingers to the Colt and drew it towards him.

Jake smiled and raised his own pistol. "You make this easy for me, threatening me with a weapon for a second time. Your pistol contains blanks."

"I don't need it. Look behind you." He nodded at the crowd of armed police and military personnel who invaded the outer office. "The President has sent help but it's not me they've come to arrest. It's you, Jake."

"Bullshitting to the end. I wouldn't have expected less of you." Jake levelled his aim the same time National Guardsmen hammered on the glass with rifle butts.

"You killed my little girl."

"War has causalities." Jake glanced behind him.

"And no winners." Wat grabbed for the SIG automatic under his jacket. Both fired simultaneously.

* * *

Seb ignored the pain in his side. The sniper was continuing to fire every fifteen seconds, gouging earth around Jody's mega cover, pausing only long enough to change magazines, clearly intent on the destruction of his target. To Seb it demonstrated the mind of a fanatic, someone without reason. He had no qualms about their confrontation, he would shoot to kill. He just prayed Jody would keep her nerve and stay down. The route he chose brought him to the rear of the second slagheap and a climb up loose and difficult shale. He stopped, tighten the bandages and checked with Navro on his position. "You closing?" he asked the American.

"I'm off the hill and ready to start up the slagheap. Back on high ground I had sight of our target. He's to the front and dug in."

"OK, I'm going up. But be careful, we don't want blue on blue."

"I got a better idea. Give me a thirty second start, that way I'll be over the brow before you. I'm going to run the surface, you'll see me. If he turns to fire, we take him from both sides."

"Roger that." Seb checked his watch and leant back against the bank, grateful for the rest as he pressed the bloodstained padding over his wound. "Jody," he called on the radio. "Cavalry's going in. Stay down." He hoisted the Heckler and started up the slope, pulling and pushing against the near vertical surface. When he reached the top, Navro was bounding at full speed across open ground, oblivious to the noise he made. Seb put the Heckler to his shoulder and aimed just as the sniper realised he was under threat. Throwing aside his camouflage cover, he drew an automatic but in the same moment Navro was on top of him, dragging him from the hide. In the next instant his neck was locked between two muscular arms. Even with the distance separating, Seb clearly heard the decisive snap of bone and sinew.

Grasping the man by his hair, Navro swung the body in a full circle, then with a screech of rage hurled it into space.

"Jody, last player down. You can leave cover."

"Roger that. Ground troops are closing. Army want to know if it's safe to bring in helicopters?"

"Sure, game's over."

Seb followed Navro up onto the railway bank. He tried to prepare himself. Bombs and heavy calibre bullets butcher people. Evidence was the blood-spattered ground. He remembered Al Razi and the torn ragdolls on the desert floor after the ambush. Seb stopped on the embankment where the girls had fallen to the opposite side. Jody knelt at the bottom, white-faced and visibly shaking. In small comfort she had folded a jacket beneath Lisa's head. She lay sprawled on her back, eyes staring to the sky, her body shivering under massive trauma, her side gaping. Juliet's crumpled form lay doubled over, her head on Lisa's chest. Blood soaked them both. Jody looked up and silently shook her head.

In his own shock and grief, Seb found himself unable to move and watched Navro slide down the bank. The man stood in useless expectation while pulling out a field dressing. Then even he saw the futility. During those seconds, Lisa spoke once. "I love you babe."

Almost in slow motion, Juliet raised herself and stretched to kiss Lisa's brow, watching her become still, her eyes vacant. Navro stood in clenched and tight control. Seb turned away, biting on his lip as he stared to the far distance and the black dotted formation of incoming helicopters, the sound of their rotors brushing over Juliet's small sobs.

CHAPTER 24

Seb's mother had told him that time heals all things but it never takes away the memory.

She looked older, still pretty but Seb could tell the past year had not been kind. She pushed a single trolley, manoeuvring round other passengers as she came through the barrier. He did not rush forward, preferring instead to observe her from the safety of seclusion. It was his training as much as caution. Reading her expression, seeing her uncertainty, he knew her confidence had been severely damaged but her eyes still shone and when the smile came it spread huge and warm. He crossed the last few yards and kissed her cheek, then her lips.

"I was worried you wouldn't be here," Juliet said as she hugged him.

Seb held the embrace and the warm pressure of her body. When he pulled back she was crying.

"Hey," he wiped her cheek. "You're supposed to be on holiday. Happy time, remember?" He took her trolley and put an arm to her shoulder as they walked.

"Memories, just memories. How are you?" She hugged him.

"Still soldiering for CAT, still chasing the baddies with Sean Fagan and Colonel Fox. I've upped rank, equivalent to a captain now." He pushed the trolley out of the terminal towards one of Heathrow's multi-storey car parks. "How's it across the pond?"

"Different. They broke up the empire. I got nothing now. I still see Eva occasionally, Jody and Navro. They're going to get married. I got a wedding invite for you. Six weeks time."

"I look forward to that. And I have to thank someone for honouring our bonus, it allowed me to buy a house."

"Thank Crawley. He's now director of Stealth Avionics, the old Walsh company. Jake's in the penitentiary, in a wheelchair." She grimaced, then clapped when she saw his car. "Still cleaned and polished, I see." Juliet ran her hand over the Jaguar's gleaming paintwork. Seb opened the boot and placed her case inside.

"Still the mechanical love of my life. How's Lucas?"

She shrugged and stayed silent until inside the car. "I'm told he's seeing the Speck-Becker girl. They're oil millionaires in Texas. She's real pretty. More important for Lucas, her family has serious money."

"Serves him right. He'll pay for every penny." Seb drove the Jaguar into raining sunshine and manoeuvred through traffic for London. "Sorry about your father," he said finally. "That must have been hard." He reached across to squeeze the small hands in her lap.

"I'm not the jewelled beetle any more, no longer in the cage but I sure wish he was around. They buried him in style. A lot of people came, including the President. They gave speeches and said he was a great man. Then they all shook my hand and went home. It hit me then but not so much as Lisa's funeral. After that I knew I was alone."

Seb glanced and saw the tears again but said nothing.

"Jody and Navro came, Eva, a contingent from the Marines. They gave her a funeral with full military honours. She had no family and after the flag was rolled they presented it to me. I cried. But in my heart I could never give the love she really wanted. She sacrificed her life for mine. When she pulled the necklace off, I was on my knees so she threw it behind, positioning herself to shield me from the blast and the bullet that struck her. If she had not done so I would be dead. Even then she used her last reserve to throw me over the embankment before falling down beside me. I will cherish her love, always suffer the guilt of not being able to give back in the nature she wanted. It's said, life only allows one true love; Lisa's love was Sapphic, but it came pure and unselfish." She sniffed on her tears and turned to him. "You going to take me swimming? Maybe we could start where we left off?"

"Sounds good to me."

ABOUT THE AUTHOR

James McKenna was born during the bombing of London in WWII and as the child of a British Army officer, spent time amidst the wretchedness of post-war Austria before travelling with his family to the Far East.

At the age of 15 he joined the British Army and attended the apprenticeship college at Harrogate, then the Royal School of Military Engineering. At 17 he passed selection for the Paras serving in the Gulf and Europe. Afterwards running his own electronic and physical protection company gave insider knowledge for his crime thrillers The Unseen, The Uncounted, The Unwanted and Global Raider.

Now a father and grandfather, in parallel to these crime thrillers, he has ventured into the action/fantasy world of the young reader aged 12+. The Mind Traveller is the first of a series where Rosie adventures deep into the unchartered universe of Mind Space.

As a fulltime writer he lives between the UK, Portugal and Ireland.

For more information go to his crime websites –

www.crimefiction-jamesmckenna.co.uk

Author's page on Amazon UK http://tinyurl.com/c9ultl3
USA http://www.amazon.com/author/jamesmckenna

Email the author at lonecloudpublishing@live.co.uk